Linda Finlay live[...] of nine novels. From lacemaking to willow weaving, each on[...] is based on a local craft which, in order to write authentically and place herself firmly in the shoes of her heroines, she has learnt to do herself. However, it is people and their problems that make for a good story and, with so much interesting material to work with, it is easy for Linda to let her imagination run as wild as the West Country landscape, which has inspired her writing. *The Girl with the Silver Bangle* is her tenth novel.

Also by Linda Finlay

The Royal Lacemaker
The Girl with the Red Ribbon
A Family For Christmas
The Sea Shell Girl
Monday's Child
Orphans and Angels
The Flower Seller
The Bonbon Girl
The Girl with the Amber Comb

The Girl with the Silver Bangle

Linda Finlay

ONE PLACE. MANY STORIES

HQ
An imprint of HarperCollins*Publishers* Ltd
1 London Bridge Street
London SE1 9GF

www.harpercollins.co.uk

HarperCollins*Publishers*
1st Floor, Watermarque Building, Ringsend Road
Dublin 4, Ireland

This paperback edition 2021

1
First published in Great Britain by
HQ, an imprint of HarperCollins*Publishers* Ltd 2021

ISBN: 978-0-00-839264-2

MIX
Paper from
responsible sources
FSC™ C007454

This book is produced from independently certified FSC™ paper to ensure responsible forest management.

For more information visit: www.harpercollins.co.uk/green

This book is set in 11/16 pt. Sabon

Printed and bound in Great Britain by
CPI Group (UK) Ltd, Croydon, CR0 4YY

To My Family

Silver Stars Shining Brightly in the Bangle of Life

Chapter 1

1910 – Camberwell, London

Although sixteen-year-old Daisy Tucker had worked at the Fun Factory in Camberwell for nearly a year, watching the scene builders assembling sets in the yard and the props being loaded onto carts ready to be transported to The Hippodrome still filled her with excitement.

The Guv'nor, Fred Karno, a successful theatre promoter, had directed the terrace of five houses in Vaughan Road be knocked through, affording plenty of indoor and outside space for performers to practise, staging and costumes created and paraphernalia stored. Now he employed many local people and offered opportunities for advancement. Although Daisy had started off washing and ironing the costumes, she had a dream and was working hard to achieve it. She'd already been promoted to one of the runners for the overseers, but her passion was drawing and painting, her ambition to work with the artists. Soon there would be a vacancy coming up in their studio and she was determined to secure the position, even if it meant competing with her fellow runner and arch-rival, Arnie Bragg. With his pointed face and dark hooded eyes, he reminded Daisy of a rat, pushing his nose into everything and telling anyone who'd listen how good he was.

Daisy, meanwhile, had decided to take a more direct approach, and as soon as she'd seen the scenery artists were under pressure to meet their deadline she'd offered to help prepare their backdrops. Now, having found a corner out of the way, she began thinly spreading primer over the large canvas, wrinkling her nose at the pungent smell of ammonia as she carefully ensured it went right to the edges.

As she worked, her imagination ran wild. She could picture the scene she'd create as clear as the sunny day. Except hers would be nocturnal. A sliver of silver moon emerging from the midnight sky, shooting stars with spangles winking to the audience from the stage and, in the bottom right-hand corner, her own trademark: a tiny white daisy.

Absorbed in her task, she didn't notice the sky darkening or the scene builders hastily pushing their sets back into their workshop until a big fat raindrop landed on her painting. 'Bloomin' August weather,' she muttered, jumping to her feet. One minute there wasn't a cloud to be seen, the next the heavens opened.

'Look sharp, Daisy, and get that out of the wet straightaway or it'll be your backside the Guv'nor'll have for his backdrop,' Stan the overseer ordered, appearing at her side and snatching the brush from her hand. Impatiently, he gestured to the props piled inside the double doors. 'And when you've done that you can get them custard pies loaded onto the cart.'

'Yes, sir,' Daisy replied, struggling under the weight of the enormous canvas.

'Oh, dear,' Arnie smirked, scrutinising the board hopefully as he passed Daisy in the corridor. 'Didn't get it wet, did yer?'

'No, thank heavens,' Daisy replied.

'Shame,' he muttered, transferring the furs and furbelows he was carrying from one arm to the other. 'Anyhow, you're a runner and should be helping me with this lot, not sucking up to them artists. And don't think you've a chance of getting that job in the studio. That's mine.'

'Been offered it then, have you?' Daisy asked, eyeing him speculatively.

'I will be,' he said, puffing out his chest importantly.

'I wouldn't be so sure about that,' she told him.

'Well, they're not going to offer it to you. Everyone knows girls get married and have babies.'

'Haven't you heard the world's changing, Arnold Bragg,' she retorted. 'And in case you hadn't noticed, some of the artists here are female.' Refusing to let him get under her skin, she hefted the canvas higher and continued on her way. Despite what Arnie said, she intended getting that position. Already the artists were asking for her as they knew she would do a thorough job. Her father had impressed upon her that a task, however menial, was worth doing properly or not at all, and she took great pride in her work. Arnie, by contrast, was slapdash, hurrying through his tasks so he could sneak outside for a smoke, for this was not allowed on the premises. He also had a mean streak and there was nothing he'd have liked better than for Daisy's canvas to have been ruined.

Daisy wrestled her way into the artists' airy studio,

3

breathing in the heady smell of paint. It was her favourite room, with a bench running the entire length, its wide shelves covered in huge jars of pigments, bottles containing liquids in every hue, and bristle brushes of varying sizes. Dodging the scenery that had been left to dry, she propped the primed canvas against the wall, ready for the design detail to be added.

'Goodness, Daisy, surely you didn't manage that all by yourself?' Scarlett asked, frowning as she looked up from her easel.

Daisy nodded, not willing to admit her arms felt as if they'd been wrenched from their sockets.

'You are a dear helping out like this.' Scarlett delved into the front of her bright-red smock, drawing out a sheet of paper and stub of pencil. 'I know how you love to draw so have these for your trouble.'

'Bet that pretty little head of yours was busy designing its own set while you were splashing on the primer,' Blue, her fellow artist, teased.

'I'll have you know I took great care to prime your canvas properly,' Daisy retorted. 'Although you know me only too well,' she ruefully admitted, pocketing the proffered gifts, which they'd assured her were perks of the job.

'Well, come on then, spill the beans; what did you dream up?' Scarlett asked, green eyes studying her curiously.

'It was a night sky, with twinkling stars and …' she stuttered to a halt as the two artists exchanged amused glances.

'The reality won't be half as romantic, I'm afraid.' Blue sighed. 'We have to create another stage upon a stage for

4

a performance up country.' Daisy watched as he distractedly wiped his hands on his own brightly coloured smock and wished she had something brighter than her white pinafore to wear.

'We've another canvas needing priming but you can do it in here, if you'd like,' Scarlett told her.

'Daisy, where the hell are you? I'll not tell you again.' Stan's roar reverberated around the high-ceilinged room. As he appeared at the open door, arms folded across his ample belly, they shot her a sympathetic look.

Dodging past him, she dived into the props room and snatched up the pies required for the slapstick comedy.

'Today, girl,' he growled.

Daisy narrowed her eyes, tempted to lob one at his pate with its combed-over wisps of greying hair. Obviously she wasn't called a runner for nothing, she thought, racing down the corridor as fast as she could manage.

It was satisfying helping the sets for the productions come together, but the mundane tasks were repetitive and she itched to be creative. Still, she'd have to bide her time. With her parents needing her wage, Daisy hadn't had the luxury of receiving any formal training, unlike Harry, her follower, who was studying at the Camberwell College of Arts and Crafts.

Although that institute was council-funded, as her father had told her, if you're learning you ain't earning. Still Daisy couldn't grumble, for her school teacher, recognising her talent, had suggested she apply for a job here, telling her father that she would then be earning while learning. Despite wanting her to work alongside him at the ginger beer factory, he'd finally given in, admitting he wanted her to be happy. She loved her job but, after paying her mother for her keep, she could hardly afford a pencil let alone a sketch pad, which was why she was so grateful for the odd bits and pieces Scarlett and Blue gave her. However, the position in the studio would mean a rise in wages, which was another reason why she was determined to get it.

Despite not having much money for luxuries, the three of them were a close-knit family, scrimping to pay the rent on a modest two-up two-down terraced house off the Northway Road close to the Fun Factory. 'We might be working class,' her mother always declared, 'but that doesn't mean we can't live in a respectable area.' It meant that Daisy could help out at home, for having damaged her legs in a bad fall, which had cost her the baby she was carrying, her mother had been forced to give up her busy job as a seamstress. Although she took in sewing, they were mainly alterations and mending jobs, which didn't make the most of her talents. However, she prided herself on keeping their house nice and serving up a hot meal when Daisy and her father returned each evening.

'Hey, look out.' The warning shout stirred Daisy from her thoughts and she just managed to duck in time to avoid being hit by a long wooden plank. As the props clattered to the floor, three apprentices emerging from the carpentry workshop grinned sheepishly.

'Sorry,' Billy shouted, endeavouring to be heard above the sounds of sawing and hammering. 'We've spent all afternoon shaping this specially to fit the backdrop for tonight's act at the Hippo. Give us a moment to load it onto the cart then we'll come back and help you with that lot,' he added, nodding to the pies that were still rolling along the corridor.

'Good job they're only meant for throwing,' she told them, grimacing at the large dent in the top of one.

'It's a shame they're not real; I'm starving,' Slim Jim said, reaching out his hand as if to check the one she was still holding wasn't edible.

'Oi, you lot, get yourselves cleaned up before you touch any of them props,' Stan bellowed, pointing to the sawdust clinging to their overalls. 'Some of them's worth more than your wages,' he added.

'That's not difficult, know what I mean?' Ted smirked, winking at Daisy as they manoeuvred the timber through the doors to the yard, where once again the fickle summer sun was shining.

'It could soon be arranged that you don't get any at all,' Stan called after them. 'Don't just stand there gawping, girl,' he added, turning back to Daisy. 'Got another canvas to prepare for them prima donnas, haven't you?'

'Yes, sir,' she muttered. Honestly, the man had ears like an elephant and missed nothing. She couldn't help smiling at Stan's scathing remarks though, for, much to his chagrin, the artists insisted on being called Scarlett and Blue instead of their real names. When he'd complained, Mr Karno had told him that if it helped them get into character that could only be beneficial for their creativity and having, once been a performer himself, he obviously knew about these things. Catching sight of the clock on the wall, she bit down her impatience. She'd have to hurry to get that canvas done if she was to get home in time for tea. Her mother didn't have many house rules but supper at six was a given.

'Here, let me help,' Kezia offered, appearing seemingly from nowhere. Her dark curls danced like a halo around her head as she scooped the pies up from the floor. Daisy smiled gratefully. It still surprised her that, despite the difference in their status, the glamorous trapeze artiste had taken Daisy under her wing, showing her where things were and introducing her to everybody. Consequently, Daisy had soon been accepted by everyone. Now they were firm friends and when she had a rare free moment, there was nothing Daisy liked better than watching the lithe figure swinging high above the practice room as she perfected her act. 'Come on, let's get these loaded before it rains again,' Kezia urged.

'Should you be here helping me, though?' Daisy asked, glancing anxiously at the overseer.

'Oh, don't take any notice of him,' Kezia whispered, giggling when she saw the man gazing appreciatively at her long legs. 'Yer like a big pussycat really, ain't you, me 'andsome,' she purred, in her attractive West Country drawl. A flush spread up the man's neck and he turned quickly away. 'See, yer just has to stand yer ground,' Kezia told her as they made their way outside.

'Thanks,' Daisy murmured as they packed the pies alongside the other props.

'Yer Harry back yet?' the girl asked.

'No, he's spending the summer holidays working at his family's ironmongers in Woolwich. I can't wait until he comes back.' Daisy sighed. Although he'd only been gone a couple of weeks, already she was missing him more than she'd thought possible.

'Well, he certainly be a fine specimen of manhood if you don't mind me saying.' Kezia chuckled, giving her a nudge. Daisy felt her face grow hot. The summer evenings had been so sultry, they'd taken to strolling around the park after supper and Harry's kisses behind the bandstand had become increasingly passionate. The night before he'd left, he'd asked her to marry him once he'd finished his course. He'd even promised to design a posie ring and engrave it with a message that signified his feelings for her. Being a talented jewellery maker, she knew it would be something really special. Recalling the tender expression in his cornflower blue eyes as he'd stared deeply into hers sent delicious tingles of excitement shivering down her spine.

'Oh Daisy, yer face is a study,' Kezia teased. 'Listen, it's my night off so why don't yer come and see the new show with me?'

'Well, I er …' Daisy mumbled, knowing she had no money.

'Timbo's promised to sneak me in, so meet me by the stage door before the performance starts,' Kezia winked.

'Alright then,' she replied enthusiastically, her spirits rising at the thought.

Hurrying back to the studio, she set about priming the other canvas. If she worked quickly, she'd have time to change out of her plain work pinafore then eat supper before meeting her friend. She hadn't had an evening out since Harry left and an opportunity to see the first night's performance would be a real treat.

She was still smiling an hour later when she joined the press of tired workers surging through the double doors. It never ceased to amaze her how many people worked at the Fun Factory, and they were all such a mix. Important-looking men in their bowler hats and dark suits pushed past boys in flat caps and rough woollen jackets, while young girls wearing bonnets, with white pinafores covering their dark dresses, smiled coyly at them. Then there were the artists, with their flamboyant smocks and berets. How she dreamed of dressing like that too.

'What are you looking so happy about?' Arnie asked, shooting Daisy a suspicious look as he appeared at her side.

Daisy shrugged. 'Just pleased to be going home.' Then she frowned, all thoughts of people's attire vanishing, as she spotted her parents waiting on the pavement beyond the gates. They were both looking anxious, and, despite the warm weather, her mother was wearing her coat. Her heart sunk to her boots, for her father was gripping the handles of a barrow, which was piled high with their possessions. Something terrible had occurred.

Chapter 2

'What's happened?' Daisy asked her parents when she finally managed to reach them.

'Come on, love,' her mother said, 'we'll talk on the way.' Ignoring the curious looks being cast in their direction, she took Daisy's arm and urged her along the street.

'But …' she began, staring at the barrow, which had obviously been loaded in a hurry.

'It's a rum do, love, and all of me own making,' her father groaned, his grey eyes bleak.

'Now, Arthur, remember no airing our linen in public,' Mabel reminded him, eyeing the crowd still spilling from the Fun Factory, before determinedly crossing the road. Although her mother's limp was pronounced, a sure sign that she was stressed, it was all Daisy could do to keep up.

'But we're going in the wrong direction,' she protested as her mother veered left into Coldharbour Lane. 'Our home's the other way.'

'Not any more, it isn't.' Mabel sighed, peering around. 'Tell her, Arthur.'

Daisy stared at her father who grimaced.

'Been given the elbow, haven't I? Didn't even get me full pay.'

Daisy frowned. 'That can't be right. You're good at your job, and as leading hand everyone looks up to you.'

'The bosses don't now. Screwed up good and proper. I've really let you and your mother down,' he muttered, giving the handle of the barrow a thump.

'Arthur Tucker, we'll have no more of that. A hero is what you are,' Mabel protested.

'Doesn't pay the rent or put decent food on the table, though, does it?'

'Will someone please tell me exactly what's going on,' Daisy cried, stopping abruptly in the middle of the pavement.

'Your father stood up for a young widow who was being bullied.'

'They were playing on her vulnerability, trying to make her do things that, well …' He shrugged, his expression telling her more than the words he couldn't formulate.

'He got sacked for saving a woman's honour,' her mother exclaimed, indignation making her voice sharp.

'Keep your voice down, Mabel. This creaking barrow's drawing enough attention as it is,' Arthur muttered, as people on the other side of the road turned their heads to stare. 'We're having to move, girl, in case you hadn't realised. Come on, I'll explain fully when we reach our new home. Not that it's much, mind,' he added, giving Daisy a warning look.

'Home is where the heart is, Arthur,' Mabel told him, and he smiled gratefully.

'But where's the rest of our furniture and things?' Daisy asked, frowning at the few bits in the barrow.

'Not getting paid meant I couldn't pay the rent so the

landlord kept your mother's favourite possessions in lieu.' Her father's mouth tightened into a line and Daisy knew better than to question him further.

As they turned down Denmark Hill, Daisy was so busy trying to take in what she'd been told that she hardly noticed the horse-drawn trams and carts, the cries of costers peddling their wares or the shopkeepers pulling up their awnings. It was only when her parents stopped outside the Cock public house and began looking around that she realised their surroundings were less than salubrious.

'We've obviously taken the wrong route,' she cried. 'What street are we looking for?'

'Tiger Yard, and if Cock Yard is by this public house then it must be over there by that one,' her father muttered, pointing ahead. 'Come on,' he added, as Daisy stared at him in disbelief.

Without waiting for a reply, he pushed the barrow through the narrow alleyway towards two terraces of run-down houses where tattered rags flapped listlessly at the windows and paint peeled from the doors. Urchins kicking a pig's bladder up the street eyed their possessions speculatively, whilst grubby toddlers playing in the dirt ignored them completely. A group of frowsy women gathered around a water pump stopped their chatting and watched as Daisy and her parents walked towards them.

'Good afternoon.' Mabel smiled. 'We're looking for number six Tiger Yard.' There was silence as the women eyed them suspiciously then finally a tall, dark-haired woman in her twenties stepped forward.

'Who wants to know?' she snapped.

'We are Arthur and Mabel Tucker and this is our daughter Daisy,' Mabel explained. As the woman gave each of them a searching stare, Daisy shivered but managed a tentative smile.

'And your business 'ere?' she asked.

'We have rented rooms to live in,' Arthur replied, colouring under the woman's appraisal.

'Didn't think you'd come 'ere for a blinkin' holiday,' she cackled, gesturing to their laden cart.

''Ere Cora, you's a card, you is,' one of the other women guffawed but fell silent when she shot her a glare.

'Must be mistaken about the number though. Rooms in number six is all taken but thirteen has empty ones on the top floor,' she said, pointing further along the yard.

'No, it's definitely the bottom floor of number six. My wife here can't manage stairs easily and—'

'Stairs!' the woman shrieked. 'Wooden steps, more like, and rickety at that. Like I says, number thirteen's the only one got any free rooms and you'll find the key in the door.'

'There must be some mistake …' Arthur began but the woman had clearly lost interest and turned back to her friends.

'Come on, Arthur, let's go and find number thirteen,' Mabel insisted, tugging at his sleeve.

'But the stairs …'

'I'll manage,' she assured him. 'And Daisy will help unload our things, won't you?' she asked.

Seeing her mother's pleading expression, Daisy nodded.

'Of course. Well, let's go and take a look,' she said, trying to inject some enthusiasm into her voice. The sooner they got inside the better, for the cloud of flies swarming around them along with the foul stench coming from the outhouses was making her nauseous. And judging from the way her mother was swaying, her energy along with her optimism was rapidly waning.

'You help Mother and I'll go and open up,' Daisy told her father, pushing open the door marked thirteen. It was dingy inside but, determinedly, she tackled the steep stairs, trying to ignore the dirt littering the hallway. On the top floor a key dangled from one of the door handles. Gingerly, she turned it and, as the wooden panel creaked open, she suppressed a shudder. The bare floorboards were filthy, one rickety chair was upended in the middle of the room, another propped up at a scratched table. A rusty range was set into the corner on which stood a battered skillet. The only other room was taken up by a torn mattress amid huge balls of dust. Cobwebs festooned the ceiling like panels of dingy lace.

'Looks like the previous occupants left in a hurry,' Mabel panted as she stood in the living area surveying everything. Letting out a deep sigh, she sank wearily into the chair by the table.

'I'm sorry, love,' Arthur said, as he followed her in. 'The man I paid the rent to definitely said it was rooms on the ground floor.'

'Well, it's too late to do anything now; we'll sort it tomorrow,' Mabel replied, forcing a smile. 'We can't sleep in this mess though. You two go and bring up the bucket, broom and some cloths and we'll make a start on cleaning this place up.' Struggling to her feet, she removed her coat, folded it over the back of the chair then rolled up her sleeves. 'Oh, and you'd better fill the kettle before you bring it up. I take it we're going to have to share that water pipe outside?'

'Looks like it,' Arthur said sadly.

How could her mother even think of staying here, Daisy wondered, as they retraced their steps. This place was worse than dreadful. When she saw the ragamuffins picking through their things, she saw red.

'Here, get your thieving hands off,' she shouted, shaking her fists at one who'd climbed onto the barrow and donned her father's cap and muffler. As she caught hold of his arm to retrieve them, he squealed loudly, alerting the group of women who came scuttling over.

'Just you take your hands off my Jimmy, you cow,' a glassy-eyed woman screeched.

'Not 'til he gives my father's things back,' Daisy insisted, hanging onto the wriggling youth.

'Why you …' the woman hissed, raising her fist at Daisy.

'Come now, ladies, we don't have much ourselves, you know,' her father said quietly, placing himself firmly between them. 'Now be a good lad and hand back our things and I'll help you down,' he continued, staring into the boy's face.

'Can get down meself,' he muttered, tossing the muffler and cap into the dirt and jumping down on top of them.

'Why you …' Daisy cried but as she went to pull him off, her father gave her a warning look and put out a restraining hand.

'Right then, we'll start unloading,' he said adopting a cheerful tone, as he bent and picked them up. Excitement over, the little crowd dispersed, leaving Daisy shaking with anger.

'How can you be so calm?' she asked her father.

'No good getting their backs up. Your mother's waiting, so fill these while I find the other things we need,' he said, handing Daisy the bucket and kettle.

'But you still haven't told me what's happened,' Daisy began. 'And you do realise there are only two rooms in that dreadful place?'

'I know,' he said, frowning. 'There's obviously been some mistake and I'll get it sorted. Now go and fetch that water. We'll have a brew when we've finished and I'll explain everything then.' Seeing he wouldn't be drawn, Daisy walked over to the pump and began filling the utensils with water. The women watched her disdainfully then went back to their gossiping.

While Daisy began the mammoth task of trying to make the rooms habitable, her mother attempted to coax the range into life. Meanwhile, her father bustled back and forth carrying up the few possessions they'd managed to bring with them. No matter how hard her mother tried, the range wouldn't catch and finally, having only succeeded in filling the room with smoke, she gave up and collapsed back into the chair. Seeing how exhausted her parents looked, Daisy filled their mugs with water then perched on a folded blanket on the windowsill.

'So, exactly what happened today?' she asked, unable to contain her curiosity any longer.

Arthur sighed, took a long draught then placed his empty mug on the table.

'For some time now, the women at the factory have been unhappy with their working conditions. Often they find themselves up to their ankles in water and apparently there's defects with their sanitary arrangements. They even have to make their tea in a bucket, would you believe? Anyhow, this woman called Annie Jacks, a widow with five children to support, dared to voice her concerns, stating that even though she'd worked there for years, her wages were well below the men's and she could no longer afford to feed her family. The supervisor took against her, making coarse suggestions as to how she could earn more. Then this morning the checking man on the gate reprimanded her for being late and threatened to dock her money. When she protested that she was on time she was sacked. It was obviously a put-up job.'

'Knowing they'd end up in the workhouse where the family would be split up, your father stood up for her,' Mabel declared. 'And I'm proud of him.'

'Except we both got the sack,' he said wryly. 'Not only that, when the other women heard what happened they threatened to go on strike so the foreman dubbed me a troublemaker and refused to pay my week's wage. Like I said earlier, the landlord didn't take kindly to me not having all the rent so he kept our best bits of furniture. I had to find us cheaper rooms but I swear the man said they'd be on the ground floor.'

'Oh Father, that's a terrible thing to have happened,' Daisy said, waving away a bluebottle that buzzed against the cracked windowpane. 'Perhaps you can sort it out with him tomorrow,' she asked hopefully.

'I should never have put my own family's future at risk,' Arthur cried, banging his fist on the table in despair.

'You did what you thought right,' Mabel assured him.

'But now we're not far from destitution ourselves.'

'At least I've still got my sewing box so perhaps I can find some alteration work,' Mabel murmured, looking towards the window doubtfully.

'And I have a bit left from last week's pay,' Daisy said, delving into her pocket and placing a few coins in front of him.

'You're a good girl,' her mother said.

'Thanks, Daisy; that'll be a help. But I'll pay you back as soon as I get another job and decent rooms for us to stay in,' Arthur said, pocketing the money. 'I'll go and see the landlord first thing, then see who's hiring,' he added.

'In the meantime, we'll just have to make the best of it for tonight,' her mother said, frowning uncertainly at the mattress through the open doorway.

'I'll bed down with a blanket in here,' Daisy offered, eager to erase the worry lines that creased her mother's brow.

Hearing the sound of voices outside, they looked at each other but then a door slammed and all went quiet.

'Must be our neighbours,' Mabel said. 'I'll introduce myself tomorrow.'

'Be careful, love, you don't know who—' Arthur began only to be interrupted by a sharp knock. Exchanging worried looks, Arthur got to his feet but as he opened the door the aroma of meat pies wafted into the room, making Daisy's stomach growl.

'Hello there,' a woman's voice greeted. 'I'm Ruby Dickin and these are my daughters Sarah and Emma. We live across the hall and thought we'd pop over and introduce ourselves.'

'Come on in,' Mabel called, struggling to her feet. Although Daisy smiled brightly at the women, she couldn't help her glance straying to the parcels they were clutching.

'I'm Arthur Tucker, and this is my wife Mabel and daughter Daisy,' Arthur said making the introductions.

'Saw we had new neighbours and thought it would be friendly to share our supper, didn't we, girls? That's if you haven't already eaten?' she added, fair curls frizzing from under her bonnet as she talked. They were all wearing simple gowns, which, although well patched, looked clean, and with their straw-like hair and pale-blue eyes, it was easy to tell they were mother and daughters.

'How kind. Truth to tell we haven't even begun thinking of supper,' Mabel replied. 'I'd invite you to take a cuppa with us but I can't get the blessed range to work for love nor money.' Mabel groaned.

'It never has done,' Ruby declared. 'And to be truthful, gin's always been Cora's tipple, if you get my meaning. She were always moaning about having to go downstairs when she needed the privy. Didn't know she'd moved though 'til we came in and saw her in number six.'

'Are you thinking what I'm thinking?' Daisy asked, staring at her father.

'I am that,' Arthur replied, his lips tightening into a line.

'And I'm also thinking I'm going to tackle her right this minute.'

'I'll come with you,' Daisy told him, jumping to her feet, ready to do battle with that horrible woman.

Just then the ring of boots on cobbles and the sound of drunken singing shattered the peace of the evening.

'What the …' Daisy began.

'That's the men returning from the pub. Drunk as skunks they'll be and looking for trouble. If I were you, Mr Tucker,' Ruby advised, 'I'd come and eat your supper and stay well clear.'

Chapter 3

'Take a pew, kettle will be ready soon,' Ruby said, ushering them into her home and removing her bonnet. Daisy couldn't help looking around and comparing it to the dingy hovel they'd moved into across the hallway. Although the furniture was sparse and had obviously seen better days, everywhere was tidy and clean. Cushions on the wooden chairs and a rag rug beside the table lent the place a homely air.

'Oh, this is lovely,' Mabel cried, unwittingly echoing Daisy's thoughts.

'Surprising what a difference a few remnants from the market can make. Shame about the outside though.' Ruby shrugged, as they heard the sound of men swearing, a shout followed by scuffling and then the slamming of doors.

'Sounds like a flippin' army on the march out there.' Arthur frowned, getting up and peering out of the window. 'Just how many men are there?'

'Generally, there's around a hundred people living in this yard,' Ruby told them.

'What, just in these two rows of houses?' Daisy gasped, her eyes widening in horror.

'Yep. It's the same in the other three yards. Most of the

men meet up in the alehouses of an evening, get drunk, fight, go to bed, sleep it off then start it all over again tomorrow. It's no wonder some of their women take to gin.'

'Luckily Arthur doesn't squander his wages like that,' Mabel said.

'Well, good for you, Arthur, though you're in the minority round here. I was given a glass of gin once. Cried my eyes out all evening and never knew what I was blubbin' about. Tea's more to my taste and I'll make us that brew right now,' she said, carrying a large brown pot over to the range as the kettle began to sing. 'Sarah, you cut up those pies and pass them round; Emma, set out some more mugs.'

As they tucked in ravenously, Daisy was pleased to see her mother's face regain some colour. Today couldn't have been easy for her. She'd lived in their little house since she'd married Daisy's father eighteen years ago, saved hard for the few good pieces of furniture they'd had, and now, through no fault of her own, she'd been forced to move to this rough area. Yet, listening to her chatting with Ruby, you'd never think her world had been turned upside down.

'So, you all work in the laundry then?' Mabel was asking.

'Yes, huge place it is. The girls help with the washing and starching, while I iron. It's backbreaking work but keeps the wolf from the door.' The woman grimaced.

'The steam plays havoc with our hair, makes it stiff as straw,' Emma groaned. 'And that lye leaves our skin red and raw,' Sarah added, holding up her mottled hands. The picture they conjured up was so graphic, Daisy imagined sketching it.

'You're both very pretty though.' Mabel smiled. 'What are you, eighteen? Seventeen?' The girls beamed delightedly.

'I'm sixteen and Emma's fifteen,' Sarah explained.

'Our Daisy's sixteen too,' Mabel replied.

'Seventeen in January,' Daisy added quickly, for she'd felt quite grown up since Harry had proposed. Not that he'd sought her father's permission yet, only having asked her the night before he left. He'd promised to do things properly when he returned in the autumn, but having an understanding in the meantime was exciting. Almost as if she was aware of her thoughts, Mabel smiled indulgently at her, then turned to Ruby.

'Have you been here long?'

'Six years now. These rooms were all I could afford after my George were taken.'

'Oh, I am sorry,' Mabel murmured.

'You get used to it.' Ruby sighed. 'And my girls are such a comfort,' she added, beaming at Sarah and Emma. 'Anyhow, things are on the up now we've got nice new neighbours. What brings you to this neck of the woods, if you don't mind my asking?'

As Arthur explained how their change in circumstances had come about, Ruby nodded sadly. 'It's true conditions for women in some of the factories are dire. Though it ain't right you losing your job for sticking up for a widow with a family to support, sometimes it's best to keep your head down.'

'But things do need to change,' Sarah cried, staring at her mother in horror.

Daisy nodded. 'Perhaps women should start speaking up for themselves.'

'Not easy though, is it? My friend Fanny works ten and a half hours each day in the jam factory lugging huge vats of boiling pulp across the floor. She's always scalding herself on the sticky syrup and her arms are a right mess. Yet it's a job, and her family need her wages so she daren't risk being sacked,' Ruby lamented, shaking her head. 'What about you, Daisy? Where do you work?'

'At the Fun Factory,' she replied. 'I began by helping to clean the costumes and now run errands, that sort of thing. I really love drawing and my ambition is to work with the scenery designers,' she added. They stared admiringly at her and she wondered if she'd made it sound grander than it was.

'You'd best be careful; sit still for two minutes and you'll find yourself in a picture,' Mabel quipped, making them laugh.

'Actually, there's a vacancy coming up that I intend going for. It'll mean more money,' Daisy said, looking to her father for approval. But his lips tightened and she realised money was a sore subject. 'Still, I enjoy it there and even get to meet some of the performers,' she added quickly.

'Have you met that Charlie Chaplin bloke?' Emma asked excitedly.

'Not yet, but I keep hoping. Lots of actors use the factory rehearsal rooms to work out their routines, so you never know who you'll bump into.'

'And do women get treated the same as men?'

'It's not something I've thought about,' she admitted. 'Although some like Scarlett, she's one of the artists, do have opportunities to progress. Mr Karno, the Guv'nor, takes on people for their talents and expertise.'

'Don't tell me we have an enlightened employer around here?' Ruby exclaimed.

'It's time women had more of a say and I'm going to join the suffrage movement for that very reason,' Sarah declared. 'They've a meeting in the halls next weekend; why don't you come along, Daisy?'

'Oh, we won't be here then,' Mabel interrupted before Daisy could reply.

'No, of course not,' Ruby agreed. 'So, what are your plans, Arthur?'

'First thing in the morning, I'm going to see who's hiring. Then I'll pay a visit to that landlord who promised me rooms on the ground floor,' he growled.

'Good for you. And what about you, Mabel?' Ruby asked, glancing down at Mabel's misshapen legs. 'Not that I'm being nosy, you understand.'

'Used to be a seamstress in Maison Fashions until a fall messed up my legs. Since then I've taken in mending and alterations but it's unlikely there'll be any work in Tiger Yard,' she said wryly. 'But then we'll not be here long.'

'Well, good luck with that. I only came here for a few months to sort myself out but time rolls on and the rent keeps going up.' She shrugged, stifling a yawn.

'I can't thank you enough for your kindness tonight. That pie and tea were lifesavers,' Mabel said, getting to her feet. 'Let me help clear away before we go.'

'Wouldn't dream of it, would we, girls?' Ruby replied. Sarah and Emma shook their heads.

'It's been fun hearing about your job, Daisy. Do you ever

get to see any of the shows?' Emma asked, looking at her hopefully.

'Oh, my Lor',' Daisy cried, slapping her forehead. 'I was meant to be meeting Kezia at the Hippodrome earlier.'

'Well, I'm sure she'll understand,' Mabel replied. 'Now come along; it's been a busy day and we must let these ladies get to their beds. Thank you again for your kindness. You must let me cook you a meal in return; hopefully it won't be next door though.'

'It's been a pleasure meeting you lovely folk. If you're still here tomorrow when we get back from the laundry, I'll pop in and look at your range. Blinkin' temperamental most of them, but you can usually get them to work. Lucky it's summer or you'd be shivering in your boots.'

Their rooms seemed even more bleak after the cosiness of Ruby's home and Daisy tried not to cringe.

'At least it's getting dark so we won't see any remaining dust,' Mabel said with forced cheerfulness.

'Or mice,' Daisy grimaced as they heard scratching coming from the corner of the room.

'Dread to think what's behind that old range,' Mabel muttered. 'Can't believe anyone could live in such squalor. You'd think that woman would have had more pride. I mean Ruby's got the same accommodation yet she's made it homely.'

'As I'm sure you would, my dear,' Arthur replied.

'I sincerely hope it won't come to that,' she shuddered. 'Now, come and help me make up that mattress in the other room. Are you sure you'll be alright in here, Daisy?'

'Yes, I'll bed down with a blanket,' she replied, grabbing

one with mock enthusiasm, for she couldn't imagine she'd get a wink of sleep.

To Daisy's surprise, despite hearing the strange noises of the building settling for the night, and the scratching and scuttling coming from behind the walls, the upsets of the day caught up with her and she soon fell asleep.

The sun was creeping above the horizon when Daisy woke. She felt stiff from sleeping on the floor and clambered gingerly to her feet, stretching to ease her muscles. Her father's cap had gone from the back of the chair so he must have crept out at first light in order to find work. Hearing her mother's gentle snores, she hurriedly dressed and slipped outside. Despite the early hour, she had to queue to use the disgusting facilities the outhouse offered. Everyone looked bleary-eyed as they shuffled impatiently from one leg to the other and clutched their precious supply of paper. Nobody took any notice of her, although one old man leered lasciviously as he came out of the privy, stopping right in front of her and making a show of doing up his trousers. Deliberately, she turned away and, ignoring his ribald remarks, hurried into the vacant cubicle.

The stench made her retch for the floor was awash with goodness knows what. How on earth could people live in such filth, she wondered, as she hurried out of the yard and retraced her steps of the previous day. She hoped her father found employment quickly so that they could move on, for she knew her mother would have trouble managing the stairs. She wished she could stay and help but her money was needed more than ever so she didn't dare risk being late for work.

As she hurried down the alley and past the public house, the disgusting smell from the outhouse seemed to stay with her, but then her attention was taken up by the volume of traffic teeming round the roads by the Green. Electric trams, their bells clanging were sparking and squeaking their way to and from the town centre; horse-drawn ones were heading out to the suburbs; the occasional motor car wove between the laden carts while wagons of all shapes and sizes jostled for position on the cobbles as they all tried to avoid the tram lines. People were rushing in all directions on the pavements in front of the shops and the noise and chaos was horrendous. Daisy realised she must have been too shocked to take it all in the previous evening.

Having weaved her way through the bustling throng, she turned into the comparative quiet of Coldharbour Lane and joined the workers making their way through the wide doors of the Fun Factory. After listening to the tales Sarah and Emma had to tell about the working conditions for women at other factories, Daisy now realised how lucky she was. However, their discussion had certainly spurred her on to ask Stan, the overseer, about being promoted. After all, the worst that could happen would be he'd say no. Determined to tackle him, she squared her shoulders and strode down the corridor.

'Surprised to see you heading towards Tiger Yard last night,' Arnie sneered as he appeared beside Daisy. 'And with that barrow being loaded up like that, anyone would think you'd moved there.'

'But I thought you lived in the other direction,' Daisy countered.

'I do,' he scoffed, stressing the words. 'Thought you did too but if you've hit hard times you've only got to tell Arnie,' he added, thrusting his pointed face closer. Immediately, he jumped back again, his nose wrinkling. 'Blimey,' he groaned, then his expression turned to one of glee.

Daisy was about to ask what was wrong when she saw the overseer bearing down on them.

'Bragg, go and tidy the props-room; Tucker, get yourself along to the studio,' he ordered.

Remembering her earlier resolve she smiled. 'Sir, I've been thinking—'

'Well, do it later. Come on, jump to it. We've important American visitors arriving any moment.'

'Yes, sir,' Daisy replied and much to her surprise, instead of arguing, Arnie shot her a jubilant look and swaggered off towards the storeroom.

Resolving to speak to the overseer later, Daisy let herself into the studio.

'Morning. I hear we have important visitors arriving soon, so what can I do to help?'

'Nice to see someone so bright and breezy,' Scarlett murmured, looking up from the floor where she was kneeling beside her canvas. 'If you could just pass me that brush,' she added, gesturing to the desk. But as Daisy turned to do so, she heard her gasp.

'Heavens, Daisy, what on earth have you got down the back of your skirt?'

Chapter 4

'What do you mean?' Daisy asked, peering down at her pinafore. 'Oh, my Lor'!' she exclaimed as she saw the ominous dark stain along the back of the hem. No wonder she'd thought the noxious stench was following her.

'Blimey Daisy, you don't smell too good either,' Blue said, holding his nose. 'If I didn't know better, I'd say you was covered in …' he stopped at the sound of footsteps approaching. From the way Stan was speaking about the scenery, it was obvious he intended showing the visitors around their studio.

'Quick, hide behind that big canvas and take off your things. I've a spare outfit you can borrow,' Scarlett cried, jumping to her feet and snatching a red smock from one of the drawers. As Daisy did as she'd been told, she heard the woman murmuring to Blue and, when she emerged, Scarlett handed her a blue beret. 'Tuck your hair under this; it looks as shaggy as a bird's nest this morning. And for heaven's sake, wipe the … muck off those filthy boots then hide your pinafore in the cupboard behind you.'

As the voices grew louder, the footsteps nearer, Daisy swallowed down her disgrace. How had she not noticed the state she was in? No wonder Arnie had looked so smug, she thought, stuffing her things out of sight. Frantically she stared around for something to do, but there were no more canvases waiting to be primed.

'Stan'll kill me if he sees me standing idle. What on earth shall I do when they come in?'

'Don't panic, Daisy. Just stand beside me and listen. I'll pretend to be tutoring you in the art of stage design,' Scarlett replied, smiling as she tilted Daisy's beret at a jaunty angle. 'You look quite the artist in that get-up, doesn't she, Blue?'

The man turned from the drawer he'd been tactfully tidying whilst Daisy had changed out of her dirty clothes and nodded.

'You look and smell decidedly better.' He grinned. 'Best paint a smile on your face though. The Guv'nor likes his visitors to see happy workers.'

'Pay attention,' Scarlett hissed, as the door opened. 'Like I was saying, it doesn't matter how long it is between productions, or which theatre they're being acted in, all the sets for the same play have to be an exact replica of each other. To ensure we get the detail correct we refer to the original sketches,' she said, her clear voice carrying as she handed Daisy the Stage Design folder.

'Make the most of this opportunity and show them what you can do,' Blue murmured, giving her a surreptitious wink. 'Ah, good morning gentlemen, do come in,' he invited, assuming his posh voice as he turned towards the two men standing beside Stan. Both were smartly dressed in well-cut jackets and matching trousers, and both tipped their trilby hats before looking intently around the room. Thank heavens she'd tidied all the paints before she'd left the previous evening, Daisy thought. Then she noticed Arnie lurking behind them, his face wreathed in ingratiating smiles, but when he spotted Daisy dressed in her smock and beret he scowled.

'Mr John Ackerman and Mr Cal Brady are friends of the Guv'nor and are here to see what we do at the Fun Factory,' Stan explained.

'Good morning, I'm John,' the taller of the men drawled as he moved to study the canvas Scarlett was working on.

'And what are you doing?' Cal, his companion, asked Daisy.

'Daisy Tucker is our ru—' Stan began.

'Apprentice artist,' Scarlett cut in, smiling at the men. 'And she's showing real promise.'

'Great stuff.' The men nodded in unison, addressing Blue.

'We know Mr Karno encourages his employees to use their talent so it's good to see you putting it into practice,' John said.

Stan puffed out his chest, his irritation at having been corrected by Scarlett turning to a self-satisfied smile.

'Of course; I always try to carry out Mr Karno's wishes to the best of my ability,' he smirked.

'And of course it's me that's in line for the promotion that's coming up here,' Arnie announced.

'Oh?' John questioned, looking straight at the overseer.

'The vacancy hasn't yet been filled,' Stan said quickly.

'So what is your apprentice contributing to this scene?' the younger man asked Blue, peering at the canvas.

'As you can see, we are painting one of the boxes for the side of the stage and Daisy will be adding the detail.'

'And I'm going to as well,' Arnie added, hurrying over to the canvas.

'Well, in that case, young man, perhaps you can explain what you need to achieve here. I take it you appreciate the premise of the show?'

'Yea, well, the picture says it all,' he replied, waving his arm around in front of the canvas.

'Hmm,' Cal responded, looking less than impressed. 'Perhaps you could enlighten me further, young lady.' Daisy looked at Blue who nodded encouragingly.

'Of course, sir. It's a representation of a music hall performance as viewed by a stage audience.'

'And you, boy, perhaps you can tell me the title of this show?' the younger man asked, turning his attention to Arnie.

'Er well, I …' He shrugged.

'It was originally *Entertaining the Shah* but now it's known as *A Stage upon a Stage*, sir,' Daisy said as a heavy silence fell over the room.

'Gee, you got to admit the girl sure knows her stuff,' the taller man told Blue.

'You say there's a promotion coming up?' Cal turned to Stan, who nodded.

'Well, let's see what their drawing's like,' he suggested. Daisy's heart flipped. Until this moment the only thing she'd put on a canvas was primer.

'That's where you'll see my real talent,' Arnie crowed.

'Is that so,' Blue muttered. 'Right, you can both replicate this crimson rose,' he said, pointing to a page in the Stage

Design folder. As he leaned forward, he whispered to Daisy. 'This really is your chance.'

'You may use any materials you wish,' Scarlett told them both.

Arnie moved straight to the centre of the backdrop and, with barely a glance at the folder, began sketching. Meanwhile, intent on realising her dream, Daisy studied the drawing to check the exact position of the rose in the scene. Nervously, she began sketching, then as the petals took shape, her confidence grew and by the time she'd filled in the graduated colour, she found she was enjoying herself. Lost in her work, she forgot she was being watched until she heard a cough.

'You can certainly paint, kiddo,' Cal whistled. 'And that vibrancy, I can almost smell its perfume.' He moved over to Arnie's image.

'As you can see, mine's bolder,' Arnie beamed. Daisy stared at his rose and her heart sank, for so much depended on how their work was judged.

'Well, Cal, you can finish up here,' John said, darting a look at his colleague. 'Perhaps you'd like to show me where the props are stored,' he added, turning to Arnie.

'Yea, cors I will. I know where everything is kept. After you, sir,' he said, and, shooting Daisy a triumphant look, followed the man from the room. To Daisy's surprise, Cal was still studying her drawing.

'Brash,' he murmured.

'Oh, I see,' she mumbled, frowning. She didn't think it was that bright, but then it was meant to be a representation of the rose in the folder.

'No, I meant that young man,' he said. 'His rose is too garish and he took no notice of the set layout. You, my dear, have got real talent,' he added, smiling at Daisy.

'We always thought she'd be perfect for scenery design, sir,' Scarlett told him, shooting the overseer a knowing look.

'I agree. And it's great to see you guys suitably arrayed for your roles. I know Fred, er Mr Karno, always says if you dress the part, you'll act it,' Cal continued. 'Although I have to say those beautiful amethyst eyes are completely overshadowed by that bright-red smock, Daisy.' He turned to Stan. 'Can't you have the costume department fit her one in a softer hue? Moss green would enhance and make them sparkle.'

'Well, I er …' the overseer blustered, but Cal had turned back to the artists.

'Forgive my obsession with detail; it's an occupational hazard. I'm here to help the head costumier put together outfits for our trip on the *Cairnrona* next month so am somewhat fired up.'

'Your opinion is most valued, sir, and we'll be delighted to act on it, won't we?' Blue said, glancing at Stan who muttered in agreement.

'I think Daisy has passed her induction with flying colours, don't you?' Scarlett added.

'Oh, er yes, of course,' Stan spluttered, a dull flush spreading up his neck. 'Well, Mr Cal, sir, if you've seen enough here shall we continue our tour of the Fun Factory?'

As he ushered the man quickly out of the studio, Blue and Scarlett collapsed into hysterics.

'Did you see Stan's face?' Scarlett spluttered. 'And as

for that Arnie, what an obnoxious little twerp. Could you imagine having to put up with him every day?'

'Not in a thousand years.' Blue grimaced. 'Anyway, well done Daisy. That really is a realistic-looking rose. But wherever did you learn all that information about the play?'

'It was written on the inside cover of the folder,' Daisy admitted, sending Scarlett and Blue into peals of laughter once more.

'Honestly, Daisy, you're such a scream. And there was me thinking you were being demure looking down like that. Oh, it's going to be fun having you in the studio with us. Welcome aboard,' Scarlett cried.

'You mean I really will be working alongside you?' Daisy asked, hardly daring to believe her luck.

'Well, Stan can hardly go back on his word now, can he?' Blue replied. 'And we'll make sure you get that new smock too. With matching beret, of course.' Daisy's heart flipped only to flop when Scarlett turned to her.

'Talking of clothes, you didn't tell us how you came to be in that filthy state this morning? I know the dirt on the streets can turn to mud but it wasn't raining.'

'Well, I ...' she stuttered to a halt, not wanting to lie yet loath to reveal the squalid conditions she'd endured that morning. However, before she could think of a plausible explanation, the door burst open and Stan appeared, his face as red as the crimson paint Daisy had been using.

'Blinkin' prima donnas,' he spluttered, 'thought you were being flippin' clever, didn't you?'

'But Stan, I thought you wanted us to impress the Guv'nor's

visitors. I mean they'll have plenty of time to swap stories about their visit on their voyage to America next month.' Scarlett smiled. Stan gave an indignant huff then turned to Daisy.

'Get back to your work. There's props need loading onto the cart.'

'Oh, but ...' Daisy began, her spirits sinking. What a fool she'd been to think she'd really been promoted to the job of her dreams.

'Hang on, Stan,' Blue said firmly. 'Daisy's our apprentice now.'

'I've not made any firm decision yet. And she knows as much about painting as one of them dog's hairs in that brush,' Stan growled, pointing to Daisy's paintbrush.

'Hog's bristles, not dog's hair,' Scarlett scoffed. 'You could at least use the correct name.'

'You and your bloomin' names,' Stan huffed.

'We like to get things correct, you know that,' Scarlett continued unabashed. 'Daisy clearly has a lot of potential and she volunteered to help when we were hard-pressed to meet deadlines.'

'Like I said, I've not made my decision as to who—'

'But it's not your decision to make, is it, old man?' Blue replied, getting to his feet. 'You seem to forget that I'm head of this studio and, as such, outrank you. We've been needing an assistant in here for weeks and Daisy's not only shown willing, she has talent and passed that impromptu test with flying colours. Which is more than that imbecile did. Daisy is now our apprentice.' Although he spoke quietly his tone brooked no argument. Seeing he'd been outmanoeuvred, the overseer edged towards the door.

'One more thing,' Blue added, stopping the man in his tracks. 'I think Daisy should go to costume and get fitted out. If those gentlemen see her sporting a new outfit, they'll know you've taken their advice,' he added, his voice conciliatory now.

'Daisy, run along to the costume department and get yourself fitted for a green smock. And don't forget to say Stan sent you. Well, don't just stand there, girl.'

Her thoughts running amok, Daisy sped along the corridor. She couldn't wait to tell her parents when she got home. But where would that be tonight? How she hoped her father had found somewhere nicer than Tiger Yard. At least if she had a new smock to wear, she could smuggle the dirty pinafore home in her bag and wash it. Her mother prided herself on the snowy whiteness of her laundry and would have a fit if she saw the state it was in.

Daisy pushed her way through the press of workers at finishing time, feeling glamorous in her new outfit. Not only did the colour suit her, the billowing smock added gentle curves to her willowy frame, the green beret highlighting flashes of gold in her otherwise nondescript fair hair. Blimey, she was even thinking like an artist now. Wait until Harry heard her news, she thought, as she scoured the crowds for her parents. But there was no sign of either of them and her spirits sank to her boots. She'd been so sure they'd be there to meet her. Dejectedly, she was about to turn towards Tiger Yard when someone yanked her arm.

'Thinks you got one over on me, do you, clever clogs?' Daisy's heart sank as she turned to find Arnie glaring at her.

'Hello, Arnie; had a good day?' she asked brightly, ignoring his taunt.

'No, I blinkin' well haven't. And if you thinks I'm running errands while you prance around in that fancy get-up, you got another think coming. Them artists like a bit of class in their studio.'

'Yes, they do,' Daisy agreed. 'And that's what they've got.'

'Hardly,' he scoffed. 'I knew something was up when I saw you coming to work looking like a scarecrow and smelling of god knows what, so I bin making enquiries. Them's higher up won't be pleased when they hear their new apprentice lives in the slums, will they?' Daisy's heart sank. She couldn't lose her job now.

'You want to get your facts right, Arnie,' Daisy retorted. 'Circumstances meant we had to stay there last night. But that was it, the one night.'

With that, Daisy hefted her bag onto her shoulder and strode off. Hearing his footsteps following, she turned right as if she was heading for their old home. Then she darted down the narrow alley between the roads, shinned over a wall, before doubling back on herself.

Chapter 5

How dare Arnie follow her, she seethed. They might have been in competition at work but what Daisy did afterwards and where she lived was none of his business. She knew appearances counted, but she'd worked hard to win her promotion and, although it had come about in an unexpected way, nothing was going to prevent her from achieving her ambition. Taking a quick look over her shoulder to ensure she'd shaken off her nemesis, she didn't see the bicycle on the road ahead.

'Hey, look where you're going!' an indignant male shouted, ringing his bell as he wobbled precariously to avoid her. Then he screeched to a stop and stared hard at her. 'Cripes, Daisy, is that you?' he added, looking at her in astonishment.

'Harry, what are you doing here?' she exclaimed, shock turning to delight as she stared into familiar cornflower-blue eyes.

'Offered to deliver this order to a special customer of Father's,' he replied, patting the brown package in the basket strapped to the handlebars. 'It's a fair hike but I thought it'd give me the opportunity to call on one of my special girls,' he explained.

'One of your special girls! Being as how you've asked me to become your wife, I should hope I'm your only girl, Harry Wylde,' she spluttered. Then seeing his lips twitching, she slapped him playfully on the arm.

'For such a slight wench you don't half pack a punch. I'm going to be a battered husband by the look of things,' he groaned. 'Wow, what's with the artist's get-up?' he asked, eyeing her up and down appreciatively.

'Oh Harry, you'll never guess what's happened,' she cried.

'Something exciting by the way you're jumping up and down. Look, I haven't got long as I've to be back in time to help Father shut up the shop. The customer lives the other side of the park so walk with me and tell me your news,' he said, vaulting nimbly off his bike and landing beside her. For a moment she thought he was going to take her hand, but the street was crowded with workers making their way home and he clearly thought better of it. However, as they sauntered side by side, the warmth emanating from his body was enough to send her pulses racing.

'Shame I haven't got one of those double bicycles; you know, a tandem. Then you could ride behind me while I'd serenade you with the song "Daisy Bell". You know, "Daisy, Daisy, give me your answer do",' he trilled, turning to her and gesturing with his free hand. His powerful voice and cheery face had people smiling as they passed by and Daisy couldn't help laughing.

'You're an idiot, Harry Wylde. For one thing I've already given you my answer and, for another, I didn't even know you could ride a bicycle,' she said, as they strolled through the gates.

'Errand boy extraordinaire, that's me,' he cried, tilting his flat cap to the back of his head so that his sandy hair flopped over his forehead. While he wasn't overly tall, his broad shoulders gave him a commanding air. 'Well, that's when I'm not counting tacks and nails or measuring lengths of chain. Those might not be the precious metals I'm being trained to craft but if I want Father to fund my second year, I must pay my way. But enough of me, fair maiden, tell me your wondrous news.' Propping his bicycle against a tree, he threw himself down onto the grass and patted the space beside him. As he surreptitiously took her hand and gave it a squeeze, their gazes locked. Tremors of excitement shivered through her and the voices of passers-by faded into the background. 'I've really missed you, petal,' he murmured, running his fingers up and down her arm.

'I've missed you too,' she whispered. Time seemed to stand still as they stared at each other and Daisy could swear butterflies were having a ball in her stomach. With a groan he broke the spell.

'Well, come on, spill the beans. Why are you prancing around like a little leprechaun? A delightful one, I might add. That green makes your mauve eyes look almost luminous.'

'Amethyst,' she corrected him. 'Well, at least that's what the American man, Cal, told me when he came to the Fun Factory.'

'Did he now?' Harry asked, frowning. 'And do I have reason to be jealous of this American fellow, Cal?'

'No, silly, he must be in his thirties at least, and quite thin,' she told him, coyly eyeing his muscular frame. 'Cal's here to assist the head costumier, so knows about colours and things. He and his colleague visited the studio and I had to pretend to be Scarlett and Blue's apprentice.' She would tell him about Tiger Yard later, she thought, and proceeded to relate the rest of her story.

'You mean you were actually reading the answers from the folder?' Harry whistled. 'Good for you, girl. That's using your initiative, that is.'

'But it did make me realise something,' Daisy explained, relishing his admiring gaze. 'Knowing the background to the story helps you see the picture – literally.'

'It's the same with all art,' he agreed. 'I've been looking into the history of Celtic jewellery and they use different shapes to signify the meaning. Any more amazing news?'

'That's it, really. For all Arnie's blustering, it was me who got the promotion. So, you are now looking at an artists' apprentice.'

'Well done, Daisy. You deserve it,' he murmured, respect shining from his eyes as he leaned forward to kiss her on the cheek. Somehow, though, his lips landed on hers and Daisy felt her passion rising.

'Sorry,' Harry gasped, moving away. 'Except I'm not, if you know what I mean,' he grinned cheekily. Daisy peered anxiously around in case they'd been seen but the few people nearby were hurrying home for their supper and nobody was taking any notice of them.

'Of course, I've got to work hard to prove myself or I might find myself back to running errands again,' she told him, trying to quell the emotions he'd stirred.

'That would be a wicked waste,' he replied, shaking his head. 'I always thought it a shame you had to work instead of going art school. You've more talent than many of the pupils there and it's good that's been recognised.'

Daisy smiled at him. 'You're like a salve to my soul, as Mother would say.'

'Glad to be of service,' he intoned, doffing his cap ceremoniously so that his sandy hair curled around his collar.

'Idiot,' she laughed.

'Seriously though, after the holidays perhaps I could help you with some of the finer points. We could come here in the evenings and sketch designs together. The natural world is inspiring and lends itself to creativity, don't you think?' he enthused, gesturing around the park.

'Oh yes, Harry, I do,' she agreed, following his gaze.

'And of course, after sitting down for so long, we'll have to stretch our legs by taking strolls around the bandstand.' He winked. Warmth flooded through her at the thought but her delight turned to dismay as he took out a gold timepiece and frowned.

'Father insisted I take this so I've no excuse for being late back,' he explained. Leaning closer, he gave her a quick kiss then jumped to his feet. 'If all goes well with this delivery, I too may have some good news when term starts.'

'Oh, what's that?' she asked, fighting down her disappointment that he had to leave so soon.

'If this comes off, you'll be first to know,' he told her. 'Sorry I can't walk you back but I daren't risk upsetting this customer. I'll see if I can arrange another delivery around here so we can spend more time together,' he promised, as he clambered onto his bike.

She was about to tell him that they no longer lived in Vaughan Road so she could accompany him to the edge of the park, but already he was pedalling furiously. She watched until he was a dot in the distance, still basking in his admiration. A talented artist himself, he'd decided to specialise in jewellery making, and his compliments about her work meant a lot. Having found herself looking at the backdrops in a different way, it seemed they now had another common bond.

It had been a lovely surprise bumping into him, almost literally, and she'd have to content herself with that, she thought, heading out of the park. Her mind was full of Harry and the emotions he aroused in her, as she hurried up the hill, dodging the carts, trams and horses. It was only as she reached the top that her thoughts turned to her father. How she hoped he'd managed to secure a new job and that her parents were packing up the barrow with their possessions. Almost as if thinking about him had made him appear, she heard a shout.

'Where've you been?' Arthur cried. 'Your mother's fretting you've been attacked or something so sent me out to find you.'

'I'm sorry I'm late, Father. Harry had a delivery to make for his father so he came to see me and …' she was about to tell him about her new job when she saw how fatigued he was looking. 'Any luck today?' she asked, although she feared she knew the answer.

'Seems no one's hiring at the moment. Although if I present myself at the gates of the brewery first thing in the morning, I might pick up some casual labour. Of course, there'll be hundreds of others doing the same. I suppose there's always them,' he muttered, gesturing to the Tiger public house they were passing.

'But you don't drink, Father. What about the landlord? Did you see him?'

'Surprisingly he wasn't available and his so-called assistant said I must have got the wrong room number.' He gave a harsh laugh. 'I'll catch up with the blighter, but for the time being we're—'

'Stuck at thirteen,' she finished for him. 'Oh, poor Mother.'

'I should never have risked my job by standing up for that woman. All those steps, the filth …' he sighed, wrinkling his nose at the stench coming from the outhouses. Daisy linked her arm through his.

'Don't worry, Father; it'll all come right, you'll see,' she told him, her heart sinking as she stared at the grey washing hanging limply from a line between the rows of houses.

'You're a good girl, Daisy,' he murmured. 'I don't know what we'd do without you.'

'Still 'ere then?' Cora sneered, leaning against her door frame. 'Thought you'd be too posh to stay.'

'Good evening to you,' Arthur called.

'Fancy a bit of fun, love?' she invited, batting her eyelashes as she looked him up and down. Arthur smiled politely, but quickened his pace. 'As for you, who do you think you are strutting around dressed like some bohemian trollop,' Cora spat after them.

Daisy felt her temper rising but, as she turned to give the woman a mouthful, her father caught hold of her arm and urged her towards number thirteen.

'How dare she! Why didn't you let me put her in her place?' Daisy demanded.

'As your mother says, we might have to stay here, but we don't have to stoop to their level.'

'But Father, she was making eyes at you,' Daisy cried. 'I don't know how you can even speak to her after what she did.' Daisy huffed indignantly as they climbed the stairs.

'Keep your voice down, Daisy; we don't want to worry your mother, do we?' Arthur implored, but she was saved from answering as Mabel called to them through the open door.

'There you are.' She was sitting in the chair picking winkles from their shells with a pin. 'You look a bit flushed, love, not sickening for something, are you?' Mabel frowned as she took in Arthur's heightened colour.

'I'm fine,' he mumbled. 'Just a bit hot out there.'

'And as for you, Daisy Tucker, I thought you'd done a runner,' she added, grinning at her little joke. 'My word girl, what are you wearing?'

'I've been promoted to artists' apprentice and this is my new outfit,' she exclaimed, her excitement returning. 'Although I'll have to work hard to prove myself,' she added quickly, seeing her father's mouth tighten.

'Well, that's grand, our Daisy,' her mother said. 'I have to say you look a bobby-dazzler in that green. Give me your pinafore and I'll see it gets laundered, though that wash-house is something else.' Mabel shook her head as she gestured to Daisy's bag.

'Don't worry, Mother,' she said quickly, 'I'll do it after supper.'

'In that case, you can butter the bread to go with these,' Mabel told her, peering bleakly down at the bowl. 'Not that you get much for your money. That fisher boy might have had scales on his barrow but I reckon he had his hand on them when he weighed these.'

'You managed the stairs alright then, Mother?' Daisy asked.

'Took me a while and by the time I got outside, there was only the winkles left.' She shrugged. 'Still your father brought a loaf home with him so with a bit of a scrape we should have ourselves some sort of meal. No luck with that rust bucket though.' She sighed, glaring at the useless contraption in the corner.

'Ruby promised to take a look when she gets home,' Daisy reminded her.

'So she did,' her mother agreed. 'Not that I can offer her a meal tonight.'

'I'm sure she's not expecting one until the range is working,' Daisy placated, knowing that repaying hospitality was important to her mother.

'Well, let's get eating. You'll find vinegar in there,' Mabel told Daisy, gesturing to the rickety cupboard hanging from the wall. 'I've given the shelf a good scrub but we'd best keep everything covered in case those dratted mice get in.'

Arthur and Mabel sat at the scratched table while Daisy perched on her blanket on the sill beside the cracked windowpane. Before long, they heard the drunken shouts of the men returning from the public house.

'I've been thinking, Arthur,' Mabel said, slice of bread midway to her mouth. 'We might be on our uppers but no good will come of you working in one of them places. Dens of iniquity, the lot of them.'

'I might not have any choice, Mabel. There's not much work around so we might be stuck here longer than we thought.'

'What about that young woman you helped, Father? Have you heard what's happened to her?' Daisy asked.

Arthur pushed his half-eaten meal away. 'It seems that like us she was unable to pay her rent so was turned out of her home.'

Daisy frowned. 'But she'll get another job, surely?'

'Word's spread. None of the other factories will employ her so with a large family to feed she's had no choice …'

'What do you mean?' Daisy persisted.

'She's had to enter the workhouse. With one daughter and four sons, they'll be separated too.'

'That's terrible,' Daisy replied.

'Oh my, the poor woman,' Mabel cried. 'And to think I've been fretting about having to leave my best bits of furniture behind. At least we're all together.'

'And I sincerely hope we can stay that way,' Arthur

murmured, passing his hand across his eyes. 'If I can't get any work and we're evicted, we might still go the same way.'

As they sat reflecting on his words, a sharp rap sounded on the door, making them jump. Daisy shivered and stared at her parents in dismay.

Chapter 6

'Coo-ee, only me,' Ruby called.

'Goodness, we're afraid of our own shadows,' Mabel murmured as they stared at each other in relief.

'I'll let her in,' Daisy said, jumping to her feet.

'Sorry to interrupt your meal,' Ruby cried, breezing through the door. She was wearing a flowery apron, her hair tied up in a scarf, a long, stout stick in her hand. 'Tools of the trade,' she explained as Mabel's eyes widened in horror.

'Oh, I thought …' Mabel began, then shook her head. 'We had bread and winkles but I'm afraid there wasn't enough to share.'

'Not to worry, we're having bubble and squeak,' Ruby told her, waving away her apologies. 'The girls are at the pump washing the spuds and cabbage while I'm here to take a look at that range of yours. My, you're all looking peaky; has something happened?' she added, taking in their pale faces.

'Just gasping for a cuppa,' Mabel replied, trying to make light of things.

'Well, let's take a gander and see what the problem is. They don't call me Ruby Repair for nothing.' The woman smiled, rolling up her sleeves. 'We're late home tonight on account of one of the boarding houses needing their sheets doing today instead of tomorrow. Means a bit extra though, so mustn't grumble. How's things with you? Any luck, Arthur?'

'No, neither on the work front nor catching up with that bloomin' landlord. Hasn't been in his office all afternoon apparently.'

'No, he wouldn't have been. From what I've heard he's been made comfortable at number six. Cora pays her rent in kind, if you get my meaning,' she said, bending down and fiddling with the range.

'You don't mean ...' Mabel spluttered, her hand going to her throat.

'Oldest trick in the book – and men like Gardner are only too happy to take advantage.'

'No wonder she was gloating,' Daisy exploded. 'And she asked Fa—'

'I'm going down to see her right away,' Arthur interrupted, shooting Daisy a warning look as he got to his feet and snatched up his cap.

'No, Arthur, we might have to stay here until you get another job, but I don't want either of you associating with the likes of her,' Mabel insisted.

'I hope you're not insinuating I might be tempted by that trollop,' Arthur spluttered, colour suffusing his face.

'Of course not. You're the most trustworthy man I know,' Mabel told him. 'But if people see you talking to her – well, all I'm saying is there's no smoke without fire and we don't want Daisy's reputation questioned either.'

'I agree with you there, Mabel,' Ruby said, looking up from

where she was kneeling beside the range. 'There's nothing Cora's gang likes better than spreading tittle-tattle.'

Daisy shuddered. Arnie would be in his element if he got a hint of what went on in Tiger Yard. With his predilection for troublemaking, it would be all round the Factory in next to no time. She wanted to make a success of her job but wouldn't be able to hold her head up if her employer got wind of any scandal, even by implication. What a place. The sooner they left here the better, she thought, staring out of the window where the filthy urchins were grubbing around in the dirt. Poor little mites, what chance did they have in life? Realising Ruby was speaking to her, she jolted herself back to the present.

'If you don't mind me saying, Daisy, although you look lovely in that green get-up, it might be better if you wore something a bit, shall we say, less flaunty round here. It don't do to draw attention to yourself in the yard.'

'But this is my new uniform,' Daisy protested. 'It goes with my promotion and sets me apart from the runners.'

'That's fine at work, Daisy, but Ruby's right: we need to look as though we fit in around here. Although we'll maintain our own standards, of course,' Mabel declared. 'Your clean pinafore is on our bed. Give me the one you've been wearing and I'll see it gets washed.' Daisy's heart sank but she was grateful for the diversion when Ruby shouted.

'Ah, I think I've found the problem, the flue's choked.' She tutted and began poking the stick vigorously up and down. Suddenly, there was a thud and a dead pigeon landed in the grate, sending a cloud of black dust billowing around the room. Coughing and spluttering, they waved their arms around to try and clear it, until Arthur managed to open the window and it finally dispersed. Gleefully, Ruby grabbed the decomposing bird and lobbed it through the window.

'Be a little feast for the cats,' she chortled, as Daisy stared at her in horror.

'Blimey, what a mess,' Mabel muttered, looking at the blanket of soot everywhere.

'I'll clear it up,' Arthur offered, snatching up the broom.

'And I'll wipe the table down,' Daisy said, grabbing a couple of cloths.

'Give me one of those and I'll clean the range,' Ruby offered. Finally, when order was restored, Mabel threw the dirty rags into a bucket and held out the kettle.

'One of you fill this and we'll find out if this old range works now.'

'I'll go,' Daisy offered, quickly taking it from her mother. 'I need the privy,' she explained when her father reached out at the same time. Grabbing the bag containing her soiled pinafore in the other hand, she rushed from the room.

The yard was deserted and she presumed Sarah and Emma had gone upstairs to cook their meal. Making her way inside the dingy outhouse that served as a washroom, she shuddered as a huge, hairy spider ran over the grimy tin bath and across the equally dirty scrubbing board which seemed to be the only amenities available. Even in here the walls were green with mould, the air rank. How she'd taken their comfortable home for granted, she thought, as she removed the offending garment from her bag. Suddenly, a long shadow loomed in the doorway blocking out the light.

'Who's there?' she called.

'Ain't yer day to use the facilities in here,' Cora snarled.

'But I need to wash my pinafore,' Daisy explained.

'Well, ain't that a shame.' The woman sniggered. 'Yer day was yesterday.'

'That's it, yer tell her.' Suddenly Cora was surrounded by her cronies and from the expressions on their faces, they were spoiling for a fight.

'But nobody else is using it,' Daisy reasoned. 'And where's the boiler for heating the water?'

'Boiler for heating the water? Blimey, girl, where do yer think yer are, The Ritz? Anyhow, like I says, it ain't yer day,' Cora reiterated, hands on hips. 'Yer can't just breeze into the yard expecting favours.' As the others muttered in agreement, Daisy felt herself becoming angry.

'From what I hear, you aren't fussy about handing out favours yourself.'

'Is that so?' Cora hissed, her dark eyes narrowing as she moved menacingly towards Daisy.

'Well, isn't that how you came to get the rooms at number six that Father paid good money for?'

'Not sure I like yer insinuations, girl.'

'And I don't like the way you spoke to my father earlier. You keep away from him; he's a respectable married man.'

'No man's ever respectable,' she spat. 'Specially one married to a dowdy old woman with a limp. Men like a bit of action in their beds, someone who can show them a good time.'

'How dare you,' Daisy exploded.

'Easily, darling,' Cora growled, moving even closer. 'Anything else rattling yer cage?'

'You called me a bohemian trollop earlier. I'm sure you know what a trollop is, but bohemian?'

'Gypsy? Cadger? Sloven? Take yer pick, love. I may not speak or dress like yer, but I ain't thick, believe yer me.'

'And I'm none of those things. Neither am I here to be bullied,' Daisy declared, taking a step towards the woman. A ripple of excitement ran around the little group as they waited to see what would happen.

'Blimey, Cora,' an older woman gasped. 'No one's ever spoken to you like that before.'

'Yea, you'd best show her who rules the yard,' another told her, obviously eager for some sport.

'For heaven's sake,' Daisy told them, pushing past Cora and elbowing her way through the group, 'the animals in the zoo at Regent's Park are better behaved than you lot.' If she couldn't use the washroom, she'd wash her pinafore in the trough beside the pump.

A deathly hush fell as, head high, she marched across the yard. Ignoring the stench coming from the slimy green water in the trough, she vigorously began pumping the handle. She could feel the glares burning into her back but had no intention of lowering herself to their level.

She filled the kettle but, as she bent to open her bag, she saw the group had her surrounded. Suddenly someone shoved her from behind, sending her stumbling. Reaching out for the pump to steady herself, she heard Cora's harsh laugh.

Seeing red, Daisy swung round and grabbed the woman by the ankles. There was a scream of outrage, followed by a splash, as Cora landed in the slimy water.

'Why, you little cow,' Cora spluttered, struggling to get to her feet. 'I'll get you back for this, Daisy Tucker, you see if I don't.'

'Slimy bath for a slimy bitch,' Daisy shouted, wiping the dirt from her hands. As the others stared in astonishment, she snatched up her things and almost ran towards their house, at any moment expecting to hear footsteps pounding behind her. Then she heard one of the women yell.

'Better get yourself cleaned up, Cora. One of your favourite customers is just coming into the yard.'

Knowing she was safe for the moment, Daisy breathed a sigh of relief.

'Cripes, that was brave,' Emma cried, when Daisy reached the door. 'I couldn't believe my eyes when I saw you pull Cora into the water,' she spluttered, shaking with mirth. 'You do look pale.'

'I'm alright,' she muttered, 'Cora deserved that for insulting my parents.'

'But where did you learn a nifty move like that?'

'Kezia showed me. She sometimes performs with the acrobats and they can do almost anything with their agile bodies. Still, it doesn't help me with this soiled pinafore. 'Is there really no means of heating water for washing?' she asked, recalling the copper in the washroom her mother shared with their neighbours.

'No, afraid not. Let's take a look,' Emma said, moving to

stand beside Daisy. 'Cripes, if that's what I think it is, it'll take more than cold water to shift that.'

'Those filthy so-called facilities, they run with ... well, you know,' Daisy grumbled.

'Yea, we found out the hard way too. Now we use them as soon as the night soil collector's been. Those dirty old drunks don't get up 'til later and it's them that makes the stinking mess. Still, it doesn't alter the fact that our day for washing is Wednesday. Can't your pinafore wait until then?'

'No, Mother will kill me if she sees the state it's in,' Daisy groaned.

'Tell you what, I could always smuggle it into work with me tomorrow.'

'I couldn't ask you to do that; suppose someone saw?'

'That's not likely. The vats of white washes we have to tackle are vast. Anyhow, should anyone ask, I can always say it belongs to me. Although we're not meant to do our own things, everyone turns a blind eye,' Emma told her.

'Well ...' Daisy began, tempted.

'Here, pop it under our washing up.' It was then Daisy noticed the huge bucket piled with crockery. 'We load everything in there and carry it in one go, saves going up and down all the time. Except we don't have enough plates so these are our breakfast ones.' The girl laughed. 'Mind you, I'm not going out there until Cora's calmed down. Blimey, Daisy, she's goin' to have it in for you even more now.'

'I know.' Daisy shrugged. 'Still, I can look after myself. It's Mother I worry about. Look, if you're sure about laundering my pinafore, then I'll take you up on it. Let me know what

I owe you,' she added, deftly tucking the offending garment beneath the plates.

'A ticket to see Charlie Chaplin?' Emma quipped. 'Only joking,' she added when she saw Daisy's worried expression.

'My friend Kezia says she can get me in to the Hippo, so if the opportunity arises, I'll let you know. Well, I'd better take this upstairs,' Daisy said, holding up the kettle. 'Your mother seems to have found the trouble with the range so they'll be spitting feathers by now.'

'More likely they'll be having a good old natter. I'll leave this little lot here and come back later when it's gone quiet. I love your green dress by the way.'

'Thanks. It's my new uniform, although it seems I'm not to wear it around here. I suppose I'll have to change into it when I get to work.'

'Like we do our aprons,' Emma told her as they climbed the stairs. 'You should see them, voluminous things they are. Makes me look like some spooky spectre. There's no chance of attracting the eye of one of the handsome carmen, I can tell you.'

'Carmen?' Daisy frowned.

'It's what they call the delivery boys. Don't know why as they use horses and carts not them automobile things.' She shrugged. 'Anyhow, I'll slip indoors whilst my mother's occupied.'

'Thanks for seeing to my pinafore, Emma, see you soon.'

'Where've you been?' Mabel cried as soon as Daisy opened the door. 'My throat's as dry as the Sahara Desert.'

'Could be all that talking you've been doing,' Arthur commented, winking at Daisy.

'Well, now the range works I'll head back next door. Hopefully, the girls will have supper ready by now,' Ruby said, as Daisy set down the kettle. 'Yep, that seems fine, although it does give off a nasty smell now it's hot, so it'll need a good scrub to clean up all that grease.'

'Give me something to do tomorrow,' Mabel told her. 'Thanks ever so Ruby, you're a pal.'

'Glad to help. Hope you have better luck tomorrow, Arthur. I'll see myself out.' As soon as Ruby had closed the door behind her, Mabel turned to Daisy.

'So, did you get your pinafore washed?'

'All sorted,' she replied, not wishing to lie. 'Emma told me they collect their dirty plates in a bucket then take it down to the pump each evening, so I thought I'd do the same.'

'Talking of the pump, I thought I heard some disturbance coming from there earlier,' Arthur said, looking at her questioningly.

'The women were spoiling for a fight,' Daisy told him quickly.

'Best stay clear,' Arthur warned her. 'I was thinking, to save your mother going down those rickety steps you could pick up something for supper on your way home.'

'Except I used the last of my money on those winkles.'

'I still have a few coppers in my bag. Luckily, I get paid on Saturday,' Daisy replied.

'And I'm determined to be first at the gates of the brewery tomorrow so I'm in with a chance of being taken on,' Arthur replied.

'That's all well and good but once I've cleaned this old

thing and tidied up, what am I supposed to do with myself all day?' Mabel asked.

'Perhaps some of the other neighbours will call by,' Arthur said hopefully.

'Yea, and I'm a monkey's uncle,' she snorted. 'You've seen the type.'

The uncomfortable silence that fell was broken by the kettle whistling as it came to the boil. 'Oh well, at least we can have a cuppa before we turn in.'

After her parents had gone to bed, Daisy settled herself down on the thin blanket under the living room window. What a day it had been. She'd started off as a runner and ended up as an apprentice to the artists. Excitement bubbled at the thought of her new job. Blue and Scarlett were both very talented and she knew she was going to learn so much from them. First thing in the morning, she'd ask them how much money she'd now be getting. Any extra would be a help, although as it was a sensitive time for her father, perhaps it would be more tactful to tell her mother.

It was thrilling to have her smock and beret to denote her new status and, strangely, wearing them made her feel much more confident. And with adrenaline still rushing through her after that confrontation with Cora, Arnie had better watch out.

Her thoughts turned to her unexpected meeting with Harry. Remembering the look on his face when he'd seen her in the green outfit, she felt a warm glow spread through her. But the best bit had been the admiration in his eyes when she'd told him about her promotion. He'd even agreed to help her with the techniques she needed to learn. It was good to think they had their creativity in common. Not only did he think she had talent, he'd suggested they work together in the park. And of course, end their evenings by the bandstand. Just thinking about it was enough to make her pulses quicken.

The full moon lit up the room, making it almost as bright as day. Too restless to sleep, she sat up and reached for her pencil and paper. Then with a blanket around her shoulders, she perched on the windowsill and began to draw.

Chapter 7

'More money?' Blue echoed, raising his brows. '*Mon dieu*, girl, you've been given this marvellous opportunity and the first thing you do is ask for more money?'

'As it's a step up from being a runner, I thought it a reasonable assumption,' Daisy replied, endeavouring to return his candid gaze. 'I was so excited yesterday, I forgot to ask how much extra I'd be getting.'

'It doesn't do to assume anything round here,' Scarlett murmured, looking up from her work.

'I'm guessing you're also assuming we shall spend our time training you in all the intricacies of the job. Time which will take us away from our own work,' Blue said.

'Come on, Blue, give the poor girl a break. You were only too keen to offer her the chance in front of Stan. Or were you just making the point that you're head of the studio?' There was an uncomfortable silence as Blue glared at Scarlett. Daisy swallowed hard. Had she just blown her chance of becoming an artist?

'Right, Daisy, we've got four large canvases to prepare for the music hall so please go and get some more gesso from the store.'

'But …' she began, then saw his mouth tighten and nodded.

Obviously, she was back to being a runner again, she fumed, as she sped along the corridor. Why hadn't she waited until she'd produced some creative work before asking about her wages? Because your father's out of work, her mind told her. But reason didn't help the way she was feeling right now.

'Hey stranger, where's the fire?'

Daisy stopped and through the open doors of the rehearsal room, she saw Kezia swinging from the trapeze by her ankles. In an instant, the girl somersaulted onto the mat, landing neatly on her feet. 'I waited ages outside the Hippo the other night.' She frowned, dark eyes flashing.

'Sorry, Kez.' Daisy sighed.

'Hey, yer look like yer got the world on your shoulders. What's up?'

Daisy looked around to make sure nobody was around, then whispered, 'Father lost his job helping a woman who was being wrongly accused of something, then we were evicted and have ended up in terrible Tiger Yard. You're the only one I've told. I don't want it getting around although I think Arnie suspects.'

'Ain't nothing to be ashamed of, lovely. Should see some of the places I've slept. Wagons, trams, even a charabanc when we've been touring the country. Wouldn't worry about arsenic Arnie neither. He's got his nose right up them Americans. Not that it'll do him any good. He's too thick to see the guys are using him as their personal runner. Though he wants to watch it cos Stan's already promoted a new runner for his department.' She laughed. 'Love yer fancy outfit, by the way. Makes yer look right womanly.'

'That's cos I've been made up to apprentice artist. Or I was until I asked for a pay rise.'

'Quite right too. Yer stick up for yerself, kiddo.'

'Kezia!' a voice barked.

'Gotta go. Kit wants to put on a double act and he's brought in another performer. Right 'andsome he be and all.' With a broad wink, she skipped back into the practice room, leaving Daisy smiling as she continued making her way to the store cupboard. Kezia was right: there wasn't anything wrong in asking for a pay rise. Though, she still wasn't comfortable admitting she lived at Tiger Yard. Perhaps her father would be successful in finding another job today, she thought, snatching up the gesso and hurrying back to the studio.

'Ah, there you are, Daisy,' Blue said, looking up from his painting. 'Perhaps you can get on with the priming. We're going to be up against it to meet the deadline, but what's new.' He shrugged.

At least he sounded more agreeable, Daisy noticed as she set about her task. She'd work hard and keep her head down for the rest of the day, she decided, dipping her brush into the clear liquid. Soon she was lost in the rhythm of her brush strokes as she ensured she applied the coating thinly and evenly.

'Right, Daisy, tell me why we use primer?' Blue asked, his voice breaking the silence as he appeared beside her.

'To make the canvas taut and diminish bounce on the surface,' Daisy replied.

'Any other reason?'

'It reduces the absorbency of the canvas.'

Blue nodded but didn't say anything, leaving Daisy none the wiser about her position. The repetitive work was soothing though, and she couldn't help her mind wandering. If Stan had already employed a new runner, where would that leave Daisy if Blue decided not to train her as an artist? She couldn't stand the strain of not knowing and vowed to speak to him before she left. The uncertainty, along with the smell of ammonia, was beginning to make her head ache when, halfway through the afternoon, Blue took out his pocket watch then got to his feet.

'Got a meeting to discuss the Guv'nor's requirements.' Scarlett waited until the door closed behind him before turning to Daisy.

'You don't want to worry about Blue. This music hall job's a bigger one than usual and he's feeling the pressure. There's always more work than week in here, if you get my meaning. Thank goodness it's payday tomorrow. I don't know about you but I always have more week than wage.' She smiled and Daisy knew she was trying to make her feel better.

'You don't think he's going to ask me to leave, do you?' she asked, the emotion of the day bursting out of her.

'Good heavens, no,' Scarlett cried, looking shocked. 'Quite frankly you're a godsend. Blue was only saying yesterday how conscientious you are. Although you are funny; I mean why wear that white pinafore to work when you look more sophisticated in your smock?'

'Mother prefers me to,' Daisy replied, not adding the reason why.

'Well, you've done enough priming for today, come and

help me with this bouquet? You do seem to have a good eye for detail.'

Happily, Daisy knelt down and, following Scarlett's example, began filling in the flowers held by the lady watching the performance.

So absorbed was she in her task she didn't hear the door open, and it was only when Blue spoke that she realised he'd returned.

'Excellent. We'll soon have you working to time as well.'

'Oh … I …' Daisy frowned.

'Don't hassle her, Blue. She's got a better eye for these flowers than I have and the more she paints the quicker she'll get.'

'I was only saying. We're going to have to work flat out to meet this deadline as someone's cancelled a show down at the halls and they've brought our opening night forward.'

'What, again?' Scarlett groaned.

'Well, young lady, you said you wanted more money, so how are you fixed for a bit of overtime?' Blue asked, turning to Daisy. 'If you can come in an hour early each morning and stay on an hour later, I'll pay you extra. Starting tomorrow?'

'Oh yes, that would be wonderful. Thank you,' Daisy cried. Knowing how much her money was needed, she didn't mind in the least working longer hours.

'And knowing you, Scarlett, you'll have no objection to earning a bit extra so you can oversee Daisy if I'm not here.'

'Yes, siree.' She smiled and gave him a salute.

'Good, that's sorted then. And Daisy, if at the end of three months I can see you have made good progress in your training, I will reconsider your basic salary.'

'Told you he wasn't so bad,' Scarlett whispered as Blue returned to his work.

To Daisy's relief, there was no sign of Arnie when she left work that afternoon. The day that had started badly had turned out well, and she couldn't wait to tell her parents about her extra money. Stopping at the butchers, she picked up some liver for her mother to fry for supper, the greengrocers for an onion and potatoes, then headed for the rooms at Tiger Yard. There was no way she could bring herself to call it home.

Her mother, sitting in one of the rickety chairs she'd pulled up by the window, gave a weak smile as Daisy entered.

'Company at last. Glad to see you're wearing your pinafore over your old dress. There's some rum-looking men round here.'

'I've got us some nice liver for our meal,' Daisy told her, shocked at how much the woman had aged in the past few days.

'You're a good girl,' her mother replied as Daisy placed her parcels on the table, which was now covered by the checked cloth they'd always used in their old home.

'That makes the place look brighter,' Daisy told her. 'Any news of Father?'

'He's been taken on at the brewery for the day, collecting and delivering beer barrels.' She sniffed. 'Stopped off on his horse-drawn dray with that straw mattress for you,' she said gesturing to the space under the window where Daisy had been bedding down. 'I told him it would encourage the vermin and such like, but he said we couldn't have you sleeping on the floor and that's the best he could manage at the moment. I've covered it with a sheet and put your old quilt on top.' For some reason seeing the brightly coloured patchwork cover spread across the lump of straw brought tears to Daisy's eyes.

'Thank you, that will save me waking up stiff as a board,' she replied, swallowing hard and forcing a smile. 'And I can see you've been busy making this place look more homely,' Daisy added, staring around the room that Mabel had evidently spent ages cleaning and polishing. And if their antimacassars looked incongruous on the backs of the old spindly chairs, so what?

'Not much else for me to do stuck up here by my Jack Jones, is there?'

'Oh, Mother,' Daisy said, putting her arms around her shoulders. 'I'm sure it won't be for long.'

'No, of course, it won't,' the woman rallied. 'Take no notice of me. We're all together and that's the important thing, although I can't stop thinking about that poor woman Arthur worked with. Right, let's take a look at that liver,' she added, struggling to her feet.

'I'll go and fetch some water then chop the onions and peel the spuds,' Daisy offered.

'Did you ask about your money?' her mother asked, as Daisy picked up the empty kettle.

'I did, and guess what? I can work two hours extra each day and get more pay.'

'They expect their pound of flesh then,' she retorted. Seeing Daisy's expression drop, she forced a smile. 'Well, I can't deny it will come in useful. Not that I like taking all your money mind, but 'til your father gets a regular job, paupers can't be pickers.'

'I don't think we're paupers yet,' Daisy scoffed.

'We're not that far off, young lady. Sitting around doing nothing all day makes me feel as useless as a wooden poker. If only I could get around like I used to,' she murmured, looking so sad, Daisy's heart went out to her.

Her mother might not have had much to do but for Daisy the next couple of weeks passed by in a blur. Getting up as soon as the night soil collector had been meant the outhouse was reasonably clean and Daisy was able to arrive at work looking presentable. There was one uncomfortable moment when her mother commented on the brightness of the pinafore Emma had secretly laundered and returned, but Daisy was able to placate her by implying it must have been one she'd washed before they'd moved. As Arthur had just told her he'd only been able to find casual labour again that day, she'd merely nodded and turned back to stare out of the window.

The overtime money Daisy earned helped pay the rent and, with judicial juggling, they managed to eat some kind of meat at least twice a week. However, it seemed as if they were marking time until her father secured a decent job and they could move on.

It was Saturday afternoon and with her pay packet secured in the deep pocket of her pinafore, Daisy made her way towards the town. With the shops closed for the Sabbath and proprietors eager to sell their perishables, Daisy was hopeful of getting something tasty for supper at a knock-down price. However, nearing the Green she was surprised to see a gathering of predominantly smartly dressed women wearing purple, white and green, shouting, 'Votes for Women'. Some were carrying banners, others handed out leaflets. The atmosphere was electric and Daisy felt compelled to stop and listen. Then, stirred by their passion, she pulled out her pencil and paper and began sketching, trying to capture the fervent expression on their faces.

'Told you the suffragette meeting would be good,' Sarah said, appearing at her side. 'Coo, that's terrific,' she cried, peering at Daisy's drawing.

'Everyone's so enthusiastic, I couldn't resist. I don't think I've ever seen so many women together before, and wearing the same colours too.'

'Purple for loyalty and dignity, white for purity and green for hope. They wear them like a uniform and consider it both a duty and privilege. Emma and me haven't got any clothes like that, but we're going to Selfridges to buy badges to support the cause. The suffragettes are planning to march through London and we intend joining them. Don't we, Em?' she added as her sister appeared.

'As long as we avoid Matilda Mitchell,' the girl replied. 'She leads the army of female shop detectives there. Looks the customers up and down like they're mud off her shoe. Thinks the store is her own domain.'

'Understandable though. Some of the suffragettes are

becoming quite militant, even smashing shop windows, but until we can make them stuck-up men in parliament take notice, what else can we do?' Sarah asked, shaking her head.

'We have to make them listen. Why shouldn't we have a say in how the country's run?' a large lady nearby butted in.

'I'd like to show my support but I can't afford to buy a badge at the moment,' Daisy admitted.

'Well, you can still come on the march with us. The important thing is to show you identify with our struggle for women to get the vote.'

'Men have had it their own way for too long,' the lady nodded. 'We need to demonstrate to them that we are people in our own right, not their property to do their bidding.'

As the crowd took up the chant, 'Votes for Women', there was the shrill sound of whistles and seemingly from nowhere policemen appeared. Brandishing their truncheons, they elbowed and pushed their way towards the bandstand where moments before the speakers had been.

'Time to go,' Sarah urged. 'Mother believes in the cause but she'd never forgive us if we got arrested.'

'Isn't it terrible that we have to go to such lengths to be heard though?' Daisy cried, quickly pocketing her sketches.

'It isn't just the suffragettes that are trying to get women more of a say,' Emma shouted over the roar of the crowd surging around them as they hurried towards the shelter of Tiger Yard; 'factory workers are threatening to strike for better pay and conditions.'

'And not before time too,' Daisy replied, thinking of the widow her father had stood up for. Even though she'd worked all the hours she could to provide for her family, she'd still ended up in the workhouse. It was high time females had a say in life and no longer had to resort to the primordial tactics that Cora did.

Chapter 8

As Daisy watched Scarlett demonstrate how everything had to be larger than life on the huge canvas, her fingers were itching to participate. Both Scarlett and Blue had been generous with their tuition and she'd already picked up more than she could ever have imagined, although that knowledge made her realise how much more she still had to learn. Rather than be daunted though, it just made her more determined.

With her extra working hours, the time seemed to fly by and being away from the yard for so long each day meant she hadn't encountered Cora and her cronies again. The memory of the woman slumped in the trough covered in slimy water never failed to make her smile when home life had little to offer.

While her father had managed to find casual work most days, he'd yet to secure a permanent position, and her mother was becoming increasingly frustrated being cooped up in the two rooms at the top of the house. With nothing else to do, she spent her time watching the goings on in Tiger Yard. The only time she'd come to life was when she'd cooked a meal to share with their neighbours. It wasn't just that she could return their hospitality, they had all become friends. Daisy wished she could think of something to help, but for the moment just concentrated on learning as well as earning, which she never thought she'd be able to do.

'The most important thing is to create realistic backdrops. Everything has to be big, bold and dramatic so that the audience becomes totally immersed in the performance,' Scarlett explained.

'It must be very rewarding to create scenes like that,' she replied.

'When it goes right; otherwise it can be frustrating,' Scarlett told her. 'And of course, we have to pass Sir's exacting standards,' she added, nodding her head towards Blue who was yelling down the corridor.

'Blinkin' runners,' he growled. 'I've been calling for ages and there's still no sign of one. At least Arnie used to appear periodically, but not anymore.' He shrugged.

'Not since those American guys arrived,' Scarlett told him. 'He's far too busy sucking up to them. And have you seen the way his backside jiggles in those gas pipes?' As Blue grunted, Daisy hid a smile, for the runner's new trousers were so tight it was surprising he could bend down in them.

'I suppose I'll have to go and get more paint myself. Honestly, what's the point of having a dog if you have to bark yourself?'

'Well, you certainly do a lot of that,' Scarlett replied, shooting him one of her looks.

'I'll go,' Daisy offered quickly, sensing the mood in the studio beginning to turn uncomfortable. 'What do you need, Blue?' she asked. In truth she couldn't help feeling sorry for him. When he got so absorbed in his work, he hated any interruption and it was true that neither Arnie nor the new runner kept their materials stocked up as she had.

'Thanks, Daisy; I'd be obliged. There's nothing worse than being thwarted mid creation.'

'Poor Picasso,' Scarlett murmured before turning back to the scene.

'You might mock but I have no qualms about being compared to such a talented artist. On the contrary, I feel quite flattered. Did you know his monochromatic paintings, mainly done in blue and green by the way, were inspired by his homeland of Spain?'

'So you've said,' Scarlett replied, raising her brows at Daisy.

'Actually, I didn't know. Did he really only use blue and green?' Daisy asked, remembering her own vision of a night sky.

'Mainly, although occasionally they were warmed by other colours, to evoke the mood, I suppose.'

'What colours would suggest your home, Daisy?' Blue asked, turning his candid gaze towards her.

Daisy thought of the filth and grimy surroundings at Tiger Yard, the ragged urchins playing in the gutter, rats scuttling over the rubbish heaps, but knew to say grey wouldn't do for the flamboyant Blue.

'If I were to paint a landscape, I'd incorporate a golden ball of summer sunshine,' she replied.

'Ah, an idealist, eh?' Blue smiled. 'Did I tell you Picasso was also a stage designer?'

'Only about a million times,' Scarlett muttered under her breath. 'Now hurry up and impart to Daisy the really important information, like what you want her to get. After all, she's meant to be helping me with this,' she added, tapping the canvas with the handle of her brush.

'I've already made a list. On the odd occasion a runner does deign to appear, they inevitably forget half of what's been asked for,' he said, handing it to Daisy. 'You'd best take the trolley; some of those tins will be heavy. Oh, and if you see Stan in your travels, tell him I want to see him. Other departments don't seem to have any trouble with their runners and I don't see why we should put up with it.'

As Daisy trundled the wooden trolley with its squeaky wheels to the storeroom, she couldn't help dreaming of the time she would become a fully-fledged artist. Neither could she wait for Harry's return when they'd sketch together in the park. Not long before his new term started, she thought, excitement fizzing up inside her like lemonade bubbles in an opened bottle.

Turning the key in the lock, she pushed open the door, inhaling the familiar aroma of paint, primer, charcoal and paper. Then her nose twitched as she detected another smell. It was similar to the one that flooded out through the open doors of the Cock and Tiger pubs as she passed by, but glancing around she couldn't see anything out of place. She consulted the list Blue had given her, then quickly loaded the trolley with the required items, marvelling again at how much material the stockroom held. It would take her months to save for even the smallest sketch pad and she was once more grateful for the scraps of paper Scarlett gave her, especially as she was drawing more these days.

As she was carefully locking the door behind her, she heard a commotion coming from the vicinity of the workshop: Cal yelling; Stan trying to placate; apprentices on the defence; and Arnie apologising.

Daisy's eyes widened in surprise for, in all the time she'd been here, she'd never heard Arnie say sorry to anyone. Should she make her presence known or remain in the shadows? But they were working to a tight deadline and Blue was waiting for his paints and paraphernalia. Besides, the squeaking of the wheels had probably given her away. Except they were all arguing so loudly, nobody heard her approach.

'Just came hurtling out of nowhere,' Billy declared.

'Didn't even see us coming out of the workshop, know what I mean?' Ted added.

'How could you?' Cal berated, snatching a swathe of golden material from the very red-faced Arnie.

'It weren't my fault,' he whined. 'Them idiots came charging out with that dangerous thing,' he added, pointing to the wooden beam protruding through the open door. Daisy's eyes widened as she saw it was festooned with golden threads and fragments of material. As if sensing her watching, Arnie looked up and shot her a look of loathing.

'Leave this with me,' Stan blustered, grabbing Arnie and the other runner by the arms. 'They'll be severely reprimanded, if not sacked,' he growled, frogmarching them down the corridor to his office. Daisy couldn't help smiling to herself when she noticed Arnie had split the back of his new trousers in the scuffle.

As the apprentices hoisted the new prop they'd fashioned back onto their shoulders and beat a hasty exit, Cal frowned, holding up the floaty dress to reveal a jagged hole in the bodice. The material was light as gossamer, golden threads shimmering in the sunlight.

'It's quite beautiful,' Daisy gasped.

'Correction, Miss: it *was* quite beautiful. And it's meant to be worn by the leading lady on opening night. Gee, what the hell am I going to do now?'

'Surely the wardrobe mistress or one of her seamstresses will be able to mend it,' Daisy ventured.

'They're working flat out to finish the other costumes. Besides, this is the star of the show so to speak. The stitching is intricate and it will take an age to repair, if indeed it can be. My first job overseas and I've failed.' He groaned, then seemed to recover himself. 'You're right, of course. I shall have to speak to Muriel, the wardrobe mistress, and see what can be done. Although she's going to kill me.' He put two fingers to his head and mimed pulling a trigger.

'I'm sure she won't,' Daisy replied, failing to suppress a grin at his theatrical gestures. 'After all it was an accident.'

'One waiting to happen with those two idiots. That so-called overseer should have more control. I don't know what they thought they were doing swaying all over the place and giggling like children.'

'Sorry, what do you mean?' Daisy asked.

'Forget I said anything. You're looking swell in that outfit and if you don't mind my saying again, you do have the most amazing eyes. Knew that moss green would be perfect for you. Well, if you'll excuse me, I'd better go and make my peace with the dragon of dresses.'

'Dragon?'

'Believe you me, that Muriel sure breathes fire like one.' He shuddered.

Smiling at his dramatic ways, Daisy continued her way down the corridor only to see Kezia gesturing to her from her rehearsal room.

'What's going on? I heard a hullabaloo but was up on me swing. By the time I got down all I could see was Stan the man shoving Arnie and the new boy into his office. I thought 'e were going to blow his stack.'

As Daisy quickly explained, her friend's expression turned to one of glee.

'About time that twerp got 'is comeuppance. 'E's been fawning around after them foreign guys like 'e's the latest film star. Anyway, glad I've seen yer before we leave.'

'Leave? Where are you going?' Daisy frowned.

'Up north. Yer know Kit brought in this new artist Joe? Well, apart from being a hunk, 'e's a talented funambulist.'

'A what?'

'It's Greek – *funis* means rope, *ambulare* to walk,' she swanked.

'Blimey, you sound like you've swallowed the dictionary,' Daisy murmured, raising her brow.

'I know, and me Pa will never believe what I've learnt. It's Joe, see, 'e knows about these things. Taught me to walk the rope 'e did. Cors I did wobble a few times so 'e 'ad to put those strong, muscular arms of 'is round me,' she said with a wicked grin.

'You're incorrigible,' Daisy laughed.

'I know, it's a failing of mine. Anyhow, when the Guv'nor saw us 'e were that impressed, 'e arranged for us to perform with the touring circus 'e used to work with. Exciting, what? Just hope I can understand them Northerners. Joe says they all speak funny up there.' Again, Daisy had to suppress a smile, for sometimes she had difficulty understanding her friend's West Country burr.

'When do you leave?' she asked.

'First thing tomorrow. We're going by train,' she cried, her face lighting up. 'It's all so exciting. I'll miss me best friend though,' she added, pulling Daisy close. 'Eh, give me yer address and I'll send you one of them postcard thingies.'

'Better not, we'll probably be moving on soon,' Daisy told her.

'Yer Pa still not found work then?' Kezia asked, looking worried.

'Nothing permanent yet, but he keeps trying so it shouldn't be long.'

'Cors it won't. Well, good luck, Dais – I'll see you when we get back.'

'Good luck with the circus,' Daisy called but her friend had already disappeared back inside the rehearsal room.

What an afternoon it was turning out to be, Daisy thought, as she trundled the loaded trolley back to the studio.

'Get lost, did you?' Blue asked. Daisy's heart sank. 'Thought

82

you'd done a "runner".' He winked and she realised he was joking.

'Sorry, Blue; there was a bit of a fuss further up the corridor.'

'Did you see Stan?'

'I did, but he was busy ushering Arnie and the new runner into his office.'

'Hope they get their just desserts,' Scarlett muttered.

'If not their marching orders,' Blue said, 'then maybe we can get some decent runners. Now if you'd bring me that cobalt, I can get on with my work. The rest can go on the shelves. I take it everything was all present and correct in the store?' He gave her a searching stare as she handed him back the key.

'Yes,' she replied, thinking it prudent not to mention the smell. If Arnie had been up to what she suspected, she could use it in retaliation if he threatened to tell where she was living.

'I'm afraid as there doesn't seem to be a runner available, it'll be back to priming for you tomorrow.'

This time Scarlett did look up.

'Not til Daisy's helped me finish this backdrop, Blue. She's coming on really well but I can't train her if you keep giving her other jobs to do.'

With Scarlett's praise spurring her on, Daisy concentrated on what she was being shown. She was even permitted to paint the luscious fluttering eyelashes on one of the women. Who would have thought that backdrop scenery involved such detail, she thought, as she cleaned her brushes at the end of the day?

Outside, the early evening sunshine was casting its rays, glinting gold everywhere. Why, she was even thinking in colour these days, she smiled. Although she would soon be back in the grey, she thought, her spirits sinking as she began making her way towards their dismal rooms.

'Hey Daisy.'

'Harry, what are you doing here?' she cried delightedly, then, seeing his angry look, her smile faded.

Chapter 9

'Harry, is something wrong? Daisy frowned.

'You tell me,' he muttered, climbing down from his bicycle. 'I waited outside here at closing time, but you didn't appear. Thinking I must have missed you I went to your house only to be told you'd moved on some weeks ago. Then as I'm making my way back home, you come out of the Factory an hour after everyone else has left. What's going on, Daisy?' As he turned to face her, she saw his eyes were dark with anguish.

'Oh Harry, so much has happened.' She sighed. 'Father lost his job and we had to move to this terrible place. I've been working overtime to help pay the rent.' As the clock chimed the quarter hour, she took his arm. 'Look, I must get to the butcher's before he closes or Mother will have nothing to cook for supper. Walk with me and I'll explain everything.'

'So, you working late has nothing to do with that American fellow you were telling me about?'

'Cal? Good heavens, no; why should it?' she asked, frowning at him in surprise.

'Well, you said he thinks you're beautiful and …' his voice trailed off and he looked sheepishly at the ground. 'He's obviously taken a shine to you.'

'He merely said I had amethyst eyes,' she corrected. 'Why Harry Wylde, I do believe you're jealous,' she added, staring at him incredulously.

'I've missed you, Daisy, and when I saw you bounding out of The Factory late and all lit up like candles on a Christmas tree, well, what was I to think? Although I see you're not wearing that charming leprechaun dress.'

'Mother prefers me to change into it at work. Now come on, if I don't get a move on everywhere will be shut.'

'Blow the shops, come here,' he murmured, pulling her into the shade of a garden gate and kissing her with so much passion she thought her racing heart would burst.

'What are you doing here anyway?' she asked when he'd reluctantly let her go and they'd resumed walking, the bicycle wheels ticking rhythmically as they went.

'Seems you're not the only one that's moved house. Remember I was going to see that important customer of Father's? Well, I actually had an ulterior motive for offering to deliver her order. She lives on the other side of the park and when I heard Father say her lodger had given notice, I thought that would suit me nicely. Mind you, when she learnt I was a student, she was dubious about letting to me, so I put on the Harry charm and naturally she offered me the room. It means we can spend more time together.'

'Is that how you sold the idea to your parents?' she asked. Although she'd yet to meet them, he'd told her they were strict and wanted their only son to do well in life.

'Of course not. I told them, truthfully as it happens, that the two hours I spend walking to college and back each day would be better spent on my work. They were reluctant at first but when I asked if I could use this bicycle instead, they said that was out of the question as the new delivery boy would need it. Clever eh?'

Daisy laughed. 'And I take it this house is nice?'

'It's more comfortable than our rooms over the shop, and, in truth, those aren't bad. So, what's your new place like?'

'The exact opposite as you'll soon see,' she grimaced. They then had to concentrate on crossing the busy flow of traffic, making any further talk impossible. 'Oh no,' she cried, her hand going to her mouth as she saw the butcher had already pulled down his blind. 'We've been living day to day and have nothing in to eat. Mother will kill me.'

'Come on, the pie shop's open. I'll treat us all to supper then you'll be in your mother's good books 'cos she won't have to cook.'

'What would I do without you,' she cried, relief flooding through her.

'I know, I'm such a saint,' he said with a wink. 'Here, hold on to the bike while I go in and order. No, it's my treat,' he added as she took out her purse.

Minutes later, with the fragrant parcel tucked safely in his delivery basket, they continued on their way. The throng of people rushing home after work had eased and, as they walked, Daisy continued filling him in on all that had happened.

'But why didn't you tell me when I saw you last?'

'I was going to but I was excited at having been promoted when I literally bumped into you.'

'And you could think of nothing else, naturally,' He grinned. Then he sobered. 'Your poor father, to think he was sacked for standing up for a helpless widow.' They were passing the Cock Public House and as the smell of alcohol and tobacco wafted towards them, Harry turned to Daisy.

'Are you sure we're going the right way?'

'I'm afraid so,' she said with a sigh, leading him down the rubbish-strewn alley that led to Tiger Yard. Harry fell silent and Daisy felt him stiffen as he stared around the insalubrious surroundings, but before she could say anything Cora, wearing the tightest dress imaginable, wiggled her way towards them.

'Well, hello, lover boy, and where have you been all my life?' she purred, putting a hand provocatively on her hip.

'I wasn't born for half of it,' he countered. She stared at him as if unable to believe what she was hearing and her look of indignant outrage made Daisy giggle. Harry joined in and they were still chuckling when she stopped outside number thirteen.

'Oh Harry, I haven't laughed like that for ages,' she spluttered.

'I'm not surprised,' he murmured, grimacing at the grimy building. 'Suppose you're on the ground floor?' he asked, pushing open the door.

'No. We were meant to be but then … well, there was some mix-up,' she said quickly. It was only as she started climbing the rickety stairs that she realised Harry had lifted his bike onto his shoulders and was carrying it with him.

'Daren't risk it being nicked,' he muttered.

'Mother, I'm home and I've brought a visitor to cheer you up,' she called breezily as she pushed open the door.

'Good evening, Mrs T,' Harry greeted the woman, his glance taking in the sparse furnishings and straw pallet in the corner of the room.

'Yes, I saw you coming and it's lovely to see you, lad, but I'm afraid you find us in straightened circumstances,' she replied, looking up from her chair, which as usual was situated beside the window.

'Daisy explained, Mrs T, and I'm sorry to hear of your troubles. It's coming to something when a man can't defend a defenceless woman. I'm sure you must be very proud of your husband.'

'I am, but pride doesn't pay the rent, Harry.' Then her nose began to twitch. 'Is that pie I can smell?' she asked hopefully.

'It is, Mother.' Daisy smiled, placing the warm parcel on the table. 'Harry's kindly treated us to eel pies for supper. Is Father not home yet?'

'No, but he'd better hurry up. I'm that hungry I could eat his as well. Do you mind if we tuck in straightaway, Harry, only I haven't eaten all day?'

Before he could reply, they heard footsteps plodding wearily up the stairs.

'Why is there a bike in the ... Harry my boy, it's good to see you,' Arthur exclaimed, shaking his hand. 'Though as you can see ...' grimacing, he gestured round the room.

'Yes,' Daisy explained, Mr Tucker, but I'm sure a skilled person, such as yourself, will soon find a permanent position.'

'Harry's bought pies for supper, Father, so if you move

Mother's chair to the table, I'll dish up. I'm afraid you'll have to perch beside me on the sill,' Daisy told Harry, as she set the kettle on the hob.

'I'm that starved, I could eat anywhere,' he added, then groaned as Daisy playfully slapped his arm.

Despite her hunger, sitting so close to him, she became acutely aware of the heat emanating from his body. She couldn't help her glance straying to her spartan bed beside them but Harry just smiled and tucked in as though he hadn't seen food for a week.

After they'd eaten and were drinking their tea, Mabel turned to Arthur.

'So how did it go today, any luck?'

'Nothing. Not even casual work. I spent the whole day going from factory to factory, even tried the hospitals, but no one's hiring. Still, tomorrow's another day, as they say,' he added as Mabel let out a long sigh. 'I hope your parents are well, Harry. How've you found working in their hardware shop?'

'Mustn't grumble, Mr Tucker. Although measuring chain and weighing nails and screws isn't exactly mind-blowing. The customers take everything so seriously.' He raised his brow. 'When one woman asked for nuts, I thought I'd try and liven things up by asking her if she'd like hazel or cobs.' She wasn't amused and told Father I'd cheeked her. Got a right rollicking, I can tell you, followed by a lecture on treating customers with respect. Talking of which, I'd better make tracks,' he said, getting to his feet. 'Night, Mrs T, you've turned this into a nice cheerful room, if you don't mind me saying.'

'Thanks, lad,' Mabel said gratefully. 'Not that I've got anything else to do.'

'Now then, Mabel, you know it's only a temporary measure,' Arthur said, and Daisy could see his patience was wearing thin. 'Thanks again for supper. Take care, son,' he added, shaking Harry's hand.

'I'll see you down the stairs,' Daisy said, eager to escape the gloom that had descended. As soon as they reached the front door, Harry propped the bike against the stairs and pulled Daisy into his arms. 'I didn't think it was the right time to ask your father's permission,' he murmured.

'I agree.' She sighed, snuggling into the warmth of his chest. 'Wait until he's found a job and we've moved somewhere decent.'

As he pulled her closer and nuzzled her hair, all thoughts of her surroundings vanished as she surrendered to his kisses. Then the sound of marching boots and ribald laughter broke the spell and with a moan, and Harry broke away.

'I hate leaving you in this place,' he murmured.

'I hate being here, but at least I'm out at work all day. It's Mother I feel sorry for, stuck upstairs in that room by herself.'

'She definitely needs something to occupy her,' Harry said, as he reluctantly pulled open the door. 'Well, you take care of yourself, petal, and I'll see you next week.'

'Wait outside the Factory, but remember I work an hour later each evening.'

'You're a good girl, Daisy, though hopefully you won't always be,' he added, giving her one of his wicked grins.

'Harry Wylde,' she retorted, trying to suppress a smile at

his cheek. 'And just you make sure you stay away from that Cora,' she ordered.

'I shall pedal like the devil herself is after me,' he promised. She was still smiling as she watched him speed away. How wonderful to think he would be living close by and they would see more of each other.

'Someone looks happy,' Scarlett trilled the next morning after Daisy had changed and settled herself down beside the backdrop they'd been working on.

'I am. I just love seeing the scene come to life. Never in all my life would I have believed I'd get an opportunity like this.'

'And never in my life have I seen such wonderful eyelashes,' Blue told her, peering over her shoulder. 'However, those two must be primed this morning or else they won't be dry in time,' he added, gesturing to the large canvases propped up against the far wall. Suppressing a groan, Daisy made to get up. 'No, stay where you are. I'm going to see Stan and insist we have a runner do them. After all you used to manage both props and priming.'

As he strode from the room, Scarlett gave Daisy a broad grin.

'Who'd have thought it: praise from the boss. However, had he even hinted you were to open the gesso, he'd have had me to deal with. I need you to fill in the elaborate detail on this woman's hat.'

Pleased with the artists' encouragement, Daisy settled down to her task and was soon absorbed in outlining a wide brim, adding ribbon trimmings and, finally, a splendid peacock plume.

'Blimey, girl, that's …' But whatever Scarlett had been about to say was lost as the door burst open and Blue stomped angrily into the room.

'It seems we have to wait until this afternoon and then we will have the honour of Arnie's services.'

'What about the new boy?' Scarlett asked.

'Dismissed yesterday after some fracas with the apprentices and costumier.'

'But Arnie was involved too,' Daisy protested, then clamped her hand over her mouth. There was nothing worse than a sneak.

'I bet he was,' Scarlett muttered.

'According to Stan, Arnie claimed the new runner deliberately pushed him into some lads coming out of the workshop carrying a prop and an expensive costume got damaged. When Stan sacked him, Arnie promised to do anything to keep his job.'

'Which means Stan will use him for his own ends,' Scarlett derided.

'As long as we get a runner, I don't really care,' Blue interrupted. 'Now let's get on, we have work to do and deadlines to meet.'

Daisy spent the rest of the morning completing the details of what she now thought of as 'her' music hall patron. She was so thrilled to be entrusted with this important part of Scarlett's work and determined to do the best job she could. Totally immersed in her task, she hardly noticed the time passing or Scarlett and Blue slipping out for a bite to eat at noon. It was only when a shadow passed over her canvas that she became aware of someone else in the room.

'Trying to get in their good books by working through yer lunch, eh?' Arnie sneered, staring with contempt at the backdrop.

'Oh, hello Arnie,' Daisy said, trying to keep her voice pleasant. 'Have you come to prime the canvases?'

'What, and be your lackey? Hardly,' he hissed, his eyes narrowing to slits. 'You think you're so clever, don't you? Well, let's see what they think of yer work now.' Before Daisy realised what was happening, he'd picked up Blue's brush and flicked paint over the woman Daisy had been working on. She watched in horror as blobs of bright blue trickled downwards.

'I saw that, Arnie,' Blue said, marching into the room and grabbing the lad by the wrists.

'How could you do such a thing?' Scarlett shouted, following behind him. 'Daisy has worked so hard on that.'

'Daisy this, Daisy that,' Arnie intoned. 'You think she's a right little goody two-shoes, don't you? Bet you didn't know she lives in the slums of Tiger Yard.'

As a heavy silence descended, Daisy stood there, wishing the ground would swallow her up.

Chapter 10

As Scarlett tutted in disgust, Daisy squirmed with embarrassment. But to her surprise the artist turned to Arnie and shrugged.

'Yes, we already know that,' she said calmly.

Daisy stared at her in astonishment, but before she could say anything Blue began taking the runner to task.

'I don't know what your problem is, Arnie, but where Daisy lives is no concern of ours. She is conscientious, an excellent worker and, above all, honest, which is more than can be said for you. Turn out your pockets.'

'I don't have to,' the boy blustered.

'Oh, but you do,' Blue told him, his eyes cold.

In the ensuing silence, Daisy watched as Scarlett poured pungent liquid onto a cloth and gently began wiping it over the canvas.

'I'm waiting and, I warn you: you are not leaving this room until you have.' As Blue stood there, arms folded, staring determinedly at Arnie, it was obvious he meant what he said. 'Unless you would prefer me to take this to Stan,' Blue added, shaking a bottle under his nose. 'Recognise it?' he asked. The boy's flushed cheeks told their own story.

'Now empty your jacket pockets.' Reluctantly Arnie did as he'd been asked and Daisy's eyes widened as he slapped an assortment of pencils, brushes and screws down on the desk. 'Theft of Factory property along with drinking alcohol in the storeroom are two grave offences. Grave enough to warrant calling in the constabulary.'

'No,' Arnie whimpered, shaking his head in despair. 'Please don't, me old man will kill me.' Hardly able to believe how the boy had gone from bully to baby in a few short moments, Daisy turned up her nose in disgust.

'Get off these premises this instant. If you're spotted anywhere near here again, I will have no hesitation in having you jailed, do you understand?'

The boy nodded and, without looking at them, fled the room.

'That's seen the end of him, Daisy,' Blue said, smiling at her.

'And not before time, the little tea leaf,' Scarlett sniffed, looking up from the canvas.

'How's that doing?' he asked.

'Almost finished but it needs to dry before I can really tell. Still, I'm hopeful we removed the paint in time,' she replied, replacing the jar and cloth on the shelf.

'Thank heavens. But how did you know about Arnie?' Daisy asked Blue.

'Suspected he'd been sneaking off for a drink for some time now. Did you not notice how he was belligerent one minute then happy or aggressive the next?'

Daisy frowned. 'Well, I knew he was moody, but didn't realise he was doing that.'

'Mood swings are typical of someone reliant upon alcohol. Anyhow, when I checked our stock, it didn't tally with my materials sheet, so I set a trap.' He pointed to the handles of the brushes and pencils, which had a yellow spot on the end. 'Gin costs money and Arnie's been pilfering and selling our wares on the market.'

'So that's why you asked if everything was alright when I came back from the stockroom yesterday?' Daisy cried. 'I thought it was a funny question.'

'I can certainly do with a cuppa after that little performance and I'm sure you could too, Daisy,' Scarlett said. 'Can't do anything more here until the canvas dries, so we'll nip to the canteen. If that's alright with you, Blue?'

'Alright, but don't be too long. I'd better go and tell Stan about Arnie.'

Her mind buzzing, Daisy followed Scarlett right to the end of the corridor where the appetising smell of food made her stomach rumble. Luckily the canteen was quiet at that time of the afternoon and the rosy-cheeked woman behind the counter greeted them cheerfully.

'Grab a table and I'll get our drinks. My treat,' Scarlett insisted, as Daisy reached in her pocket for her purse.

'Did you know what Arnie was up to?' Daisy asked, when they were sitting with steaming mugs and a plate of teacakes before them.

'Not until Blue mentioned it a couple of weeks back. He was hoping to have a quiet word with Arnie but he just went too far.' Scarlett sighed. 'I think he was secretly trying to save him.'

'What do you mean?' Daisy frowned.

'Well, I can't divulge any secrets, but let's just say Blue got in with a rough crowd when he was younger. The Guv'nor found him ... er ... misbehaving, and offered to train him for a job if he promised to reform. He's worked like a Trojan ever since and made quite a name for himself. Of course, he does have a modicum of talent, but don't tell him I said that.' She winked then took a bite of her teacake. Daisy tucked into hers, revelling in the taste of the creamy butter and moist fruit before taking a sip of her tea. It seemed strange to think of the fastidious Blue ever being wayward. However, Arnie had been downright spiteful and Daisy was still reeling from his malevolence.

'How did you know I was living in Tiger Yard?' Daisy asked, remembering their earlier conversation.

'One of the writers saw you coming to work that day covered in – well, you know. Anyway, he was concerned and mentioned it to Blue who asked me to keep an eye out for you. He's quite a softy underneath that veneer, you know.' Daisy nodded then took another bite of her cake.

'What will we do about the backdrop?' she asked, thinking of the hours they'd both spent working on it.

'Hopefully, I caught it in time. We'll have to see when we get back. Accidents do happen sometimes so don't look so worried.'

'But that was no accident,' Daisy retorted.

'No, it wasn't,' Scarlett agreed. 'But Arnie will find it hard to get a job without a character, so ...' she shrugged. 'That tea's gone straight through me, so I'll just nip to the you-know-where and see you back in the studio,' she added, getting to her feet. 'And no more worrying about where you live. As Blue said, it's you and the quality of your work we're interested in.'

Feeling better for both the refreshment and Scarlett's reassurance, Daisy finished the last of her drink and was about to make her way back when she saw Cal, mug in hand, weaving his way towards her.

'Gee, Daisy, it's good to see a friendly face,' he murmured, flopping into the chair Scarlett had just vacated.

'Hello, did you get that beautiful dress mended alright?'

'Oh boy, did Muriel tear me off a strip, even though she'd passed it to that stupid runner to pack in the hamper.' He shook his head as if remembering. 'The good news is she found a matching piece of material to replace the bodice; the bad news is she's gone home ill. The others are juniors unable to do anything beyond hemming or sewing on buttons, and this will require intricate stitching. So, there you have it, yours truly is well down the swanny.' He looked so wretched that Daisy's heart went out to him, for hadn't he been instrumental in getting her new green outfit?

'I'm sure my mother would be able to help. She used to be a seamstress for a well-known store and has made some really gorgeous dresses.'

'Really? Gee, that would be swell,' he cried, his face lighting up. 'Where can I find her?' Daisy stared at the well-dressed man, with his immaculate suit and shoes buffed to a mirror shine, then thought of their shabby rooms. Despite what Scarlett said, she had no desire to show anyone where they lived.

'I can take it home with me. Er, Mother's a really skilled worker …' she added, looking at him hopefully.

'That would be a huge relief, Daisy. I'll have it packaged and sent to your studio before you leave. Of course, I'll pay the going rate so get your mother to bill me.'

'I will. Now, if you'll excuse me, Blue and Scarlett will be wondering where I am,' she said, jumping to her feet.

Daisy's spirits soared as she made her way back to the studio. Not only would her mother have something to do again, she would be able to contribute to their budget. Things were looking up at last.

Blue and Scarlett both looked up and smiled as she entered the studio.

'We'll be getting a new runner tomorrow,' Blue told her. 'I let Stan know in no uncertain terms that he should have kept a better eye on Arnie.'

'I can't believe he volunteered one just like that, though,' Scarlett frowned.

'Well, he couldn't afford to have the Guv'nor find out what had been going on, could he?' Blue winked.

'You're incorrigible,' Scarlett cried. 'Anyway, I have good news too. As you can see, most of those splashes of cobalt have gone, apart from on the woman's outfit, so I was thinking we may as well go with it and give her a blue dress. It'll match the peacock feather in her hat and, if we paint the brim blue too, it will look as if we've co-ordinated the look.'

'What about the flowers?' Blue asked, squinting objectively at the canvas.

'We could turn them into violets,' Daisy cried. 'I've seen the sellers with them and know what they look like.'

'Great idea,' Scarlett squealed, clapping her hands in delight. 'You change the flowers; I'll paint the dress.'

Clutching the parcel tightly, Daisy made her way home through the afternoon traffic. With only a few coppers left in her purse it would have to be tripe for tea. Still, she knew her mother would be pleased when she heard about the repairs required to the dress. She'd always loved to sew and it would now give her a sense of purpose, as well as some cash.

'Hey, who was that handsome hunk you were kissing in the hallway?' Roused from her reverie, she smiled as Emma bounded up to her.

'Emma!' Sarah remonstrated. 'Sorry, Daisy, she can't help being nosy.'

'That's alright,' Daisy replied as they moved onto the pavement, trying to avoid the usual chaos of carts, costers and trams. 'That's Harry, he's … well, my good friend.' She smiled thinking it prudent not to mention their intention to marry until he'd spoken to her father.

'You dark horse,' Emma cooed. 'Has he got any mates?'

'Emma,' Sarah warned, but her twitching lips gave away her amusement at her sister's curiosity. 'There's another rally on the Green next Saturday. Will you be there?' she asked Daisy.

'We're going to buy our badges this weekend,' Emma said proudly.

'I'll certainly be making my way there as soon as I finish work,' Daisy promised. 'And I found a scrap of ribbon in Mother's workbox so I can make my own. Now I must go and get something for supper.'

'Mother's visiting a friend so we're going to treat ourselves to a drink over there,' Sarah said, pointing to the coffee house. 'But don't tell or she'll kill us for wasting the money she gave us for food.'

'But we gotta enjoy life and, who knows, there might be another good-looking chap like that Harry of yours in there,' Emma cried.

Still grinning, Daisy purchased the tripe and hurried home. She couldn't wait to see her mother's face when she saw the golden dress.

'Oh Daisy, it's so beautiful,' Mabel gasped, running her fingers gently over the delicate material. 'Shame about that hole though.' She frowned, holding the garment up to the window where it shimmered in the light.

'But you'll be able to use the extra material to replace the bodice?' Daisy asked.

'Of course I will,' Mabel said indignantly. 'It'll take time, but they've provided the golden silk for stitching, so, with a bit of strategic pleating, it will look good as new. I'll spread it out on the table and take a proper look after supper. Which is what?' she asked, staring hopefully at the brown package Daisy was still holding.

'Tripe, I'm afraid. It's all I could afford,' she added, as her mother groaned. 'However, the good news is that Cal, who's over here from America to see about the costumes, has said he'll pay the going rate.'

'Who's paying the going rate?' They looked up to see Arthur standing in the doorway. They'd been so busy chatting they hadn't heard his footsteps on the stairs.

'It's so exciting, Arthur. Not only have I been asked to repair this beautiful gown, they're going to pay me to do it,' Mabel cried, her face lighting up for the first time since they'd moved here.

'That is good news,' Arthur replied, kissing the top of her head as she leaned contentedly back against him.

'Our fortunes may be about to change,' she whispered.

'Yours perhaps—' he groaned '—but as I've only managed to pick up an hour here and there at the timber and stone yards, it looks as if I shall have to content myself with being kept by my wife and daughter.' Although he tried to make light of it, Daisy knew he felt his position as man of the house had been eroded.

That night, as fingers of silvery moonlight filtered through the grimy windows, Daisy settled herself down on the straw mattress. She prayed her father would soon find permanent work so they could move somewhere decent, for she missed having her own room and comfortable bed. Still, with factory workers increasingly voicing their dissatisfaction at their pay and conditions, bosses weren't hiring new staff. She did admire his tenacity though.

And she was pleased for her mother. Seeing her come to life made Daisy realise just how low she'd sunk. She'd get enormous satisfaction restoring the gown to its former glory, and, of course, the icing on the cake was she could now contribute to the household budget. Although her father was pleased for her, Daisy knew it was yet another blow to his manly pride. Still, they were a strong couple and would weather the storm until he'd secured another permanent position.

As for her own work, it was going to be much nicer without Arnie around. She still couldn't believe that Scarlett had been able to salvage the spoiled backdrop and all their hard work hadn't been wasted. Goodness, she had so much to tell Harry when she saw him.

Dear Harry … how exciting that he'd soon be living in Camberwell. Her heart flipped to think they would be able to spend more time together. He'd mentioned sketching together in the park and she couldn't wait to show him all she'd learned whilst he'd been away. Although Harry was going to wait until her father had secured employment before asking him formally for her hand in marriage, the thought of being Harry's wife sent tingles of anticipation through her. For the first time in ages, she fell into a contented sleep.

Chapter 11

'That's very good,' Harry told Daisy, looking over her shoulder.

'Do you think so?' she asked, staring at her drawing.

'I do, those prickles look positively lethal. I've never seen such a realistic-looking hedgehog before.'

'But it's meant to be that conker,' Daisy wailed, pointing to the spiny green case of a chestnut, which had fallen from the tree. Hearing a snort, she looked up to find him trying to contain his laughter.

'Oh you,' she cried, slapping his arm.

'There, told you I was going to be a battered husband.' He shook his head helplessly.

It was a glorious day in early October, and as had become their habit since Harry's return, they were stretched out on the grass trying to capture on paper the vibrant colours of the autumnal scenery around them. Although her work made her happy, this was Daisy's favourite time of the week: she and Harry together, drawing inspiration from the landscape.

'What are you doing now?' Harry asked.

'Adding my mark. Instead of signing my pictures, I draw a little daisy in the corner.' He stared at it and frowned. 'Do you think that's pompous?' she asked anxiously.

'No, I think it's terrific, and will be instantly recognisable when you become an artist of renown,' he told her. Certain he was teasing, she opened her mouth to protest, but, smiling, he leaned forward and kissed her lightly on the lips. 'Have faith, little one. I'm sure we are both going to shine in our respective fields, and the way you draw your mark has given me an idea.' He bent his head over his pad and began sketching furiously.

Lips tingling, Daisy leaned back, and watched as, under his skilled fingers, the bold strokes formed a circle in the centre of which was a perfectly formed flower. Finally, he looked up, his eyes sparkling as he smiled at her.

'We've been studying all things Arts and Crafts where everything created should be beautiful. I intend incorporating that philosophy into my work. Beautiful jewellery for a beautiful lady, and what could be better than the white of enamelled petals against the gleaming gold of a ring.' He winked, sending warmth flooding through her. 'Although I might be governed by the metals my tutor says I can use.'

'It sounds wonderful, Harry. Will you really be able to make my ring as part of your course?'

'Yep. It'll make a great project, as we have to prove we've learned our craft, with the best works being displayed in exhibitions up and down the country. I'm working under the guidance of a master craftsman who belongs to the Guild of Handicrafts and has just moved up from Newlyn where he was an instructor. It's a good way of promoting the school while getting our names out there.'

'Goodness, I hadn't realised,' Daisy murmured, staring at him admiringly.

As Harry made some notes on the side of his drawing, she stared down at her hand, imagining the ring he'd just described on her finger. How special it would be to wear something he'd made just for her. Nearby children were laughing as they kicked up the leaves that had already fallen. Their happiness was infectious and she found herself smiling.

'You look content,' Harry said, putting his drawing to one side. 'What are you thinking?'

'How much I love this park.'

'And me, I hope?' His twinkling eyes told her he was teasing.

'Yes, and you,' she agreed, running her finger down his smooth cheek to the tiny, moon-shaped scar under his chin. Shivers of delight ran through her as she caught the tang of the lemony soap he used. Then seeing an older couple approaching, they sprang apart like guilty children.

'Everything's so beautifully set out,' she said, trying to regain her composure. 'I'll never run out of inspiration for drawing.'

'The park was named for John Ruskin who used to live around here,' Harry told her. 'He was a talented water-colourist, writer, poet, who championed green spaces. His detailed sketches of plants, birds, landscapes and ornamental structures are impressive. Like the pagoda over there,' he said, gesturing beyond the bowling green surrounded by yew hedging, from where the eastern-looking building rose majestically. Daisy shook her head. He never failed to surprise her, one minute teasing her, the next imparting snippets of information.

'How do you know all that?' she asked.

'Just my natural genius,' he quipped. Before she could reply, a breeze rustled the gold and russet leaves in the tall trees. 'Come on, it's getting chilly. Let's go and explore what else this wonderful place has to offer,' he suggested, packing pad and pencils into his bag, then jumping to his feet and holding a hand out to help her up.

'I've been thinking,' he said as they ambled along. 'I really must speak with your father. He knows, of course, that you're safe walking out with a respectable gentleman like myself, but I'd feel better letting him know my intentions are honourable.'

'Respectable gentleman? Honourable? Whoever are you talking about, Harry?' Daisy exclaimed, remembering their ever-increasing passionate embraces behind the bandstand.

'I'm mortally wounded,' he murmured, thumping his chest.

'Seriously, Harry, Father still hasn't secured a permanent position and is growing more despondent by the week. I think it would be better if we waited. I mean, it wouldn't be tactful to start planning our future home when the best he can provide are those dreadful rooms.'

'Steady on, Daisy. I was only going to ask for your hand.'

'Oh, and what's wrong with the rest of me?' she quipped, playing him at his own game.

'Absolutely nothing, petal. Well, at least from what I've seen so far,' he countered, eyes glittering suggestively so that her heart gave a flip. 'However, it'll be another year before I leave college and then I will have to work hard to establish myself. Of course, it will be worth the wait as you will be marrying the finest jewellery maker in all the country, but until then …' He shrugged.

'Oh you,' she said, sighing. 'So, what were those notes you were scribbling beside my ring?'

'If you must know, I was working out the finer details of the design. I know you think I'm always joking but I want this ring to be perfect for you,' he said, his cornflower eyes bright with emotion.

'Oh Harry, that sounds wonderful,' she cried, taking his hand and giving it a squeeze. 'Except, I don't actually know what a posie ring is.'

'The name itself comes from the word poesy, which means short rhyme or poem. A posie ring is decorated on the outside of the band and inscribed with a message inside.'

'And what message will you engrave?' she asked, eyeing him curiously.

'Potty Petal perhaps?' He grinned.

'Oh, very romantic,' she retorted. But he refused to say any more and by tacit agreement they wandered on, the sun's rays making shadows along the path as they filtered through the trees. They stopped beside the oval pond and although it was bordered by shrubbery and weeping willows, the ripples on the water were clearly visible.

'That would make a good picture,' Daisy said. But Harry was peering up at the dark clouds that had gathered.

'Looks like we're in for a soaking.' Sure enough, just at that moment, raindrops began falling. 'Come on, my rooms are only a couple of streets away.'

Hand in hand, they ran to the nearest exit and along the wet pavements. By the time Harry pushed open a little wicket gate that led up to a three-storey house, the rain was coming down in torrents. Pushing open the front door, he stood back to allow her to enter. Shaking the worst of the water from her hair, Daisy scuttled inside. The hallway was narrow, with black and white tiles on the floor and a console table housing an aspidistra, its broad tapering leaves reaching out as if to entrap her. She shivered.

'You're cold,' Harry said, removing his flat cap and smoothing down his hair, which sprang in curls around his collar. 'I'll go and ask Mrs Meddler for a hot drink.'

'Did I hear my name, Harry dear?' A thin woman came bustling out of a room at the end of the hallway. However, when she saw Daisy, the smile of welcome vanished. 'Who is this?' she asked, beady brown eyes glinting.

'Allow me to introduce my good friend Miss Daisy Tucker,' Harry replied. 'Mrs Meddler is my landlady and a splendid one she is too,' he added, seemingly unaware of the woman's disapproval.

'This is a lodging house for gentlemen and female guests are not permitted, Miss Tucker,' she sniffed.

'I didn't realise,' Daisy replied, suddenly anxious to leave.

'It's pouring buckets, Mrs M, and I'm sure you wouldn't want Daisy to catch her death,' Harry reasoned. From the look on the landlady's face, Daisy was sure she wouldn't care if she caught pneumonia. 'If I promise to fill the coal scuttle for you later, would you permit us to sit in the front room until it clears?' he cajoled.

'Well,' she began, clearly liking the idea of having the dirty chore done for her, 'as you're a gentleman, I'll make an exception on this occasion,' she conceded, pushing open a door to the left of the stairs. The room was crowded with furniture and more of those evil-looking plants in ugly planters that reminded Daisy of chamber pots. Pictures of flowers lined one wall, all standing stiffly to attention as though they daren't move for fear of incurring the wrath of the indomitable Mrs Meddler. Although a fire was laid in the grate, she doubted the woman would deign to light it.

'Any chance of one of your splendid cups of tea?' Harry asked as his landlady stood, hands on hips, watching. Without answering, she went over to the sash window and peered through the net curtains where the rain still lashed against the panes.

'Do you have far to go?' she asked, turning and addressing Daisy.

'I live in Tiger Yard,' Daisy replied and took childish satisfaction in seeing the woman purse her lips. Darting Harry a pitying look, she left the room.

'I think we might have to whistle for our tea,' Harry groaned.

'Perhaps you should have told her we're betrothed,' she whispered.

'But I've yet to speak with your father. Might as well take a pew while the old bat's out of the way,' he said, grimacing as he sat on one of the hard-backed chairs.

'I can assure you there are no bats in here,' the woman said reappearing. With a knowing look, she sat on the chair beside him, leaving Daisy no option other than to take the seat by the door. 'And what does your father do for a living, Miss Tucker?'

'Erm, he's …'

'Looking to improve his position,' Harry said quickly. 'Now, Mrs M, I've never been in here before and I was just thinking what a charming room this is.' As Daisy stared at him in astonishment, the woman smiled.

'Why thank you, Harry. I do my best, but being a woman by oneself is not easy.' She sighed. 'That's why I do business with your father. He's such a considerate man, and your charming mother a respectable pillar of the community. And they obviously want the best for their only son, sending you to that School of Arts and Crafts.' The woman shot Daisy a sly look and it took all her willpower not to put out her tongue.

'I realise I'm lucky to be given the opportunity, Mrs M.'

'We make our own luck,' the woman replied.

'I want to ensure I can provide well for my future wife and family,' Harry told her, winking at Daisy.

Her eyes widened and her heart quickened. She hadn't even thought about children.

'Well, you make sure you choose wisely, young man. A man needs a wife who will stay at home and look after him. Not like those suffragettes. Hussies, the lot of them. Votes for women indeed. I've never heard the like of it,' she sniffed.

'But women should have a say in how the country's run, surely?' Daisy asked.

'Fiddlesticks. A woman's place is in the home, always has been, always will be.'

As the woman narrowed her eyes at Daisy, she felt her blood boil. It was antiquated thinking like that the politicians were relying on to continue having their own way. Then she realised the room had grown brighter. The rain was no longer hammering on the window and the sun was shining once more.

'Well, thank you so much for your kind hospitality, Mrs Meddler,' she said, jumping to her feet.

'My pleasure,' the woman replied, seemingly oblivious that Daisy was being sarcastic. 'You will bring in my coal now, won't you, Harry dear,' she simpered in the little girl voice she obviously used to get her own way.

'Of course, Mrs M. I'll just walk Daisy home first whilst the weather's dry.'

Ignoring the woman's indignant look, they let themselves outside. The air was cooler now and Daisy welcomed the breeze on her hot cheeks and the refreshing smell of wet soil and flowers from the gardens they were passing. She didn't know what had been worse: the patronising tones of the bigoted landlady; or her cloying, claustrophobic front room. How her hands itched to commit her to paper. She could just picture a caricature of the woman, hair sprouting from her chin like a spiny cactus.

'I'm sorry, Daisy,' Harry said, as they headed towards the shops on their way to Tiger Yard. 'I can't think what got into Mrs M. She's usually so charming.'

'Well, she didn't approve of me and would have thrown me

out if she knew I'd been at the suffragette rally on the Green yesterday. She's horribly old-fashioned. I mean, a woman's place is in the home, indeed!'

'Quite right too,' Harry agreed soberly.

'Harry … that's as ridiculous as saying you're a gentleman,' she shrieked, only to see his lips twitch. 'Oh you,' she murmured, slapping his arm. He gave a wry grin but, as they continued walking, he lapsed into silence. Then just as they reached the shops, he turned to Daisy.

'I know we agreed to wait until your father had secured a proper job before I spoke to him about our future, but …'

'But what, Harry?'

'I've been thinking,' he muttered.

'Dangerous pastime that,' she teased. But instead of returning her smile, he took her hand and gazed intently at her.

'You're right; Mrs M would have been more welcoming if I'd introduced you as my betrothed, wouldn't she?'

'She might have looked on me more favourably if she'd thought I was more like your mother rather than some perceived gold-digger.'

'What do you mean, more like my mother?' he frowned.

'According to Mrs Meddler, your father's considerate, your mother charming, so they obviously have a happy marriage and comfortable home.'

'That's what I mean about perceptions, Daisy. My parents might present a happy front to the public, but in private they argue like cat and dog. Give me a loving marriage like your parents have any day of the week. It's people that matter, not where you live.'

'Oh,' she murmured.

'I love you, Daisy, and what others think of you matters to me. So, with your permission, I'd like to speak to your father this evening, and assure him I'll be in a position to take good care of his beloved daughter.'

Chapter 12

Butterflies fluttered in Daisy's stomach as they climbed the stairs. She was excited and pleased Harry wanted to ask her father's permission, but was now the right time? However, the door was thrown open by a jubilant Arthur.

'Come in, the pair of you,' he beamed. Daisy stared past him to her mother who, instead of sitting on her chair beside the window, was stirring a pan on the range from which a fragrant aroma wafted. Her face was wreathed in smiles and Daisy thought how much younger she looked.

'Your father has found a permanent position at last,' she exclaimed.

'That's wonderful. Congratulations, Father,' Daisy cried.

'And you're just in time to join us for a special meal to celebrate.'

'If you're sure then I'd love to join you. Thank you, Mrs T,' Harry replied then turned to Arthur. 'Well done, sir; you must be relieved.'

'I am that, lad,' Arthur agreed.

'Come and sit yourselves down, although I'm afraid it's still the windowsill for you two,' Mabel told them, as she began dishing up meat coated in a glistening, rich gravy.

Again, Daisy was conscious of her straw bed so close by. But this time, rather than worrying what Harry thought of their primitive arrangements, she couldn't help imagining the two of them lying side by side, kissing, cuddling and … Feeling her face growing hot at where her thoughts were leading, she glanced at him from under her lashes. Unusually though, he was toying with his food, and if she didn't know him better, she'd have said he was nervous.

As soon as they'd finished eating, Harry asked if he could have a word with Arthur.

'Sounds serious,' her father replied, giving them both an appraising look. 'Better go into the other room.'

Expecting it to be merely a formality, Daisy set the kettle to boil then made tea.

'Seems we might have two things to celebrate this day,' Mabel said, smiling at Daisy.

'I don't know what's taking them so long,' Daisy cried, frowning at the door, which had remained obstinately closed for the past twenty minutes. 'This brew will be stewed.' Although they could hear the murmur of voices, it was impossible to make out what was being said.

'Well, pour out ours and we'll have a chat while we're waiting. Your father will be making sure Harry's plans for the future are satisfactory. You know how thorough he is, especially where his precious daughter is concerned,' Mabel replied, patting Daisy's shoulder reassuringly. As they sat at the table sipping their drinks, Mabel turned to Daisy, her eyes alight for the first time in months.

'Your father's taking me out to celebrate as soon as he gets paid. It'll be a rare treat to spend some time together. And we're going on a tram too,' she cried delightedly.

'That'll be really nice for you, Mother. I hope you have a good time,' Daisy told her.

'And your father's giving notice on this place, thank heavens. Now he's found a permanent position, it will be easy to find somewhere decent to live. Who knows, we might even be able to go back to Vaughan Road,' she said happily.

'Well, stranger things have happened and—' Daisy began only to stop as the door opened and her father and a grinning Harry emerged.

'Well, Mother, it seems our Daisy and Harry are to become betrothed,' Arthur announced grandly. 'Although, not until Harry has finished his course and secured a job, of course. However, he has assured me he has good prospects and so I've given my blessing.'

'Oh Father, thank you,' Daisy cried, jumping to her feet and throwing her arms around him, then finding Harry's hand.

'Congratulations, the pair of you. I hope you will be as happy as Arthur and I,' Mabel cried.

'Thank you, Mrs T.' Harry grinned. 'You have my word that I will always take care of Daisy,' he assured her solemnly.

'I know you will, lad,' Mabel replied. 'I couldn't ask for a nicer son-in-law. And of course, I will ensure Daisy is well equipped in the housekeeping department.'

'Oh, Mother,' Daisy groaned. 'Come on, Harry; I'll see you out,' she added, suddenly eager to be alone with him.

'Phew, your father certainly put me through my paces,'

Harry admitted as they skipped down the stairs. 'But when he asked me about my prospects, he seemed pleased with my answers so …'

'Oh Harry, do stop chatting and kiss me,' Daisy murmured, snuggling into him.

'As my wife-to-be wishes,' he said, grinning, pulling her close and nuzzling her hair. Then his lips moved lower until they claimed hers and, once again, they were lost in their own world.

'I know how important this rally is to you, Daisy, so as you've worked hard all week you may leave now,' Blue told her at noon on Saturday.

'Thank you.' Daisy sighed with relief, for they'd been putting in long hours to get these backdrops finished.

'I'm really pleased with your work, Daisy. You've shown a real understanding for what stage scenery entails. Not many artists grasp the fact they're actually painting the story of the show.'

'Why, thank you.' Daisy's eyes widened in astonishment for, while Blue was generous with his tuition and not afraid to point out when something wasn't working, praise was as rare as a heatwave in January.

'From next week you will be working on your own backdrop,' he told her. She stared at him in astonishment, excitement pounding through her veins. 'Off you go now. Can't have those suffragettes accusing me of being a chauvinist, or, worse, hitting me over the head with their parasols,' he quipped.

'Thank you, Blue,' Daisy managed to murmur. 'See you on Monday,' she called and hurried from the room.

Despite the cold and drizzly November weather, by the time Daisy reached the Green it was already crowded. Most of the supporters were huddled in shawls and cloaks, but all sported ribbons or badges in purple, green and white. Sarah and Emma were waiting for her by the pathway and together they stood listening to the shouts for women to be given the vote without further delay. The speaker was so passionate and articulate, she soon had the crowd whipped into a frenzy.

'Are we just going to stand back and let those bigoted ministers refuse to take the Conciliation Bill further? The Bill that would allow we women the right to vote?'

'No,' the tumultuous crowd roared.

'Then join us on the eighteenth of November, when suffragettes from all over the country will converge on the House of Commons to make our feelings heard in the name of suffrage.'

'Yes!' The cry was deafening.

Sheltering under a tree, Daisy took out her pencil and began drawing the woman speaker. With her aquiline nose and bright eyes that seemed to seek out and address each of them individually, she was a compelling subject.

'And we will be united in our stand against the police who have violated our sisters by pinching their breasts, lifting their skirts and, worse, subjecting them to sexual interference. It is contemptible and unacceptable. We are well into the twentieth century and the time men consider us to be their property is over. Ladies, it's time we made a stand for justice for women.'

'Cor blimey, we'd best not tell Mother about that or she'll never let us go,' Sarah muttered.

'My lips are as sealed as our boss' wallet,' Emma replied. 'Hey, that's good. You've really caught the likeness of her,' she added, staring at Daisy's sketch.

'Do you think so? I struggle getting some of the finer details right.' Just then as always happened at these rallies, there came the shrill sound of whistles as the police, truncheons in hand, converged on the crowds.

'Come on, let's beat it before we get collared,' Emma urged. 'We said we'd meet the boys in the coffee shop at four. What about you, Daisy?'

'I'm meeting Harry but I'd better go and change first,' she told them, staring at her green smock, which hung down from under her shawl. 'Father's taken Mother out for the day to celebrate. He's got a new job at last and found us a better house. By this time next week, we'll be living somewhere decent.'

'I'm pleased for your father but don't suppose you'll talk to us then,' Sarah moaned.

'Of course I will. You've been real pals and I don't know how Mother would have coped without Ruby. But ...' she frowned, not wishing to be insensitive.

'We know, you hate the yard. I can't say we love it, but we have no choice,' Emma lamented.

'It's really good news for your mother and father, though,' Sarah said. 'We will see you before you move, I hope.'

'You bet. We'll have a night to remember,' Daisy told them. 'And of course, we can all go on the march together.'

Daisy hurried towards Tiger Yard, her thoughts whirling faster than the litter being blown along the pavement. Things had definitely taken a turn for the better. And it had all started with the golden dress. Impressed with the repair her mother had made, Cal had asked if she would make costumes for the next show. Then, before sailing for America with the Guv'nor, he'd set up a home-working contract for her. Her father had secured a good job at the Stone Works and she couldn't believe she was going to be entrusted with her own backdrop. Wait until she told Harry.

And then there was their wedding to plan. Although it wouldn't be for a couple of years, when Scarlett had given Daisy a supply of surplus paper, she couldn't resist making sketches for her special outfit. Life was on the up at last, she thought, as she scuttled down the alley towards number thirteen.

But no sooner had she reached the house than the door was opened by an agitated Ruby. The woman looked ashen and she threw her arms around Daisy's shoulders. Daisy could feel her trembling.

'Oh Daisy, love, there you are,' she cried.

'Whatever's the matter?' Daisy asked, fear flooding through her.

'I'm afraid there's been a terrible accident. Everyone's been talking about it. Even made the front page of the early papers. I'll show you, come inside and sit down.'

'No, tell me what's happened,' she pleaded, her voice coming out as a squeak.

'A tram overturned earlier, people were trapped,' the

woman told her. 'They've got some out and they've taken the injured to the infirmary. Of course, your parents might not be involved but I fear …'

'What?' Daisy cried, cutting in. ' I must go and find out if they're alright,' she mumbled, shaking her head in bewilderment yet knowing instinctively her parents had been involved.

'I'll let Harry know,' Ruby called after her, but Daisy hardly heard as she dashed back outside, fear gnawing at her heart.

The streets were crowded. When, gasping for breath, she eventually reached the hospital, it was bustling with activity. Shocked people were frantically milling around the reception desk desperate to find out information about their loved ones. Ignoring their protests, she began elbowing her way through the crowds only to be stopped by an officious-looking man, who was marshalling everyone into an orderly line. Hopping from one foot to the other, she had little option other than to wait her turn. The smell of disinfectant was overpowering and she was sure she was going to be sick, but then finally, she found herself at the front.

'My mother and father, the tram accident,' she wailed, clutching at the counter for support.

'Name?' the woman asked briskly, frowning at Daisy's paint-stained fingers.

'Daisy Tucker. My parents, Arthur and Mabel Tucker. Where can I find them? Are they alright?' The woman's expression was guarded as she consulted a long list.

'Please take a seat over there,' she told Daisy, darting her a sympathetic look. 'Someone will be with you shortly.'

'I can't sit down, I need to know …' she insisted, fear clutching at her heart. 'Please tell me …' but the woman had disappeared. Moments later, a tired-looking man wearing a white coat appeared by her side.

'Miss Tucker?' he asked. Daisy nodded.

'My parents, the tram accident …' she began, then stopped when she saw his grave expression.

'I'm Dr Booth. Look, there is no easy way to tell you this: I'm afraid your father was one of those killed.'

'No,' Daisy whispered. 'Not Father. Are you sure?' she asked, swallowing down the bile that rose in her throat.

'He was trapped beneath the wreckage. As was your mother,' he said gently.

Daisy swayed on her feet and, as the ground came up to meet her, he put out his arm to steady her then gently pushed her down onto the seat.

'Your mother is Mabel Tucker?' She nodded. 'She's been taken up to the ward—'

'I must see her,' Daisy cried.

'She is still unconscious and, as yet, we've been unable to establish the extent of her injuries. We'll know more when she comes around. Although …' he hesitated.

'What?' she asked, her heart almost stopping.

'You might have to prepare yourself for the fact that she won't. I'm afraid I can't tell you any more at the moment. The next few hours are critical so we'll just have to pray.' He winced as someone almost knocked him off his feet in their urgency to reach the desk. 'Look, it's mayhem down here. Go home and come back in the morning,' he suggested.

'I can't go home,' Daisy screamed. 'She's my mother. I must see her now,' she insisted.

The doctor gave a resigned nod.

'Very well, I'll get someone to show you to the ward. But don't expect too much. As I said, she's still unconscious.' He signalled to a passing porter and, in a daze, Daisy followed him through a blue of corridors. She hardly noticed the clang of trolleys being wheeled past, their patients hidden under swathes of white, or the nurses hurrying about their business. Finally, she was shown through swing doors where, by contrast, all was deathly quiet. With a brief smile, a nurse pulled back the curtains drawn around one of the beds.

'Just two minutes. Mrs Tucker really is poorly,' she said quietly, giving Daisy a compassionate look before hurrying away again.

'Mother?' Daisy whispered, as she stared down at the figure in the bed. A livid red wound on her cheek contrasted with the ghostly pallor of her skin. There was no answer and her breathing was so shallow Daisy had to bend forward to check she was actually still alive. Tears sprang to her eyes as she remembered how excited her mother had been that morning.

And now her father was dead and neither of them would ever see him again, she thought, choking back a sob. She couldn't break down now. Her mother needed her.

'Please wake up,' she implored.

'Miss?' She turned to find the nurse gesturing for her to leave. Leaning forward, she gently kissed the parchment-white cheek, then, tears running freely, she followed the young girl out of the ward.

'My father? What will happen to his … ?' Daisy stuttered to a halt, unable to utter the word body. The nurse patted her arm.

'Come back tomorrow; Sister will be able to tell you what arrangements are being made.'

'I'm not leaving here until Mother regains consciousness. I must be here when she wakes.'

'If you insist. I'll show you to the waiting room.' She walked briskly along the corridor and threw open another door. Heads snapped up hopefully, then looked glumly down at the floor again. Daisy took an empty seat and waited with the other relatives and friends who were either dry-eyed and staring, or weeping into their handkerchiefs. She lost all track of time as shadows crowded the corners and the room grew steadily colder.

'Daisy, Daisy.' Lost in thoughts of her poor parents, it was some moments before she realised Harry had appeared. 'Ruby told me about the accident. I came straight here.'

'Father's dead …' Daisy's voice broke on a sob.

'Poor Arthur,' he murmured, squeezing in beside her and pulling her close. 'They say your mother is holding her own,' he added. 'So many people have been hurt. They're working flat out trying to contact next of kin.'

Chapter 13

All through that long night, they sat together. Harry refused to leave Daisy and although she drew comfort from the warmth of his embrace, thoughts of her poor father still plagued her. Had he known anything about the accident? Had he suffered? Had he known her mother was hurt? So many questions, so few answers.

'Can I get you something to eat?' Harry asked, fidgeting on the hard chair as the first fingers of sunlight filtered through the blinds.

'I'd be sick,' she murmured. 'You go and get something.' But he shook his head and pulled her close again. As the day dragged on, she was only vaguely aware of low voices, people coming and going, the odd wail of distress. When Harry gave her a nudge, she almost jumped off the seat. A nurse was standing in the doorway beckoning to her. Daisy's heart began thumping so hard in her chest she had to take a deep breath.

'The doctor has just examined your mother and says there's no change. Sister insists you're to go home, rest and get something to eat. You need to keep your strength up. You'll be no use unless you do.'

'Sister's right, Daisy. Come on, I'll take you home,' Harry said, taking her arm.

Reluctantly she let him lead her along the streets where, to her surprise, everyone was bustling home after the day's business.

'I'll come in and light the range,' he offered, opening the door.

'No, please go home. I need to be by myself,' she urged. 'I must try and get my head round what's happened.'

'Alright, only if you promise to get some rest. But I'll be back with something for your breakfast in the morning,' he said, kissing her gently on the cheek.

Closing the door, she was hit by the sound of silence, a feeling of emptiness filled the room. A sharp rap made her jump and Ruby bustled in with a steaming bowl.

'Here you are, dearie. Why you look frozen to the marrow,' she exclaimed, setting the soup down on the table then taking Daisy's arm and leading her to the chair. 'You sup some of this while I light the range. Then you can tell me how your poor parents are.'

'Father's dead,' Daisy muttered.

'Oh no,' Ruby cried, her hand going to her mouth. 'And your poor mother?'

'Still unconscious. Look, Ruby, I don't mean to be rude but I need to be by myself,' she burst out, swallowing down the bile that rose in her throat.

'Well, let me know if you need anything,' Ruby replied, eyeing her doubtfully as she made for the door. Although the woman meant well, Daisy really did need to be alone.

As if a magnet was drawing her, she went into her parents' room. Boxes lined the wall where her mother had begun packing up their few things in readiness for their move. The bed was made, their nightclothes neatly folded on the pillows. Impulsively, Daisy snatched up her mother's nightdress and held it to her face. Breathing in the familiar smell of her, tears coursed down her face.

'Please get better, Mother,' she cried, collapsing onto the bed.

She stayed like that until dawn broke the next morning, then, frozen and stiff, she struggled to her feet and made her way back to the hospital. Please let Mother be awake, she prayed, but there was no change in her condition.

The waiting room had emptied since the previous day, and, slumping onto a vacant chair, she suddenly felt very alone. How she wished Harry was with her. Then, as if she'd conjured him up, he appeared beside her.

'Any news?' he asked.

She sighed. 'No change.'

'I bought you a pie,' he said, handing over a warm parcel wrapped in paper. 'And before you refuse it, exam or no, I'm not leaving until you eat it. You'll be fainting at my feet if you don't have some nourishment.'

'I'd forgotten about your exam,' Daisy admitted, quickly taking a small bite to please him.

'I have to go or they'll throw me off the course, but I'll be back during my lunch break,' Harry promised, pulling her close and kissing her forehead. 'Keep strong.' And then he was gone, leaving her alone with her thoughts. What were they going to do when her mother recovered? If she recovered. Daisy shivered. And what about her poor father's body? The thought made her feel sick again, and she threw the rest of the pie in the bin.

The time dragged as she waited for news, the clock on the wall never seeming to move.

'Your uncle is here, Miss Tucker.' Roused from her reverie, she looked up to see a tall man with a moustache, dressed in a dark coat, top hat in his hand, smiling gravely down at her.

'Who?' Daisy frowned.

'You remember me, Daisy – Uncle Rich, your father's brother.'

As she stared at him, she had a brief recollection of this man visiting them in Vaughan Road when she'd been a young girl. The serious grey eyes staring down at her reminded Daisy of her father and she swallowed hard. 'I caught the first train this morning as soon as I received the telegram about poor Arthur.'

'Your uncle's details were in your father's wallet along with your mother's, Miss,' the nurse explained to a perplexed Daisy. 'But of course, with your mother being unconscious … well—' she shrugged '—Sister will see you both now.'

Daisy felt as if she was surrounded by a bank of mist as she followed them down the corridor.

'Sister, this is Mr Tucker and Daisy his niece,' the nurse announced.

'Take a seat,' the prim woman commanded, her stentorian tones brooking no argument. 'I understand you have already identified Mr, er, Arthur Tucker,' she stated, consulting the notes in front of her. Daisy stared at the man in surprise.

'It's a sad business and I thought it would save my poor

niece from having to do it,' he agreed. 'I gather Mrs Tucker still shows no sign of regaining consciousness.'

'Not yet, no. Which leaves us with Daisy here. I understand you are sixteen years of age,' she said, looking up from consulting her notes again. 'Do you have any older brothers or sisters?'

'I have no siblings. Mother lost the baby she was carrying when she fell and hurt her legs.'

'Hmm. Do you have any other relations living locally?' she asked, her penetrating stare unsettling Daisy further.

'No,' she admitted, 'but my betrothed Harry lives nearby. He's studying at the School of Arts and Crafts.'

'So, obviously not earning. You can see what the problem is, Mr Tucker.'

'Which is why I am here, Sister. As soon as I was informed of that dreadful accident, I caught the first train up from the West Country. I shall be happy to offer my dear niece a home there until such time as her mother is restored to health.'

'That's very kind of you but I'm capable of taking care of myself,' Daisy cried, suddenly filled with fear.

'I'm afraid the law doesn't permit that, Miss Tucker,' the woman said, shooting her a look. 'It would appear you have two choices: accept the generous offer your uncle has made to provide you with a home; or I'm afraid it'll be the workhouse.'

Daisy's eyes widened in horror as she stared from one to the other in disbelief.

'Come home with me, Daisy,' her uncle urged. 'Surely you can see that's the best thing for you at this time.'

'But I can't just leave Mother,' she cried.

'You'll be of no use hanging around here.' Sister tutted then consulted her papers. 'There will also be the matter of a burial fee for Mr Tucker and hospital charges for Mrs Tucker, which have already mounted up considerably.' Daisy's heart sank. She had no money and, as of the next day, no home either.

'Send the bills to my address,' her uncle instructed, rising to his feet. 'And include a note on Mrs Tucker's progress if you would. Now, if you'll forgive us, we have a train to catch. Come along, Daisy, you'll need to tell the driver where you live so you can pack your things.'

This couldn't be happening, Daisy thought as she stared through the rain-lashed window of the hansom cab her uncle had hailed.

'I never realised my brother had fallen on such hard times,' Uncle Rich said, wrinkling his nose as they pulled up by the alley leading to Tiger Yard. 'Wait here,' he instructed the driver. 'We'll be five minutes and then you must take us to Waterloo station fast as you can.'

'I'll not wait a moment longer; them ragamuffins will be all over my vehicle if I'm not careful,' the cabby advised him, waving a fist at the advancing rascals.

They made their way along the filthy yard, trying to avoid the dirty puddles and pleas from the begging urchins who were sitting in the mud. 'It probably explains why Arthur didn't let me know you'd moved,' her uncle muttered.

'Actually, Father gave notice and we were to leave tomorrow,' she whispered, swallowing down the lump in her throat as she thought of him.

'Then, it's opportune I turned up today, or you'd have found yourself out on the streets,' he replied.

Feeling as if she was wading through treacle, Daisy led the way up the stairs. She paused outside Ruby's in the hope she would appear, but of course the woman was at work. With a resolute sigh, Daisy pushed open the door that led straight into the main room, trying to ignore her uncle tutting in disapproval as he stared around.

'Thankfully, I can provide you with much better accommodation than this,' he told Daisy, as he frowned down at her straw bed. Although he was trying to reassure her, a prickle of apprehension ran down her spine for she didn't really know him, did she? 'Pack your bag with whatever you need, we must catch the next train if we're to make it back to Devon by evening. Hurry up now, you won't need much,' he urged.

Encouraged, she did as he asked. If she didn't need to take lots with her then she couldn't be staying long which surely meant her mother was expected to recover soon.

They were making their way back down the rickety stairs when Harry burst through the outer door.

'Daisy. Where are you going, and who's this?' he asked, frowning from her bag to her uncle.

'This is my Uncle Rich and he's offered me a home until Mother recovers,' Daisy explained.

'Oh? Is that far from here, sir?' he asked politely.

'I reside in Devonshire,' the man replied.

'But that's counties away,' Harry cried.

'It is certainly a world away from this squalor,' her uncle agreed. 'I'm guessing you must be the gentleman Daisy mentioned.'

'Harry Wylde, sir. I am Daisy's betrothed and as such

consider it my duty to look after her,' Harry told him, taking hold of Daisy's hand. She looked at him gratefully, a spark of hope fluttering in her breast.

'I'm sure you have Daisy's best interests at heart, young man, but let's be sensible about this. Do you have a job? Can you provide her with somewhere to live?' Harry shook his head.

'I'm a student at the School of Arts and Crafts,' he admitted. 'But I'd do anything to help Daisy.'

'Then you'll appreciate she'll be better off in a nice home rather than the workhouse.' As Harry opened his mouth to say something else, the man put up his hand. 'I'm sorry but we need to be practical. I'll give you two minutes to say your goodbyes, then we have to leave.' Taking Daisy's bag from her, he walked briskly outside.

'I didn't know you had an uncle.' Harry frowned, pulling Daisy closer.

'I haven't seen him since I was little, but the Sister at the hospital said as next of kin he'd been informed of Father's …' she swallowed down the tears that threatened. 'They can't tell when Mother will come around, and if I don't go with him, they'll send me to the workhouse.'

'Oh Daisy, I can see you have no choice, especially as your father gave notice here. I'm going to miss you terribly,' he murmured, kissing her gently on the lips.

'I feel dreadful leaving you and poor Mother. What will happen when she comes round?'

'I'll visit her as often as I can,' he promised. 'Write with your new address and I'll reply straightaway and let you know how she's doing.' She nodded and they stood staring into each other's eyes as though imprinting every detail until the next time they met.

'Daisy.' They jumped as her uncle's impatient shout broke the spell.

'Please take this,' Harry muttered, reaching into his pocket and drawing out a roughly wrapped package. 'I made it for your Christmas present and was going to put a bright-red ribbon round it and give it to you then. Wear it and think of me. Like the posie ring I'm designing for our wedding, the hoop stands for eternal love. A circle with no beginning or end is a symbol of infinity, endless and eternal as our love will be.'

'Why Harry, that's a beautiful sentiment,' she whispered, the breath catching in her throat. 'And this is just exquisite,' Daisy whispered, staring from his eyes, now almost navy with passion, down to the silver bangle etched all the way round with a delicate chain of daisies. Gently he took it from her and slipped it over her wrist where it shimmered in the dingy hallway.

'It won't be for long,' she assured him as her uncle's exasperated call came again. 'I love you.' She leaned forward and kissed him passionately on the lips. All she wanted was to sink further into his embrace but, knowing she must be strong, resolutely she tore herself away.

Chapter 14

The journey to the station was slow with traffic nose to tail, with her uncle peering at his pocket watch every few minutes.

'What's the hold-up, cabby?' he called as they shuddered to a halt again.

'It's them suffragettes, sir; all over the bloomin' place they are, holding up their placards and shouting about Women's Rights.'

'They should leave running the country to us men who know about these things,' her uncle replied. Daisy stared at him incredulously but thought better of responding. Instead she sank back against the wooden seat.

'Please step on it, driver, I've a train to catch,' her uncle barked, shaking her back to the present.

Although the cabby did his best, by the time they reached the station, the guard had his flag raised ready to signal to the driver. Everywhere was noisy and dirty, with steam and smuts of smoke from the engines billowing in great clouds around them. Her uncle dived into a carriage and held out his hand to help Daisy. In a daze, she sank into a seat beside the window while he stored her bag in the rack above them. There was the shriek of a whistle and the carriage juddered forward.

As the train picked up speed, so did Daisy's apprehension. She'd never been outside London before. And yet she had no choice for her wages weren't enough to pay for rent.

'Oh … my job,' she gasped. Everything had happened so fast she hadn't had time to let Blue know.

'Don't worry, Daisy, as soon as we arrive in Devonshire, you can write and tell them what's happened,' her uncle replied, lighting a cigarette and inhaling.

Pulling her shawl tighter, Daisy settled back against the padded seat. They were still gathering speed, the wheels clicking and clacking as they rattled along the tracks. Wiping the steamed-up window, she watched as densely packed terraced houses and factories gave way to more salubrious surroundings where homes had long gardens that meandered down to the railway lines. She wondered what their new home was like, then remembered her father was no longer here. Pain seared through her and she had to bite her lip to stop herself from crying out. Despite her grief, exhaustion caught up with her and she felt her eyes growing heavy.

When she woke, the gas lamps had been lit and were casting an eerie glow over the crowded carriage. Her first thoughts were for her mother and she sent up a prayer for her speedy recovery. She fervently hoped it wouldn't be long so she could return home. Thank heavens dear Harry had promised to keep an eye on her.

The gleam of silver caught her eye and she ran her fingers over the cool, smoothness of the bangle, tracing the daisy chain he had painstakingly engraved. She wondered what he was doing. How she was going to miss him, she thought, jumping as she saw her uncle watching her.

'Nearly there, my dear,' he told her gently.

Moments later, the train began to slow, and as they shuddered to a halt alongside the platform the guard called, 'Seaton Junction.' Her uncle rose and lifted down her bag.

'We change trains here,' he said, helping her from the carriage then clambering into another train. 'Only two more stops and then my stable boy will be waiting to collect us. It's only a few miles from the station where a nice warm meal and bed will be waiting,' he told her.

It wasn't until they were trotting through the darkened lanes in the trap, lanterns shining dim rays of light onto the puddles that pooled in the ruts, that a thought occurred to Daisy.

'How will we know when Father's funeral is? I must be there. I will, won't I?' she asked, peering at her uncle through the gloom.

'Because it was a public accident, there'll have to be a post-mortem. The hospital will keep me informed.'

'And Mother?' she asked. 'Hospitals are expensive and …'

'Now, don't you worry, niece,' he said, patting her hand. 'Everything's been taken care of,' her uncle murmured, and there was a click followed by a pinprick glow as he lit another cigarette. 'All you need to do is settle into your new life here in Devonshire.'

'But I won't be staying long,' she told him.

'God willing your mother will soon recover,' he murmured. 'In the meantime, my home is your home.'

'Thank you, Uncle. So, what is it like? What is your wife

called and how many children do you have?' she asked, realising that, although he was her uncle, she knew nothing about him or his family.

'Family life isn't for me, my dear. I work hard at my business. They don't call me Rich for nothing,' he chortled.

'Oh, I thought it must be short for Richard,' she replied, then had to grip the sides of the trap as the pony veered sharply left. Slowly, they began descending a steep hill, the trees on either side so tall their stark branches almost met in the middle. Apart from the lanterns, everywhere was pitch-black and Daisy shivered, her fingers caressing the silver bangle for comfort.

'Fallen tree down that lane, master, so we'll take the next,' the lad announced, gesturing with his hand.

They came out of the tunnel of trees, passed a huddle of cottages, then a church and further on a few more cottages. Everything seemed so spread out unlike the tight confines of Tiger Yard. They rounded a bend, finally coming to a halt outside a large thatched building with flickering lamps shining out from the many, tiny paned windows. Through the gloom, she could just make out the dark shapes of other buildings further along but they looked much smaller.

'Goodness, I had no idea your cottage was so large, Uncle,' she gasped. Again, his laugh rang through the night.

'It's the biggest around here,' he told her proudly, before grabbing her bag and jumping down onto the wide path. 'Come along, I'll show you where you'll be staying. Stable the horse then come indoors,' he ordered, turning to the young lad.

Endeavouring to keep up with her uncle's brisk footsteps, Daisy was nearly knocked off her feet when a portly man, obviously worse for drink, knocked into her.

'Scenery's lookin' up,' he leered before letting out a loud belch.

Charming, Daisy thought, but her uncle was already disappearing through a heavy wooden door. She followed him into a large room with low beams and a fire burning in a wide inglenook. Everywhere smelled of ale, tobacco and cooked food. She wrinkled her nose. What was this place her uncle had brought her to?

'Polly, where are you?' her uncle called. Daisy could hear muttered voices but before she'd had time to take in her surroundings, she was being ushered down a narrow hallway.

'Why Master Rich, there you are,' declared a plump woman. She was wearing a shapeless dress and was wiping her arms on her voluminous apron. Her lank hair hung in rats' tails to her shoulders but her dark eyes were piercing as they fixed Daisy with a calculating stare that made her shiver.

'This is my niece, Daisy. She'll be staying until her mother recovers,' her uncle told the woman, dumping Daisy's bag on the flagstones. 'You'll have to excuse me, my dear, but the journey took longer than I expected and there are things I must attend to. Polly here will look after you.' As the woman opened her mouth to protest, a look passed between them that Daisy couldn't fathom. 'See Daisy has a hot meal and then it would be better if you showed her where she'll be sleeping,' he added. 'After that, perhaps you could serve up whatever delights you've concocted in the back parlour.'

'As if I ain't got enough to do,' the woman muttered. 'Besides, you said ...'

'We will discuss arrangements in the morning,' her uncle said briskly, cutting her short.

'Long as we do,' Polly told him. 'And Ginge'll have to carry her bag upstairs. Me back's playing up after doing all that clearing up by myself.'

'I'm really not hungry so if you could show me to my room,' Daisy said quickly, not wishing to cause any trouble. 'And I can carry my own things,' she added, picking up her bag.

'You must eat, my dear, I'm sure Polly can rustle up some bread and ham,' her uncle insisted, ignoring the woman's snort. 'We'll have a good chat over breakfast. Sleep well,' he murmured, patting her shoulder before disappearing through another door.

'Come along then,' Polly muttered, snatching up a candle and glaring at Daisy before she began climbing the stairs. Not sure why the woman had taken against her, Daisy tried to make conversation.

'Is my uncle entertaining tonight?' Daisy asked, wondering if that was why he'd hurried away. But then that didn't explain the drunkard who'd nearly knocked her down outside.

'He's always entertaining. That's what a tavern's for,' the woman chortled.

'You mean this is an alehouse?' Daisy cried. The woman paused and shook her head.

'What was yer expecting, Buckingham flipping Palace?' she muttered, before puffing her way up the next flight. Still reeling from the shock, Daisy followed her in silence and was relieved when, on reaching the top, Polly threw open a door and stood back so Daisy could enter.

''Fraid there ain't no servants so you'll 'ave to deal with yer own slops. Privy's in the yard,' she told Daisy, stooping to light the candle beside the bed with her own. Then, muttering to herself, she disappeared back down the stairs.

The room under the eaves was little more than the tiny attic space a maid would have used, but it had a small window and seemed warm. There was a bed with a patchwork cover, a tiny cupboard for her things and a washstand on which stood a jug of water and a cloth. A fly-spotted mirror hung above it. Having spent weeks sleeping on a straw mattress, this was a great improvement and she'd make the best of things until her mother had recovered enough for her to return. And she'd be sure to stay away from any customers.

Wearily, she emptied her bag then changed into her nightdress and climbed into the bed with its sagging mattress. She lay under the thin cover, gently stroking her silver bangle. In all the turmoil, she hadn't even had time to ask Harry how his exam had gone. She'd write to him about it first thing in the morning, giving her new address, and enquire after her mother. Hopefully he would reply by return and the news would be good.

A pang cut through her as she thought of her poor father, his life cruelly cut short just as things had been looking up for him. At least he'd be pleased his brother Rich was looking after her, she thought, wiping away a tear. It was strange they hadn't seen him for so many years, but no doubt his business kept him busy. Anyway, she'd return home very soon, Daisy thought, as exhaustion overtook her and she fell into a troubled sleep.

Daisy woke with a start. The candle had guttered and it was pitch-black. She could hear voices, laughter, raucous singing. Then came a tap, tap, tapping against the window and she froze. It came again, tap, tap, tap. Gingerly, creeping out of bed, she peered through the dirty glass. All she could make out was the empty pathway and a couple of cottages further along the road. Then, seemingly from nowhere came a gust of wind and that insistent tapping as the slender branch of a tree was blown against the glass. About to laugh at her stupidity, the sudden screech of an owl made her jump, sending her scurrying under her cover. How she wished she was back in London with her family, Harry and friends around her. Except family life as she'd known it would never be the same again.

Chapter 15

Bleary-eyed after her disturbed night, Daisy made her way down the two flights of stairs.

'Ah niece, I trust you slept well,' her uncle greeted her. This morning he was dressed in a woollen jacket, a colourful scarf peeking through the open neck of his shirt.

'Thank you, Uncle,' she replied, not wishing to admit she'd been awake for most of the night.

'We will breakfast together in here,' he said, ushering her in to a small room where a fire was blazing. 'Bring eggs, bacon, toast and a pot of tea, Polly,' he called down the hallway. 'Now sit yourself down,' he said, pulling out a wooden chair with a patchwork cushion for her. 'I'm sorry to have left you to your own devices last night, but evenings are our busy times.'

'I didn't realise you ran an alehouse,' Daisy replied. He eyed her closely for a moment then smiled.

'Is that disapproval I detect, young lady?' he asked, stroking his moustache thoughtfully.

'Well, Father always …' she began before remembering.

'Arthur always did have idealistic notions, if you'll forgive my saying so. However, I prefer to think of Masons as a tavern, offering hospitality to the community. Villagers, some lonely, some unable to afford to heat their humble cottages, come in here to partake of a drink and something to eat while warming themselves and catching up with friends. Is that so wrong?' he asked.

'Well, not when you put it like that.' Daisy frowned, thinking of the rough alehouses she passed on the way home from work.

'Breakfast,' Polly announced as she waddled into the room carrying a loaded tray. 'Though for some of us who've been up since the crack of dawn, it's more like lunchtime,' she puffed, plonking their plates noisily down in front of them. 'I take it yer can manage to pour?' she asked Daisy, her voice oozing sarcasm.

'Well, yes, of course,' Daisy said, smiling at the woman.

'Thank the lord for that. Got enough to do without playing nursemaid.'

'Polly,' her uncle warned. 'That will be all. We'll speak later.'

'Too right we will,' she muttered, glaring at Daisy before making her way back down the hallway.

'She doesn't seem to like me,' Daisy ventured, as, seemingly oblivious, her uncle began tucking into his food.

'Don't worry. Bit of a misunderstanding,' he replied, through a mouthful of egg.

'Oh?' Daisy asked but he continued eating and didn't answer. Valiantly, she tried to force down the food but the eggs were overdone, the bacon soggy and they stuck in her throat. Giving up, she pushed her plate away and poured their tea into mugs that were none too clean. Her uncle looked up, raised his brow at her breakfast, then promptly emptied it onto his own plate.

'Don't believe in waste,' he muttered. She sat there sipping her tea until he'd finished. 'Right,' he said, spooning sugar into his mug and stirring it, round and round. The clinking sound was beginning to make Daisy's head ache when he stopped abruptly, took a slurp of tea then stared directly at her with those grey eyes reminiscent of her father. Except his had been clear grey while her uncle's were dimmer. Feeling he was expecting her to say something, she swallowed.

'I do appreciate you looking after me like this, Uncle.'

'The least I can do, niece. Now, the first thing you should do is write to your intended. There is a post box in the wall outside, which is emptied at ten o'clock, which is in …' he looked at the grandmother clock standing in the corner. 'About thirty minutes. Do you have stationery? Stamps?' he asked.

'No, Uncle,' she admitted. 'And I need to let Blue, my boss at the Fun Factory, know too.'

'Right. Wait here,' he said, getting to his feet and disappearing. She heard him call to Polly and by the time, with much muttering and glaring, she'd cleared away their things, he'd returned carrying paper and envelopes upon which he'd already stuck postage stamps.

'Thank you, Uncle,' she replied as he set them down in front of her. 'What exactly is the address here?'

'Masons of Bransum will find us,' he replied. 'I'll leave you to write and post those. You can write, I suppose?' he asked.

'Of course, I can,' she cried, outraged that he should think otherwise.

'All right, keep your hair on. There's some round here who can't, that's all.'

'Really?' she asked, staring at him in surprise.

'Thick as planks a lot of them. Comes in handy though.' He grinned, tapping the side of his nose with his finger. Not understanding what he meant but not wishing to appear 'thick' either, she smiled and took up the pencil he'd provided.

Dearest Harry,

I miss you already and can't wait to see you again. How is Mother?

Please write and let me know how she is. I'm staying at Masons, Bransum, Devonshire. It is a tavern but Uncle Rich explained he provides a service for the community. He told me there has to be a post-mortem on Father as he was killed in an accident, but that I can return for the funeral. I'm not sure how long these things take, so please let me know when it is to be.

I adore my silver bangle and think of you when I feel its smoothness and trace the pretty daisy chain with my finger. I won't ever take it off. Hope your exam went well.

Please, please write soon with news of Mother.

With all my love,
Daisy

She read it through, placed it in the envelope and addressed it. Glancing at the clock she saw she had only ten minutes left and quickly, she penned a note to Blue at the Fun Factory, apologising for her absence and explaining about the accident. As she got to her feet to find the post box, her uncle reappeared.

'I couldn't help notice you were looking peaky, my dear, which is not surprising after all you've been through,' he said. 'I suggest you get your shawl and, after posting your letters, take a walk around the hamlet. It's not very big but a bit of fresh air would do you good. I have business to attend to,' he told her.

'Thank you, Uncle,' she replied, thinking it was just what she needed to clear her head.

The wind from the previous night had died and the air smelled fresh after the rain. She walked along, looking for the post box and listening to the sparrows chirping in the hedgerow. It was all so quiet with the only traffic being a horse and cart that plodded sedately past, the driver raising his cap in greeting.

Crossing the road, she found herself in a small square lined with shops. Rows of stone-built cottages fronted lanes that led off in all directions. A group of women, bonneted heads bent close in conversation, looked up curiously as she passed.

'Good morning, I wonder if you could direct me to the post box?' she asked, holding up her letters.

'It be just be down there, my dear,' one lady replied, gesturing along the lane.

'Thank you.' She smiled and was gratified when they all smiled back.

'Yer be staying in Bransum, then?' the woman asked.

'Yes, with my Uncle Rich over there,' she replied, nodding back towards the alehouse.

Immediately, the women's smiles changed to looks of disapproval and, without another word, they bent their heads close again.

Well, that's given them something else to chat about, she thought, making her way past a cobbler's with leather boots and shoes on display.

Further along she came to another shop and, peering through the tiny windows, she could see piles of vegetables and fruit on a counter, while stockings, knickers and petticoats lined the dresser behind. A woman with a woollen cloak thrown over her shoulders and a basket on her arm came out and nodded, then hurried on her way, but Daisy knew her birdlike eyes had taken in every detail of her appearance, which would no doubt be shared with the others when she met up with them.

Spotting the red post box built into a stone wall, under which grew clusters of the prettiest little mauve blue flowers she'd ever seen, she crossed the road. Then holding Harry's letter to her lips, she kissed it for luck before popping them both through the slit. Thinking the flowers would make a delightful sketch, Daisy bent to study them then noticed a slender woman, a crimson and black scarf draped over one shoulder, watching her. Or rather she seemed to be staring at her wrist. Daisy jumped up, her eyes widening in shock.

'Sorry if I startled you. I couldn't help admiring your beautiful bangle.' There was no doubting the sincerity shining from the woman's hazel eyes and Daisy smiled.

'My friend Harry made it for me. He's studying at the Camberwell School of Arts and Crafts,' she told her proudly.

'Really? I studied there, too,' the woman told her.

'Goodness, what an amazing coincidence,' Daisy replied.

'Not really, it's a bit like a circuit as artists tend to gravitate together to work in beautiful places.' She laughed. 'When our tutor left to start his own workshop, he invited some of us to join him. Let me introduce myself: my name is Grace Mullins. I paint and make jewellery,' the woman explained.

'And my name is Daisy, hence the chain Harry engraved,' she replied, holding the bangle out for the woman to see.

'He is obviously very talented,' Grace murmured, studying it closely. 'What about you, are you studying at the school too?'

'No, I'm not an artist, although I do love to draw,' she admitted. 'I work at the Fun Factory helping to prepare scenery for the music halls.'

'Well, that sounds artistic to me.'

'That's why these delicate little flowers caught my eye,' Daisy admitted. 'They remind me of the posies women wear on their dresses when they visit the music halls.'

'They're violets and grow well in the damp Devon climate. Despite their fragile appearance, they flower throughout the winter. Are you here visiting?' she asked.

'I'm staying with my uncle while my mother's in hospital.'

'Oh, I do hope she is recovering well?'

'She was still unconscious when I left.' Daisy sighed, her eyes clouding. 'I only arrived yesterday. My father was killed, you see, and my uncle said I was too young to stay by myself.'

'Well, I'm sorry to hear that, but at least you have your uncle to care for you. I'm afraid I have to get back to work now, but perhaps you'd like to come and see the work we produce, meet the others? We're down there—' she gestured towards a lane behind '—and you'd be welcome anytime.'

'I'd love to but wouldn't you need to ask your boss first?' she asked. To her surprise, the woman laughed.

'Our workshop is run as a co-operative so we're all equal. We work closely together giving each other mutual support and encouragement. Do say you'll come?'

'I'd love to,' Daisy cried delightedly.

'Good, we can discuss our crafts over a nice warm drink. Where are you staying, by the way?'

'My uncle runs the tavern up there,' she replied, gesturing back towards the way she'd come. To her consternation, Grace's expression turned from delight to despair.

'Well, make sure you take care of yourself,' she told Daisy, then with a little smile hurried on her way.

Daisy stared after her, wondering why mentioning where she was staying should have precipitated such a change in everybody's manner.

She didn't have time to dwell on it, though, for, as she entered the tavern, she saw it was busy with customers. Without glancing right or left, she hurried through the tap room, ignoring the ribald remarks thrown in her direction. Her uncle met her in the hallway, a worried look on his face.

'Is something wrong, Uncle? Have you heard from the hospital?' she asked, her heart thumping so wildly she thought she was going to be sick.

'Just a minor domestic problem,' her uncle replied.

'Minor,' Polly sniffed, hurrying past with a tray of food. 'Won't be blinkin' minor if I gets no 'elp.'

'Sorry, Daisy, as you can see, we're run off our feet. The new girl hasn't shown up and ...' he shrugged, running a hand distractedly through his hair.

'Can I do anything?' she offered.

'Oh, niece, I couldn't possibly expect you to work in the kitchen,' he demurred, shaking his head.

'I don't mind. I'd be pleased to help pay for my board,' she told him.

'Well, if you could, just for today, I'll see we get someone for tomorrow. Polly,' he called, gesturing for her to come over. She finished setting down the dishes, then, hips swaying, made her way towards them.

'Good news, Polly,' the man told her. 'Daisy has offered to assist. Isn't that kind of her.' They exchanged another of those unfathomable looks.

'Yea, cors.' She smiled. 'Come on then,' she muttered, leading the way down the hallway and into a large kitchen.

The square table in the centre was cluttered with boxes. Steam rose from the bubbling pans set on an old range, their contents hissing as they spilled over. In the corner was a stone sink piled high with dirty dishes, while glasses and plates littered the less than clean work counters. The smell of stale fish pervaded the room, making Daisy's stomach turn over.

'Rich has been promising to get me help ever since the last wench left,' Polly said, darting her a meaningful look.

'I only offered because the new girl didn't turn up,' Daisy told her, anxious the woman didn't get the wrong idea. But Polly tossed her a voluminous apron and told her to slice bread, ham and cheese for the ploughman's lunches.

The young lad who'd driven the trap was in the scullery area washing pots and pans as if his life depended on it. Daisy could see he was much younger than she'd first thought, probably no more than ten or eleven years old and looking in dire need of a good meal.

'Time to serve the stew,' Polly announced, lifting the lid off one of the pans.

'Blimey, that smells ripe,' the boy cried, holding a wet hand to his nose.

'Why, you little ...' She flapped her dirty tea towel at him but continued to ladle out the foul-smelling gloop. Daisy swallowed hard.

'Well, don't just stand there, girl, take these dishes through,' Polly ordered. 'The punters in the window seat are waiting.'

Glad to be out of the steamy, stinking kitchen, Daisy carried the tray through to the bar. The room fell silent as the customers all turned to look at her. Then, as she made her way towards the window, one man let out a piercing whistle.

'Would yer look at that,' he called. Embarrassed at being the centre of attention, Daisy hurried over to the table.

'Ay Rich, things are really lookin' up in here,' a man shouted.

'You mind your manners, Toby, or you'll be out on your ear,' her uncle replied, hurrying over. 'Tell Polly she's to do the rest of the waiting, Daisy. I appreciate your help but please stay in the kitchen.' Relieved, she hurried back and relayed the message to Polly.

'So, he expects me to put up with their leering, does he?' she hissed.

'Give over, you love every moment of it, Pol,' the lad chuckled, dodging as she swiped at him with her filthy cloth.

'Well, I ain't about to do all the waiting on tables for the rest of the day so yer'll have to 'elp me,' she told him. 'And yer can wash the dirty pots,' she added, turning to Daisy.

Chapter 16

As Polly and the lad carried loaded trays through to the bar, Daisy stared around, noticing the room was even filthier than she'd first thought. Her mother would have a fit if she saw it. She felt that twinge stabbing at her insides as she remembered the accident. Had her mother recovered consciousness by now? How she wished she was by her side, holding her hand. But she wasn't, and as she couldn't be, it was some consolation knowing Harry would be visiting her. All she could do was wait to hear from him.

'Well, get a move on,' Polly snapped, dumping more dishes beside her. 'Them pots won't clean themselves.'

The rest of the day passed in a frenzy of pot washing, peeling endless potatoes, then helping to serve up the suppers. As no food was offered and, having eaten nothing since breakfast, she had to make do with hastily devouring a slice of ham and bread when Polly was taking yet more plates of food through to customers. Her back and feet were aching but still there was no let up.

'I've bin slavin' away since first thing so I'm goin' for a bit of a lie-down,' Polly announced, when, finally, the last meal had been served.

'Thank you for your help, Daisy,' she muttered to her back, as the woman disappeared through the door.

'Yer can get put away for talking to yerself,' the lad said, appearing with yet more glasses to be washed.

'I might as well be. When I offered to help out, I didn't expect to be treated like a skivvy,' Daisy retorted. 'Goodness, you look all in,' she added, noting that, despite his exertions, the ginger-haired boy was looking ashen beneath his freckles. 'What's your name?'

'They calls me Ginge,' he replied. 'And you be Miss Daisy.'

'Just Daisy's fine. Well, Ginge, it's nice to see a friendly face.'

'Thanks for helping with the pots. I'll take over now or your skin will get all sore.' Daisy looked down at her reddened hands and grimaced. Then hearing the sound of bawdy singing outside, she turned to Ginge.

'Tell me, is it always like this?' she asked, as she began stacking the dishes on the shelves.

He nodded. 'They'll all be tight as boiled owls come midnight.'

'Sorry?' Daisy frowned.

'Drunk as skunks,' he explained.

'Oh.' Daisy shuddered.

'That's just the way tis,' he muttered and returned to his pot washing. 'You go on up now, just Daisy, I'll finish off here.'

'Won't Polly be back?' she asked.

'Nah, probably warming the master's bed by now,' he replied with a wry grin. ''Er room be the one down there, next to the cellar,' he said, pointing to the floor. 'But she 'ardly uses it, if yer gets my meanin'.'

'Oh, I see,' Daisy replied. Although she thought he must be mistaken, for she couldn't imagine her smartly dressed uncle associating with that slovenly woman. 'Is your room down there too?' she asked. He shook his head.

'I prefers to sleep in the stable with the 'orses. Tis warm in there. And 'orses don't orders yer about.'

'Goodnight then, Ginge,' she said, lighting a candle from the one on the table.

'Goodnight, just Daisy.'

Candlestick in hand, she wearily plodded up the stairs then, too tired to undress, slid under the bedcover. Snuffing out the flame, she lay back on the saggy mattress and stretched her aching legs. Never had she worked so hard before. Yet she didn't dare complain for her uncle had taken her in after that terrible accident. A pang of despair shot through her as she thought of her poor father. As hot, salty tears rolled unchecked down her cheeks, she'd never felt so bereft. How she longed to feel Harry's arms comforting her.

A deafening bang woke Daisy with a start. It was followed by clanking and crashing and then her bed began to shake as what sounded like an avalanche of rocks came thundering down. As the room vibrated again, she shot out of bed. The noise was definitely coming from outside and, hastily throwing her shawl around her shoulders, she fled down the stairs. The kitchen was empty but the back door was blowing back and forth in the wind. Surely that hadn't been enough to wake her?

As she stood there shivering, wondering what to do, Ginge appeared.

'Mornin', just Daisy,' he yawned. 'Yous up early.'

'I was woken by some terrible crashing and banging. Must have been the door, I suppose,' she said.

'Na, that were the draymen delivering,' he told her. 'Twice a week they has to come or the place'd 'ave no ale. Tis my job to count the barrels as they roll um down, in case they short-change the master. Now I 'as to make tea and butties for 'em.'

'Doesn't Polly do that?' she asked.

He gave a harsh laugh. 'Yer won't see 'er this time of day,' he snorted.

'What about my uncle?'

He shrugged. 'The same of cors.'

'Well, I can help you while I'm waiting,' she offered. 'You have to start work early,' Daisy said as he began riddling the ashes in the range and adding more kindling. 'I can make the butties for you if you show me where the bread is.'

'Mole will be 'ere in a mo, 'e as to 'ave the bakery fire lit and the bricks 'eating lit by four in the mornin'.'

'Mole?' Daisy frowned as she watched Ginge move the large kettle onto the hob.

'Yea, 'e 'as a nose for things, see? Baker's boy 'e be. We was friends at the orphanage. They says it would be good for us working near each other but we never gets no time off.' He shrugged. ''Ere 'e is now,' he added, snatching up a basket as they heard the persistent tinkling of a bell.

While the boy dashed to the door, Daisy stood by the range to warm herself.

Ginge staggered back with a basket full of bread and placed it on the side. Then taking out a crusty loaf he went to set it on the board that still had crumbs and blobs of goodness knows what on from the previous night.

'Hang on,' Daisy said quickly, picking up a cloth and giving it a vigorous wipe. 'What do they have on their butties?'

'Butter,' he said, pointing to the dish on the side with one hand while tipping boiling water into a huge brown pot with the other.

'Anything else?'

'Na, dems don't pay nuffin so that's all they get.'

As the aroma of freshly baked bread wafted around the room, Daisy's stomach grumbled loudly.

'Yer starving same as me,' Ginge chuckled. 'Tis the best time of day to snatch a bite, before them tight-fisted … er I mean … the master and her comes down.' He snatched up a freshly buttered slice and stuffed it into his mouth. Daisy watched in astonishment as he gobbled the piece whole, leaving a glistening yellow film on his lips. Unable to resist, she popped a piece into her mouth and stood savouring its sweet, yeasty taste. Ginge grinned, then began pouring tea into tall mugs.

'Weak as gnat's p— well, we ain't allowed to use more than half a spoon of leaves, see,' he explained, when he saw her looking aghast at the barely coloured liquid. 'Don't worry, though, by the time I've taken them out to the draymen it'll have brewed a bit more so we'll have a decent cuppa.' He tapped the side of his nose and, as he carefully carried out the loaded tray, Daisy smiled. Well, she couldn't fault his logic, she thought, cutting another slice of bread and taking a large bite.

When the boy returned, they stood side by side in front of the range warming themselves whilst they sipped their tea. Heavy footsteps thundering down the stairs made her jump, sending hot liquid spilling over her hand.

'Bring some tea through to the tap room, boy. And make it snappy, my throat's as scratchy as the bottom of a bird's cage.' Hearing her uncle's voice, Daisy wiped her hand on the apron, then turned to Ginge.

'I'll do it,' she told him, pouring the hot liquid and taking it through to him with the rest of her own drink.

'Here you are, Uncle,' Daisy said, placing the mug in front of him, and trying to ignore the overpowering smell of stale alcohol and tobacco.

'Thank you. You're up early,' he said, looking up from his newspaper. He appeared a bit rumpled this morning, she noticed. 'I trust you're well,' he mumbled.

'Actually, I'm feeling weary. Not only was I working in the kitchen until nearly midnight, I was woken first thing by the draymen delivering.'

'Ah well, luckily it only happens twice a week,' her uncle replied.

'I was wondering if you had time to tell me a bit about what my father was like when he was younger,' she asked him. The discussion with Ginge about the orphanage had unsettled her. Her uncle stared at her for a long moment then shrugged.

'Let's take our drinks through to the back parlour. Never

know who's listening in here,' he said, staring around the seemingly empty room.

'So, what do you want to know?' he asked, when they were seated next to each other at the table.

'What was he like as a young boy?' she said, realising her father had never spoken about his childhood. 'Did you live here?'

'Good heavens no,' he snorted. 'We were brought up in a two-up two-down not far from Camberwell as it happens.'

'What was he like?' she urged, suddenly desperate to build up a picture of her father.

'Serious, always had his head in a book, learning his sums. I preferred skiving off and helping down the market. Father was forever saying he wished I was more like him. Then Arthur met and married your mother and worked all hours to better himself.'

'But you've done well for yourself, having a place like this,' she said, looking around as she sipped her drink thoughtfully.

'I suppose I have,' he said, staring about as if seeing it for the first time. He frowned. 'Although your father wouldn't have approved of a den of iniquity like this.'

'He might have, if he knew you were providing a service for the community.'

'Yer what? Oh yes, of course. Well, I always try and do my bit. Like paying for his burial and your mother's hospital fees. And that won't come cheap.'

'Well, you know I'll help in any way I can,' Daisy said, trying to blink back the tears that were never far away these days. But talking about her father had made her emotional and they spilled over and rolled down her cheeks. 'I loved him so much. And what happens if Mother doesn't recover?' she sobbed.

'There, there,' her uncle murmured, reaching across and putting an arm around her. 'I'm sure the hospital's doing their best and you'll soon be hearing from that Harry of yours,' he added, pulling her closer.

'Well, well how cosy,' Polly muttered, hands on hips as she stood glaring at them.

'Morning Pol, didn't hear you come down. Daisy's feeling low this morning so I was just trying to console her,' he said, quickly removing his arm.

'Yea, I bet you were.'

'I think I'll go back to bed for half an hour,' Daisy said, jumping up and heading for the stairs.

Reaching the privacy of her room, she was seized with the urge to see the faces of her beloved mother and father again. Delving into her bag, she took out the pictures she'd drawn of them a few months earlier and carefully untied the string around them. But seeing them smiling up at her made her feel even worse as it suddenly hit her that, if her mother didn't recover, she'd be an orphan just like poor Ginge. Wretchedly laying them down on her bedcover, she took out the one of Harry but, as she caught sight of his cheeky grin, she was overwhelmed by a sense of loneliness. How she missed him, she thought, running her hand along the smooth coolness of her bangle. Was he thinking of her too?

Desperate for some fresh air, she jumped to her feet. As she did, she caught sight of her crumpled pinafore and realised she'd been in such a hurry to find out what the disturbance had been that morning that she'd forgotten to put a clean one on. Quickly changing, she rinsed her face and hands then tidied her hair. Wrapping her shawl around her shoulders, she tripped back down the stairs.

Her uncle and Polly were still arguing so, taking a deep breath, she went through to the tap room.

'I think I'll go for a walk, get some fresh air,' she told them.

'And who'll be helping me in the kitchen then?' Polly asked, hands on hips.

'Well, your new girl's starting today,' Daisy told her.

'Yer what?' the woman cried.

'That was what you told me, wasn't it, Uncle?' she asked.

'Er yes, of course,' he muttered, looking quickly down at the newspaper on the bar before him.

'Oh no yer don't, Rich Tucker,' Polly said, snatching it away. 'Yer've got more explaining to do,' she retorted.

'I'll be off then,' Daisy murmured, making a quick escape. It was strange that for someone supposedly in charge of the tavern, her uncle seemed quite fearful of Polly.

Chapter 17

Although a weak sun was shining, the days were growing noticeably cooler; winter was on its way. Glancing at the post box as she passed, Daisy crossed her fingers there'd be a letter from Harry today. Staring down at the clusters of little mauve flowers, she again thought what a lovely picture they would make and vowed to return with her pencil and paper.

She made her way through the funny little square, marvelling at how quiet everywhere was in contrast to the busy streets of Camberwell. Thoughts of home reminded her of the tragic circumstances that had led to her being here and she sent up a silent prayer that her mother was recovering. Then she spotted the group of bonneted women gossiping outside their cottages, and wondered if they'd been there ever since she'd last passed by.

'Good morning,' she called. Although they looked up and nodded, nobody spoke, no doubt unwilling to be associated with someone who was staying in an alehouse.

She passed the little shops then spotted the lane where Grace had told her they had their studio. Desperate to see a friendly face, she made her way towards the row of tumbledown cottages, then hesitated outside wondering whether or not to knock on the door. Although Daisy had been invited, she didn't wish to intrude if they were busy. Just then the door opened and Grace appeared, beckoning to her.

'You found us then.' She smiled.

'Are you sure it's convenient?' Daisy asked.

'Of course, come on in,' she said, red skirts rustling as she led the way. 'Thought you'd changed your mind when you saw the state of the building. I know it's not much but, the rent is low and the old place has been converted in such a way, we can all work at what we love.'

'That must be very rewarding,' Daisy replied, realising how much she was already missing her sketching.

'We might not be well-off in the monetary sense, but we're rich in spirit and always have a welcome for friends,' she explained.

As she inhaled the familiar smell of paint and ammonia, along with the slight tang of metal, Daisy blinked in surprise, for the building had indeed been altered with all the interior walls having been opened up to form arches, giving the appearance of one long room.

One man was hunched over a table, tiny hammer in his hand, while a lady, older than Grace, was sitting at a high bench beside a window, no doubt to take advantage of the light. A more mature man with auburn hair and bushy beard flecked with grey was perched on a stool in front of an easel. Although his canvas was daubed with colourful swirls, Daisy guessed, from his position beside another of the windows, he was painting the view. Cupboards and shelves stacked with materials, boxes and bottles ran the length of the back wall.

A heavy workbench with a vice sat in one corner, black iron tools hung on nails above. It reminded Daisy of the studio at the Fun Factory and she sighed as she remembered she should have been starting work on her own backdrop this week.

'This is Daisy, everyone,' Grace announced. 'She likes to draw, and guess what? Her betrothed is only a student at the School of Arts and Crafts in Camberwell.' They all looked up and smiled warmly, and Daisy felt welcome for the first time since she'd arrived in Bransum. Grace turned to the older woman. 'This is Mae; she used to teach at the very same school. That was before Sean seduced her and brought her back here to his lair,' she teased.

The woman, wearing a man's checked shirt, her brown hair tied in a thick plait that fell to her waist, looked up from a workbook in which she'd been sketching an elegant design for a brooch, and proffered her hand. 'Hello Daisy, nice to meet you.' As Daisy shook it, her bangle caught the light and Mae's eyes widened in appreciation. 'If your young man made that for you, he is certainly very talented and if that delicate etching is a daisy chain, he obviously has a sense of humour. Always a good trait in a man.' Daisy smiled, for that was one of the things that had attracted her to Harry.

'Thank you, Harry gave it to me before I left,' she explained.

'I agree, it is beautifully done,' Grace agreed. 'Daisy is staying with her uncle whilst her mother recovers from an accident.' Murmurs of sympathy echoed round the room and Daisy could feel their compassion radiating towards her. 'And this is said seducer Sean, who, naturally, has an instinctive feeling for natural forms.' She chortled, gesturing to the man at the table, who put down the silver dish he'd been beating.

'Which is why I'm delighted to be working with the two most beautiful women for miles around,' Sean replied, in a musical voice that rose at the end of his sentence. With his clear-blue eyes twinkling, he stood up and bowed. 'Or might that about to be three?' he asked, winking at Daisy who was mesmerised by his lilting accent.

'Not everyone falls for your charms, darling,' Mae snorted.

'Daisy works at the Fun Factory,' Grace told them.

'Fred Karno's place?' The man swivelled round from his easel and surveyed her with eyes that reminded Daisy of jade. 'Met him once, wonderful chap. Comes from Exeter, a few miles from here. Small world, as they say. So, Daisy, what do you do in Fred's inimitable factory of fun?'

'I help create the backdrops, although I began by priming them,' she explained.

'A very important job. Proper preparation of the canvas is vital or you'll never achieve a good result. I'm Claude, by the way.'

'Claude loves to paint our glorious scenery, although sometimes his work is open to interpretation,' Grace chaffed.

'Alas this girl is unable to appreciate sheer genius when she sees it,' he lamented, throwing up his hands in despair. 'So, Daisy, what do you like to draw?'

'Flowers and folk mainly, although I have difficulty getting a good likeness of some people,' she admitted.

'Capture the character, that's the secret,' Claude told her.

'Except they all run away from Claude.' Mae laughed.

'Poor Daisy, all you've heard is us teasing each other when you must be dying for a drink. I might be unenlightened in the interpretation of impressionism, Claude, but I am hospitable,' Grace quipped, holding out her hand for Daisy's shawl. 'You'll not feel the benefit when you go out otherwise,' she said, reminding Daisy of her mother even though Grace couldn't be more than twenty-three or four. 'Now, who wants a tisane?' she asked, moving gracefully towards the stove upon which a copper kettle was heating.

'Yes please, all the dust round here's making me thirsty,' Claude replied.

'I'll have mint, please,' Mae replied. 'You should try some, Daisy. Grace's tisanes are wonderfully refreshing.'

'And being the chivalrous gentleman that I am, I'll have whatever's going.' Sean grinned.

'If you're that much of a gent you can go outside and pick the mint while I set out the mugs,' Grace told him. 'Oh, and you can bring in some onions and carrots from the store while you're about it, then we can have soup for supper.'

'That's right, take advantage of my good nature,' he grumbled, grabbing a wicker basket and theatrically raising his eyes to the heavens as he went outside.

'Anyone hungry?' Grace called, as she opened the stove and prodded at some blackened potatoes before removing them to a plate. 'We try to be as self-sufficient as possible here,' she explained, when she saw Daisy's eyes widen. 'We grow most of our vegetables and herbs in the patch outside, while the potatoes thrive up on the plats.'

'The what?' Daisy frowned.

'It's what the locals call the plots of land up on the cliff tops.'

'Cliff tops? You mean the sea is near here?' Daisy gasped.

'It's only a few minutes' walk away. Did you not know?' Grace asked, looking surprised.

'I had no idea. This is the first time I've been to Devonshire,' she explained.

'Well, let's eat and then we can go and explore.'

Daisy's heart flipped with excitement. She'd never seen the sea before. 'What can I do to help?' she asked, as Grace pushed tins and jars of brushes out of the way before setting out plates on the cupboard.

'You can cut these spuds in half and place a knob of butter in each,' she said, handing Daisy a dish.

'Are you sure you've enough?' Daisy asked, her mouth watering at the sweet aroma wafting her way. It had been hours since she'd stood eating bread in the kitchen with Ginge and she was ravenous, but didn't wish to impose.

'Darling, whoever happens to be here when we eat, gets fed. It's the way we live,' Mae said, dragging her high-backed stool across the room.

'It's only coming down in sheets again,' Sean said, drops of rain beading his hair and shoulders as he stepped back inside. 'Here you are, oh task mistress,' he quipped, placing the laden basket on the floor beside Grace. Deftly she plucked a handful of the mint.

'Chop this then, if you're feeling so hard done by,' she said, raising her brow at Daisy.

The others pulled up chairs and moments later they were

seated, plates on laps, enjoying the warmth of the stove. Daisy tucked in hungrily then took a sip of her drink. As the minty freshness hit the back of her throat she smiled in appreciation.

'We might live simply but we live well,' Claude told her when he saw her expression. 'Nourish the body, nurture the soul, ignite the inspiration.' He grinned, rubbing his hands together.

'Anything's got to be better than those bags of mystery we had the other day.' Mae grimaced. 'Gave me jip all night, they did.'

'What was in the bags?' Daisy asked, never having heard of anyone eating such a thing before.

'To be sure that's the question,' Sean groaned, shaking his head. 'Never had so-called sausages like that before. Nobody knows what Bert the butcher puts in them, hence the name. I'm sticking to what we grow from now on. Don't know how the villagers can eat his stuff.'

'Well, they are a funny lot.' Mae shrugged. 'Shunning us like they do.'

'Why is that?' Daisy asked, remembering the looks she'd received earlier.

'Can't abide newcomers,' Claude replied. 'Intruders, they call us.'

'They think we're shameful because we all live here together,' Grace explained.

'Instead of being Miss Grace you're a Dis Grace,' Sean hooted.

'You'll have to forgive our dear friend,' Claude told Daisy. 'You're staying here because your mother had an accident. Nothing too bad, I hope?'

'Father was killed in the tram accident which left Mother unconscious. She still hadn't come round when my uncle came for me, so I don't know how badly hurt she is. I didn't want to leave her, but I had no choice.' She shrugged, trying to quell the pang that was becoming familiar. Again, there were murmurs of sympathy. 'I've written to Harry giving him the address of where I'm staying. He promised to visit her and let me know how she is, you see.'

'Oh, you poor darling,' Mae murmured, leaning over and giving Daisy's arm a squeeze. 'Still, at least your uncle's looking after you. Is he anyone we know? What?' she frowned as Grace shook her head.

'His name is Rich Tucker and he runs Masons.' In the ensuing silence, Daisy saw them exchange looks. 'What is it?' she asked.

'Well, it's not really an appropriate place for him to take a young girl like you,' Claude said finally, fiddling with the handle of his mug.

'It was that or the workhouse,' she admitted.

'Not much difference from what I've heard,' Sean muttered.

'But my uncle has been kind and taken care of … well, the formalities,' she told them, anxious to make them understand. 'Besides, he says he runs Masons as a service to the community,' Daisy told them. Sean snorted and the others looked at each other again.

'Well, I suppose he does offer jobs to orphans,' Grace said quickly.

'And expects them to work all day every day without

paying them,' Sean retorted. Daisy thought of the long hours Ginge worked, his bony body and the way he'd wolfed down the bread that morning.

'And he leaves paying the local traders until the very last moment, even though he makes a nice fat profit on their goods,' Sean added.

'Surprised they continue delivering to him,' Mae snorted.

'He's got the biggest business round here.' Sean shrugged, then seeing Daisy's horrified look, added, 'I'm sure your mother will recover soon but, meantime, you're welcome to visit us anytime.'

'Thank you.'

'Well, that was delicious Grace, but I must return to my easel before the light goes. Want to see what I'm doing?' Claude asked Daisy.

'I'd love to, but shall I wash the dishes first?'

'Goodness no. As Claude says, the days are growing ever shorter and we need to get back to work. I'll put them outside the door and let the rain clean them,' Sean said, jumping up and hurriedly collecting the empty plates.

'When you've had enough of Claude trying to explain his work, come and see what you think of my new design,' Grace said, dragging her chair back to her bench and peering out of the window. 'I'm afraid it's much too wet to explore the beach now.'

'Or paint *en plein air*; that's in the open air,' Claude explained, seeing Daisy's puzzled look. 'It's what I prefer. You get to feel and smell the natural environment, which translates onto the canvas.'

Daisy was fascinated as Claude went on to explain how he used small, thin yet visible brush strokes along with accurate portrayal of the changing qualities of light in his landscapes.

'It's the exact opposite of the way we paint the backdrops,' she told him. 'We have to use big, bold strokes and colours so the audience feel part of the scene.'

'That is an interesting concept,' Claude said, nodding. 'This way gives me the freedom to use colour in the way I want. Take that tree outside, for example. Half close your eyes and tell me what colours you see.' Screwing up her eyes, Daisy was surprised to see how the red and gold of the leaves clinging to the dark branches merged into swirls of vibrancy just as Claude had painted.

'Yes, I get it,' she cried.

'You must be the only one who does then.' Grace laughed. 'You'd best come over here and look at my sketches before Claude's head grows larger than it already is.' As the man snorted and returned to his painting, Daisy joined Grace.

'These are beautiful,' she enthused, admiring the flowing lines of the flowers and fern fronds Grace had drawn in her workbook. Turning over the page she exclaimed at the tiny clusters of hazelnuts and ivy leaves with veins that looked so realistic she wanted to reach out and stroke them.

'I'm glad you approve.' Grace nodded. 'And from the way your fingers are twitching, I see you're itching to draw something yourself.'

'I am,' Daisy admitted, staring down at her hands.

'Have you brought any of your work with you?' Claude asked, looking up from his painting.

'Sketches of my mother, father and Harry, but they're in my room,' she replied.

'Bring them next time you visit us. I'd love to see them,' he said. He turned to peer out of the window. 'It's stopped raining but the light's beginning to go. I think you should be getting back before darkness sets in.'

'Oh goodness, I'm sorry. I didn't realise I'd been here so long,' Daisy cried. 'Thank you so much for luncheon and showing me your work,' she added, retrieving her shawl and throwing it around her shoulders.

'You've not seen mine yet so you'll have to come again, darling,' Mae told her.

'Would you like me to walk you back?' Claude asked, looking serious. Conscious he was eager to make the most of the light which was now fading fast, Daisy shook her head.

'Thank you but there's no need, I know the way. Bye, everyone. See you soon,' she called.

'I hope your mother recovers quickly,' Grace said, showing her to the door. 'Don't worry too much about what the others said about your uncle. None of us have been here long; it's probably just hearsay. You know where we are if you need us.' She smiled but, this time, it didn't reach her eyes.

As the door closed behind her, Daisy shivered and it wasn't just from the chill of the late afternoon air.

Chapter 18

As Daisy walked briskly up the lane, carefully avoiding the puddles that had gathered in the ruts, she couldn't help pondering on what Grace had said. Or rather what she hadn't. Surely her uncle wasn't as bad as they'd all made out, but then the artists had all seemed sincere? Even though it was late afternoon, the little square was eerily quiet, the keepers having locked their shops, lights flickering in cottage windows.

Passing the post box, her heart flipped. There might be a letter waiting from Harry. The thought made her heart sing, and she crossed her fingers there would be good news about her mother and she could return home.

Reaching the alehouse and not wishing to spoil her wonderful day by encountering any more drunkards, Daisy made her way round to the back entrance that led into the hallway by the kitchen. Even from outside, she could smell the unsavoury odours pervading the air and wrinkled her nose. Why anyone should want to eat here, she couldn't imagine. She pushed the door open then stopped in her tracks for her uncle and Polly were engaged in another bitter argument.

'I said leave it to me, Polly,' Rich snapped, 'and I mean it.'

'But yer promised me some help …' Polly wailed.

'And if you hadn't pushed her too hard as soon as she arrived, she'd be … oh hello,' her uncle said, looking up suddenly and seeing Daisy standing in the doorway.

'Where the hell have yer been all this time?' Polly yelled, her face contorting with rage.

'I went out for some air then had a look around the neighbourhood,' Daisy replied.

'Oh, how nice for yer and that took all day, did it?' she sneered. 'Whilst yer've been gallivanting, missy, I've been slaving away here all by myself.'

'Didn't the new girl turn up?' Daisy asked. But the untidy kitchen with unwashed crockery and pots on every surface told its own answer.

'Oh yea, her turned up alright, but it seems her don't do work …'

'Polly,' Rich warned, his voice cutting through her tirade. Her uncle turned back to Daisy, his voice softer now. 'I, er, we were worried about you.'

'Sorry, I didn't realise. Did a letter come from Harry?' Daisy asked, letting Polly's ranting go over her. But her uncle shook his head. 'What about the hospital?' she persisted.

'The hospital?' He frowned, his bushy brows joining together in bewilderment.

'Have they been in touch with news of Mother?'

'Ah, I received a bill for her hospital fees to date and your father's burial, which of course I'll be settling immediately. But they didn't say anything about your mother's condition. No news must be good news, eh?' He smiled and patted her shoulder.

'Thank you, Uncle. But they will let you know when Father's funeral is?' Daisy asked.

'Yes, of course,' he said quickly. Although the thought of it was heartbreaking, she needed to pay her last respects to the man who'd brought her up. It would be an opportunity to return home, wherever that might be now, for, of course, she would need to find accommodation for herself and her mother.

'You find us in a bit of predicament, I'm afraid,' he said, jolting her back to the present. 'It's been really busy here and we've both been rushed off our feet. Then the new help failed to materialise …'

'Again, Uncle?' Daisy frowned, only to hear Polly snort.

'Yes, it's unfortunate for there's a bar of people screaming for Polly's wonderful food but …' he gestured helplessly around the chaotic room and sighed. 'It's too late to get someone else today but I'll sort that first thing. A fine hostelry we've turned out to be. My reputation will be ruined if the punters don't get fed and they decide to go to the one up the top of the village. I really don't know what to do.' He groaned and looked at Daisy in despair.

'I suppose I could help clear up again …' she began, then saw the look that passed between her uncle and Polly, but before she had time to add that this really would be the last time, his mood had brightened.

'Oh, would you?' he cried, putting an arm around her shoulders. 'We'd be so grateful, wouldn't we, Pol?' Seeing the woman's accusing glare, he quickly removed his arm and strode from the room.

'So, where've yer been all day?' Polly growled, throwing a grubby apron at her.

'When I went to post my letter the other day, I met a lovely artist called Grace. We got talking and she invited me back to her workshop to see her designs. There are four of them and ...'

'Corrupt, the lot of they,' the woman cut in. 'It's immoral all living together under one roof like that, and not one of them married.' She sniffed.

'But they're really nice and ...' Daisy began.

'Ain't got time for idle chit-chat. Now yer've deigned to turn up, you can peel them tatties. Then when you've set them to boil, you can make a start on the pots. Don't know where that lazy good-for-nothing's got to, but he'll feel the back of my hand when I see him.'

Shrugging off her shawl and hanging it on the nail beside the door, Daisy grimaced at the stained apron, but knowing it would protect her pinafore, reluctantly tied it around her waist. She worked quickly and was cutting up the potatoes when Ginge appeared. Putting his finger to his lips he gave Daisy a pleading look as he crept across the kitchen. It was then Daisy noticed he was limping.

'Well, look what the cat's dragged in,' Polly sneered, looking up from the ploughman's plate she'd been putting together. Then without warning her arm snaked out and cuffed the boy's ear so violently, he had to grab hold of the sink to stop himself from falling. 'Lazy good-for-nothing, they'll be no supper for yer,' she hissed, picking up a tray and waddling through the door.

'Are you all right?' Daisy asked, hurrying over to him.

'The 'orse cast a shoe so I had to take 'im to the smith. 'E were busy so I was late getting back. I got a right kicking,' he groaned, rubbing his thigh.

'You poor thing,' Daisy sympathised.

'You gets used to it, just Daisy,' he muttered, picking up the cloth and making a start on the dirty pots. 'Got bloomin' big feet though. I can feel the bruise already.'

'Well, horses are large,' she replied, only to receive a quizzical look from the boy. 'Mother always put butter on mine to bring it out,' she added, trying to help.

'Sooner eat it on some bread, just Daisy,' he said, giving a wry grin. 'Missed me tea tonight, though.'

Without hesitating, Daisy went over to the loaf and cut off a thick slice which she slathered in butter.

'Here, eat this before Polly returns,' she urged.

'Coo, ta,' he replied, his eyes lighting up as he grabbed it gratefully. Just as earlier, he wolfed it down in one go. Then hearing the sound heavy footsteps, they quickly returned to their tasks.

'Right, who's nicked some of me bread,' the woman demanded, her eyes narrowing when she saw the remains of the loaf on the board.

'It was me, Polly; I cut Ginge and myself both a slice,' Daisy said. 'Nobody thought to tell me what time supper is and we were so hungry, we couldn't do any more work without food.' Her voice tailed off as the woman looked as if she was about to explode.

'This ain't no hostelry, yer know,' she cried.

'Why, Polly, I thought Uncle Rich said that's exactly what this place is,' Daisy replied, smiling demurely.

'Don't yer get clever with me, missy. It might be for the punters but they pays good money. Yer'll eat when everyone's been served, if there's anything left. Yer got them tatties boiling, yet?' she asked.

'Just about to put them on, Polly.' She smiled. Perhaps if she got on the right side of the woman, she'd find out more about what went on here. What the artists disclosed had unsettled her. Father had always taught her they should pay their way and if they couldn't afford anything, they went without.

Placing the heavy pan on the range, she jumped back smartly as the woman removed the lid from a fish kettle. The foul smell along with clouds of billowing steam made her eyes water and she had to turn away.

'Don't you turn yer nose up, missy,' she declared, taking up a spoon and slopping indeterminate grey lumps onto a plate. 'I'll have yer know this fish is fresh the day,' the woman retorted.

'Yea, but which day,' Ginge snorted, turning to Daisy and miming being sick. He looked so comical she had to bite her lip to stop herself laughing out loud.

'Don't know what yer thinks funny, girl, as yer've been so slow doin' them tatties this'll have to go out with bread instead,' Polly snapped, glaring at Daisy. 'The man at the table beside the fire is getting impatient and we can't afford to upset him of all people. Put his food down in front of him and come straight back,' Polly ordered.

'Uncle said I'm not to go into the bar again,' Daisy told her. 'And I only offered to help out in the kitchen.'

'Yer'll do as yer bloomin' well told, missy.'

'You seem to have forgotten my uncle's in charge and he brought me here to look after me,' Daisy retorted, eyes blazing as she rounded on the cook.

'Yer uncle ain't given to charity and the sooner yer realise that, the better for yer,' Polly replied, her voice oddly gentle. But before Daisy had time to question her remark, the woman was back to her usual bossy self. 'Now scoot before the food goes cold.'

Snatching up the plate, Daisy marched down the hallway, grimacing as the smell of ale and tobacco smoke hit her. Surprisingly there was nobody drinking in front of the bar; instead the locals were seated in a cluster at the far end of the room. The only customer waiting to eat was a man with dark hair and a neat moustache.

'Is this your niece, Rich?' he asked pleasantly. He was softer spoken than the others and had placed his bowler hat and fine wool coat on the seat beside him.

'Is nothin' bloomin' private?' Daisy heard her uncle mutter. However, he looked up from the drink he was pouring and said genially, 'Yes, this is Daisy. Although I don't like her being in here,' he added. Looking unusually nervous, he walked over and set the man's tankard down before him.

'Quite right too. It's hardly the place for a delightful young lady,' the man said, smiling at Daisy before looking down at his plate and grimacing.

'Send Polly to see me, please,' her uncle told Daisy as she hurried back to the kitchen.

'Ain't I got enough to do?' the woman snapped, looking up from the tatties she was beating to a pulp, as Daisy relayed her uncle's message. 'Carry on with these,' she said, shoving the pan in front of her.

'I don't think they need any more mashing,' Daisy laughed, staring at the greying pulp.

'You ain't paid to think. The finer you mash 'em the further they go.' And with a sniff, she pulled her top lower and swayed from the room.

'Wouldn't mind if I was paid at all,' Daisy told Ginge, who nodded ruefully.

'Can't prise money from tight fists,' he snorted.

'Is my uncle really that bad at paying people?' Daisy asked but, before the lad could answer, Polly stamped into the room.

'Get them glasses cleared and the tables cleaned in the bar,' she snarled at Ginge before disappearing. As he let out a groan, they heard her heavy steps thudding down the stone stairs.

'Going to her own room? That's a bad sign,' he muttered as he picked up a tray. 'She won't be back tonight so I'd escape while you can, just Daisy,' he told her, limping towards the door. 'Perhaps you'll get a letter tomorrow,' he added.

'I do hope so,' she replied. 'But you get off and I'll finish clearing up here; you look all in.'

'Thanks, just Daisy, I am,' he muttered as he dragged himself out to the stables.

Later, up in her room, Daisy sank onto the bed and put her

head in her hands. What a day. She'd been so sure there'd be a letter waiting from Harry. Still, as Ginge said, perhaps one would arrive tomorrow. She hoped so, for it was dreadful not knowing how her mother was. And she missed Harry so much, she thought, running her fingers over her silver bangle, recalling his strong hands as they'd gently placed it around her wrist. Remembering his caresses behind the bandstand, she felt her body grow hot and, suddenly needing to see him, reached under her bed for her sketches. Lying back against the pillow, in the flickering light of the candle, she untied the string then traced the outline of Harry's face. Although she'd captured his cheeky grin quite well, now she thought about it, his ears looked slightly out of proportion. Perhaps she could ask Claude's advice on getting the scale right. She smiled at the little daisy monogram she'd drawn in the corner, remembering how Harry had teased her about thinking herself a professional artist. 'I love and miss you so much,' she murmured, pressing her lips to his.

Sighing, she turned to the picture of her father and had to swallowed down the raw emotion that threatened to engulf her. The thought of never seeing him again was almost too much to bear. Blinking back the tears, she picked up the one she'd drawn of her mother before they'd moved to Tiger Yard. How contented she looked, Daisy thought, praying she'd soon get well and they'd be reunited. Stifling a sob, she retied the string, placed the pictures back under the bed then changed into her nightdress and blew out the candle.

Although she was weary, sleep evaded her. Meeting the artists had made her impatient to begin working on her first backdrop. Always supposing Blue had kept her job open for her. When she next visited the workshop, she'd take along her sketches as Claude suggested. Perhaps he could offer advice on how to improve her drawing then she'd be able to show Blue how ambitious she was. And Harry and she could go out sketching together again, she thought, stroking her silver bangle until she fell asleep.

Chapter 19

Another week passed and still there was no word from Harry. Daisy's impatience turned to anxiety and she began to fret.

'What can have happened? Why hasn't he written?' she wailed, as once again her uncle, having sorted through the morning mail the postman had delivered, shook his head. 'He knows I'll be desperately waiting for news of Mother and promised to reply as soon as he got my address. I shall write again this very minute,' she told him. Her uncle reached across the breakfast table and patted her hand sympathetically.

'I'm sure there's a good explanation,' he murmured. 'But I agree it would be a good idea to write again. Then you'll know for certain he has your new address.'

'The only trouble is, Uncle, I've been giving all my wages to Mother for the rent and don't have enough money to buy paper or a stamp,' she admitted. He gave her a speculative look then smiled.

'Don't you worry, niece. I'll give you the necessary.' He paused then added, 'As I did last time.' Feeling he was trying to make a point, Daisy opened her mouth to remind him how much work she'd done in the hostelry, then closed it again. He was providing her with a roof over her head and some food to eat, even if it was less than appetising, she thought, glancing down at the remains of her egg and bread that was swimming in grease.

It didn't seem to worry her uncle though, for he cleared his plate then, taking out a handkerchief, wiped the fat from his moustache. Slowly, he got to his feet, rummaged in the drawer and took out a sheet of writing paper and envelope.

'Ah, out of stamps. Never mind, I have to go to Idbury later so I'll post it for you there.'

'Thank you, Uncle,' she replied, trying not to flinch as his hand rested on her shoulder.

'It's the least I can do,' he told her.

'Is there still no sign of any new help?' she asked, hurriedly taking the paper.

'That's one of the reasons I'm going to the next village. Seems none of the local girls are interested in good, honest work – idle wenches.'

'I'll pen my note to Harry in my room.'

'No need, my dear. Besides, I shall be leaving very shortly.'

'If you don't mind, I find it easier to think by myself. But I'll be quick,' she assured him, all but running up the two flights of stairs. Although she was sure he was just being friendly, his touches were becoming more frequent and there was something about the way he stared at her she found unnerving. Throwing herself down onto the bed, she rested the paper on her pillow and began to write.

Dearest Harry,

I know you are busy with your course, but I'm anxious that I've not had a reply from you. I'm missing you so much and desperate for news of Mother. Please, give her my love and please, please write to me at Masons, Bransum, Devonshire, as soon as you receive this.

Your loving Daisy

ps: Sorry this note is so short but Uncle is just leaving for the next village and has promised to post it for me.

Hastily folding it into the envelope, Daisy ran back down the stairs. She could hear Polly and her uncle having a heated conversation in the tap room. Wrinkling her nose at the stench of tobacco smoke, ale and the seemingly ever-present odour of stale fish, she went to join them. He was wearing his long woollen coat and, from the way he kept glancing towards the door, was anxious to get away.

'Yer knows we've a large party in today and I can't do everything by myself,' Polly cried, folding her arms defiantly across her ample bosom.

'Ah yes, the lunches,' he murmured, brightening. 'That'll bring in some money at any rate.'

'Well?' Polly snapped, looking pointedly at Daisy.

'Make a start in the kitchen while I have a word with my niece,' he told her and yet again Daisy saw that look pass between them.

'For God's sake make yer meaning clear this time. I can't be doin' with her high-falutin' ways. Besides yer said …' Polly began.

'Alright, alright,' he cut in. As, muttering under her breath, the woman waddled away, her uncle cleared his throat then turned to Daisy.

'Ah yes, your letter,' he said, smiling as he took it from her and put it in his pocket. 'As I said, I need to go into Idbury. You see, I've received a letter from my bank manager. It seems the cost of your father's burial along with your mother's hospital bills, which are ongoing by the way, have left my funds somewhat depleted.'

'You don't mean you're going to stop paying for her to be treated in hospital?' Daisy cried in alarm.

'No, no, it won't come to that, I'm sure,' he said, patting her shoulder. 'But it has left me with a problem.' He heaved a sigh. 'You see, we're now into the shooting season.'

'Shooting season!' Daisy exclaimed. 'You don't mean people kill each other round here?'

'I forgot you're a townie, my dear,' he replied, with a ghost of a smile. 'No, we're not quite that barbaric. You see, gentry from all around descend on the manor to shoot pheasant, partridge and other game birds. The squire puts on a spread for the toffs, but the beaters and helpers come here for refreshments after their morning's exertions. It's a busy but profitable time for my business and I have to make the most of it. Things go quiet after Christmas when there's not much work around and nobody has any money.' Again, he fixed her with an imploring look.

'So, what exactly are you trying to tell me?' Daisy asked, a suspicion already forming.

'Until this, er, situation with my bank is sorted, I can't afford to pay for extra help. So, there we have it.' He shrugged. 'I suppose you could say I'm a victim of my own kind-heartedness, but with Arthur having been my brother, it seemed only right to help out his family.'

'And I do appreciate your kindness, Uncle,' Daisy said quickly. 'So, you'd like me to prepare these lunches with Polly in the kitchen today?' A spark gleamed in his eyes and he took both her hands in his.

'That would be a real help,' he cried. 'As I say, it's our busy time and I can't expect Polly to see to everything by herself. Obviously, as soon as my cash flow improves, I will hire someone else. In the meantime, you'll be doing your bit to ensure your mother's hospital expenses continue to be met.'

'You mean you want me to help out every day?' Daisy retorted, visions of her visiting Grace disappearing.

'I can see you're a fair person, niece,' he replied. It was only when he squeezed her hands that she realised he was still holding them. Quickly she pulled away, although she couldn't help thinking that she'd metaphorically played into them. In helping her family, he'd put himself in a difficult position and now, it seemed, they were in his debt. Decency decreed she help repay it.

'The beaters will be here at one o'clock, so perhaps you could go and help Polly right away. You know how she frets. Now, I really must leave,' her uncle said, picking up his hat and striding to the door.

'You won't forget to post my letter, will you?' she called after him.

'Understand things now, do we?' Polly asked, as soon as Daisy entered the kitchen.

'Yes, Uncle explained.' She sighed.

'Good. Do as I say and we'll get along fine. Just like we does, eh boy?' she said, turning to Ginge who was bent over the sink, a large pointed knife in hand. He seemed to grip it tighter for a moment, then shrugged and continued what he was doing.

'I'm sure yer uncle told yer how busy we'll be over the next few weeks and if I'm serving punters in the tap room until all hours, I can't be expected to be up at the crack of dawn as well.'

Weeks? Daisy gulped then caught a glimpse of what Ginge was doing and nearly fainted. Fur and fluff were piled up along the worktop and the sink ran red with blood.

'Yer finished skinning them coneys yet, boy?' Polly asked, clicking her fingers impatiently. 'I'll need to get cooking if we're going to be ready in time. Them beaters always eats like they've never seen food before. Right, missy, get dicing them vegetables,' she snapped, gesturing to the corner of the room. Daisy looked at the sacks of carrots, onions and turnips lining the floor and grimaced.

'What, all of them?' she gulped.

'Yep, then there's the tatties. Got to pack the casserole out, ain't we? Good meat costs money, yer know.'

'Not when yer gets it free,' Ginge muttered but the woman was already scrabbling in the pantry and didn't hear. 'She exchanges them for somethin' Terry the trapper wants, if yer gets my meanin'?' He winked. 'Quite clever, really, giving him a gratis then charging the master.'

As Daisy stared incredulously at him, he gave a sly grin and went back to viciously dissecting the coneys, which she now realised were rabbits. Swallowing down her revulsion, she began preparing the vegetables.

'Yer'll have to go faster than that,' Polly snapped, dragging two large sacks behind her. 'Here's the tatties and I need to see through the skin when yer've peeled them. I'll have no waste in my kitchen.' Daisy peeled and diced until all she could see was red and white cubes in front of her eyes. Her fingers were stiff and sore yet still Polly wasn't satisfied.

'Come on, girl,' she cried. 'They want their lunch today, not next week.'

Finally, she reached the bottom of the sacks and leaned back against the wall to stretch her back.

'What the hell are yer doin'?' Polly sniffed. 'Get them vegetables into the stew pan.'

'Easier doing a stretch in the clink,' Ginge murmured, looking up from the huge pan he was stirring and giving her a sympathetic look as Polly went to check everything was laid up properly in the back parlour.

'I trust you're not speaking from experience,' Daisy joked.

'Nah, no such luck,' he muttered, beads of sweat running down his face. 'Blimey, I'm thirsty,' he muttered. Daisy stopped what she was doing, poured water from the jug into a mug and held it out to him.

'What the blazes are yer doin'?' Polly screeched, reappearing in the doorway. 'The party's arrived and we've got twenty-five or more lunches to dish up. Right boy, yer set out the dishes; Daisy, ladle out the stew, half a dish each and make sure it's mostly veg. I'll take them through. Come on, hurry up,' she snapped. With the woman's eyes watching, Daisy automatically dished out the food, the smell only marginally better than when it was fish.

Then Polly took off her apron, pulled down her top and began ferrying the food up to the parlour.

'Poor chaps. Don't know what they're in for,' Ginge muttered. Whether he meant Polly or the food, Daisy wasn't sure, and she was too busy to care. Finally, as the woman took the last tray through, Daisy collapsed into a chair.

'Phew, I need a cuppa after all that,' she groaned.

'And you shall have one,' Polly replied, waddling back into the room, 'when you've washed the pots and cleared away.'

Finally, just as Daisy thought she'd drop from exhaustion, Polly announced they could stop and have something to eat.

'Make a brew, boy, while I cut some bread to go with that left-over stew,' she told Ginge. Daisy watched in horror as she flicked bits of food from the table onto the floor with her cloth, ran it over her face and then wiped the knife with it.

'Ain't no use yer screwing up yer face like that,' she told Daisy. 'Yer either want to eat or yer don't.' Although she was starving by now, the thought of eating rabbit turned her stomach.

'Is Uncle back yet?' she asked.

'Yes, and he's in a foul mood, so I'm keeping clear and if you've any sense you will too, missy,' Polly told her.

But Daisy needed to ensure he'd posted her letter and, removing the filthy apron, she hurried to find him.

He was leaning against the bar, staring morosely into a glass of whisky.

'Ah niece,' he said, brightening when he saw her. Then he looked down at her pinafore and frowned. 'Perhaps you should change before you come in here,' he said, glancing round at the two men standing beside the fire. They were deep in conversation and whether their faces were flushed from the flames or the drink it was hard to tell. However, they didn't even look up and Daisy turned back to her uncle.

'Did you post my letter to Harry?' she asked. His eyes darkened.

'Cors I did,' he grunted.

'Thank you. And did your meeting with your bank manager go well?' she asked politely.

'No,' he muttered, downing the rest of his drink. 'But that's not for you to worry your pretty little head about. From what I can make out the lunch went well today but you seem to be wearing a lot of it,' he chortled, pointing to her stained clothing. As he studied her, she was conscious of her heat-frizzed hair and red face. 'Haven't you got anything, well, more grown-up, you could change into?' he asked.

'Not really, Uncle, I had to pack so quickly,' she replied, glad she'd left the green smock behind yet not wishing to admit she only possessed two presentable pinafores. 'I'll try to find time to wash this later then perhaps it could dry overnight in front of the fire.' He studied her thoughtfully and Daisy had to suppress a shudder as he slowly looked her up and down.

'Don't worry, niece, leave it with me.' Although the smile he gave her was warm, Daisy felt a sense of disquiet spreading through her.

Chapter 20

As Daisy made her way up to bed that night, she spotted something white hanging from the door handle. Picking it up, she saw it was a smart blouse and underneath was a long blue skirt. Her uncle must have put them there, she thought, remembering their earlier conversation.

Hurrying into her room, she held them up against her and looked in the mirror. They were certainly a great improvement on her own clothes, which were spattered with grease stains and even grimier than she'd realised. She couldn't accept them though, could she? But then what choice did she have? Her uncle clearly hadn't wanted her to hang wet clothes in front of the fire in the bar. He'd explained he couldn't pay her for helping out in the kitchen so perhaps this was his way of thanking her for all her hard work.

Still, it was with some reticence that, next morning, Daisy dressed in the new things. Standing in front of the mirror, she frowned at the frizz of fair hair that now fell about her shoulders. It badly needed cutting, but her mother had always done that for her before. Carefully, she braided it then, using the string from around her pictures, neatly tied the ends. As she worked, the flashes of silver from her bracelet made her smile. If only you could see me now, Harry Wylde, she murmured. Perhaps there'd be a letter from him today, she thought as her spirits lifted and she tripped lightly down the stairs.

'My dear, you look positively charming,' her uncle beamed, looking up from his newspaper as she appeared. 'And they fit perfectly.'

'Thank you, Uncle,' she replied. 'It was kind of you, although I don't know how you could possibly have known my size.'

'Oh, I'm a good judge,' he winked. 'I've asked Polly to bring breakfast through to the parlour.'

Realising she was hungry, she eagerly took her seat in the comfortable back room, hoping that by some miracle the food wouldn't be swimming in grease.

'I couldn't help noticing the rain has stopped, Uncle, so will I be allowed to go out this morning?' she asked.

'Gracious, my dear, this is not a prison you know.' He smiled. 'Whilst I appreciate your help with the shooting lunches, you can certainly go for a stroll before then.'

Daisy was about to say she'd actually like to spend the day at the workshops when Polly, tray in hand, entered. Seeing Daisy, her eyes widened and her lips pursed.

'Them fancy clothes ain't goin' to be no good in the kitchen,' she snapped, slapping the plates down so hard on the table, the fried egg, in its pool of fat, slid precariously to the edge of the plate. Quickly Daisy put out her hand to prevent it from landing in her lap.

'Up to our tricks again, are we?' Polly hissed at Rich, who coloured under her glare.

'Don't know what you mean,' he replied. 'And do be care-ful how you set those plates down. Can't afford new ones,' he joked.

'Only new clothes, eh?' she retorted, narrowing her eyes. 'Perhaps you could afford to pay me seeing as how I've not had any money in months. As for you, missy,' she said, turning back to Daisy, 'fancy clathers or no, yer'll be in the kitchen at ten sharp or yer'll have me to answer to.'

'And that would be a fate worse than death,' her uncle chuckled as Polly stamped away, her ample hips hitting the stone walls as they swayed from side to side. 'Good job those are as thick as she is,' he added, before turning his attention to his food.

Disconcerted by the showdown, but not knowing what to say, Daisy picked up her knife and fork. Why had her new clothes upset Polly, she wondered, her stomach turning at the sight of the grease congealing on the plate. Then she noticed her uncle staring at her thoughtfully as he chewed. Feeling uncomfortable, she jumped to her feet.

'I'm not really hungry so, if you'll excuse me, I'll go outside and wait for the postman.'

'Goodness me, there's no need for that. The robin always brings it in. It's part of his job, after all.'

'Well, I, er thought I'd make the most of being in the coun-try and draw the delightful flowers I saw growing nearby,' she replied, ignoring his obvious witticism.

'As you wish, my dear.' Her uncle shrugged and turned back to his food.

Running up to her room, Daisy threw her shawl around

her shoulders, took the paper and pencil from her pinafore pocket, then hurried down the stairs and outside. Although it was cold, thankfully it wasn't raining and as she breathed in the fresh air, she began to feel better. She really didn't know what was worse, her uncle's intense gazes or Polly's dreadful cooking. How she longed to be back home, sitting at the table with her father while her mother dished up a tasty meal.

The pain caught her unawares as she remembered that would never happen again. Poor Father, and poor Mother having to cope without him. If she recovered. Please let there be a letter from Harry today. How she hated this strange place. She wanted to go home, back to familiar faces, familiar places, she thought, blinking back the tears which surfaced once again.

Swallowing hard, she strode up the narrow lane then, kneeling down beside the clump of dainty mauve flowers, began to sketch. It was incredible to think these fragile little violets could survive all the weather winter threw at them. Lost in her drawing, she didn't hear the footsteps behind her and jumped when someone spoke.

'Good morning.' Looking up, she saw the gentleman she'd recently served in the bar.

'Good morning,' she replied, getting to her feet.

'So, you draw as well as wait on tables?' he asked, staring admiringly at her picture. 'You've really captured their likeness.'

'Thank you. I was surprised to see them out at this time of year but I guess they must be resilient,' she replied.

'Indeed, they are.' He smiled, a spark lighting his dark

eyes. 'Some of their species originated in warmer climes but I guess they must have the survival instinct to adapt to their new environment.'

'Yes, I suppose they must,' Daisy replied, looking at him in amazement, for wasn't that what she needed to do? Then realising she was staring, she asked, 'Are you an artist like Grace and Claude?'

'I'm not an artist, no.' He shrugged. 'That doesn't mean I don't appreciate beauty though,' he added, staring directly at her.

'Oh well,' she said, looking away quickly. 'So, what is it you do then?'

'Explore,' he said, laughing.

'And there's much to see around here?' she asked, sure he was jesting.

'You'd be surprised. Which reminds me, I'm meant to be seeing someone, so I'll bid you good day,' and with another smile, he tipped his hand to his hat and strode away.

It was only as she walked back inside the tavern that she realised she hadn't seen the postman. Her uncle was nowhere to be seen either.

'Has a letter come for me?' she asked Polly hopefully, as she entered the kitchen.

'Not that I've seen,' she said with a shrug. 'Now yer might not have paid for them fancy clathers, but yer can at least look after them,' she added, throwing another filthy apron across the room. Daisy tried not to grimace as she tied the garment round her waist. From his station at the sink, Ginge shot her a sympathetic look but seeing the pile of pots he had to tackle Daisy couldn't help feeling he was the one in need of sympathy.

While Daisy tackled another mountain of vegetables, she thought about her conversation with the dark-haired man. Although he'd been referring to the violets, his words could have been directed at her, for didn't having the survival instinct to adapt to a new environment describe her present circumstances exactly? And like those dear, little flowers, that was exactly what she was going to do.

'Stop yer daydreaming and get them vegetables in the pan,' Polly hollered, snapping Daisy back to the present. 'Don't do to fret over a male, yer know. That Harry's probably found another girl to keep him warm.'

'No, Harry's not like that. He doesn't look at other women,' she protested, the very thought making her go cold.

'All men are like that and they all like looking at other women, as yer'll find out,' Polly sneered. 'They don't say out of sight, out of mind for nothin', you know. Now I'm going to lay up the back parlour and while I'm gone yer can think on why his nibs up in the tap room should be giving you them new things.' Shooting Daisy a knowing look, she snatched up a tray of cutlery and waddled from the room.

'I thinks yer look lovely, just Daisy,' Ginge said as soon as the door shut behind the woman. 'And I wouldn't want anyone else if yer wos my girlfriend,' Ginge added, giving her a shy smile.

'Why Ginge, that's sweet of you, but you're much too young to be thinking about girls yet.' She smiled.

'I'll 'ave you know I'll be fourteen next birthday,' he retorted, puffing out his bony chest.

'Goodness, really?' she exclaimed, for she'd thought him to be no more than ten or eleven years old. He was obviously more malnourished than she'd believed. 'When is your birthday?' she asked, seeing him waiting for her to reply.

'Dunno 'xactly. I was dumped in the doorway of St Winifred's and the vicar took me to the orphanage in the next village. They reckoned that as I was only a few days old and it was Christmas Day, that could be my birthday. Good job they didn't call me Jesus though or I'd never 'ave lived it down. Still, don't suppose 'e 'ad ginger 'air and freckles.'

'Here this ain't no blinkin' party, yer know,' Polly snarled as she stomped back into the kitchen. 'Take them clean glasses up to the bar, boy, and mind yer don't drop any.'

'I've finished cutting up the vegetables; shall I add them into the stew?' Daisy asked, looking at the mountain in front of her.

'Well, them ain't goin' to jump in by themselves, are they?' Polly replied, lifting the lid and standing well back from the steam. When the pot had been given a good stir, Polly turned to Daisy. 'I'm parched. We've just time for a cuppa if you can squeeze the pot.' As Daisy stared at her in astonishment, she sighed. 'We won't have time if yer just stands there.'

Not sure what to make of the sudden change in her manner, Daisy did as she'd been asked, trying not to frown as the woman swept the peelings and crumbs onto the floor with her hand. They sat sipping their tea in silence for a few moments until Polly put down her mug and turned to Daisy.

'Look, dear, I know yer thinks …' she began, then stopped as she spotted Rich trying to creep past the open door. Seeing he was being watched, he smiled and beckoned. 'All I'm saying is things ain't always what they seem round here, so watch out,' she whispered, struggling to her feet.

'No, stay where you are, Polly; it's Daisy I want,' he called. Immediately the woman's demeanour reverted to her former, sullen self.

'Don't bloody be long, there's still work to be done,' she snarled as Daisy hurried after her uncle. Had there been a letter from Harry, she wondered, her heart leaping. She was so excited that for once she didn't even mind the smells emanating from the tap room as she passed. Her uncle was waiting for her in the back parlour, which surprised her as the tables were already laid up for the shooting lunch.

'Goodness, are we joining the party?' she joked.

'What? No … although thinking about it, that might not be a bad idea,' he murmured, stroking his moustache as he eyed her thoughtfully.

'So, is there a letter from Harry?' she asked eagerly.

'No, I'm afraid not. The thing is,' he hurried on when he saw her crestfallen look, 'I saw you outside with that stuck-up bloke.' Her thoughts full of Harry, she stared at her uncle blankly for a moment.

'Oh, you mean the dark-haired gentleman.'

'Wouldn't call him no gent,' he snorted.

'Really, Uncle, he was only talking to me.'

'Oh yes? What about?' he asked, giving her a searching look.

'Flowers, actually. Do you know—'

'Is that all?' he interrupted.

'Yes, Uncle. Oh, other than when I asked him if he was an artist, he said he wasn't.'

'Oh? Did he say what he was then?'

'Not really, no,' she replied, reluctant to divulge any more.

'Well, as your uncle, I insist you don't speak to him again. In fact, for the next few days I want you to remain on the premises.'

'Why?' she frowned.

'There are some dodgy people around here at the moment and I'd feel better if I knew you were safely indoors,' he said, patting her shoulder. 'Now, this morning I happened to notice your hair.'

'My hair? What's wrong with it?' she asked, her hand going to her braid.

'Nothing. In fact, it's rather lovely,' he said, his hand reaching out to stroke it. Instinctively, she moved away. 'Which is why, when I was out this morning, I purchased this,' he said, pulling a bright blue ribbon from his pocket. 'Better than that bit of old string, eh?'

'Why, thank you, Uncle,' she said, taking it from him.

'Would you like me to put it in for you?' he asked, grey eyes shining.

'No,' she said quickly. 'I mean, it might get ruined so I'll do it later.'

'I'd rather you put it in now, before you go back to the kitchen.' She frowned, then thinking it could do no harm, she untied the string and replaced it with the ribbon.

'There, you look even more becoming than ever,' he said, grinning with delight.

'Thank you. Now I'd better get going before Polly calls,' she said, hurrying back down the hallway. What a strange man, she thought. Still, it seemed to make him happy and you didn't get given a ribbon every day.

'Oh, so that's the way it is, is it?' Polly barked, glaring at the blue trimming. 'Well, don't say I didn't try to warn yer.' Before Daisy could ask what she meant, the woman slammed down a pile of dishes in front of her and removed her apron. 'I can hear them beaters arriving so yer can dish up for a change. I'll go and serve in the bar,' she announced, patting her hair and pulling her top lower.

'Blimey, one minute I'm meant to be in the bar the next I'm sent back 'ere to bring out the dishes of food,' Ginge moaned, as he entered the kitchen minutes later. ''Er ladyship's acting like she owns the place up there, laughing and fawning over the blokes. It's unsavoury.'

Daisy shrugged as she continued dishing out the food. If anything was unsavoury it was the so-called stew, she thought.

'That's gopping,' Ginge cried, pulling a face as he picked up the tray.

The next ten minutes were hectic as they endeavoured to get all the meals served and they'd just finished when the door banged open. Slamming a tray down so hard it set the dirty glasses clinking and wobbling precariously, Polly glowered.

'Bloody men,' she hissed.

'What's up?' Daisy asked.

'Nothing and that's the trouble. Those men treat me like I'm invisible these days. Don't yer dare grin, my lad, or yer'll feel the back of my hand,' she growled, raising her fist.

'But you told Daisy men liked looking at women,' he murmured and Daisy had to hide a smile as Polly looked even more disgruntled.

'And yer can wipe that smile off yer face,' she snarled at Daisy. 'He wants yer serving in the bar.'

'What?' she gasped. 'No, you've got that wrong, Polly. My uncle said—'

'Yer to work in the bar,' she repeated.

Chapter 21

'You still don't get it, do you?' Polly said, blocking the way as she made to pass.

'What don't I get?' asked Daisy.

'That your uncle is beginning to use you.'

'But he's paying for Mother's hospital bills, which means I'm beholden to him.'

'There's beholden and being abused,' the woman replied, shaking her head.

However, Daisy didn't have time to ponder on her words: her uncle was waiting for her at the entrance to the bar.

'There you are, niece,' he said impatiently. 'The men and I have urgent things to discuss so I want you to entertain that dark-haired bloke.' He gestured to the fire, where the gentleman in question was sitting in his customary place, an untouched tankard of ale before him. He was facing the door while in the far corner a group of men were huddled over their drinks.

Daisy frowned. 'But you said I wasn't to speak to him.'

'Needs must. He's started showing up when we have a meeting arranged so whether there's a snitch around here or he's just blinkin' nosy, I don't know.'

'So, what's his name?' Daisy asked, realising he hadn't introduced himself.

'We call him Pigeon; stool pigeon, get it?' he guffawed.

'I can't address him like that,' she gasped.

'Well, don't call him anything then. Just keep him entertained. A pretty young woman like you shouldn't find that difficult,' he added, as she opened her mouth to protest. 'Now off you go,' he urged, moving so close she could smell the alcohol on his breath. Then, he gave her a nudge so that she almost fell into the room. Trying not to wrinkle her nose, she made her way through the fug.

'Can I get you another drink, sir?' she asked. As he had his back to her, he hadn't seen her coming and looked up in surprise.

'Thank you, but no,' he replied, his eyes oddly guarded. Far from being pleased to see her, it was almost as if he resented her presence.

Not wishing to intrude, or to upset her uncle by leaving the bar, she looked around for something to do. Seeing the tables badly needed wiping, she picked up a cloth and quietly moved from table to table, conscious of the man's glance following her. Yet when she looked up, he'd gone. Feeling she'd lost an ally but not understanding why, she began cleaning the remaining table next to the group. They'd obviously all had a fair bit to drink and were so engrossed in conversation, they didn't notice her. Then she heard her uncle, who had now joined the men, gloating about a boat coming over from France. Brandy casks being left in the cellar. A fat profit for Christmas.

'How did you manage that?' one man asked.

'Easy mate, the tunnel under the cellar runs right down to the beach and the sea's not froze yet.' His booming laugh and bragging manner were enough to let Daisy know that, despite the early hour, he'd been drinking heavily.

'Cor that's a good un, Rich,' the other man roared, slapping his hand on the table so that their ale slopped over. 'Surprised it weren't discovered years ago when the revenue men down Seaton carried out all them checks on cellars.'

'Oh, it were checked alright, but here's the thing—' her uncle lowered his voice so that Daisy had to edge closer to hear '—one barrel's empty. Twist the tap on the front and, hey presto, door swings open. Leads right …' Eager to hear more, Daisy didn't notice the stool as she inched closer, sending it clattering to the floor. As the men turned in her direction, Daisy's heart flipped right over.

'What the … oh, I'd forgotten about you,' her uncle frowned. 'Sent the pigeon on a wild goose chase so take the rest of the day off,' he said, waving his hand magnanimously.

Before he had a chance to change his mind, Daisy hurried from the bar, ignoring the whistles and ribald laughter that followed her. Up in her room, she threw herself down on her bed.

Who was the dark-haired man? And after their earlier conversation, why had he been so cool then disappeared without saying goodbye? And what had Polly meant about her being beholden and abused? Why did she feel she was missing something? How she wished she was back in Camberwell with friendly faces instead of being miles from home, in a hostelry where who knew what went on.

Oh Harry, I miss you so, she thought. Why haven't you written? You know I'll be fretting for news of Mother, she sobbed, her finger tracing the daisy chain on her silver bangle.

Impulsively, she snatched up her pictures, and, after glancing at Harry's profile, she found a scrap of paper Scarlett had given her and began pouring out her feelings.

Dearest Harry,

I am so unhappy not to have heard from you. Surely you must realise I need to know how Mother is? The thought of never seeing Father again cuts through me like a knife and if I were to lose Mother too, I don't know what I'd do. The idea of being an orphan is too dreadful to contemplate. Please, please write SOON and let me know how she is.

Only a few short weeks ago we were happily planning our wedding. I've even drawn a sketch of the dress for Mother to make up for me. But will she even be here to make it? Will there even be a wedding? Polly says you've probably found someone else by now, but I can't bear to think of you with anyone else so please write and put me out of my misery.

I think of you all the time and as you can see from this scrap, I have run out of paper to write to you and cannot afford to buy more. For although I work in the kitchens here, Uncle has to settle the hospital bills for Mother so hasn't the money to pay me.

*I'm sorry if this is a miserable letter but I needed to
get my thoughts down on paper. Please write, Harry.
I love you and miss you so much.*

Ever yours,
Daisy

With hot tears running down her cheek, Daisy took up his
picture and kissed his lips, then, emotionally drained, lay back
against the pillow and sobbed herself to sleep.

Daisy had no time to dwell on her problems, for there was
no let-up in the work over the next few weeks. As soon as
the shooting lunches finished, the bar filled up with workers.

'Why are customers coming in so early?' Daisy asked.

'Gets dark halfway through the afternoon this near to
Christmas so they finish work early and come in for a warm
and wet. Cors, after a few bevies, most forget they got homes
to go to. Still, I suppose it's all dough in the drawer, which
keeps his lord and master happy,' Polly told her. To Daisy's
surprise, the woman had become friendlier of late, which
made life easier, especially as there was still no word from
Harry. Her earlier comment about him finding someone else
niggled away at the back of her mind.

However, what Polly had just said set Daisy thinking. If her
uncle was taking so much money, he could afford to hire help.
She'd been rushed off her feet these past few weeks and, apart
from going to the privy and drawing water from the pump,
hadn't set foot outside. If she didn't have a break from here

soon, she'd go mad. Knowing their cheerful banter would lift her spirits, she wanted to visit Grace and her friends.

'I'm too old for this caper,' Polly moaned, breaking into her thoughts. 'Where's that stupid boy got to?' she grumbled, as someone rapped sharply on the back door.

'You sent him out to get more eggs,' Daisy reminded her. 'I'll see who it is,' she volunteered, glad of the excuse to escape the steamy room.

'I ain't got time to see no one,' Polly called after her.

Daisy opened the door to find a stocky man of middle years waiting on the step.

'Mornin', me luvly. Polly about, is she?' he asked.

'She's busy cooking at the moment,' Daisy told him.

'Ah well, praps yer'd give 'er these then,' he said, holding up a bundle of brightly coloured feathers. Then Daisy saw the glossy blue heads, closed eyes and shiny beaks glinting at her and nearly screamed.

'But they're …' her voice faltered, clutching at the door for support.

'Pheasants, that's right, me dear. Shot only an hour since so still nice and warm,' the man continued, seemingly oblivious to her discomfort as he waited for Daisy to take them. ''Ang 'em straightaway and they'll make a right tasty Christmas lunch, specially if yer gets rid of their guts first.' Daisy's stomach turned a full somersault; then, just as she thought she was going to keel over, Ginge appeared on the path behind the man. Seeing Daisy's expression, he thrust a basket into her hands.

'Take these eggs into Polly before she gets in a scramble.'

He chuckled, then turned to the man. 'Morning Terry, you had a good shoot then. Let me take those beauties.'

'Ta, give Polly Poodles my love and tell her I'll be waiting later,' the man told Daisy, giving her a knowing wink.

On legs like jelly, Daisy carried the wicker basket into the kitchen. They certainly had strange ways here in the country. And what was it the man had called Polly? Poodles?

'Ah the eggs at last,' Polly said, frowning over Daisy's shoulder. 'Where's that boy got to? Yer can't tell me the flippin' chooks collected those themselves?'

'Ginge asked me to bring them in while he took the pheasants from Terry.'

'Terry? He's here? Why didn't you say, girl?' Polly gabbled, throwing off her apron and patting her hair into place before hurrying outside.

''Ey, that were funny,' Ginge chuckled as he hurried into the room.

'I didn't think so,' Daisy retorted, relieved to see he hadn't brought the gamebirds in with him. 'He said they were still warm.' She shuddered.

'I didn't mean you, just Daisy. I meant old Pol haring after Terry like a bi— well, like she were about to miss out on somefink.' He grinned. 'Still, she'll be busy for a good while yet so we can have something to eat. You cut some bread and I'll dish,' he said, lifting the lid off the pot and ladling generous portions of rabbit stew into two dishes.

'Good idea,' Daisy said, eagerly picking up a spoon. It was a treat to eat food that wasn't overcooked or stewed to a mush and for once she enjoyed her meal. It was then she remembered what her uncle had been bragging about in the bar.

'Is there a tunnel underneath here?' she asked Ginge.

'Yea, the door's in the cellar by Polly's room. But yer don't want to go down there. Spiders and cobwebs are scarier than pheasants, just Daisy.' He chuckled, then stopped as Polly ambled into the room, her cheeks red as apples.

'Blimey, you look happy,' Ginge sniggered, quickly sliding their dishes under the cupboard. 'Anyone'd think yer been kissed.'

'Less of your bloomin' cheek,' the woman snorted, yet couldn't hide her grin.

'Just going to see if there's a letter for me,' Daisy said.

'Best you forget about that boy,' Polly muttered, but Daisy was already making her way down the hallway. Her uncle was sitting on his usual stool.

'I'm afraid there's still no letter from your young man,' he said, looking up from his newspaper.

Daisy swallowed down her disappointment. Harry might be busy with his course, but surely he could have penned a quick note? She hoped he was finding time to visit her mother. As the niggle that he'd found someone else surfaced, her hand went to her bangle for reassurance.

'Was there something else?' her uncle asked, looking her up and down in the way that made Daisy uncomfortable.

'We've been really busy these past weeks and takings have been good, so I was wondering how soon you'll be hiring more help?'

'Ah, I intended speaking with you about that.' Reaching

out, he took her hands in his. 'Today I received a communication from the hospital. Your mother requires an operation on her legs.'

'Poor Mother. I really must go and see her,' Daisy cried, pulling her hands away. 'If you can pay me for all the hours I've worked, I'll catch the tr—'

'If only it were that easy,' he interrupted, heaving another sigh. 'Sawbones don't come cheap and they won't operate until they receive their fee. I was going to arrange it today but if you'd rather have the money instead …' he shrugged, leaving the rest of his sentence hanging in the air. Daisy shook her head impatiently.

'Obviously Mother's operation is more important so please arrange for the money to be sent straightaway, Uncle. And can you find out how she is? I'm going mad not knowing.'

'Of course.' He paused, then put his arm around her shoulders. Cringing at his closeness, she pulled away and he narrowed his eyes. 'You must understand this new bill will wipe out any profit I've made from the shooting parties. It will be some time before I can afford to hire anyone so …'

'Surely …' she began, but he ignored her.

'It's nearly Christmas and we have the Boxing Day Meet to prepare. It's a busy time but will bring in more money. The hunt assembles in the courtyard for the stirrup cup, so I'll be needing your help. Still, at least you know you're helping Mabel.'

Knowing she had no choice, Daisy nodded. She desperately wanted to be with her mother, but again her hands were tied for she had no doubt that if she didn't stay and help, he'd stop paying the hospital bills. Although it was sad she had to stay in the infirmary over Christmas, at least she'd be getting the necessary care.

As for Christmas, that was when she and Harry had met, shared their first kiss and agreed it would always be their special time of year. Surely, he wouldn't forget that? He'd be breaking up from the college any day now so, perhaps, he'd come and visit. Her heart leapt at the thought.

'Maybe there'll be a letter from your young man tomorrow,' her uncle called after her.

'But postie said …' Ginge began, appearing with a tray of glasses.

'Shut it, boy. See nothing, hear nothing, say nothing, remember?' her uncle warned.

'Yea but …'

'Want another kicking?' he barked, raising his leg threateningly.

'Ain't recovered from the last one,' the boy muttered as, with a fearful glance at Daisy, he dashed back to the kitchen.

'Are you sure I haven't had a letter from Harry?' Daisy asked her uncle.

'The boy's obviously mistaken. He's got about as much head on him as last night's ale.'

But Daisy couldn't help feeling her uncle was lying and vowed to have a quiet word with Ginge.

Chapter 22

A gamut of emotions running through her, Daisy hurried back down the hallway. Polly looked up from the pan she was stirring and scowled.

'Got lost, did we, missy?' Polly sniffed. 'Well, get them tatties mashed then you can help Ginge pluck and draw those pheasants.'

Daisy stared at her in disbelief.

'Why do you want a picture of them?' she asked, only to hear Ginge snigger.

'Oh, I bloomin' give up,' the woman exclaimed, shaking her head as she picked up the plates and waddled to the door. 'Being the season of goodwill let's hope the punters are feeling generous,' she cackled. Ginge waited until the sound of her footsteps had faded then joined Daisy beside the table, which was littered with drips of stew from Polly's slapdash plating up.

'Oh, that were a cracker, that were, just Daisy. Draw a picture of the pheasants,' he chuckled. 'Ain't laughed like that for ages.'

'What did she mean then?' Daisy asked, feeling foolish.

'Gutting their innards,' he said, laughing as she grimaced.

Then, looking over his shoulder, he edged closer. 'I swear there were a letter—'

'I warned you, boy.' Her uncle's growl made them both jump and looking up they saw him glaring from the doorway. He was red-faced and shaking with rage but before they could say anything, he'd crossed the room and lifted Ginge clean off his feet.

'Get to the stables,' he hissed.

'But Uncle …' Daisy began.

'Back to your work. You've hospital fees to earn, remember,' he told her, his eyes so cold Daisy wondered how she could ever have thought they were like her father's. By the time she'd recovered her composure he'd already gone. Worried about the way he'd spoken to Ginge, Daisy made for the door only to bump into Polly returning from the bar.

'You ain't going nowhere, missy,' she hissed. 'People's waiting to be served so get dishing them veg. But I'm doing the waiting and them swine had better watch out if they don't cough up a Christmas tip or two.'

'But Ginge …' she began.

'Not our concern. Come on, we ain't got all day. Then you'll have to make a start on the pots.'

Although Daisy was rushed off her feet, she kept looking towards the door hoping to see Ginge. Had there been a letter from Harry? Ginge would have no reason to lie but perhaps he'd misunderstood what the postman had said. Yet instinct told her he hadn't.

Even when the demand for food ceased, she still had the washing up to do and by the time she'd finally cleaned down the work surfaces, her head was throbbing, her hands red and raw. She knew she'd have to tackle her uncle again, but it was no good doing it this time of night for he'd be three sheets to the wind and nasty with it. She'd come to recognise his changeable moods and couldn't determine which was worse: his pathetic pawing or rampant rages.

Daisy crawled up the two flights of stairs and lay shivering under her thin cover, hoping Ginge was alright. She realised now why he'd given her a scathing look when she'd mentioned him getting kicked by the horse.

The sound of voices rising on the night air broke into her thoughts. Surely that was Claude followed by Sean's lilting tones. Daisy sprang out of bed but, by the time she reached the window, all she could see were the regulars staggering down the path.

'Happy Christmas,' they called out drunkenly.

Happy Christmas indeed, Daisy thought. She offered up a prayer that her mother's operation would be successful and that her father was at peace. Then her thoughts turned to Harry. Bitter tears fell as she thought of his bright-blue eyes and cheeky grin. She'd give anything to feel the warmth of his arms around her now. Gently, she ran her finger along the outline of the delicate daisy chain, drawing comfort from knowing he'd made it especially for her. She missed him so much, her chest hurt.

As if to echo her despondent feelings, Daisy woke to hear rain pounding on the roof. Quickly rinsing her face, she dressed, tidied her hair then went downstairs intending to speak to her uncle over breakfast. But he was already propping up the bar, a glass of amber liquid in his hand.

'Merry Christmas, Uncle,' Daisy said brightly. Although miserable being so far from home and the ones she loved at this special time of year, she made an effort to be cheerful. Hopefully, if she appealed to his better nature, she could escape and see Grace for a few hours later. But he studied her morosely through bloodshot eyes.

'Ah, niece, if only that were true.' He shook his head. 'Went to see the boy this morning only to find he's upped and gone, which means more work for us.'

'Ginge has left?' Although after yesterday she wasn't surprised, he was the only one around this place who ever smiled and she'd miss his cheerful banter.

'That's what I said,' her uncle retorted. 'The barrels still need bringing up from the cellar and with my lumbago …' he winced, his hand going to his back. 'Anyway, I know I can rely on your help. Polly always puts on a bit of a spread for the regulars around noon, so you'd best get to the kitchen.'

'Yes, of course.' She hesitated. 'Did the artists Claude and Sean come in last night, by any chance?'

'Those mavericks? Won't have them anywhere near the place. Why?' he asked, staring at her through narrowed eyes.

'I thought I heard their voices,' she replied, holding his gaze.

'Well, you thought wrong,' he snapped, taking a gulp of his drink.

'And was I wrong to think there had been a letter from Harry, after all?' she asked, fighting to keep her voice calm.

'How many times have I got to tell you?' he snarled, downing the rest of his drink in one. 'I'm tired of you pestering me, so stop asking, alright? I'll tell you if and when one comes, though I doubt it will,' he added, pouring more drink into his empty glass.

'As it's Christmas, I thought I'd pay my friends a visit. After I've helped with the lunches, of course,' she added hastily.

'You'll do no such thing,' he declared, his lips tightening. 'Look, you don't understand the likes of those people. They're undesirable not to say unpredictable. You're in my care and I have a duty to your dear departed father to see you don't come to any harm. I insist you stay here where you'll be safe.'

'But …' she began, feeling that pang in her chest at the mention of her beloved father.

'No buts. Now run along or we'll both have Polly to answer to.'

Daisy hurried down the hallway and pushed open the door to the kitchen. Unusually, there were no pots steaming on the range.

'Merry Christmas, Polly,' she greeted the woman, who was sitting hunched over the table, a mug of tea cradled in her hands.

'Nothing merry about it. That good-for-nothin' boy's scarpered and me with the festive luncheon to serve.'

'Where's he gone?' Daisy asked.

'Who knows.' The woman shrugged, then lapsed into silence. 'I'm goin' back to bed for a while. Make up plates of bread, ham and cheese; the punters can make do with them today.'

Realising she hadn't eaten since the previous lunchtime,

Daisy cut herself a thick slice from the loaf, piled on some pink meat and sank gratefully into a chair. Although the food made her feel better, she couldn't help wondering where Ginge had gone and hoped he was alright. She was just setting the cheese on the board, when the door burst open and she saw her uncle swaying in the doorway.

'Don't feel like opening up today so tell Polly I've locked the front door and not to bother with food,' he slurred, then noticed the plates laid out on the table. 'Take some of that through to the bar for me.'

Tempted to ask why he couldn't do it himself, Daisy did as he said and by the time she returned to the kitchen, it was empty. She tidied the food away, thinking how eerily quiet it was. When Polly still didn't reappear, knowing her uncle would be in a drunken stupor, she decided there was no reason why she shouldn't slip out to visit her new friends. However, when she went to turn the knob on the back door it wouldn't move. No matter how much she twisted and tugged, it wouldn't budge. She'd been locked in.

Seething with anger, she went through to the bar but there was no sign of her uncle and she had little alternative other than to spend the rest of the day in her room. Some Christmas this was, she thought, snuggling under her cover for warmth and thinking of happier times past.

Boxing Day dawned bright, cold and clear. Hearing the sound of raised voices, Daisy quickly rinsed her face, threw on her clothes and tripped down the stairs. A curious spicy, alcoholic aroma drifted along the hallway as she made her way towards the kitchen. Polly was standing at the range stirring a large pot of ruby liquid while her uncle was setting out an assortment of slender glasses and pewter cups onto silver trays.

'Ah Daisy,' her uncle beamed, only his bloodshot eyes betraying the excesses of the previous day, 'I trust you are well this morning.'

'Ye, but I am unhappy, Uncle. I was locked in yesterday.'

'Don't tell me that back door's sticking again,' he tutted, going over and giving it a tug. Immediately it opened. 'There, it's alright today. Perhaps you didn't pull hard enough,' he told her. Daisy opened her mouth to say she had given it a huge tug but he carried on talking.

'I want you to serve the men their stirrup cup. It'll brighten their morning seeing a pretty young girl, like you.'

'But I always do that,' Polly protested.

'Not anymore. Face it, Polly, you're looking quite crinkled round the edges these days. I'll go and set up a fresh barrel in the bar for later. Hopefully, the hunt will be successful, the riders thirsty.' Rubbing his hands in anticipation, he hurried away.

'You stay where you are, missy. It's always been my job to hand round their drinks and today's no different,' Polly told her. 'There's them now,' she added, as they heard the ring of horses' hooves and baying of hounds outside. Quickly the woman poured a jug of water into the pan and gave it a brisk stir. 'There that'll make it go further,' she added tipping the diluted drink back into the jug. 'Dish this out.'

As Daisy carefully poured the now pink liquid into the waiting cups and glasses, the woman patted her hair into place then pinched her lips and cheeks. With a satisfied grin, she snatched up the first tray and waddled out of the door. Clearly it wasn't sticking at all today, Daisy thought. Curious at the noise coming from outside, she peered through the window at the assembled men. Resplendent in shiny black hats, many in red coats and white breeches they sat astride the tallest and glossiest horses she'd ever seen. A pack of mottled brown and white hounds, their pointed faces alert, barked and howled as they waited impatiently beside them.

She saw Polly weaving her way incongruously through the crowd. Seemingly unaware of the cold as, beaming widely, she held out the tray for the men to take their drink, allowing them glimpses of her ample cleavage in the process. What she didn't see were the raised brows, or hear their ribald remarks, as she waddled her way back indoors. Why would a woman demean herself like that? Daisy wondered

'Still got it, I has,' Polly crowed, as she reappeared. 'Crinkled round the edges indeed,' she retorted, downing a drink. Then, snatching up the other tray, she made her way back outside again, hips swaying wildly as she went.

'What are you doing?' her uncle demanded, glaring at her from the doorway.

'I was just watching. I've never seen a hunt before,' she explained.

'I meant what are you doing in here? I thought I told you to serve the men their stirrup cup.'

'What is the stirrup cup exactly?' she asked, hoping to deflect his anger.

'A hot drink to toast the success of the hunt,' he muttered, frowning at the pot on the hob. 'Which is usually stronger than this. Has …' But the rest of his sentence was swallowed up by the sound of a horn, followed by the baying of hounds and ringing of horses' hooves on the stones as the hunt began.

'Here it only be snowing,' Polly puffed as she shuffled her way back into the room, dumped a tray of empty cups on the table then sank into a chair. 'Ooh I needs another one of them,' she added, pouring the rest of the drink from the jug into a cup and downing it in one.

'When you've quite finished perhaps you would make a start on the luncheons. Then I need to speak with you,' her uncle snapped.

'Yes, siree,' the woman slurred, shooting him a salute. With a look of disgust, he stormed from the room. 'Don't just stand there,' she told Daisy. 'Get them glasses and cups washed. Oh, and as Ginge ain't here, you'll have to see to the bread delivery in the morning. I can't get up at dawn at my age,' she whined, changing from femme fatale to helpless woman.

Daisy stifled a sigh as she set about her seemingly endless chores.

'Yer know, Daisy,' the woman said, looking serious, 'yer and me might have had our differences but you ain't a bad kid. Yer won't let Rich take advantage, will yer?'

'What do you mean?' Daisy asked.

'I might not be here much longer and well, yer a bit naïve, ain't yer? I've seen the way he gawps at yer. Believe it or not, that's how he used to look at me in the beginning. All I'm saying is, watch out. Now I'd better go and report to his lordship. He's in a foul mood cos this weather scuppered his plans. No doubt that's why we haven't seen the stool pigeon around either.'

And she waddled from the room, leaving Daisy to ponder on her words. It might have been the drink talking, but there was no denying her uncle did touch her more these days. She'd have to make sure she wasn't alone with him any more than she had to be.

Chapter 23

Shivering in the cold of dawn, Daisy waited for the ring of the bicycle bell before tugging open the back door. Then she blinked at the dazzling brightness, for the entire yard was covered in snow.

'Mornin',' Mole murmured, taking fresh loaves from his carrier and placing them in the basket Daisy held out. 'I won't say good cos I'm sad about Ginge.'

'I don't suppose you know where he's gone?' Daisy asked, hefting the heavy basket onto her other arm.

'Probably in Bert's bags of mystery by now,' Mole groaned.

Thinking he was joking, Daisy chuckled.

'Don't do to laugh. Yer doesn't know what goes on round 'ere,' he muttered before peddling off through the deep snow like the hounds of hell were after him.

Discomforted, Daisy carried the basket indoors and was unpacking it when she heard steps coming up from the cellar. To her surprise Polly appeared, looking glum.

'Bloomin' freezing down there. How's a body expected to get any sleep?' she moaned, slamming the kettle on the hob. 'In future, have this boilin' when I come up, will yer?' she growled.

Daisy put a fresh loaf onto the board ready for the woman to slice, but didn't reply. She'd heard her uncle and Polly arguing last night but, as they were both hot tempered, she was sure it would soon blow over.

Having washed the glasses from the previous evening, Daisy took herself off to the tap room where her uncle was banging barrels and muttering under his breath. The smell of stale beer and cigarette smoke hanging in the air turned her stomach and she wondered if she'd ever get used to it.

'Morning, Uncle. I've brought you a mug of tea,' she told him, placing it carefully on the bar. 'Has the postman been yet?'

'Yes, he has and, no, your fellow hasn't written,' he muttered without looking up.

'Have you heard how Mother's operation went?' she asked.

'It seems she's come through it very well.' He smiled.

'Thank heavens,' Daisy cried, clapping her hands excitedly. 'She'll be released from hospital soon and I'll be able to go home.' Her spirits soared only to plummet when her uncle shook his head.

'That was the good news, niece. She's very frail and needs more nursing. They want to move her to a convalescent home, but of course that will cost money and ...' he shrugged.

'You need me to continue working here in order to pay the fees,' she finished for him.

'I wish it could be different but ...' he let out a long sigh and went to put his arm around her shoulder. Recalling Polly's warning, she quickly moved away. 'No need to be like that,' he muttered. 'Like I said before, it must make you feel better to know you are enabling her to receive the best treatment. As well as keeping her from the workhouse.'

'The workhouse?' Daisy exclaimed, staring at him in horror.

'Hospitals can't afford to keep recovering patients on their wards, so if I didn't cough up enough dough for the convalescent home, that's where she'd end up.'

'Really?' Although what he said made sense, once again Daisy had the feeling she was being manipulated. Would she never be free from this place, she wondered, as she made her way back down the hallway?

Through the window, she could see snow falling in fat, feathery flakes, covering the ground in a soft, white carpet. Staring down at her worn boots, she grimaced. They'd be worse than useless if she ventured outside.

'Goodness, would you look at these,' Polly said. She was standing at the table staring down at an open package on the table. 'Blimey, old Bert's made some sausages in his time, but I've never seen any this colour before.'

Glancing down at them, Daisy felt her stomach turn over. They were bright orange. She remembered the baker's boy's earlier words. And what was it Ginge had said about his friend? He ain't called Mole for nothin', he's got a nose for things.

The snow continued to fall throughout January and everywhere ground to a halt. The insides of Daisy's window were deeply frosted with fern-like patterns. Although they looked beautiful, it was far too cold to stand and draw them.

With her uncle and Polly still refusing to speak to each other, the atmosphere inside the alehouse was as frosty as the air outside. Fed up with relaying messages between them, Daisy wished she could escape, but being situated deep in a valley, the hamlet of Bransum was completely cut off from the surrounding towns. Other than Mole, who now called on foot with their bread, there were no deliveries. To her dismay, when Daisy asked the boy if he'd seen Ginge, he always shook his head and hurried off.

Daisy worried constantly about her mother but knew it was no use asking her uncle for any news and if her thoughts strayed to Harry, she pushed them firmly away. Like her surroundings, her heart was frozen. So hurt was she by his silence, she'd removed her silver bangle and wrapped it inside her precious drawings. She hadn't even sent the letter she'd written.

'Yer learning,' Polly told her, eyeing her bare wrist as they sat sipping tea in front of the range. 'Next time make sure he's a keeper before yer gives yer heart away. Like I has at last,' she chortled, then lapsed into silence.

'Do you mean you're courting?' Daisy asked, staring at the woman in surprise.

'Yep. Wasted too much of me life on that bast—' she said, jerking her head towards the bar. 'Cors he was different when I first met him.' She sighed deeply then turned to Daisy. 'We only get one life so don't waste yours.'

After that, Polly was strangely absent from the kitchen and Daisy supposed she was out with her new man. Luckily the hostelry was quiet and with no deliveries, so she had few meals to prepare.

Late one afternoon, Daisy was passing the bar, which was empty apart from the group of men huddled over their ale talking to her uncle. There was something about the way they kept glancing furtively around the room that triggered her interest. Taking a sheet of paper from her uncle's drawer and ensuring she was hidden behind the door, she began sketching. Remembering Claude telling her that capturing the character was important when portraying a likeness, she focussed on their features. Then, she moved onto her uncle, who as usual was gesticulating as he talked. With his brilliantined hair, curling moustache and fierce expression, he made an interesting study. She was so absorbed in her work, she didn't notice him, tankards in hand, striding towards the bar to replenish their drinks.

'What are you doing in here?' he snarled.

'I heard voices and wondered if anyone needed food,' she said, hiding the picture behind her back.

'Good to see you now understand your position here, niece,' he replied. 'However, we men have business to discuss so I'll see you in the morning.'

Breathing a sigh of relief, Daisy fled upstairs and hid the picture at the bottom of her bag. Then, on impulse she fetched the others from under her bed and added those too. Whatever had she been thinking of, she wondered. Although she hadn't been able hear what they'd been saying, it was obvious the group were up to no good.

February dawned cold, bright and white; and throwing her shawl around her shoulders, Daisy hurried down to the kitchen to riddle the ashes into life and set the water to heat.

'Dozy cow's gone off with that bleeding poacher,' her uncle growled, appearing in the doorway. 'Better count last night's takings. Be just like her to scarper with them. Bring me tea and toast, mouth's like the droppings in a bird cage this morning.' Before Daisy could ask any questions, he'd gone.

As she sliced the remainder of the previous day's loaf and poured boiling water into the pot, Daisy mused on what the woman's departure would mean. While she wished the woman well, no doubt her uncle would expect Daisy to do more chores. She was right. As she set his tray down on the bar, he looked up from the money he'd been counting and let out a moan.

'Business has been so quiet we haven't taken enough to cover the bills. You'll take over the dozy dollop's work, of course.' Daisy held her tongue, knowing complaining would only prompt him to remind her that he paid the fees for the convalescent home.

'Yes, Uncle,' she murmured, turning to go.

'Let's console ourselves with a little cuddle?' he suggested, snaking his arm around her waist.

'Uncle, please don't do that,' she scolded, pushing him away.

'Women, all the bloody same,' he snorted. 'Don't know why I kept Polly on anyhow, she outlived her usefulness months ago. Might as well shut the bar after the noon stampede. We can keep each other company,' he told her. Not if she had anything to do with it, Daisy thought.

She spent the next few days playing cat and mouse with her uncle but with few visitors to the bar, it was difficult keeping out of his way. He seemed to lurk in the shadows of the hallway, and she could feel his eyes watching her as she passed by. There was no escape. Although the thaw had begun, snow was still banked up in drifts, the fields frozen. Her uncle told her the whole country had been affected by the weather and that some trains had even been cancelled. She was just wondering how and when she could get away, when he appeared in the doorway.

'Bad news, niece,' he said, coming over and drawing her close. 'I'm afraid your mother's dead.'

'No,' Daisy whispered, moving away from him and clutching at the table for support. 'How?'

'Wasn't strong enough, I suppose. Don't worry, my dear, I'll look after you,' he leered, and there was no mistaking his meaning. 'I'm alone, you're alone so we take care of each other.' Seeing her look of horror, his demeanour changed. 'And you look right comely in those clothes I bought for you. How old are you exactly?'

Daisy was about to say sixteen then realised that, in the turmoil of the past few months, her birthday had come and gone without her realising it.

'Seventeen,' she admitted.

'Old enough to take care of my needs,' he said, his breathing heavy as he moved closer.

'No,' she whispered, her mouth too dry to make any sound.

'Yes,' he nodded. 'But don't worry. I'll be gentle,' he told her, his arm snaking around her waist. 'We'll go up to my room.'

'No.' This time it came out as a scream. Desperate to

escape, she made a dash for the door but her uncle was too quick for her. Grabbing hold of her wrists, he placed his wet lips on hers. Fighting down the nausea, she summoned all her strength and kicked out.

'Why you little …' he panted. 'Want a fight do you.' Roughly he pushed her back against the table, pinning her against it with his body. The smell of sweat and alcohol made her feel sick. 'Come on, you owe me,' he said, groping her chest.

Fighting her revulsion, she reached out until her hand closed around the handle of a pot. As he began fumbling with the buttons on her blouse, she brought it down on his head as hard as she could. His eyes widened in disbelief, his mouth gaped open and then with a groan he fell back onto the stone floor. Her hands flew to her mouth and she could only watch in horror as he lay there, dead to the world. Dead! Dear God, she'd killed him.

Breathing heavily, she dashed up the stairs, frantically threw her few things into her bag, then throwing on her shawl she fled back down the stairs and through to the bar. But the doors were locked. Hysteria rising, she dashed to the back door but that was locked too.

What should she do, she wondered, staring fearfully at his body which hadn't moved. She had to get away and fast. But was there any way out? The tunnel, she thought, recalling her uncle bragging to his friends.

Hurrying as quickly as she dared down the slippery steps, she made her way into the cellar. She had to try quite a few barrels before she found the tap, then heart in mouth she turned it, breathing a sigh of relief as the secret door with a loud creak, swung open. With fumbling fingers, she managed to light the candle on the shelf, then, lantern in hand, made her way gingerly inside. The stench of damp was almost overpowering and trying to avoid the ice on the puddles, she made her way cautiously along the passage. The floor and walls, roughly hacked from the rock, seemed to go on forever as she tried to avoid the drips that trickled from the roof. Any moment, she expected to hear footsteps following, feel a hand on her shoulder, but finally, she made out the faintest glimmer ahead and her heart skipped. She was nearly there.

But her elation was short-lived for when she reached the end, she was greeted by a misty veil. She could smell salt on the wind, could hear water lapping close by, but only by leaning precariously out, could she make out the froth of waves before they swept into the cave and covered her boots. Jumping back in disbelief, her heart sank. What should she do now? There was no way she could go back to the alehouse, she thought, setting the lantern and her bag down on a ledge then perching beside them. The cold and damp seeped through her clothes as she stared into the bank of swirling grey. And then the flame flickered and died.

Chapter 24

How long she sat there, watching the water rising, she didn't know. She lost all sense of time as she grew ever colder. It was only when she realised the roar of the sea had lessened that she looked down and saw the water receding. To her relief the mist was lifting and she could see a stretch of wet shingle just wide enough for her to walk on. Stamping her feet and blowing on her hands to bring some life back into them, she finally managed to struggle to her feet. What a way to get her first sight of the sea, she thought, snatching up her bag and stumbling over the stones until she came upon firm ground.

Surprisingly, there was no sign of any snow here. Wet through, and shivering from shock and the cold, she stumbled up the lane, relieved to see the tumbledown cottages housing the workshop. But as she got nearer, her heart nearly stopped, for outside was a horse and cart. Claude and Grace, dressed in their warm outer clothes, were loading boxes onto the back.

'Where are you going?' she gasped.

'Daisy, what are you doing here?' Claude asked, staring at her in astonishment.

'Gosh, child, you're chilled to the bone,' Grace murmured, taking Daisy's bag from her and helping her inside. 'Mae, pour Daisy a hot drink,' she called to the woman, as she propelled the shivering Daisy towards the stove. 'Whatever's the matter?' she asked.

'I've killed him,' she muttered as her teeth began to chatter.

'Hush now, let's get that wet shawl and boots off you before you catch your death,' she fussed, gently pushing Daisy onto a chair and throwing a blanket over her. Mae handed her a steaming mug, holding it steady as Daisy began trembling. 'Come on, I've added some brandy, it's good for shock.'

'What's happened?' Grace asked, taking the mug from her when Daisy had managed to sip some of the fiery liquid which burned the back of her throat, but did stop her shaking.

'My uncle ... he ...' she swallowed hard.

'Your beautiful bangle's missing ...' Mae began, as she took Daisy's wrists to rub some circulation into them. Then she saw the vivid, black bruises and her hand flew to her mouth. 'Oh, my poor darling,' she cried, throwing her arms around Daisy's shoulders and hugging her tight.

'Did your uncle do this?' Claude asked, looking grave. Daisy nodded.

'He told me Mother's dead,' she sobbed, beginning to shake again.

'Have another sip, darling,' Mae urged, holding the mug to her lips. 'There, that's better.' As the laced tea took effect, Daisy began to feel calmer and warmer.

'Now, in your own time, tell us exactly what happened,' Claude insisted.

'He said I had to ... had to ... take care of his needs ... he ...' she gulped. 'He tried to undo my ...' Her hand went

236

to her chest and there was a collective gasp as they stared at each other in horror. 'So, I hit him hard on the head with a pot and he fell to the floor. He didn't move. I've killed him,' she sobbed.

'Well, good riddance, I say,' Mae muttered.

'But I could go to prison,' Daisy sobbed.

'Only if he really is dead,' Claude frowned. 'I can't believe a slight little thing like you could inflict much damage on a big bloke like that. We need to find out though.'

'But I can't go back there,' Daisy cried, terrified at the thought.

'Of course not. Don't worry, you're safe with us,' Mae soothed, putting her arm around her.

'The best thing would be for you to get away from here,' Sean said.

'Do you have any money for your fare home?' Claude asked, green eyes serious as he studied her. Daisy shook her head.

'Even if I did, I don't have any home or family to return to.' She swallowed hard as the sobering fact hit her.

'What about your fellow? Harry, isn't it?' Mae asked gently. 'He must be worried about you.'

'He never wrote. Polly reckoned he'd found somebody else, probably someone more glamorous on his course.' She sighed. 'If he doesn't want me, I certainly don't want him or his pity.'

'Well said, darling,' Mae murmured, crossing her legs, which as usual were encased in trousers. 'It's no good us women campaigning to be equal to men if we expect them to pander to our emotions. We have to stand on our own two feet or we'll never get anywhere.'

'That's all very well, but this isn't helping Daisy's predicament, and Claude and I need to be leaving if we're to reach Exeter before dark,' Grace told her.

'Could I come with you?' Daisy asked, looking at them hopefully.

'Well, I don't know,' the woman frowned. 'Our lifestyle is somewhat unconventional and we intend staying on Bodmin Moor to gather inspiration for our work, before travelling on to Lamorna Cove.'

'I see,' Daisy murmured, picking up her bag and trying to rise to her feet. 'Don't worry, I'll manage,' she said smiling bravely.

'You can't go anywhere in those, they're full of holes,' Mae said, pointing to her boots where, after catching them on the rocks, the soles were coming away from the uppers. 'We look about the same size so you can have my spares.' Jumping up, she scrabbled through a cupboard then thrust a pair of buttoned boots at her. Daisy stared at the soft leather then shook her head.

'I can't possibly take those, they're beautiful.'

'And so are you, darling,' Mae said, squeezing her arm gently.

'They're so soft,' she murmured, marvelling as the pliable leather with its velvety lining enveloped her feet like a warm hug.

'Just like Mae,' Sean said, looking lovingly at the woman. 'At least she would be if only she'd wear a dress,' he sighed theatrically, making them all laugh and relieving the tension.

'Hurry up and put them on or we'll have to go without you,' Grace said.

'You mean I can come with you?' Daisy asked, hardly daring to believe her luck. 'But what about my uncle? The police will be after me.'

'All the more reason for us to get going,' Claude told her, draping her shawl around her shoulders.

'Don't forget this,' Mae said, lifting a basket from the table. 'You'll be hungry before you get halfway.'

'Thanks, Mae,' Grace murmured, embracing her friend before taking it from her. 'And thank you for everything,' she added, going over and pecking Sean's cheek. Then Daisy found herself swept up in Mae's arms.

'Be bold, be brave,' she murmured. 'And we'll be down to see you when the weather warms up. We're not hardy like those two,' she added, gesturing towards the door where Claude and Grace stood waiting.

'Or foolish,' Sean added. 'Be sure and take care of yourself,' he said, bending and kissing Daisy.

'Well, that'll make sure she leaves right away,' Mae quipped.

'As a precaution, lie on the floor and I'll hide you with the cover,' Claude said, helping Daisy into the cart. She just had time to make herself reasonably comfortable when everything went dark as the tarpaulin was thrown over her. Then she felt a jolt as Claude and Grace climbed up in front. She heard them all calling their farewells, Claude's brisk 'walk on' and the horse began to move.

'Just stay where you are and keep quiet,' Grace called

softly. 'We don't want to risk you being spotted until we're well clear of the village.'

As the shock of what she'd done set in, Daisy hardly dared breathe and couldn't have moved if she'd wanted. It was only now, as the cart slowly started to trundle its way out of the village, that she realised what a risk her friends were taking on her behalf. She owed them a huge debt and, if they managed to get away, she vowed she'd do anything she could to repay them.

Grace kept up a running commentary to let Daisy know where they were as they made their way past the alehouse, the church and then climbed the steep hill out of the village. Although exhausted after her ordeal, she was too petrified to sleep but, as they plodded along, her eyelids grew heavy and she fell into a doze.

She was jolted awake as the cart lurched to a halt, then there was a flash of light as the tarpaulin was pulled back and she saw Claude smiling down at her.

'We're well on our way to Exeter and there's not much traffic, so you can sit with us now,' he said, holding out his hand to help her.

'Are you alright?' Grace asked, as after an anxious look behind, Daisy squashed in beside her.

'A bit shaky,' she admitted.

'Well, we're miles away from Bransum now, let's have something to eat,' Grace said, reaching down and pulling the basket onto her lap. 'Although you might just want a drink,' she added, as Daisy looked over her shoulder again.

'You mustn't worry, Daisy. After all you acted in

self-defence. Besides, your uncle's as tough as old boots so will probably have woken up by now,' Claude said.

'Hopefully with the mother of all headaches,' Grace chuckled. 'Come on, you need to eat after all you've been through. You're safely away from that brute now.' As she held out the open basket, the aroma of baked bread wafted upwards and, surprisingly, Daisy realised she was hungry.

She was free from her uncle's clutches at last and, reassured by Claude and Grace's encouragement, Daisy began to relax, although she couldn't help looking back from time to time.

They were pulled up on a grass verge at the side of the road, rolling hills dotted with sheep spread out on one side while on the other steam rose from ruby red cattle housed in a thatched linney. Everywhere was a lush green, and fortified by her food, Daisy gazed around in wonderment. She'd never seen so much open space before. In the distance, she could even make out the shimmer of water.

'Is that the sea?' she asked excitedly.

'No, my little townie, that's the River Exe. Starts in Exmoor and meanders its way through Devonshire until it reaches the sea at Exmouth way over there,' he said, gesturing to his left. 'I painted the estuary last year, and it was a spectacular sight.'

'What, the scenery or your picture?' Grace asked, her lips twitching. 'Now, Mae's packed a bottle of mint tea; who'd like some?' As Daisy sipped her drink, she felt her body coming back to life.

'We really thought you'd returned to London weeks ago,' Grace told her.

'I wish,' Daisy murmured. 'I wanted to come and see you again but Uncle forbade me. He even locked me in.'

'Bastard,' Claude exclaimed. 'Sean and I braved the ale-house to ask after you. He told us you'd returned home, then sent us packing.' So, she hadn't been mistaken, Daisy thought, wondering how many other lies her uncle had told her. Still, it was good to know she was in the company of real friends.

'How do you feel about coming to Cornwall with us?' Grace asked. 'We're a little unconventional in our ways, but we work hard then play hard so you're guaranteed lots of fun.'

'After the past few months, that sounds like heaven,' Daisy assured her, then she frowned. 'But I don't have any money to pay my way.'

'We'll work something out.' Grace smiled, patting her hand.

'Yes, when we reach Bodmin, we'll need someone to hunt and fish for our food,' Claude murmured, then laughed when Daisy stared at him aghast.

'Don't scare the poor girl,' Grace admonished. 'Seriously, Daisy, we all muck in and share everything. Anyway, it's time we were on our way again,' she added, returning their empty cups to the basket. 'We've booked into the coaching house so Maxwell here can have a good feed and rest,' she added, gesturing to the bay horse.

'So called, because Grace thought he had the look of artist Maxwell Armfield, her paramour, who alas married another.'

'Don't remind me,' Grace groaned. 'That was years ago

and I'm wedded to my jewellery designing now.' Daisy looked from one to the other.

'So, you two …' Daisy began, then stopped, realising it was none of her business.

'Are the best of friends,' Claude finished for her.

'And being twenty years older than me, Claude is more of a father figure,' Grace chuckled.

'Thanks,' he muttered. 'But you must admit your illustrations have improved enormously since we've been working together.'

'True,' Grace agreed then turned to Daisy. 'Although our relationship is platonic, for economy reasons we've booked just the one room.'

'So now I'll have the pleasure of bedding down with two beautiful ladies,' Claude chuckled as Daisy's mouth dropped open. 'Don't worry, you'll be quite safe with Grace as chaperone.' Daisy smiled, for already she was feeling safer than she had for months.

'The coaching house should be up here on the left.' Daisy stared at the tall buildings rising before them and the traffic that had appeared seemingly from nowhere. Although different to Camberwell, the bustle was more like she was used to. 'There it is,' Grace added, squinting in the gathering gloom.

'Thank heavens we made it before dark; we've no lamps on the cart. Ah, here's the ostler,' Claude added, jumping down as a boy hurried towards them. 'We're staying the night, so see old Maxwell here is looked after,' he said, tossing a coin through the air. As the lad neatly caught it, Daisy caught sight of his beaming face.

'Ginge,' she cried delightedly, jumping down and hurrying over to him. 'You're alive.'

'And kicking, just Daisy.' He grinned. 'That last booting from yer uncle nearly did for me, so I lied low with Mole. 'E got me a lift and well 'ere I am, ostler in this fine place. Much better than the dump in … oops sorry, I were forgetting, just Daisy,' he mumbled.

'I'm so relieved to know you're not sausage meat,' Daisy said, now understanding Mole's reticence to talk about his friend.

'I were nearly a goner, but not that far. Mole fed me more bread and pies than I ever seen in me life before,' he winked. ''Ow's things with yer, just Daisy?'

'I've just heard Mother died,' she admitted, the tears welling. 'And I never did get a letter from Harry. But Polly went off with her fella.'

'Coo, would loved to 'ave seen yer uncle's face,' Ginge chortled. At the mention of her uncle, Daisy shivered, automatically peering around in the gathering gloom. 'Gotta go,' Ginge muttered as another lad appeared to help with their luggage. Claude, who'd been watching their exchange intently, looked grave.

'If your uncle is still alive, and instinct tells me he is, I think it's time the authorities were informed about his nefarious activities,' he told Daisy. She nodded, for she couldn't bear anyone else being treated as she and Ginge had. 'Apparently, he's been under surveillance for a while now but they haven't been able to pin anything on him. However, if they were to hear about that tunnel, well …' He shrugged.

Was that what the dark-haired man had been doing, Daisy wondered. Yet that didn't explain his coolness towards her that last time in the bar.

Grace and Claude decided on an early night, telling Daisy to use the facilities whilst they were shown to their room. Then, after smuggling her in, the three of them bedded down. Relieved to be away from the hostelry, Daisy lay in the dark, thinking of her poor mother. As the tears fell, she prayed her parents were happily reunited in heaven.

Chapter 25

After bidding Ginge a fond farewell, they set off soon after sun rise. At first, Daisy couldn't help looking anxiously behind in case they were being followed. However, as they plodded out of the city and houses gave way to open fields, she felt excitement pulsing through her veins.

'The buildings are even more remote than Bransum,' she remarked as they passed a farm and headed towards the undulating hills in the distance.

After a long, slow climb, the road descended into a sprawling verdant valley. Daisy, who'd been relaxing after her recent ordeal, leaned forward eagerly, when Claude turned into a wide, tree-lined driveway.

'Goodness,' she murmured, gazing at the manicured lawns edged with golden daffodils and crimson tulips that bobbed in the breeze. A man weeding the herbaceous border turned and saluted as they passed. Moments later, they drew up outside the grandest house Daisy had ever seen, its granite walls and stone mullions were topped with a slate roof and broad chimneys. The way the gables rose at each end over the upper latticed windows reminded Daisy of neatly shaped eyebrows, and the turret over the entrance a stumpy nose.

'Whoever lives here?' Daisy gasped.

'My sister Joy, and we're staying with her tonight,' Grace explained, as they clambered down.

'Was that her husband we saw tending the garden?' she asked.

'No, that was the gardener.' Grace smiled. 'Joy's husband works in the city and is away a lot.'

'Shall I stable the horse, sir?' A man dressed in a rough jacket, his cheeks as red as the tulips, appeared from behind the house and looked questioningly at Claude. Then Daisy saw a woman, dark hair swept up in a chignon, standing in the doorway, waving. In her high-necked lace blouse and sweeping navy skirt, she looked elegant, almost regal, and Daisy stared down at her crumpled pinafore in dismay. Although she'd managed to launder it after Polly had left, it was threadbare and she felt like a street urchin.

'Come on in,' she greeted them warmly. 'I've asked Ginny to prepare a tray.' There was no denying her likeness to Grace as she ushered them into the hallway. 'Barden will bring in your things, and don't worry, Claude, he has been instructed to be careful,' she teased.

'Joy, this is Daisy,' Grace introduced. 'Daisy, this is my sister Joy.'

'Lovely to meet you, Daisy,' the woman greeted with a gracious smile. Her eyes, the same soft hazel as Grace's, swiftly appraised her, making Daisy even more aware of her unkempt appearance. 'Ginny will take your wraps,' she said as a tall, thin woman in a black dress appeared. 'We'll go through to the parlour,' Joy told them, leading the way along an elegant hallway resplendent with chandeliers and gold-framed pictures, into a room where a log fire was burning brightly. Seeing Daisy's appreciative look, Joy smiled. 'The winds round here can be decidedly nippy. Now do take a seat everyone and Ginny will pour tea.' Daisy looked around the room, its curved furniture and velvet drapes as stylish as its owner.

Daisy perched on a tapestry-covered chair, trying not to stare at the dainty sandwiches and fancies that Ginny wheeled in on a trolley. They looked delicious and the fresh air had made her hungry. She sipped the fragrant tea, trying not to grimace at the slice of lemon floating on the top.

'Let me look at that beautiful lace,' Joy said to Grace, moving closer to her sister and inspecting the collar and sleeves of her blouse.

'The patterns are a work of art in themselves. It was the flower motifs that attracted me. I swapped a length of lace for one of my brooches,' Grace admitted.

'You must tell me from whom you purchased it. I'm in need of some new blouses and will set my dressmaker to work.'

'Honestly, Joy, there's no need. It's quite simple to stitch a couple of frills onto the cuffs and collar of any existing one. I have some lace in my bag so I could do it for you later,' Grace offered.

'Oh, I couldn't possibly let you do that,' Joy protested, her eyes lighting up.

'I insist. As a thank you for putting us all up for the night. I'm assuming you don't mind if Daisy shares my room?'

'Of course not.' She smiled at Daisy graciously. 'Would you really sew some for me, Grace?' Joy asked, clapping her hands together in delight. 'You're so clever at that kind of thing and I have to entertain some of William's business associates next week.'

While the sisters chatted, Daisy stared at the portrait on the wall above the fireplace. It was of a young man, his hand resting on the shoulder of a pretty young girl. The twinkle in his blue eyes reminded her of Harry and her heart gave a lurch. Automatically, her hand went to the bangle on her wrist. But of course, she was no longer wearing it. Would she ever stop thinking of him, she wondered.

'There's about an hour of daylight left, so while you and your sister catch up, I'll take a stroll, stretch my legs and get some inspiration,' Claude said, getting to his feet. 'Want to join me, Daisy?'

'I'd love to,' she replied, grateful for the distraction.

'Good idea. The moors look spectacular when the sun sets. But take your shawl, it gets cold quickly up here,' Grace told her.

They walked in silence for some minutes, climbing the steep path behind the house that led to the moors. Daisy marvelled at the peace surrounding them and couldn't help thinking how Harry would love sketching this landscape that was so different to Camberwell. Then she saw dark shapes looming ahead and stopped abruptly.

'What's wrong?' Claude asked, frowning at her.

'I thought I saw men over there,' she whispered.

'They're not men, silly, just shadows from the tors. Come

on,' he said, taking her arm. 'There, see?' He smiled, as they neared the prominent rocky outcrops glowing like dark copper in the evening light. 'Very therapeutic to paint when you have the weight of the world on your shoulders,' he added, turning to look at her. 'You'll be safe with us, Daisy, I promise.'

'But if, as you think, my uncle is alive, he might come looking for me.'

'Hardly, Daisy. He's too tied up with his own affairs.' Daisy stared at him, realising what he said was true. And yet after the events of the past few months, her emotions were all of a jumble. 'You've had a tough time recently, Daisy, why don't you tell me how you're feeling?'

Daisy bit her lip. Sometimes she wondered if Claude was psychic, the way he tuned into her feelings.

'Sad, bitter, guilty and scared,' she admitted. 'Sad that I will never see my parents again, bitter that Harry never replied to my letters and guilty that I didn't go and see Mother in the hospital and, despite what you say, scared in case I've killed my uncle. I should never have listened to him, but he was so convincing,' she burst out.

'Why? What did he say?' Claude asked, turning to look at her.

'That he couldn't afford to pay Mother's hospital bills as well as employing someone to help Polly in the kitchen, so I had to do it instead. I honestly thought I was doing the right thing. But I wasn't, and now it's too late.'

'We can only ever do what we feel is right at the time, Daisy,' Claude murmured. 'Your mother wouldn't want you to be unhappy, would she?'

She sighed, knowing he was right. 'But I'll never get to see her again,' she cried, the tears welling up.

'You did what you thought was your duty. No one can do more than that,' he told her, patting her shoulder.

'But all the people I loved have gone. Even Harry didn't care enough to keep in touch,' she retorted.

'That's hard to accept,' he admitted, 'but you mustn't let bitterness consume you. The only person you'll hurt is yourself and you're young with your whole life ahead of you.'

'You understand what it's like to be hurt?' Daisy asked.

'Yes, Daisy.' He nodded then lapsed into silence.

Lost in their own thoughts, they stood staring over the moors that stretched out in every direction.

'Spring is on the way,' Claude said, finally breaking the silence. 'A time of hope and renewal. The trees unfurl their buds, squirrels come out of hibernation, birds build nests to lay their eggs. It makes you appreciate the cycle of life. And up there—' he gestured to the darkening sky where one lone star was beginning to shine '—is a heavenly body bravely making its own way in life. Be brave too, Daisy, and do that with yours.'

'Like you and Grace have?' she asked, remembering what he'd said about Maxwell.

'We've both had to decide whether we let sadness overwhelm us, or be courageous enough to let it go. Bitterness sours the soul and stifles creativity. Come on; Joy always puts on a splendid supper.'

'Thank you, Claude.' Daisy smiled, wiping away her tears. She would carve out a new life for herself and make her mother proud. For all Daisy knew, she might be that lone star shining down on her.

Next morning, the sun shining brightly from a clear cobalt sky, the little group set off for Bodmin. Daisy was excited and full of optimism for the journey ahead, both physically and metaphorically. Her talk with Claude had helped ease her conscience about her beloved mother. And now, having come to terms with the fact that Polly had been right and Harry had found someone else, she would make something of her life. If only she could be sure she hadn't killed her uncle.

'I don't know what your sister put in those bags, but they must have been heavy,' Claude commented as Maxwell lumbered up the hill.

'You know how generous Joy is. She can't believe we'll be able to survive without a few home comforts and a stash of food. Poor Ginny was up early turning the remains of that game casserole into a pie.' Grace smiled. 'It'll be perfect for our first meal at Peacehaven.'

'Is that where we are going?' Daisy asked.

'That's what we call our retreat on Bodmin Moor. It's just a tumble-down cottage really, but we love the serenity and solitude it affords, and find it inspiring,' Grace continued, hazel eyes alight with enthusiasm.

'Sounds wonderful,' Daisy replied. Peace and quiet would be bliss after the recent turmoil and if this cottage was isolated, nobody would know she was there. Despite what her friends said, she couldn't help worrying that someone was searching for her.

Shaking her head to banish the dreadful thought, she stared around at the seemingly endless moor. With its wind-stunted trees bending like little old ladies, it looked bleak in places yet it undoubtedly had a mystical charm. Grace's sister was lucky living in such an idyllic location.

'Joy's home is like a fairy tale palace, isn't it?'

'It's certainly comfortable, but I wouldn't call it a home, and Joy pays a heavy price for such luxury,' Grace replied. 'Her husband spends more time in London with his mistress than with her. Joy was hoping that starting a family would refocus his attention, but regrettably a baby remains elusive. I guess the moral of that story is, material riches don't guarantee happiness.'

'It's spiritual fulfillment that's really important,' Claude added. 'Now, let's discuss what we are going to do over the next few weeks. We might eke out a pitiful existence in our lowly moorland shack, but we always have fun.'

'We certainly make the most of our time,' Grace gigged, suddenly appearing younger and softer.

As Grace and Claude debated ideas for the exhibition later that summer, Daisy found their excitement infectious.

'Did you bring your sketches with you?' Claude suddenly asked.

'They're in my bag, although they've got a bit creased. I was hoping you might show me how to get Harry's ears right; they're a bit lopsided at the moment,' she admitted.

'It's about scale and proportion. Get those wrong and everything looks out of kilter. Mind you, one lady I was commissioned to paint insisted I give her a more voluptuous bustline as she wanted to impress her future husband. Poor chap must have been disappointed when he got to see the real thing.' He chuckled. His words brought a flush to Daisy's cheeks, which made them laugh.

'Don't worry, my little innocent,' Claude told her. 'You'll get used to our ways.'

As they passed through tiny hamlets of lime-washed thatched cottages and alongside fields intersected by ragged hawthorn hedgerows, the sun rose higher. Finally, when it was overhead, they stopped for the picnic Ginny had packed.

Replete, they continued their journey, passing through a large market town dominated by an ancient round fort, rising up barren rolling hills with tussocks of grass bleached almost straw-coloured from the winter snow and gales. The air was crystal clear and, for the first time in months, Daisy felt truly alive.

As the late afternoon sun gilded the sky a glorious fusion of crimson, amethyst and gold, Claude veered off the main path and onto a winding track that seemed too narrow for the cart to travel along. They stopped beside a strange wall that looked as though it had been made by cobbling boulders and vegetation together. Behind it was a grey stone building, its matching porch leading to a wooden door with a pile of kindling to one side. Although the slate roof was bowing under the weight of a crooked chimney on one corner, and the windows looked like they were at odds with the walls, Daisy thought it looked charming.

'Isn't it heavenly?' Grace cried, clambering down and

gesturing to the rising moors beyond. 'And listen?' she added, putting a hand to her ear and smiling.

'I can't hear anything,' Daisy frowned.

'Exactly: peace and quiet.'

'Solace for the soul,' Claude added, as he unhitched Maxwell, who immediately began munching the tufts of grass sprouting from the funny wall.

'Why is that wall wonky?' Daisy asked.

'That's a Cornish hedge. It takes a craftsman to erect a work of art like that,' Claude told her. 'Now, let's unload and get a fire lit before it grows too dark to see anything.' He pulled back the tarpaulin and began lifting out their bags.

The interior was cool and dim, yet as soon as she stepped over the threshold, Daisy felt a sense of tranquillity enfold her. It really was a haven of peace and she could understand why Grace and Claude had named it such.

'You can have the upstairs room at the back,' Grace told her. 'It's small but has stunning views down to the lake. Just mind those as you go up,' she said, gesturing to the steep flight of steps, 'they're uneven to say the least. By the time you've settled in we'll have a blaze going down here. This place might be compact but it takes next to no time to get warm.'

Daisy's room was just big enough for a single bed and chest, but the outlook down to the water, dark and shimmering in the gathering dusk, more than made up for it. She set about unpacking, frowning at how shabby and threadbare everything had become. Disconcerted by her uncle's ogling, she'd stopped wearing the close-fitting clothes he'd given her, then in her haste to leave, had left them behind. Not that she'd ever wear them again, she thought, shuddering at the memory. Diving into her bag to retrieve the sketches, she gasped as, with a jingle and flash of silver, her bangle fell to the floor and disappeared through a gap in the floorboards.

Chapter 26

Desperately Daisy tried to retrieve her bangle but couldn't push her fingers through the space in the uneven planks. Almost mockingly, it just sat there, gleaming up at her. Cursing her clumsiness, she looked round for something with which to grab it, for perversely, although she hadn't wanted to look at it for weeks, she now wished to hold it. Remembering the wire hooks hanging from the beams in the kitchen, she dashed downstairs past a surprised Grace and retrieved one. It was just thin enough to slip between the boards, so she lay flat on her stomach and, after much twisting and pulling, finally managed to seize it.

Relief flooding through her. She sank onto the bed and wiped it on her pinafore, running her fingers around the delicate chain of daisies. Remembering Claude telling her she shouldn't be bitter, she slipped it over her wrist. It might have been the rays from the setting sun peeping through the window, but suddenly she was filled with a sense of warmth. Picking up the picture of Harry, it seemed as if his eyes were twinkling with mirth. Yes, very funny, she thought, setting it down on the deep sill and placing the ones of her mother and father beside it. Once they had been her life and now, in the space of a few months, they were all gone. Onwards and upwards, she told herself as she placed the sketch of her uncle and his cronies beneath the others.

Realising she'd been some time, Daisy quickly combed her hair and made her way back down the funny stairs. She was greeted by the smell of woodsmoke, and the orange flames dancing in the stone fireplace made the living room warm and welcoming. A kettle had been placed on the trivet in the hearth and Grace was setting out plates on the table by the window. Candles stood on the sills ready to be lit.

'Everything alright?' Grace asked.

'Yes,' Daisy said, hanging the hook back and holding up her arm. 'My bangle dropped through a gap in the floor.'

'So, you've decided to wear it again,' Grace said, staring at her knowingly. Daisy just smiled and changed the subject.

'It's a lovely room and I see what you mean about the view. It felt as if I was expected, what with the bed being made and everything.'

'We share this cottage with other co-operative members, the agreement being that we always leave it ready for others to use. Hence the wood pile by the door.'

'Sounds wonderful.'

'It works well. We all get to have a holiday and arrive knowing we can just fall into bed if necessary. Claude is settling Maxwell in the old stable so we'll eat when he comes in.'

Perching on cushions and toasting their feet in front of the fire, they tucked into the game pie and bread that Joy had pressed upon them. Contented, but too tired to make conversation, they sipped their hot drinks before retiring. Whether it was the journey, her new room or the peace that had enfolded her, for the first time in ages, Daisy fell into a deep sleep, her hand clasping the silver bangle.

They were all up early the next morning, eager to make the most of what Grace referred to as their restorative retreat, although Claude insisted on calling it their curative kickstart to creativity.

'Don't know how you work that one out, you never stop sketching or painting wherever you are,' Grace teased as they prepared their materials to take down to the lake. Picking up a box, Grace handed it to Daisy. 'Joy wondered if these might be of use.'

Although it was said casually, it was obvious from the woollen tops, stockings and thick skirt that the parcel had been thoughtfully put together.

'That's so kind of her,' Daisy gasped, touched that a woman she'd only just met should have thought of her. 'Oh, my, this is beautiful,' Daisy marvelled, holding up an emerald-green velvet cloak. It had ruffles at the collar and she couldn't resist throwing it around her shoulders.

'And very necessary this time of year,' Grace told her, pulling the hood up over Daisy's hair. 'The wind whistles right through your ears up here.'

'Goodness, who is this vision of beauty,' Claude enquired, looking up from the easel he was strapping onto a canvas bag. 'Whomever she is, I quite want to paint her.'

'Oh Claude,' Daisy demurred, although his teasing made her feel good.

'It's true. Now come on, let's make the most of this beautiful weather.'

Daisy followed them down the track towards the lake, marvelling at the sweep of undulating reed covered moors that seemed to enclose them.

'Probably too cold to swim today,' Claude observed.

'You swim in that?' Daisy gulped, peering in distaste at the black waters.

'It's the peat that gives it that colour,' Grace said, laughing at her expression. 'Although it's hard to believe, the water reflects the moorland and clouds which makes swimming a relaxing experience and is good for the metabolism. It's also thought to help restore hair, which is why Claude bathes as often as he can,' she teased, ruffling the man's head affectionately.

'Remember who digs the peat out and dries it for burning on the fire,' Claude muttered.

'And remember who bakes the bread you love so much,' Grace countered.

'This is called Dozmary Pool, by the way,' Claude told Daisy. 'King Arthur's last battle was fought near here and his sword Excalibur is meant to lie in its depths. Legend decrees a hand can sometimes be seen rising out of the water,' he warned, lifting his arm dramatically in front of her.

'Oh,' Daisy shuddered, then realised he was teasing her again.

'It does feel melancholy when the mist hovers,' Grace murmured, gazing out over the still waters.

'Must make the most of the light,' Claude announced,

setting up his easel by the side of the pool and beginning to sketch.

'Fancy a walk?' Grace asked Daisy.

'As long as I'm not stopping you from working,' Daisy replied, conscious that's why her friend was here.

'I'll gather ideas and materials along the way.' Leaving their bags with Claude, they set off at a brisk pace for the wind was indeed cold. 'Look at those,' Grace cried, bending to examine a clump of pale lilac flowers.

'They're just like the ones outside the hostelry in Bransum.'

'So they are,' Grace replied. 'Although, I think they might be slightly different.' She frowned, inspecting them closer.

'Some of their species originated in warmer climes,' Daisy told her, remembering what the dark-haired man had told her, but Grace was already taking a notepad and pencil from her pocket and didn't hear. Daisy tried to recall what else the man had said. Something about them having the survival instinct to adapt to their new environment. Well, that was what she was doing now, wasn't it? But thoughts of the dark-haired man reminded her of Bransum and she shuddered. In her mind's eye, she could still see the image of her uncle lying still as a stone on the kitchen floor.

'Look, Daisy, this shape would be perfect for a brooch,' Grace enthused, breaking into her thoughts. 'See how the delicate petals curve?' Daisy watched admiringly as, with a few deft strokes, Grace captured the shape perfectly.

'I wish I could draw like that,' Daisy murmured.

'I try and get down as much detail as possible, although translating it into my design work is more complicated.' She scribbled a few words about the colours and outline of the veins alongside the sketch, then turned to Daisy. 'Come on, this fresh air is making me hungry. I wonder if Claude has braved the water.'

'But it's so cold.'

'That won't put him off,' Grace laughed.

They retraced their steps to find Claude swimming across the lake. He raised an arm and Daisy was about to wave back when she noticed his clothes scattered at the water's edge.

'But he's ...' she gasped, her hand going to her mouth.

'We did tell you we do everything au naturel, didn't we?'

'I didn't realise you meant ...' Daisy began, swallowing hard and turning away.

'Oh Daisy, you're such a little innocent,' Grace chuckled. 'We like to feel at one with nature, not that you have to join in, of course.'

'I'll go and prepare the food,' she called, all but running back to the cottage.

By the time Claude and Grace appeared, Daisy had regained her composure.

'Sorry, Daisy, I should have warned you. Still not many females can resist the splendid sight of Adonis in all his glory.'

'That's as may be,' Grace replied, 'but a cavorting Claude is a different matter.'

'I'll have you know I was not cavorting,' he retorted, looking so indignant Daisy had to laugh and the tension was broken. 'But out of respect to our virtuous little visitor,

I shall spend tomorrow fishing for our supper. Have you ever fished, Daisy?'

'No,' she admitted.

'Then your education is sadly lacking and I shall teach you,' he promised.

However, when Daisy woke the next morning, she could hear rain lashing against the roof. Peering out of the window, she saw grey mist covering the moors like a shroud. Shivering, she quickly pulled on a warm jumper and long skirt that Joy had given her. It felt nice to be wearing something stylish and although Daisy didn't consider herself particularly vain, as she looked into the tiny mirror above the bed, even she could appreciate the soft violet colour made her skin look brighter, and her eyes sparkle.

'Well, look at you,' Claude exclaimed, looking up from the magazine he was reading, as Daisy clattered down the steep stairs. Already a fire was burning brightly in the grate, the kettle on the trivet singing. 'Quite the country lady.'

'You look delightful,' Grace said, looking up from setting the table.

'These clothes have hardly been worn and are obviously of high quality. I feel very guilty not giving Joy anything for them,' Daisy admitted.

'Ah, but you have. According to my dear sister, you have spared my reputation,' Grace chuckled. 'Appearances are everything to Joy. She considers my being unmarried and sharing a house with mixed company quite immoral enough but when she heard I intended staying here with Claude she declared everyone would think I had the morals of an alley cat. However, when I pointed out you would be with us, she calmed down, declaring you would make the perfect chaperone.' Daisy stared at Grace in surprise.

'I know, archaic, isn't it? I did remind her this is 1911 not 1811. Now, sit yourselves down, I've made porridge for breakfast.' Remembering the offering Polly had provided, Daisy's heart sank but she needn't have worried for, when Grace placed a dish in front of her, it looked smooth and appetising with a swirl of glistening golden cream on top.

'Just like Nanny used to make,' Claude exclaimed, sighing with appreciation.

'Don't get too used to the good life, *mon ami*,' Grace warned him. 'Although Joy has been generous, the supplies won't last forever. We've plenty of pie and cold meats left for later and I've put potatoes in the ashes to bake for luncheon but when the rain lets up, we should go for a walk and see what we can forage. In the meantime, I thought I'd transfer the sketches I made yesterday into my workbook. And the colour of your top will make the perfect aide-memoire, Daisy,' Grace said, bubbling with enthusiasm.

'I intend capturing the mood of the mist masking the moors,' Claude murmured, peering morosely out of the window.

'I'm happy to clear away,' Daisy volunteered, gathering up their empty dishes. 'And you must let me prepare our meals as payment towards staying here.'

'We all muck in together, Daisy, but if you can wash up this time, we'll be able to make some use of the day, uninviting though it is,' Grace added.

'And later we can take a look at those pictures of your Harry, see if we can address his unbalanced ears.' Claude laughed.

'Shame you can't do something about the inside of his head while you're at it,' Grace muttered, picking up her things, and curling comfortably in the big sagging chair beside the fire.

Daisy was happy to be spending the day indoors, and, having tidied the little kitchen, she went to get her pictures. By the time she returned, Claude had set his easel at an angle to the window and was peering out gloomily.

'Ah, let's take a look at these masterpieces,' he said, brightening as he turned to Daisy.

'They're not very good,' Daisy murmured, suddenly conscious she was showing her amateur offerings to a professional artist.

'I'll be the judge of that,' Claude said, patting the chair beside him. She sat staring at the patterns the rain was making as it trickled down the glass while Claude studied the pictures of her mother and father.

'Although I never knew them, Daisy, I can see from these they were loving people. You've captured the warmth in their expressions. Not an easy thing to do at the best of times, so well done,' he said, smiling encouragingly.

'Thank you,' she whispered, wiping away the tears that had welled when she saw their dear faces staring up at her. She handed him the one of Harry then sat listening to the logs crackling in the grate while Claude took his time scrutinising it.

'Well, he certainly looks like a cheeky chap, and again

you've managed to convey a sense of character,' he finally pronounced.

'His ears are all wrong though, they're much too big,' she muttered.

'Technically I would agree, although I would imagine you drew him just as you saw him. Did you know, the Chinese consider people with big ears to be lively and energetic?'

'No, but Harry was certainly that.' Daisy sighed, remembering some of his harebrained schemes.

Chapter 27

As thoughts from her past surfaced, Claude smiled knowingly.

'Perhaps it would be better to try something else today,' he suggested, tearing a sheet of paper from his board and passing it to her. 'The mist is beginning to lift and I want to capture my impression of it before it disappears. Why don't you sketch the view as you see it?'

'Oh yes please do, Daisy. It would be nice to have a proper picture to look at, instead of splodges of colour,' Grace said, shooting her a grin.

Claude snorted as he furiously began mixing different colours together on his palette. Then, as if consumed by some monster, he started splashing them randomly onto the paper.

Daisy focussed on the crooked gate that led to the gentle swell of the field beyond, but the slant of the wind-bent trees proved challenging and she furrowed her brow. Seeing her struggling, Claude leaned across and, with a few deft strokes, showed her how shading gave her the depth she was looking for. After a few false starts, Daisy managed to reflect the darkness of the branches. Growing more confident, she drew in the rolling moors beyond.

'That's good,' Grace said, as she peered over Daisy's shoulder.

'It is, but Daisy has a most unusual way of drawing,' Claude observed. 'I've never seen anyone work up the page before.'

'Well, however she did it, at least I can make out the detail, which is more than can be said about your depressing swirls and whirls,' Grace replied, winking at Daisy.

'*Mon dieu!*' he exclaimed, throwing down his brush. 'I'll have you know those swirls and whirls, as you call them, are deliberate broken brush strokes, a mix of pure and unmixed colours.'

'But they're all blobby,' Grace insisted.

'Not blending them together gives a sense of intense colour vibration. That swirl of ochre there is the transient effect of the one burst of sunshine that broke through the cloud earlier,' he explained, pointing with the end of his brush.

'Well, Daisy's is a truer representation of what I can see outside,' Grace laughed.

'Right, let's see your masterpiece then,' Claude challenged, grabbing her sketchbook. 'Oh, a drooping flower, and that's not depressing?' he scoffed, although Daisy could tell he was scrutinising every detail.

'A flowing flower,' Grace corrected. 'The violet represents modesty, with its elemental association water. I'm going to make an enamelled brooch with a curved stem and open petals staring downwards to represent the shyness of its wearer. The markings for the face will be little seed pearls for tears of joy.'

'That sounds amazing,' Daisy cried, clapping her hands in delight.

'Don't know why you have to incorporate tears, even if it's meant to epitomise a woman,' Claude snorted, the look in his eyes betraying his admiration for his friend's work.

'I wouldn't expect you to understand sentiment,' Grace laughed.

'Maybe not. However, I was reading in *The Studio* that pieces incorporating the sinuous curves of plants and flowers are proving popular, so you could be on to something for the exhibition. Right, I'm going out for a walk and then I'll ride Maxwell into Bodmin,' he announced, snatching up his hat and coat.

As the door shut behind him, Grace shook her head.

'Poor Claude, he's having a bad day. He doesn't often get like that now, but when he does, it's best to let him be until he's worked the angst out of his system. I'm sure he'll tell you about it one day,' she added when Daisy looked at her questioningly.

'Is this the magazine he was talking about?' Daisy asked, picking up the pamphlet from the table.

'Yes, it details the latest news, events and exhibitions and keeps us up to date with what's going on in the art scene. Claude asked Ginge to pick up a copy when he posted his letter in Exeter.' She turned to look at Daisy. 'He's informed the authorities about your uncle as he doesn't want anyone else suffering as you have.'

'If Uncle is still alive,' Daisy muttered, staring around the room as if he might suddenly appear.

'Huh, it would take more than a bang on the head to kill that one off. And as Claude pointed out, you're such a slight little thing you couldn't possibly have inflicted much harm. I don't know why you're worrying, he's a thoroughly nasty piece of work.'

'But he did take me in and pay for all my parents' expenses,' Daisy said, wanting to be fair.

'He used you, Daisy,' Grace corrected. 'Thank heavens you got away before he …' her voice trailed off as she frowned at Daisy's arm. 'So, do you want to tell me what prompted you to wear your bangle again?'

'When it rolled under the floorboard, I felt the sudden urge to wear it,' she admitted.

'As you've kept it on, I'm guessing you still love Harry.' Daisy nodded, and Grace patted her hand. 'You say he didn't reply to your letters but how many times did you write?'

'Three, but I only sent two,' Daisy admitted. 'The third one's still in my bag.'

'Well, I'm sure you had your reasons.' She hesitated, obviously wondering whether to say any more. 'As you still care for him, wouldn't it be worth writing again?'

'But he never wrote to me so why should I?' Daisy burst out.

'You don't know that he received your letters though, do you?'

'But I posted them, well, the first one anyway. And I checked with Uncle every morning to see if he'd replied.' As she was talking, she remembered what Ginge had said and realised her uncle might well have been lying.

'Look, all I'm saying is don't let pride stand in your way,'

Grace advised. 'Here's some paper,' she added, tearing a sheet from her notebook. 'Write to him now while I get an envelope from the kitchen drawer.'

Daisy stared at the paper. Should she write again? She had her self-respect after all. But then perhaps she should give him another chance, she reasoned, pulling it towards her. But she only got as far as writing *Dear Harry*, when Grace reappeared, holding out an envelope.

'Here you are. Claude's just walking up the path so if you're quick he can post it in Bodmin.' The door opened and Daisy stared at Claude in dismay.

'Well, that's a nice greeting,' he told her. 'I can always go out again.'

'No,' she exclaimed. 'I mean, how soon are you leaving?'

'Now, whilst it's not raining. I just popped in to say I'll eat my potato when I get back.'

'Could you wait just one moment?' Daisy asked. Now she'd made up her mind to communicate with Harry again, she needed to do it straightaway. Without waiting for Claude to reply, she bounded up the stairs and retrieved the letter from her bag. Then quickly penning a note with her new address, c/o of Claude, she folded them both into the envelope.

Back downstairs, Grace snatched it from her and handed it to Claude.

'Post that for Daisy, will you?' she asked, giving him a knowing look. 'And while you're gone, we'll go foraging for something tasty for your supper.'

*

The air was fresh with the smell of wet grass as Daisy followed Grace through the gate. Although it was nice to be outside, she couldn't help wishing Claude was with them and she looked anxiously around for any sign of movement.

'I don't suppose you ever foraged in London, did you?' Grace asked Daisy, taking her arm as if sensing her worry.

'No, and I can't imagine what you'd find round here either,' she replied. 'All I can see is grass and weeds.' Laughing, Grace bent and picked a bunch of green leaves on long stalks.

'Smell,' she ordered, thrusting them under Daisy's nose.

'Yuk,' she grimaced, making them laugh.

'Alexanders, introduced to this country by the Romans who used to pick and eat it on their long journeys to keep up their strength. They make a tasty soup or you can add them to dough when baking bread. We might find some nettles or wild garlic to add to them.'

'I'm not eating nettles, they'll sting my mouth,' Daisy cried, staring at her in horror.

'Baby nettles don't sting,' Grace laughed. 'We use lots of plants in our cooking so know what we're doing. By the time you leave here you'll be bursting with energy and creativity.' They walked on until they reached the darkness of the woods where Daisy became uneasy again.

'I don't suppose you had many trees in Camberwell,' Grace said, breaking into her thoughts.

'Harry and I used to walk in the park and sketch the trees there,' Daisy told her. She closed her eyes, thinking back to those happy days of autumn when they had seemed so close. No, were so close. He wouldn't have asked her to marry him otherwise, would he? Or make her a pretty bangle, she reflected, her hand automatically going to her wrist.

'Memories are bittersweet, aren't they?' Grace murmured and Daisy knew she was thinking about her Maxwell. 'I bet these beautiful trees don't harbour dark musings, just dryads, the nymphs who look after the forest and health of the trees. There's some wild garlic over there, they'll go perfectly with our Alexanders,' she said.

'Something's smelling good.' Claude sniffed the air appreciatively as he entered the cottage.

'We've made Alexander and wild garlic soup,' Grace told him.

'Go nicely with my potato.' He smiled. 'Here you are, Daisy,' he said, handing Daisy her a slip of paper. 'I asked the postmaster for a receipt.'

'But I don't have the money to repay you,' she cried, her hand flying to her mouth.

'I don't want your money, you chump. That's proof your letter is winging its merry way to Harry.'

'Oh, I see, thank you,' Daisy replied. 'I didn't know you could get such a thing.'

'More's the pity,' Grace muttered.

That night her dreams were of Harry. Harry kissing her. Harry on bended knee proposing to her. Harry placing her bracelet so tenderly over her wrist.

Chapter 28

Although Daisy was happy doing domestic chores to pay for her keep, her friends insisted she also embark on her own projects. They gave her paper, pencils and paints and before long, under their guidance, she could see her pictures improving. She really enjoyed sketching the local flora and spent hours perfecting the detail. While she worked, her thoughts frequently turned to Harry but to her disappointment the postman never called.

As the weeks passed, Daisy tried to come to terms with the loss of her beloved parents. Whilst it still hurt to think she'd never see them again, she gained comfort from knowing they were together. The weather grew warmer, the days longer and Daisy spent her time painting by the pool or wandering the woods where, much to Claude's amusement, Daisy sought refuge when he and Grace swam naked. However natural they found it, to her it was unusual and made her feel uncomfortable, so she contented herself with paddling in the shallows when they were working elsewhere. She never strayed too far though, for although as time passed thoughts of her uncle receded, they never totally disappeared.

Then one day, the postman appeared on his bike and

Daisy's heart flipped in anticipation. However, the envelope was addressed to Claude and as he took out the letter and read it, his expression turned grim.

'Just as I thought, Daisy Tucker: you are a weakling,' he said, smiling as he scanned the letter.

'What do you mean?' she frowned.

'Your uncle is alive and literally kicking everyone in sight. I asked Sean to find out and let me know,' he told her. It took a moment for her to realise what that meant.

'I won't be sent to jail,' she cried, relief flooding through her.

'No, so you can relax now,' Grace said. It was good news, of course, but whilst she'd accepted her parents were dead, not knowing why Harry didn't respond gnawed away at her. She even contemplated returning to Camberwell but thought better of it. For one thing she had no money and, for another, if Harry had found someone else, she didn't want to see them together.

Then one morning, as they were preparing for another day sketching and painting, the postman called again. Despite her resolve, Daisy's heart flipped but, once again, the letter was for Claude.

'Fantastic,' he cried, eagerly scanning the page. 'We leave for Lamorna first thing tomorrow.'

'How exciting,' Grace beamed, clapping her hands excitedly. 'Although I've loved being here these past weeks, I'm itching to translate my sketches into pieces of jewellery. And there's nowhere better to draw the May flowers,' she added, turning to Daisy who was watching them apprehensively.

'You mean I can come too?' she asked anxiously, her hopes rising.

'Well, we're not going to leave you here at the mercy of Ted and Toby. They'd eat you for breakfast, my little friend,' Claude told her.

'They are vacating Chy an dowr and will travel by rail to Bodmin. We're to leave Maxwell and the cart at the station for them, then catch the train. No disrespect to the old nag, but it will be much quicker. Of course, we'll have to speak nicely to the guard about stowing our equipment in his van but he'll be putty in your hands when you turn your captivating charm on him, Grace.'

'But trains cost money,' Daisy pointed out.

'This place needs a final clean before we leave so you can earn your fare that way,' Grace told her. 'How will we get from Penzance to Lamorna?' she asked, turning back to Claude.

'They're leaving their pony and jingle with the station master,' he said, consulting the letter. 'And in return for one of your delicious loaves, they'll put pasties in the pantry for our supper.'

'Can't say fairer than that. I'll make two so we can take one with us,' Grace replied.

'And if you're still worrying about money, young Daisy, local businesses will be looking for people to fill their summer vacancies,' Claude told her.

'I'll feel happier when I'm earning,' Daisy admitted. Although it was their ethos to share everything, she didn't wish to take advantage of their good nature. Besides, it was time for her to make a new life for herself.

*

The first thing Daisy saw when they got off the train at Penzance was an island rising up from the shimmering sea.

'That's St Michael's Mount,' Grace told her. 'It's a place of pilgrimage and at low water you can walk across the causeway.'

'I'd love to do that,' Daisy cried excitedly.

'Well, we're staying not far from here. Ah, Claude's found our transport.' Grace smiled as a brown pony hauling a jingle trotted towards them.

'Going to be a tight squeeze.' He jumped down and started to pack everything into the tiny cart. Then, they squashed in alongside and set off along the bustling harbour. This was the start of her new life, Daisy thought, suddenly feeling all bubbly and happy inside. The salt-laden air was refreshing after their sooty train journey and she stared in wonder at the boats pitching up and down on the rolling waves.

'Are they all fishing?' she asked, seeing their nets spread.

'Mostly,' Claude replied. 'But it's an unreliable industry. Years back, when bad weather prevented the fishermen from putting to sea, a Mr Mackenzie established the Newlyn Industrial Class, offering them instruction in enamelling, embroidery and metalwork. Some craftspeople stayed and others moved away to teach at the new authority-funded art schools. Now, their pupils vie to have their work displayed, for some have made their names exhibiting here. So, you see, there's hope for us all.'

'Because this area is renowned for its arts and crafts, people travel from all over the country to show their works,' Grace said.

'Like you,' Daisy replied.

'Yes. And, who knows, if you continue working hard, perhaps you will too.'

Daisy looked at her in astonishment. Impoverished girls like her didn't do things like that.

'It's true, you show great promise,' Claude insisted, misinterpreting her look. 'It just takes perseverance and determination.'

'Both of which you've shown over these past weeks.' Grace smiled.

Warmed by their encouragement, Daisy turned her attention to the esplanade with its granite cottages and vast expanse of sea. They were passing a tall hotel when Daisy thought she glimpsed a figure she recognised. Peering over her shoulder, she flinched when she saw dark eyes staring directly at her.

'It's alright, you're safe now,' Claude said, patting her arm.

'But …' she began, reluctantly turning around.

'Relax, Daisy,' Grace murmured. 'Enjoy this marvellous scenery. It's very different from Camberwell, isn't it?'

'Yes,' Daisy agreed, sneaking a peek behind, but the hotel had been swallowed up by the crowds. There were so many people, perhaps she'd been mistaken.

'Look at that pavilion,' Claude said, gesturing to the ornate building they were passing. 'And now we're approaching the fishing port of Newlyn.' Knowing her friends were trying to put her at ease, Daisy smiled and obediently looked around. Then excitement took over again as on reaching the top of a steep hill she saw the boats in the harbour below bobbing up and down like tiny models. Moments later they were trundling through lush countryside before entering a densely wooded valley filled with lichen-covered trees of greenish grey.

'What a composition,' Grace cried, gesturing to the rich banks of grass speckled with creamy primroses and white anemones.

'Best not stop today,' Claude said. They rode on, passing the milk factory and Clapper Mill with its babbling water turning the wheel.

'The Wink? What a funny name,' Daisy cried, pointing to the tavern sign showing a man wearing a strange hat.

'The kiddlywink was a term for a Cornish alehouse licensed to sell beer or cider. A wink to the landlord signalled you were prepared to pay for something strong and illegal. Afternoon Colonel,' Claude called to the man in tweeds walking towards them.

'Afternoon, Claude, Grace. Good to see you back,' he responded, raising his stick in greeting. 'You've brought a friend, I see.' He smiled politely at Daisy, his piercing eyes giving her a searching look.

'This is Daisy Tucker, Colonel,' Grace told him. 'She's staying with us at Chy an dowr, if that's alright with you?'

'Of course,' he said with a nod, whistling to his dog and continuing on his way.

'Is he really a colonel?' Daisy asked.

'Certainly. Owns most of the land round here. Only way to purchase a property is to get on with him,' Claude told her.

'You mean you're going to buy somewhere?' Grace exclaimed.

'With a garden.' He chuckled. 'Can't think of anything better than growing vegetables in my old age. Let's show Daisy the cove before we settle in to the cottage.' He gestured to a granite building they were passing. They were halfway down the steep hill with buildings dotted on either side, when a bay of the brightest blue topped with crystal waves opened out before them.

'It's beautiful,' Daisy gasped, leaning forward to get a better view. 'But I hadn't expected there to be so many people.' She frowned, staring around.

'Lamorna is quite magical and attracts many artists,' Grace admitted, as they pulled to a halt beside a row of cottages that faced the sea.

'It's a lovely name,' Daisy admitted.

'Cornish for valley by the sea. As you can see it's aptly named, and peaceful now they no longer quarry the granite.' She gestured to the huge riven rocks protruding from the remains of workings high above the cottages. But Daisy had spotted pale shapes recumbent on the rocks.

'What are those women doing?' Daisy frowned.

'Modelling. Look,' Claude said, pointing to the water's edge where easels were set up and artists sat painting.

'But some of them are naked,' she exclaimed, staring aghast.

'As the day they were born,' Claude chuckled. 'The human body is an art form in itself, Daisy. Perhaps you'd like to sit for me one day.'

'No, I would not,' she retorted.

'I didn't mean unclothed, my little cherub. You've really

blossomed these past few weeks and would make a most attractive subject. Think about it.'

'Don't pester, Claude,' Grace chided. 'Come on, let's go and unpack. I'm dying for a cuppa.'

As they trundled back up the hill, Grace called out to an older lady, silver hair escaping the knot on top of her head, while purple cotton skirts flapped around her bare feet. She seemed to stare right through them.

'Sorry,' she muttered, bright cerulean eyes widening in surprise. 'Perplexing conundrum to work out.'

'Wondering who to kill off next, Edna?' Claude asked. 'She's an author,' he added, laughing at Daisy's horrified expression.

The slow climb gave Daisy time to peer through the windows, where she saw figures hunched over easels or benches, working on their creations. To think she was going to be part of all this, she thought, excitement fizzing inside her like sparkling wine. Already her fingers itched to sketch the pink flowers she'd spotted sprouting from the rocks.

'Welcome to Chy an dowr, or house by the water,' Grace announced, gesturing to the cottage they'd passed earlier. It stood sideways on to the road and was almost surrounded by woodland. With its ivy-clad walls, four windows and door in the middle, it looked like something out of a story book.

'Come on,' Grace said, jumping down. 'It's so hot I'm tempted to cool off in the stream.' She gestured towards the trees where the sound of rushing water could be heard.

'I'll see to Penny here and then take our equipment into the studio,' Claude told them.

Grace opened the cottage door, which led straight into a beamed living room. It was cool and bright with an ingle-nook and mismatch of comfy chairs to one side. On the other was a long table with upright chairs in differing styles. Bright-yellow curtains adorned the windows while a red rug covered the floor. The fact that nothing matched lent it a cosy charm.

'The kitchen's through here,' Grace said, indicating a narrow galley, just wide enough to house a couple of cupboards, range and sink. 'I don't know about you but I'm starving,' she added, reaching into the pantry and pulling out a plate of golden pastries. 'Good old Toby. Nobody makes pasties like he does.'

'What can I do to help?' Daisy asked, her stomach rumbling at the sight of the food.

'This place isn't big enough for more than one person to work in so why don't you take your things up to your room. The one to the left of the stairs is small but overlooks the stream and woods.'

The little room had a low ceiling and a window that had the most glorious views out over the wooded valley. The bed looked comfortable, its cover matching the soft green curtains. There was a tiny cupboard for her clothes and a washstand with a ewer on top. It had a welcoming feel, Daisy thought, thankfully shrugging off the velvet cloak she'd been obliged to wear due to the lack of space. She unpacked, thinking it was the nicest room she'd ever occupied.

Later, as they sat sipping tea and munching pasties in contented silence, Daisy thought they'd have an early night after their journey, but she couldn't have been more wrong. They'd just finished eating when the door burst open and a babble of excited people, all dressed in brightly coloured clothes, pressed into the room. She was introduced to artists, jewellers, writers and potters. Everyone was friendly, wine was proffered in an assortment of drinking vessels and within moments a party was underway. Claude was in his element, circling the room, topping up everyone's glass while Grace caught up with the local news.

'You don't seem to have a drink,' a soft voice said.

'I'm fine, thanks,' she told the man, for in truth she was enjoying herself. She remembered being introduced to him earlier but couldn't remember his name.

'Well, Daisy Tucker, why don't you tell me about yourself,' he invited, ebony eyes gazing intently at her as if seeing into the depth of her soul.

Chapter 29

Daisy woke to the sound of tinkling water and it was some moments before she remembered where she was. She lay back against her pillow, thinking back over the impromptu party the previous evening. The dark wavy-haired man called Cadan had been attentive, although she'd found the way he'd looked at her with those fathomless eyes disconcerting. Or perhaps that was the way the small glass of wine Claude had persuaded her to have made her feel.

When the clamour of the party had become too much, Cadan had suggested they take a walk in the garden. It was cool under the canopy of trees that bordered the stream where bluebells spread out like a velvet carpet.

Daisy had felt as if she was in a fairy glade and couldn't wait to draw them, but her first priority was securing a job.

Carefully she dressed in the white blouse and tailored skirt that had been a gift from Joy. As she pinned up her hair, her bangle gleamed in the sunlight and, having given up expecting to hear from Harry, she was tempted to remove it for good. Then she told herself it was time to stop thinking with her heart and be practical. The silver added the finishing touch to her outfit and it was important she make a good impression today.

'You and Cadan seemed to hit it off last night,' Claude said, as they sat eating toast spread with golden honey.

'He showed me the campion and ferns and told me the flowers growing in the cliffs were called thrift, or sea pinks because of their colour.'

'Makes a change from etchings.' Claude smiled.

'He also told me that Susan, who runs the boarding house up the hill, is seeking help and thought I might be suitable,' Daisy told him, ignoring his remark.

'It's unusual for Cadan to pass comment like that,' Grace mused.

'Well, he is a Cornish Charmer,' Claude added, quirking a brow. 'Sees right into people's souls. Must have seen some quality in you, Daisy.'

'From the way he was staring at my bangle, I think he was more interested in that. Besides, it was an impromptu party so I'll probably not see him again.'

'Don't you believe it. The artists here are a sociable lot and throw parties most nights,' Claude chuckled.

'Really?' asked Daisy, staring at him in surprise.

'Life in Lamorna is lively, to say the least.'

'Well, I'm off to see about this job,' Daisy replied. The sooner she could pay her way, the better she'd feel.

'You're looking very smart; I'm sure you'll be snapped up. Be a love and call into Ma Brown's for some milk on the way back, will you?' Grace suggested, pointing to a pail with a hinged lid by the door.

'Good luck. We'll be in the studio if you need us,' Claude told her.

Although the hour was early, it was already warm and Daisy could smell the tang of the sea as she climbed towards the boarding house. Walking briskly up the driveway, she saw the cottage was much larger than the one they were staying in, the granite walls completely covered in ivy. The flowers in the borders were a riot of colour but needed weeding, the lawn mowing. Ringing the bell, she was dismayed to hear a scream followed by a shrill voice. Perhaps she shouldn't have arrived unannounced, she thought, gripping the handle of her pail tighter.

'Yes?' The woman who answered the door was clearly harassed but it was the overt stare of the sandy-haired young lad that caused her to frown.

'Excuse me …' she began.

'What's your name?' the boy asked, his green eyes boring into her.

'Daisy. What's yours?' she asked him.

'Simon. How old are you?'

'Now Simon, that's rude,' the woman chided. 'Sorry, he's a bit—'

'I'm twelve,' the boy butted in and, as he inched closer, Daisy saw he was taller than she'd first thought. 'Well, how old are you?' he repeated.

'I'm seventeen,' Daisy replied.

'Why are you here?'

'You know it's rude to ask so many questions, Simon,' the woman chided, then turned back to Daisy. 'Please come in. Simon gets put out when a stranger comes to the door. Strange, I know, when this is a guest house, but he's as good as gold once he gets to know you. I'm Susan, by the way.'

'Come on, I'll find you a biscuit,' the boy told Daisy, running down the hallway.

'Well, I never,' Susan murmured, blinking at Daisy in surprise. 'He's taken to you already.'

Placing the milk container beside the step, she followed them into a bright airy room where the homely smell of cooking hung in the air.

'Goodness, you've been busy already,' Daisy exclaimed, her eyes widening when she saw the pies cooling on the side.

'Biscuit,' Simon said, shaking a tin in front of Daisy.

'Thank you, Simon.' Daisy smiled, selecting one of the homemade cookies.

'You have to sit down while you eat it,' he told her. Daisy looked at Susan who smiled apologetically, and pulled out a chair from beneath the farmhouse table. Under Simon's unwavering gaze, she took a bite.

'That's the tastiest biscuit I've ever eaten,' she told Simon. He nodded gravely.

'The tea's freshly brewed,' Susan said, pushing a steaming mug across the table towards her. 'Perhaps you'd like to tell me why you called?' she asked, sinking thankfully into a chair opposite.

'I'm seeking work and someone said you may have a vacancy.'

'Who might that be?' the woman asked, green eyes so similar to her son's, staring at Daisy curiously.

'Cadan. I'm staying in the cove with Claude and Grace.'

'I like Claude; he's funny,' Simon remarked, nodding in his serious little way.

'If Cadan sent you then you must be alright,' Susan said. 'I've five bedrooms, usually let out for a week or fortnight, although some of the artists stay longer. I'm looking for someone reliable to clean, cook and generally help …'

'I do the man's work,' Simon butted in, puffing out his chest importantly. 'I don't have a father you see,' he stated, staring at her candidly.

'Simon is a great help. I don't know what I'd do without him,' Susan said, getting quickly to her feet. 'If you've finished your tea why don't I show you around?'

'That's my job,' Simon declared, jumping to his feet. 'Come on.'

Daisy looked enquiringly at Susan, who nodded.

'This is where people sit and chat,' he said, pushing open the door to a room with comfy chairs and settees set around a large stone fireplace. The furnishings were old, but everywhere was spotless. 'Through there is the bathroom. We were one of the first to get an indoor privy,' he said proudly.

'The colonel thought it necessary if we wanted to be successful,' Susan explained. 'I rent the property from him you see.'

'That's the glasshouse where we grow vegetables,' Simon said, pointing through the window that overlooked the back garden. 'Come on, I'll show you the bedrooms. Those Fairings are done,' he told his mother.

'Ginger biscuits, ready to welcome our guests,' Susan explained, seeing Daisy's puzzled expression.

'The first biddy's coming tomorrow,' Simon told her, leading the way up the stairs. The rooms were slightly shabby yet clean, and exuded a homely feel. 'That's it.'

Daisy grinned at Simon's energy as he bounded back down the stairs.

'She'll do,' he announced to his mother.

'Will she now?' Susan replied, turning to Daisy. 'Usually I would ask for references but you've obviously won Simon's approval, which is important. I can't pay much, but there's vegetables from the garden along with leftovers to take home.'

'And you can have lunch with me,' Simon told her.

Although the money wasn't as much as she used to earn, it was enough to pay her board and if she provided fresh produce and leftovers to supplement their meals, Claude and Grace would be pleased.

'When would you like me to start?' she asked.

'Tomorrow? Simon, put the biscuit tin back in the pantry please,' she said, showing Daisy down the hallway. 'Simon's a good lad but a bit slow, if you get my meaning. He needs routine or he throws tantrums. I hope that won't put you off?' she asked, a frown lining her forehead. 'His father couldn't cope and left when he was very young so it's just the two of us. Plus, a house full of summer guests, of course.'

'I think Simon's lovely,' Daisy assured her. 'See you first thing tomorrow,' she added, retrieving her bucket and making her way back down the path.

The days passed quickly with Daisy working long hours at the boarding house. But the atmosphere was congenial as the guests enjoyed their holidays beside the sea. Simon greeted her as soon as she arrived, then followed her around like a puppy. As anything out of his routine unsettled him, Daisy tried to ensure she carried out her tasks in the same order each day. He was a keen watcher of people and some of his observations had her in stitches.

'The colonel wants to kiss my mother,' Simon told her one morning.

'Oh?' Daisy murmured, not sure she should encourage such talk.

'Yes. When he called yesterday, she gave him a cake to take home and he said, I could kiss you, Susan.'

'I see,' Daisy replied, hiding her smile as she bent to tuck in the sheet of the bed she was making. As was his way, he took everything literally, she thought, making her way to the next room. It had surprised her that there were no locks on the doors, but Susan had assured her that it was unnecessary as all the guests were honest.

'Then he asked Mother how you were doing,' Simon continued, following after her. 'She said you did the work of three men. I said that was plain daft cos anyone can see you're a woman,' he snorted. 'Don't know why they laughed.'

'I hope Simon's not getting in your way,' Susan said, when she went down to the kitchen to help serve luncheon. The aroma of cooking meat wafting up the stairs had made her hungry. Susan's food was superb and her guests were eagerly waiting in the dining room.

'Not at all, he's good company,' she replied truthfully.

Susan smiled. 'If you could mash the tatties, I'll dish up the stew. Even though it's hot, the guests do like a nourishing meal. By the way, as it's your day off tomorrow, I've prepared a basket of produce and you can take the remains of the stew to go with them; I know Claude and Grace are busy with their projects.'

'They're both working long hours in the studio.'

'Everyone's preparing for the exhibition in Newlyn. Nancy Noble's sent me a letter requesting a room for the rest of the season. She does the most exquisite embroidery to exhibit. I've had to move Simon in with me in order to accommodate her, but it's all money in the pot.'

'I'm enjoying talking to the guests,' Daisy replied, loading plates onto a tray. 'They have some fascinating stories to tell.'

Daisy hummed happily as she walked home in the late afternoon sunshine. At last she had money in her pocket and a purpose in life. But as she was admiring the beautiful blue of the bay in front of her, she felt a prickle creeping up her spine.

Someone was watching her.

Chapter 30

Daisy spun round, but there was no one there. Thinking she must be overtired after working so hard, she let herself into the cottage where the silence told her Claude and Grace were still working. Knowing better than to disturb them, Daisy put the stew on a gentle heat, then began preparing the vegetables.

Deciding to make the most of the sunshine, she changed into a lighter top, snatched up the pad she'd bought with part of her first week's wages and took herself out into the garden. Absorbed in drawing the blue blooms that grew on the upper slopes, she jumped as a shadow loomed over her.

'Not bad,' Claude commented. 'Agapanthus, or Lily of the Nile, are difficult to replicate. Now if you just—'

'Leave the poor girl alone,' Grace said, stretching as she came out of the studio. She inhaled deeply. 'Ah, the fragrance of honeysuckle, and is that stew I can smell cooking?'

'Yes, Susan sent it. I just need to cook the vegetables,' she said, snapping her pad shut and jumping to her feet.

'So, how's your job going?' Grace asked, following her indoors.

'Great, although cleaning the bathroom's a bit …' Daisy

sniffed. 'Still, Susan's easy to work for, the guests are friendly and Simon makes me laugh with his tales.'

'But it's not stimulating,' Claude observed, watching as Daisy moved pots and pans around on the hob.

She shrugged. 'Anyway, it's my day off tomorrow, so I shall sit on the beach and seek inspiration.'

'I'll come with you,' Claude offered. 'I've a brilliant idea and you're just the person to assist,' he added, looking at her hopefully.

'I'm not posing nude,' Daisy warned, narrowing her eyes.

'Of course not,' he laughed

'I know that look, Claude,' Grace said, shaking her finger at him.

'When inspiration strikes.' He shrugged. 'An actress offered the loan of a rather sensational costume that would suit you a treat, Daisy. It would be the perfect subject for my exhibition piece, so what do you say?' he asked, staring at her hopefully.

'Let me see this outfit first,' Daisy replied cautiously. It wasn't that she didn't trust Claude but that twitch of his lips signalled he was up to something.

Daisy adjusted the lace parasol to shade her eyes from the fierce rays of the midday sun. Dressed in a pink and white striped blouse and matching flounced skirt, red ribbons at the neck and waist, she was uncomfortably hot and had cramp in her calf. She'd been perched on this rock for hours, listening to the gulls screeching and watching the white-tipped waves coming in, and the novelty had worn off.

'Another minute and I'll be finished,' Claude called, distracting her from her thoughts. He was perched on his stool, sketching furiously, and Daisy was dying to see what he'd done. Then she intended going for a long walk to stretch her legs before they seized up.

'You've captured Daisy's expression perfectly. It's grand to see you've returned to portraiture, my friend.' Recognising the Cornish burr, Daisy turned and saw Cadan admiring Claude's work on the easel. She hadn't seen him since the night she'd arrived in Lamorna and wanted to thank him for recommending the job at the boarding house.

'Might as well finish now that you've moved,' Claude growled.

Daisy smiled and jumped down beside them. 'Thank heavens, I felt like a statue up there. Oh, is that really me?' she exclaimed, staring at the picture in surprise. 'I look all ... well, grown-up.'

'Haven't I been saying you've blossomed these past few months,' Claude laughed.

'The epitome of the Edwardian Lady,' Cadan nodded. 'And your silver bangle sits well on that outfit.'

'It might look pretty; I've been standing still for so long, it's sticking to my body,' she groaned.

'Talking of standing, I was heading to the menhir if you fancy a walk,' Cadan suggested. As he stared at her, Daisy felt a tremor pulse through her body.

'Good idea, Daisy,' Claude agreed. 'I've enough detail to work on for today.'

'I'll go and change,' Daisy said. 'It wouldn't do to get these fine clothes dirty.'

'You can brush off any dust later; it's much too hot to go up the hill and back again.'

'There'll be more shade on the coast path,' Cadan told her.

'I'll see you both later. There's a party at Edna's this evening; she wants to celebrate getting together with Talan.'

'But she's …' Daisy stopped, her hand flying to her mouth.

'You're never too old, if that's what you were going to say,' Claude replied, raising his brow suggestively. 'Must be something in the air; even Grace is taking a day off to go *somewhere with someone*, as she put it, and she never lets anything get in the way of her work.'

'I was only suggesting a walk,' Cadan said quickly.

'Of course, and I'd love to come with you to this menhir, whatever it is,' Daisy replied. 'But I'm leaving this with you,' she told Claude, placing the parasol beside his stool.

As they strolled across the beach to the path that led up the side of the cliff, Daisy tried to avert her eyes from all the nude models in their various poses.

'What possesses them?' she asked.

'Money,' Cadan replied. 'There's not much work around here in the winter so they have to grab every opportunity.'

'Oh, I understand now,' Daisy said, nodding. While she wouldn't do that herself, being able to pay her way in life was important.

They climbed in companionable silence, listening to the waves pounding the cliffs below and inhaling the briny air.

'I feel like a bird,' Daisy said, throwing her arms wide.

'Wouldn't try flying off the cliff if I were you,' Cadan replied, laughing at her antics.

'I'll have to make do with sketching these then. Do you know what they are?' she asked, taking the little pad and pencil from her bag and kneeling down beside some thistle-like plants with blue flowers.

'The locals call them blue buttons. They can be boiled up and used to ease respiratory ailments.'

Carefully she noted his comments alongside her drawing. 'And what about those white ones?'

'Chamomile, which not only smell gorgeous when trodden on, but make a poultice for wounds and skin complaints. The leaves can be dried and used to make a soothing tea.'

'Wouldn't mind a cup of any tea right now,' she replied, quickly sketching the outlines and jotting down their uses. 'I do love all their funny names and the characteristics associated with them.'

'So how are you liking life in Lamorna?' he asked as they wandered on.

'Busy, but I love working at the boarding house; thank you for suggesting it. Susan is easy to work for and Simon's a love. He follows me around and tells me what everyone's been doing. I don't think that boy misses anything.'

'I knew you'd be on the same wavelength,' Cadan said, smiling knowingly. 'Your eyes have lost that haunted look they had when I first met you, and yet …' he paused as if considering his words. 'I feel that deep within your soul lies something that's still unresolved.'

'I didn't know I'd had a haunted look.' Daisy frowned, her hand unconsciously going to her arm.

'If I'm not mistaken, it has something to do with that

bangle,' he said, ignoring her comment. 'May I?' he asked, gently catching hold of her hand and running his fingers along the pattern. As heat seared up her arm, Daisy stared at him in surprise.

'He often thinks of you, you know?' Cadan murmured softly.

'What makes you say that?' she gasped, snatching her hand away. 'You don't even know who gave this to me.'

He gave another little smile then turned away.

'See that rock pool down there?' he said after a moment. 'When the tide goes out the fish are trapped until the water floods back in. They have to wait until the time is right.'

'Are you trying to tell me something?' Daisy asked, feeling she'd somehow missed the point.

'It's about biding your time. You'll understand one day,' he told her.

Further along their walk Daisy noticed bustling activity ahead.

'What are those people doing with the donkeys?' she asked.

'Harvesting potatoes. The narrow plots are known as quillets and those red fuchsia hedges protect the crops from the wind.'

'Fascinating. Claude mentioned something similar called plats when I was in Devonshire.'

'What an education you're getting. Come on, while we walk you can tell me about how you came to be here.'

Daisy explained the events leading to her arrival in Cornwall, and, when pangs of pain made her falter, he patted her arm in sympathy.

'Sorry, I thought I'd come to terms with the accident.' She sighed, swallowing hard.

'One day you'll find yourself remembering the happy times. Do you have any pictures of your parents?' Cadan asked, staring intently at her.

'A couple of sketches. Why?' she asked, the turn of conversation taking her by surprise.

'I'd be interested to look at them. Now, this is what we've come to see,' he said, gesturing to a strange stone almost hidden in a hedgerow. 'Look around and you'll see many more.'

'What are they doing here?' she asked, astonished to see stones of varying heights dotted around the open fields.

'They're the Menhir, the bodies of raiding Viking warriors who were turned to stone by the witch of Kemyel. But as she leapt back over the wall to her cottage, the first rays of morning sun froze her figure. That twisted thorn tree is supposed to be her,' he said, pointing ahead.

'Yea right, and I'm a monkey's uncle, as my mother used to say,' she snorted, then felt another pang.

'Come on, the sun's setting; it's time we were heading back. I don't know about you, but I'm hungry.'

'Surprisingly, even after all that claptrap you've been telling me, I am.'

'I'll have you know I stick to facts, young lady.'

'And witches are fact, are they?' she scoffed.

'There are many different kinds,' he told her. Seeing her incredulous look, he shook his head sadly and started walking.

By the time they'd returned to the beach, people were heading towards the large cottage at the bottom of the hill.

'Ah, Edna's party,' Cadan said. As they drew nearer, they were swept up in the crush surging inside.

'Come in, darlings,' Edna called. She was dressed in her customary purple, this time with a matching scarf swathed around her head. 'Help yourselves to refreshments through there,' she said, before turning back to gaze adoringly at the curly-haired man beside her.

'The new paramour,' Cadan whispered.

'Well, I hope they'll be very happy together.'

'They will, at least for the next few weeks. Then, it will probably be all change again. Must be something in the water.' He grinned, gesturing at the guests who were milling around with glasses full of amber liquid. 'Don't worry, it's not compulsory,' he added, chuckling at her shocked expression.

'Goodness, I thought writers were supposed to be poor,' Daisy exclaimed, taking in the large room with its inglenook fireplace and luxurious furnishings.

'Edna's very successful. Readers love her unique stories, which manage to combine grisly murders with a quirky sense of humour,' Cadan murmured, reaching out to steady her as yet more people pressed into them. 'Let's go and help ourselves to some food.'

Before they'd reached the table where a succulent-looking ham, cheeses and salads were laid out, they heard Claude's voice calling to them.

'Daisy, come and meet Sybella. She's the actress who kindly loaned me that outfit,' he explained, gesturing to her pink and white attire.

'Hello Sybella, how are you?' Cadan asked the woman, who tossed her blonde curls.

'Glad to be here, darling. Last night's performance had to be seen to be believed. We're playing at the Pavilion in Penzance and well ...' she shrugged, her tinkling laugh rising above the clinking of the glasses. 'You look ravishing in that,' she said, turning to Daisy. 'It sets off those eyes a treat.'

'Thank you; I've been sitting for Claude,' she explained.

'I'm sure you make the perfect model,' Sybella purred. 'Is this for the exhibition?' she asked Claude.

'Certainly is. Thought I'd call it *Portrait of an Edwardian Lady*.'

'That's not very inspiring, Claude. What's the setting?'

'Daisy's been perched on a rock and ...' Claude began.

'Oh, no darling, that will never do. That's what all those nude painters are doing. You need to be different, create a background that stands out. With Daisy's profile she should be standing to show her and that outfit off to best advantage. Are you using the parasol?' she asked. Daisy nodded.

'Then you must use the cliffs as your backdrop, Claude. Have Daisy peering pensively out to sea in the hope of catching sight of her paramour approaching in his boat.'

'You're a genius, Sybella,' Claude exclaimed, slapping his thigh.

'I know, darling; it's a fault of mine,' she trilled. 'And, if I might make one other tiny suggestion?'

'Of course,' he agreed.

'Have Daisy wear this ensemble around the cove all summer. People will notice and when the exhibition shows they'll recognise Daisy and the location. You'll be halfway to being famous, Claude – well, more famous than you already are, of course,' she amended, fluttering her eyelashes at him.

'But I thought I was only sitting for Claude the once, then I was going to return your outfit,' she told the woman.

'Keep it, darling. It suits you far better than it ever did me, and the wardrobe mistress will never notice.' She laughed. 'Just promise to help Claude regain the recognition he once had and deserves to … oops, have I made a booboo, darling?' she asked, as Claude reddened and began to cough.

'Excuse us, we were about to choose something from this delectable spread,' Cadan told them, taking Daisy's arm and steering her towards the table.

'What was that about?' Daisy asked as, plates in hand, they made their way out to the garden.

'It's not my story to tell Daisy. I'm sure Claude will enlighten you when he's ready. Now, let's enjoy our food.' He bit into his bread and chewed thoughtfully. 'We all have secrets or things we shy away from, don't we?' he murmured, and once again Daisy felt the full force of his gaze.

That night, as she lay in bed thinking back over her day, Daisy realised that, in the excitement of the evening, she'd forgotten to show Cadan her pictures. She'd have them ready when he called to take her to the Merry Maidens for the summer solstice celebrations, although, she wouldn't bother with the one of Harry. Even if, as Cadan suggested, he'd been thinking of her, he hadn't bothered writing, had he? Automatically her hand went to the cool silver of her bangle and, to her dismay, she felt hot tears welling.

Chapter 31

The next day, having promised Claude she'd pose for him again that evening, Daisy hurried towards the guest house, only to meet Grace coming in the opposite direction.

'Isn't it a simply gorgeous day?' she gushed, waving one hand around whilst the other clutched her travelling bag.

'Er yes,' Daisy replied, staring at her friend in surprise. She was looking radiant, and, unusually for Grace, somewhat dishevelled. 'Where've you been?' she asked. To her surprise, the woman tapped the side of her nose and giggled like a naughty schoolgirl.

'Tell you when the time's right. Don't want to put a hex on anything.' Before Daisy could reply, she hurried on her way, leaving Daisy staring after her.

'Where've you been?' Simon shouted, unwittingly echoing her words to Grace moments earlier. Daisy inhaled deeply taking in the delicious smell of baking mixed with the aroma of meat simmering on the hob.

'That's no way to greet Daisy,' Susan chided. 'I told you she was having a day off, didn't I?'

'Can't have a day off,' he retorted.

'Sorry, Simon, I should have said I wouldn't be here,' Daisy replied, silently reproaching herself for forgetting the boy needed any change in routine explained to him. 'I do have something for you though.'

'Oh?' he asked, staring curiously at the bag Daisy held out to him. 'What is it?'

'Why don't you open it and find out?' Susan suggested. 'Cuppa before we start?'

'I'll make it,' Daisy said, seeing how tired the woman was looking.

'Yum, sausage roll. I love sausage rolls. I'll enjoy it with my cup of tea,' he announced, his serious adult manner making them laugh as he settled himself onto a chair.

As was their custom, they sipped their drinks while catching up on what had happened at the guest house during Daisy's absence. And, as usual, it was Simon who filled in details of the times everyone had arrived and departed.

'Yesterday afternoon, Miss Noble rang the bell at two thirty,' he announced. 'She was thirty minutes late but she did say sorry.'

'That's the lady I told you about,' Susan added. 'She likes to spend her days sitting by the window with her embroidery, but doesn't mind us cleaning the room around her. Perhaps you'd like to start there?'

'I'll show you the way,' Simon volunteered, jumping to his feet. While Daisy grabbed her cleaning things, he folded the empty paper bag neatly. 'Ready,' he called, and she followed him up the stairs then waited while he knocked on the door.

'Come in,' a pleasant voice called.

'Morning, Miss Noble. This is Daisy and she's come to make your bed.'

'Hello, Simon. Nice to meet you, Daisy,' the woman replied, looking up from her stitching. Just as Susan had said, she was sitting in front of the wide bay window, a length of cloth on her lap.

'Will it disturb you if I clean while you work, Miss Noble?' Daisy asked politely.

'Not at all, and please, call me Nancy. Miss Noble makes me feel old, although I probably look ancient to you, young man, don't I?' she asked turning to Simon.

'Yes,' he said with a nod, studying her closely. 'You've got a nice face but it crinkles when you smile,' he told her.

Daisy held her breath, hoping the woman wouldn't be offended by his candour. To her relief Nancy laughed, and Daisy realised she was probably about the same age as Claude.

'Well, crinkles sound better than wrinkles. Now, if you look in that tin on the dressing table, you might just find a mint humbug.' As Simon scuttled across the room, Nancy gestured at the garden beyond. 'It's so inspirational here.'

'What are you making, if you don't mind my asking?'

'I'm embroidering a bedspread to show at the exhibition in Newlyn at the end of the summer. I'm trying to replicate those irises in the flowerbeds in the Arts and Crafts style. Now, of course, I can look at your amethyst eyes. They really are quite remarkable.'

'Thank you,' Daisy replied, flushing as the woman's words catapulted her back to life at the Fun Factory and the American costumier.

'I did the drawings last time I was here, then spent the winter working out the design. It was challenging to say the least, for you have to consider how it will look in the larger context. How big is the room? The bed? How large should the spread be? How many flowers and leaves to each pattern? How many pattern repeats will give a pleasing effect? You get my meaning?'

'It sounds complicated,' Daisy frowned.

'Not really. But living in a town, I don't get to see blooms like these, so I use Grandmother's pendant for reference.' Nancy gave a sad little smile. 'She died last year and I want this bedspread to be a tribute to her,' she added, pointing to the table beside her where a large purple-blue stone, shaped like the flower, glinted in the sunlight.

'That's beautiful,' Daisy enthused. 'As are the vibrant colours of your silks.'

'Why, thank you, my dear.'

'Is it worth a lot?' Simon asked, munching on his sweet as he picked up the locket and studied it.

'To me it's priceless,' Nancy replied, not in the least put out by his question.

'Right, young man, it's time we cleaned Miss Noble's room so she can get on with her embroidery,' Daisy told him. 'Then we've the others to do.'

'There's another guest coming this afternoon. We'll have to see if she's late as well.' Daisy and Nancy exchanged knowing smiles.

Daisy had just cleaned up the kitchen after luncheon, when the doorbell rang.

'Be a love and get that, will you?' Susan asked, looking up from the cake she was icing.

'That's my job,' Simon announced. 'At least this one's on time,' he added, squinting at the clock on the wall. He ran down the hallway and opened the door. 'Wait there,' he commanded before closing it and scuttling back to them.

'Well, where is she? Didn't you ask her in?' Susan asked, wiping her hands on the tea towel.

'No,' he growled. 'Didn't like her. She can go straight back home.'

'I'll go and greet her,' Daisy said, quickly leaving Susan to explain to a sullen Simon that the lady was a guest. It was strange, though, for she'd never seen the boy behave like that before.

The bell sounded again and Daisy hurriedly opened the door. Before she could say anything, a woman of about twenty-five, her hair a riot of red-gold curls, stepped inside and dumped her bags on the carpet.

'Little blighter, needs to learn some manners. Coo, it's hot out there; I could murder a cuppa.'

'I'll take you through to the lounge then, er?' Daisy quirked her brow enquiringly.

'Tulla. 'Ere, don't tell me you're from London too?'

'Camberwell,' Daisy replied, smiling at the familiar tones.

'Well, stone me,' the woman exclaimed. 'I'm just down the road in Bermondsey.'

'Welcome to our guest house, Tulla. My name is Susan and I'm the proprietor. I've set the kettle to boil so, if you'd like to follow me, I'll show you to your room,' Susan said, appearing beside them.

'Don't know why you're smiling,' Simon mumbled, when Daisy walked back into the kitchen. 'She's horrid.'

'We must be nice to all the guests,' Daisy told him, ignoring his comment as she spooned fresh leaves into the pot.

'Don't see why,' he glared.

'Because their money pays our bills,' Susan replied, appearing in the doorway. 'Now Simon, go and pick some tomatoes from the glasshouse for our tea. The lettuce and radishes are ready too,' she told him, holding out a basket.

'No doubt you've got an exciting evening planned?' Susan asked Daisy.

'Claude wants me to pose for him. Not in the nude,' Daisy added quickly, seeing her shocked look. 'He sketched me yesterday but his friend reckoned the composition wasn't right for the exhibition.'

'Everyone around here seems to be working on something for that. Goodness that was quick, Simon.' She smiled as the boy staggered into the room, his basket overflowing. 'Take some home for your tea, Daisy.'

As Daisy put some of the fresh produce into her bag, Simon turned to her.

'You are coming back tomorrow, aren't you?'

'Of course.'

'Good, cos I don't trust her,' he snorted, jerking his head towards the staircase.

'Hello again.' Tulla smiled.

'I'll take your tea through to the lounge,' Susan said, picking up a tray.

'Ta. Is there any night life round here?' Tulla asked.

'The artists hold parties most nights,' Daisy told her. The woman's eyes lit up. 'But tonight, I'm posing for Claude on the beach.'

'Yea? Might walk down that way meself later,' Tulla said, following Susan through to the other room. Daisy nodded then turned to see Simon scowling.

'See you tomorrow,' she told him, as, placing her basket of produce over her arm, she let herself outside.

The sun was shining, the air gloriously warm, and Daisy was just thinking she'd enjoy an hour's drawing in the garden, when she again felt the sensation of being watched. Yet when she spun around, the road rising to the tavern was empty. Shrugging, she headed towards the cottage, telling herself she was getting as fanciful as Simon.

'You're nice and early.' Claude smiled, opening the gate and taking her basket. 'Salad for tea, we are spoilt these days. I'm looking forward to when I can plant my own. Perhaps this new picture will make my fortune and I can move somewhere with a suitably large plot,' he said, staring round the garden where the plants ran wild. 'Grace is busy in the studio making up for lost time, so I thought we could go straight down to the cove and make a start.'

'I'd better go and change then,' she replied. He looked so eager she didn't have the heart to disappoint him.

Dressed in her candy-striped outfit, parasol in hand, Daisy followed Claude down to the beach where he stared thoughtfully around. As usual, there were artists at their easels, models perched on rocks whilst others combed the shore for driftwood and sea glass to use in their creations.

'Over there, I think,' he told her. 'Sybella's right, you peering pensively out to sea would make a more interesting picture, so if you wouldn't mind,' he added, gesturing to the disused pier. By the time she'd walked to the end, Claude had already set up his easel and placed his jacket on the back of his folding chair.

'Like this?' Daisy called, holding up her parasol with one hand while gazing out under the other.

'Perfect. Hold that pose. I'll be as quick as I can.'

'Good, because I'm starving,' she called.

'Don't move,' he ordered.

Daisy sighed; it was going to be a long evening.

She stared out at the rolling waves for seemingly ages, then, just when she thought rigor mortis was setting in, she heard someone talking to Claude.

'Hey, that looks just like her.' Recognising Tulla's voice, Daisy turned, her eyes widening in astonishment. For there she was, red-gold curls, leaning against Claude's shoulder as she studied his work. He seemed to have forgotten Daisy, and, shivering now the sun was going down, she marched back along the pier towards them.

'Sorry, Daisy, I should have told you I'd finished for today,' Claude murmured, when she reached them.

'I was just telling Claude how good his work is.' Tulla smiled, straightening up. She was looking so pleased with herself that Daisy wondered what Claude had said to her. 'And if you ever want a proper model, I'd be happy to pose for you. I'm sure you'll agree, I have just the figure for it and I wouldn't charge as much as some.' She smirked, running her hands over her shapely hips. But Claude was looking distracted as he shrugged his jacket back on.

There was a collective gasp as the first ray of crimson peeped above the horizon, shining on the stone circle known as the Merry Maidens. It was the summer solstice, and Daisy and Cadan had joined with wayfarers and other artists in keeping vigil overnight to greet the rising sun.

'This is the time to draw strength and energy from the Sol Invicta,' Cadan told her. 'Focus on your outgoing energies and direct your desires to the universe.'

'Mother used to say if you bathed in the dew of the new day you would see who you were going to marry,' Daisy whispered, suddenly aware the others were standing in silence.

'Just close your eyes and wish,' he urged. Glancing around, Daisy saw most people were either gazing fixedly at the rising sun or had their eyes tightly shut. Even Claude and Grace looked spellbound, so perhaps there was something in it, she thought, lowering her lids. Immediately she saw bright cornflower eyes and that cheeky grin. Then his expression changed to one of pleading, his hand beckoning her.

'Oh,' Daisy gasped, her eyes flying open. Feeling a warmth against her wrist, she glanced down at the silver bangle which gleamed gold in the shafts of sunlight. Cadan moved closer and she saw him smiling knowingly.

'Tell me again what these stones are called and how many there are?' she asked quickly,

'Dans Meyn or Merry Maidens. They represent the nine-teen local girls who, having broken the rules of the Sabbath by dancing, were turned to stone. Come on,' he added, as the pure notes of a flute rose on the morning air and everyone held hands and encircled the stones. The circle began to move, slowly at first then gathering pace until Daisy was laughing and out of breath. As quickly as it had started, the music stopped, the gathering came to a halt and the disparate groups of people began to disperse.

'Until tonight,' someone called.

'We'll build the biggest bonfire in Cornwall.' This was greeted with a cheer and Cadan turned to Daisy.

'You'll come?' he asked, smiling when she nodded.

'Wouldn't miss it for the world.'

'Work beckons, we'd better be getting back.'

'What is it you do exactly?' Daisy asked, as they joined the throng leaving the field.

'I suppose you could say my job is to help people.'

'You're a doctor?' she exclaimed, thinking his gentle manner would make him a fine one.

'Not exactly, although I am drawn to those who need me.'

As they made their way back through the village, something struck Daisy.

'It's strange how all the artists get together socially, yet work by themselves.'

'That's because they're competitive and fiercely guard their creations. Don't forget everyone's working towards the exhibition. Shall we look at your pictures?' he asked as they reached Chy an dowr.

'I've got them out ready,' she told him, leading the way inside. 'Although, I warn you, they're a bit amateurish.' She watched nervously as Cadan studied the one of her father, the sight of his beloved face bringing tears to her eyes. Slowly Cadan ran a finger over the man's forehead.

'He lies with many others,' he murmured.

There were always lots of people buried in cemeteries, Daisy thought, as he moved on to the sketch of her mother.

Again, he traced the outline, this time shaking his head. 'I feel the heat of life. This woman lives.'

'Uncle said she'd died.' Daisy assured him, the familiar pang tightening her chest.

'The vibrations tell me otherwise, Daisy,' he murmured, gazing at her so intently, she was tempted to believe he was telling the truth. 'Surely you returned home?' he asked, his look turning incredulous when she shook her head.

'I had no money. Then my uncle turned nasty. I had to hit him to escape …' she paused, a lump rising in her throat as the memories flooded back. 'As I told you, Claude and Grace brought me to Cornwall with them,' she explained, not wishing to revisit that time, yet unable to bear Cadan thinking ill of her. He put a hand on her trembling shoulder.

'I'd never think badly of you,' he replied as if reading her mind. 'Now this is your young man.' He examined the picture of Harry, this time trailing his fingers from the mouth upwards. 'I see miscommunication, a troubled mind. You are always in his thoughts. Things are not as you think, Daisy. Go home and discover the truth,' he urged.

Chapter 32

As Daisy made her way to the boarding house, she was still shaken by what Cadan had told her. Could her mother really be alive? But why would her uncle have told her otherwise? And if Harry had been thinking of her, why hadn't he written? Nothing made sense, she thought, and her head throbbed from trying to puzzle everything out. Perhaps she should go home like Cadan had suggested. If she saved her wages, by the time the season ended, she'd have enough for the train fare.

'My, you look like you've had a rough night,' Susan greeted Daisy as she entered the kitchen. Then seeing her dazed expression, asked. 'Did you celebrate the sun rise?'

'Yes,' she admitted, forcing a smile. 'Is everything alright here?' she asked, noticing the woman staring out of the window.

'Simon refuses to stay indoors. Says he can't stand that Tulla. He's in the glasshouse so perhaps you'd go and help him pick some salad things for luncheon. Thank heavens I boiled the ham yesterday. It's turning out to be one of those days.'

Glad of the fresh air, Daisy wandered down the garden path, greeting guests as she went. Even in the time she'd been here, the whistling jack and columbines had bloomed, adding an array of bright pinks and mauves to the already colourful flowerbeds.

'Hello, Simon, how are you?' she asked, wiping her brow as she stepped into the hothouse. It was certainly aptly named, she thought, as she breathed in the sweet aroma of ripe tomatoes and cucumber.

'I've filled the basket but I'm not coming indoors 'til that Tulla goes out,' he told her defiantly. 'I asked her why she was calling the colonel "you darling man", and she called me a nosy brat.'

'That wasn't very nice,' Daisy admitted, thinking the woman probably didn't understand his ways.

'He was checking his pocket watch against the clock in the lounge as he always does at seven o'clock, and she asked him how it worked. Her eyes were on stalks as he showed her.'

'Well, maybe she hadn't seen one like it before,' Daisy said.

'No need to cuddle right into him though.' He grimaced.

'Perhaps she was just being friendly. Anyway, she's in the lounge at the moment, so why don't we sneak upstairs and clean the bedrooms. Miss Noble might have another sweet for you,' she coaxed.

The rest of the day was so hectic Daisy didn't have a moment to think, and it was only when she was back at the cottage that she remembered her conversation with Cadan. Claude was studying her pictures when she went inside. He looked up so quickly, Daisy had the feeling he'd been waiting for her.

'Not like you to leave these out. Erm, I've been meaning

to speak with you. The other evening when that woman, er, Tulla, mentioned people receiving fees for modelling, it occurred to me that I haven't offered you anything.' He looked at her awkwardly and Daisy was just about to say it didn't matter when she remembered her resolve to purchase a train ticket home. Her spirits rose, only to sink again when he added, 'The truth of the matter is that I have a proposition in the offing which will take all my savings.'

'But you see …' she began

'I will pay you, of course,' he said quickly. 'In fact, I intended giving you something on account, but I can't seem to find my wallet at the moment. If you could wait until I've sold my work, it would help enormously and, of course, there'll be extra for you parading around in that costume all summer. You will be wearing it again tonight?' he asked anxiously.

'I'll go and change now,' she said, hurrying up the stairs. He'd been so good to her, she couldn't really argue, could she? But she was determined to get her fare together somehow.

'When people see your portrait at the exhibition, they'll be excited to think they know you,' Claude said, brightening when she reappeared in the candy-striped attire. 'Anything that creates an interest will attract attention from buyers. Oh, here's Cadan,' he added.

'Are you alright?' Cadan asked, as they walked down the lane. 'I wasn't sure I should have left you so soon after looking at your drawings.'

'I'm fine and had to get to work anyway. But you're right, I do need to return home and discover what has been going on. I intend saving my wages until I have enough for the train fare.'

'I'm pleased, Daisy, I really am. Come on,' he said, taking her arm and leading her towards the others making their way to the field. She saw Tulla laughing with some of the artists and felt pleased she'd made some friends. A huge bonfire had been built since they'd left that morning and, as the last flickers of the setting sun gilded the gorse, it was lit to celebrate the summer.

'Similar beacons will be blazing on hilltops the length of Cornwall,' Cadan told her. 'Here comes the lady of the flowers,' he said, as a maiden dressed in a flowing white robe with white blossom in her hair made her way through the crowd. On reaching the fire, she tossed a garland of herbs and flowers into the flames and everyone cheered.

'Good luck for another year,' Cadan announced as they turned for home.

'Well, I can certainly do with some of that,' Daisy replied, her hand automatically going to her bangle. Cadan stopped and stared at her, those fathomless eyes boring into her very soul.

'Storm clouds hover but sunshine will follow,' he said enigmatically. 'Keep your bangle close and all will come right in the end.'

'Oh,' she frowned. They walked on in silence, Daisy trying to work out what he'd meant, but, before she could ask, they'd reached the cottage. 'Thanks for a lovely evening. I love all these local traditions and funny stones you have around here.'

'Those funny stones are megalithic and neolithic sites. Want to see some more on your next day off?'

'Yes, please, I'd love to incorporate those symbols into my drawing.'

'Then you shall,' he promised, kissing her gently on the cheek and disappearing into the night.

Daisy was getting ready for work the next morning, when there was a brisk rap on the front door. She heard Claude's greeting followed by the low rumble of male voices. Whoever it was sounded serious, Daisy thought, as she tripped down the stairs only to come to a halt when she saw a uniformed constable and the dark-haired man from Bransum.

'Hello, Mr Pigeon,' she exclaimed. The man frowned.

'Daisy Tucker?' he asked, gravely.

'You know I am,' she replied. 'We met in my uncle's tavern.'

'Seems you were right, Mr Crawford,' the constable said.

'Chief Preventative Officer Crawford and Constable Wise from Devon Constabulary wish to speak with you on a serious matter, Daisy,' Claude said. 'Do sit down, gentlemen,' he invited. 'Can I offer you some refreshment?'

'No, thank you,' the constable replied, gesturing for Daisy to be seated before sinking into the chair beside her and taking his notebook out of his pocket. 'Your uncle is Richard Tucker?' he addressed Daisy.

'Yes,' she replied, wondering what was going on. Had he died after all?

'And you resided with him at Masons? Bransum in Devonshire, until earlier this year?'

'Yes,' she confirmed.

'We have been making enquiries into his, er, activities for some time and, following a tip-off, he was arrested and interviewed at the police station, in Exeter. He claims that you,

Daisy Tucker, knocked him unconscious without provocation, stole his takings along with items of jewellery, including one silver bangle with flowers engraved on it,' he said, looking pointedly at Daisy's wrist.

'But Harry made that for me,' she exclaimed. 'We are to be married, or were …' she stuttered to a halt.

'Are? Were? Don't you know if you're to be wed?' the constable snorted, staring disbelievingly at her.

'But Mr Crawford met me in Bransum,' she cried.

'Which is why he is here. To identify you.'

'So, it was you I saw in Penzance.' She frowned. 'Have you been following me?'

'We are investigating a number of things at the moment,' the constable said quickly. 'So, Miss Tucker, did you or did you not hit your uncle over the head then make off with property belonging to him?'

'I admit I hit him, but I'm no thief,' she told him. As the constable began scribbling furiously, Claude held up his hand.

'If I might interrupt. It was me who wrote that letter to the authorities. Daisy's uncle was making demands on her, demands no young lady should ever have to entertain. It was only when he forced his attentions on her that she retaliated. She was acting in self-defence. After escaping she sought refuge at our workshop in Bransum, and my colleague Grace and I brought her with us to Lamorna. She came to us with no money, and no jewellery apart from her bangle. My colleague Sean Sullivan who shares the co-operative with us can confirm that's true.' As the two gentlemen exchanged looks, Daisy's heart almost stopped beating. Was she to be charged, put in prison?

'This is all very well, sir, however to wrap up our case against Mr Tucker and his cronies we need further information,' Mr Crawford said. 'Although, I witnessed your uncle meeting with these men, Miss Tucker, regrettably some of them have subsequently disappeared. Naturally nobody else in Bransum is willing to say anything, and without proof we cannot bring them to justice.'

'My drawing!' Daisy cried, jumping up. Immediately the constable sprang to his feet and stood in front of the door as if to prevent her escaping.

'I hardly think a picture of some violets, however pretty, will prove anything,' Mr Crawford exclaimed, but Daisy was already halfway up the stairs. She reappeared moments later clutching the sketch she'd done of her uncle with the group sitting in the bar at Masons.

'Well, I'll be,' he muttered. 'It looks just like them. This could be just what we need to verify their identity when they're apprehended,' he said, opening his case and slipping it inside. 'Is there any other information you have that may assist us?'

Daisy explained in detail all she had seen and heard at the tavern, from her uncle's temper, the muttered conversations about bringing in brandy and silks in exchange for other goods, to how she found out about the tunnel and how to gain access. She also told them where they could find Ginge who would be happy to corroborate all she'd said.

'That does seem to correspond with the facts as we know them, sir,' Constable Wise confirmed.

'Does that mean I'm not being accused of anything now? I wouldn't help if I was involved, would I?'

'Ha, all criminals will turn their accomplices in if they think it will save their neck,' the constable said.

'But I haven't done anything.'

'Well, that remains to be seen,' he replied. 'Until we have completed our investigations, we would caution you, Miss Tucker, that you are not, on any account, to leave Lamorna.'

'One last thing before we leave, Miss Tucker: why did you think my name was Pigeon?' Mr Crawford asked.

'Ah,' Daisy said, colouring. 'Uncle referred to you as stool pigeon, so I suppose it must have stuck in my memory.'

While the constable stared studiously at the ground, Daisy saw Mr Crawford's moustache twitch.

'I see,' he replied. 'Another offence to be set at Mr Tucker's door then. We will be in touch soon, Miss Tucker.'

As the men took their leave, Daisy sank into the nearest chair. Dear God in heaven was there no end to her nightmare? She'd really been enjoying her time in this beautiful cove, but now she wished she was back in the tranquillity of Peacehaven.

'Don't worry, Daisy,' Claude said quietly. 'There's not a shred of evidence against you, and Mr Crawford in particular seemed very happy with the information you gave him.'

'Thanks, Claude. Oh heck, look at the time,' she cried, jumping up and heading for the door.

Although she didn't think she'd be able to concentrate on work, she couldn't let Susan down. Besides she needed her wages to pay her train fare home.

Chapter 33

'Blimey, girl, you look like death.' Daisy looked up to see Tulla coming towards her, a brightly coloured bag over her shoulder.

'I'm fine.' She smiled. 'You're out early.'

'Can't stand all those old biddies chattering over breakfast. And I thought this place would be peaceful,' she snorted.

'Me too,' Daisy murmured.

'We seem to be on the same wavelength,' she remarked. 'Shame you have to work all the time.'

'Not all the time,' Daisy corrected. 'Saw you up at the bonfire; did you enjoy the ceremony?'

'Must have been mistaken, me old duck. You'd never catch me at anything like that. Posing in the buff for that handsome artist, now that's different.' Tulla laughed and before Daisy could answer, she hurried on her way. How strange, Daisy thought. She could have sworn she saw her red gold curls in the crowd. And why hadn't Claude mentioned he was painting her?

Thinking how much she needed her morning cuppa and chat with Susan, she was surprised to find the woman waiting for her on the doorstep. She was looking grim and didn't greet Daisy with her usual smile.

'Is something wrong?' Daisy asked.

'Miss Noble's pendant went missing yesterday. She claims she only left her room briefly while she went out to check some detail on the flowers. It was only later she realised it was no longer on the table where she always placed it.'

'How awful!' Daisy frowned.

'Yes. Obviously, I contacted Constable Penpraze. When I asked him to investigate, he wanted to know who else worked here so I gave him your details.'

'But you can't think I had anything to do with it?' Daisy cried, hardly able to believe she was about to be questioned by the authorities twice in the same day.

'It's you who cleans the rooms,' Susan pointed out, her gaze cool as she stared directly at Daisy.

'I told him I was always with you and that you'd never steal anything, Daisy,' Simon declared stoutly.

'And I wouldn't. Surely you believe me?' Daisy vowed, staring Susan straight in the eye.

'I want to, of course, but I never saw any references. This place is my livelihood and I can't afford for word to get out.'

'Well, I'd best go then,' Daisy told her.

'No,' Simon cried. 'That's not fair,' he told his mother.

Just then the guests began wandering in for their morning drinks, and, letting out a sigh, Susan turned towards the kitchen. 'Make a start on the rooms,' she called. 'Simon, you can—'

'I'm going with Daisy,' he said, slipping his hand into hers and dragging her up the hallway. 'Don't worry, we'll find out what's been going on,' he declared so adamantly that despite the gravity of the situation Daisy found herself smiling. But as he knocked on Miss Noble's door, her stomach was churning.

'Come in,' the woman called. 'Ah, Daisy and Simon,' she acknowledged. 'You'll have heard about my pendant?'

'Yes, I'm sorry, I know how much you valued it. Would you prefer me not to clean your room today?'

'Oh no dear, you carry on, though I've little heart for my embroidery.'

'Don't worry, Miss Noble, me and Daisy are going to find your stone,' Simon declared.

The woman ruffled his hair affectionately. 'There'll be a big bag of humbugs if you do,' she told him. 'But meantime, see what you can find in my drawer.'

While Daisy made the bed and tidied the room, she was sad to note the woman just sat looking forlornly over the garden.

The day dragged and, despite all the residents still being amenable, Daisy was on tenterhooks expecting the doorbell to ring at any moment. But by the time her shift ended, the constable hadn't appeared. She wondered if he'd be waiting when she arrived back at the cottage, instead it was the colonel standing by the gate.

'Pleasure doing business with you, Colonel,' Claude said, shaking his hand. 'You can be sure I'll pay my dues as soon as my wretched wallet shows up.'

'I hope you'll be happy in your new home,' he called, beaming at Daisy in passing. New home? Claude was leaving? Daisy stared at him in dismay.

'Great news,' Claude enthused, rubbing his hands together. 'Especially as Grace is deserting us.'

'Someone taking my name in vain?' Grace trilled, as she tripped lightly down the stairs, bag in one hand, coat over the other.

'But where are you going?' Daisy asked Claude. 'I thought you'd be down on the beach painting Tulla.'

'Whatever gave you that idea?' he frowned.

'She told me she was posing for you – in the buff, as she put it.'

'No fear; not a provocative minx like that. Once bitten and all that,' he snorted, then, seeing Daisy's puzzled expression, let out a long sigh. 'You might as well know that when I was in France a couple of years back, I was taken in by the physical assets of someone just as vain and hot-headed as Tulla. Caused no end of trouble, and I vowed never to paint another woman again.'

'But you're painting me?' Daisy quizzed.

'That's different. Your sweetness and naivety show in your face, and that's exactly what I'm trying to capture. Along with the vision you make in that outfit.'

'I wish Susan thought I was sweet and naïve.'

'Why shouldn't she?' Grace asked.

'Miss Noble's pendant's gone missing,' Daisy groaned.

'What, the lovely mauve one you were telling me about?' Grace asked.

'Yes. It was her grandmother's and she said it was priceless,' Daisy murmured. 'Susan's called in the police.'

'Constable Penpraze doesn't let the grass grow so I'm sure he'll soon have it sorted,' Claude told her. 'Anyway, you'd better go and pack your things.'

'I heard the colonel say you were leaving, but do I have to move out straightaway?' she asked, looking bewildered.

'Don't you want to come with me?' Claude asked. 'I mean, I understand if you don't. It's a fair way from the beach.'

'Daisy doesn't know what you're talking about, Claude,' Grace told him.

'Oh sorry. The colonel has agreed to me renting one of his properties. It has more rooms and a large garden already planted with vegetables and fruit bushes.' His excited expression made him look younger.

'Claude's hoping the peace and solitude will enable him to concentrate on his painting without the interruptions he gets here.'

'Especially as the annual swapping of partners is in full swing. Happens every year and causes no end of disputes. For some reason people come to me with their dilemmas,' he muttered.

'Being older, they probably think you're wiser, mistakenly, of course,' Grace chuckled. 'Anyway, the poor girl still doesn't know exactly what's going on,' she added, turning to Daisy. 'I'm moving in with my dear friend Denzil ...'

'Denzil the Druid,' Claude snorted.

'His love of trees, and communing with nature, is as much a part of him as painting is to you. He's someone from my past and we should have got together long before now,' she continued.

Daisy smiled, remembering Grace enthusing about the trees on the moor.

'Claude's hoping you'll move with him.'

'To keep house and cook in return for your board. It would afford me more time to paint and tend the garden. Regrettably with the higher rent, I won't be able to pay you anything until I sell some work. But I really have great hopes for that picture of you. You've already created much interest parading around in your striped outfit.'

'Do say yes, Daisy,' Grace urged. 'You'll have time to practise your own drawing and I won't have to feel so guilty about deserting my dear friend here.'

'If you're sure,' Daisy replied. After all, she needed some-where to stay, didn't she?

'Let's pack our things into the jingle then. We can give you a lift as far as Rosemerryn, Grace, and you can catch the horse-bus from there.'

'By the way, I've heard Mae and Sean are travelling down for the exhibition. It will be good to see them again, although I just know Mae will say I told you so, when she sees me with Denzil.' Grace grimaced.

Daisy smiled. She was fond of Mae and hadn't forgotten the woman's generosity in giving her those boots. Taking herself upstairs, it took no time at all to pack her few belong-ings. She would miss this dear little room with the sound of the stream rushing past the window and the view out over the garden.

As the pony pulled the laden jingle slowly up the hill and past the turning to the guest house, Daisy pondered on how she could find out who'd taken Miss Noble's pendant. For although nothing had actually been said as such, it was obvious she was under suspicion. Lost in thought, she jumped as Claude tugged on the reins. They'd pulled up outside an elegant two-storey stone and slate house surrounded by tall trees.

'Elm and sycamores, I'm jealous,' Grace cried, jumping down and grabbing her bag. 'I'll borrow a cart and return for my tools and equipment in a day or so. Meanwhile, Daisy, don't go worrying about things. They'll get sorted; you'll see.' With a wave she walked jauntily towards the dairy.

'We'll unpack and then I'd like you to change into your outfit as I feel the muse upon me,' Claude said, raising his hands theatrically. 'You're upstairs on the right. Oh, and you won't need the parasol, it's your eyes I wish to concentrate on.'

The eventful day had left Daisy drained but she forced a smile and hurried to settle herself into yet another room. To her delight this one was spacious and comfortably furnished, although her few things looked pitiful in the large walnut wardrobe. Shaking out the creases, she changed into her pink and white outfit then checked her appearance in the cheval mirror. She glanced out of the window, delighted to see the same little babbling brook meandering down one side of the rose arbour. Its chuckling sound never failed to raise her spirits and the continuity was comforting.

Under Claude's direction, she sat on the lawn in the evening sun while he added more detail to her features.

'I know we are not down at the cove but try and look as if you are waiting for your paramour,' Claude instructed. Whilst endeavouring to do as he asked, Daisy stared across the garden, with its abundance of flowers and shrubs. How she wished Harry really would appear, she thought, then chided herself. His silence spoke volumes and, although her heart still yearned for him, she needed to put the past firmly behind her.

Her thoughts had unsettled her and, after a restless night, Daisy had to hurry to work. The walk, although level, took longer and when she finally arrived at the boarding house, a uniformed young man was waiting impatiently on the doorstep.

'Miss Daisy Tucker?'

'Yes,' she confirmed. Although she'd been expecting the visit, her heart was thumping alarmingly.

'Constable Penpraze,' he announced. 'I've just been to Chy an dowr but, despite being told by Constable Wise you were cautioned not to remove from Lamorna, it was empty,' he said, his tone frosty.

'That's because Claude has rented Rosemerryn and we moved there yesterday evening. That's still in Lamorna, so I didn't think that would be a problem,' she told him, returning his stare.

'It's actually in the hamlet of Trove,' he told her. 'However, I've wasted enough time this morning so if you wouldn't mind stepping inside, Mrs Hendry suggests I interview you in her office so as not to alarm the guests.'

'Yes, of course,' Daisy replied, endeavouring to keep calm as she led the way inside. 'Good morning,' she called to Susan, who was furiously rubbing fat into flour in the kitchen.

'I trust this won't take long, Constable?' she asked.

'So do I, Mrs Hendry,' he replied, opening the door into the room housing a table littered with papers and two chairs. 'Take a seat, Miss Tucker. I understand you clean the rooms here?'

'I do,' she confirmed.

'And you are aware that money and certain items of jewellery have gone missing?' He sent her a penetrating stare.

'I understand Miss Noble's pendant did, yes.'

'Well, Miss, after you left work yesterday, other items were reported stolen.'

'What are you inferring?' Daisy asked, not liking the tone of his voice. 'I'll have you know I would never abuse my position.'

'Did I suggest you would?' he said mildly. 'You say you removed to Rosemerryn yesterday. Presumably that was after you left here. Can anyone confirm this?'

'Well, Claude and Grace. Oh, and the colonel, of course. He was finalising the details when I arrived home after work.'

'You saw the colonel yesterday?' he asked, his expression changing to one of surprise.

'Yes, why?' she asked but he was scribbling in his notebook and didn't reply.

'Well, I won't keep you any longer, Miss Tucker. But should you decide to remove again without telling us, be certain we will be after you,' he said, getting to his feet and striding from the room.

Susan looked up from the pan she was stirring on the range and Daisy was horrified to see how pale and drawn she looked.

'This is all so embarrassing and will damage my business if we don't find the culprit soon,' she groaned. 'Miss Noble has already left, saying she has no heart for the exhibition now.'

'Oh no, poor Miss Noble. Is it only here that things are going missing?' Daisy asked.

'Apparently the constable's investigating another report.'

'Daisy,' Simon cried, appearing with a basket full of fresh potatoes. 'I've been waiting for you. There's been more thefts.'

'Simon,' Susan admonished. 'He's right, though.' She turned to Daisy. 'Mrs Cawley says money's missing from her purse. Now our remaining guests are sitting in the lounge with their handbags on their laps.'

'And the colonel can't find his watch,' Simon announced.

'Heavens, let's hope he finds it soon,' Daisy cried. 'Well, I'd better make a start on the rooms.'

'Simon will go with you,' Susan said firmly.

'Like I always do,' he said, before Daisy had a chance to comment.

It was strange cleaning Miss Noble's room without her cheery presence and Daisy hoped her pendant would turn up. She stripped the sheets from the bed as Simon chattered away.

'No more humbugs,' he muttered, looking wistfully at the drawer. 'I'm sure Tulla took Miss Noble's pendant.'

'What makes you say that?' Daisy asked, staring at him in surprise.

'Every time she goes out, her shoulder bag is empty but when she gets back it's full. I asked her what was in it and she told me to bugger off. That's rude, isn't it?'

'Very,' Daisy agreed.

'I guessed she was up to something so I followed her and watched as she chatted to the men on the beach. She makes gooey eyes at them and they're so taken in they don't notice her putting things in her bag.'

'Are you sure?' Although she asked the question, she knew Simon always related things just as they happened. It just wasn't in him to fabricate.

'Yes, she does it like this,' he said, fluttering his eyelashes and putting on a sickly smile, while demonstrating taking something from her pocket. Was that how Claude's wallet had gone missing whilst he'd been on the beach she wondered?

'Have you told your mother?' she asked.

'She thinks I'm a bit, well, stupid.' He sighed, looking so forlorn Daisy couldn't help throwing her arms around him. 'Yuk,' he said, pushing her away. 'That's just what that Tulla does to the colonel.'

Chapter 34

As soon as they'd finished cleaning the rooms, while Simon went out to weed the front garden, Daisy hurried through to the kitchen. What he'd told her about Tulla was weighing heavily on her mind and she decided to speak to Susan whilst the guests were relaxing over their morning drinks.

However, no sooner had they sat down with their cups of tea than they heard the thunder of feet haring along the hallway.

'Daisy, Daisy,' Simon shouted. 'Tulla's in Miss Bassett's room.'

'Are you sure?' Susan frowned.

'Yes,' Simon gasped. 'I saw her from the garden. Besides, Tulla's room is at the back. Come on,' he urged. 'Hurry up.'

Footsteps pounded down the stairs and they jumped to their feet just in time to glimpse Tulla, heavy bag in hand, disappearing through the front door.

'Stop, thief,' Daisy shouted, as all three of them gave chase. Just as Tulla reached the gate a loud voice boomed.

'In a hurry, are we, Miss?' On the pathway stood Constable Penpraze and the colonel, who had his shotgun pointed at her.

'I ain't done nothing,' the woman screeched. 'Get out of my way.'

'Let's see what we have in here, shall we, Miss,' the constable said, reaching out and trying to take the bag from her. But Tulla refused to let go and a tussle ensued.

'Drop it, girl,' the colonel commanded, as if talking to his dog.

'Yer wouldn't dare shoot me,' she scoffed.

'Used to clearing vermin off my land,' he replied, cocking the hammer. The click sounded loud in the morning air, and, shocked, Tulla cowered down.

With a satisfied smile, the constable bent over and flicked the catch that opened the capacious bag.

'Well, well,' he said, pulling out a wad of paper money, the purple pendant, various wallets and the colonel's gold pocket watch. 'I think you'd better accompany me to the station, Miss,' he said, pulling handcuffs from his pocket and snapping one around her wrist.

'I said it was her,' Simon cried.

'You 'orrid brat,' she shrieked. 'I'll bleedin' skin yer 'ide.'

'Why is she speaking like that?' he asked.

'Because she's showing her true colours,' the colonel told him.

'Why, what colour should she be?' Simon asked, staring the woman up and down.

'Don't worry, Simon, it just means she's proving what a nasty woman she really is,' Daisy told him.

'A few nights in gaol should cool you down,' Constable Penpraze told her.

'But my bag with my things, the money ...' she squealed.

'Will go some way towards recompensing Susan for all the

trouble you've caused.' Susan coloured as the colonel placed a comforting arm around her. 'If I might have my timepiece, please, Constable.'

'Of course, Colonel,' he replied, handing over the pocket watch. 'The rest of the stolen property will be returned to its rightful owners, and then, and only then, will you get your bag back,' he told Tulla. 'By the way, Miss Tucker, Chief Preventative Officer Crawford has concluded his investigation and says you are no longer restricted to Lamorna,' the constable declared.

'Thank heavens,' Daisy cried.

'Now you'll be able to check your watch against the clock in the lounge at seven o'clock this evening,' Simon told the colonel.

'I will indeed, young man,' he smiled. 'And with your observation skills I think you have the makings of a fine detective.'

As Simon grinned, Daisy felt her heart grow warm. He might have his peculiar little ways but nobody could deny his meticulous eye for detail had helped clear her name.

'It was lucky you and the constable were passing,' Susan told the colonel.

'Actually, we've been keeping an eye on the guest house,' he replied, flushing as he glanced at Daisy.

'You mean me?' she spluttered. 'But why?'

'Firstly, because of your association with Mr Tucker,' the colonel replied. 'Then when things went missing whilst you were posing on the pier, we wondered if you had an accomplice.'

'However, from my enquiries I discovered this woman—'

Constable Penpraze gestured to Tulla '—was apprehended for pickpocketing in Newquay last summer. So, Miss Tucker, it appears you are in the clear.'

'I should hope too,' Daisy cried.

After all the turmoil, Daisy was pleased to have the next day off. She loved Rosemerryn with its large square kitchen, and sang as she bustled around preparing their breakfast.

'That was the best scrambled eggs ever,' Claude told her, patting his stomach. 'Now I think we should return to Lamorna and put the finishing touches to your portrait. I can collect my wallet from the constable on the way. Should have known that scheming minx was up to no good.'

'I thought it strange Tulla should lie about you painting her, but never realised she was thieving from people all around the cove.' Daisy shook her head. 'At least Susan won't have to worry now.'

'But I still can't believe you've been under suspicion.'

'I felt I was being watched a few times, but reckoned it was because of my uncle's activities.' She sighed. 'I never realised the authorities thought I might also be linked to the thefts here. In fact, I feel quite indignant about it.'

'Well, you've been exonerated, my dear Daisy. In fact, I can see your halo shining from here,' he chuckled. 'Come on, it's much too nice a day to waste.'

It was a beautiful day, and, as they plodded along in the jingle, Daisy found herself relaxing for the first time in ages. After stopping at the police station Claude reappeared, beaming widely.

'And not only have I got my wallet back, it still has some money in it,' he said, taking out a note and handing it to her.

'But …' she began.

'Please take it. Although it's not as much as I'd hoped to give you, I know you are saving for your fare home. Obviously, when I sell my picture, I'll make sure you're well recompensed.' He smiled. 'Now let's get this portrait finished.'

Daisy had been religiously setting her wages aside and hoped that by the time the season ended, she'd have enough to pay for her ticket back to Camberwell. Cadan still insisted her mother was alive, and although she had great difficulty believing him, she knew she wouldn't rest until she'd found out the truth.

She didn't have time to dwell on the matter for her weeks were busy both at the guest house and Rosemerryn, and the time sped by. Before she knew it, exhibition day dawned and it was time for them to load the jingle.

'I can't wait to see Grace again,' Daisy told Claude as they made their way past the tall church in Paul.

'Me too. You'll like Denzil; he's right for Grace, although it's taken her long enough to realise it,' he said, shaking his head. 'And we'll be meeting up with Mae and Sean too.'

'Wonderful,' she cried happily.

'And since most of the artists in Lamorna will be there, we'll be in for a few parties.'

'But I thought you moved to Rosemerryn to get away from them,' Daisy said, looking at him in surprise.

'Work is done, time to play.' He grinned. 'And, of course, I'm hoping to have something to celebrate,' he added, putting his hand behind him and stroking the covered portrait reverently.

As they turned down the hill towards Newlyn, the bay spread out before them and the miniature boats on the sparkling sea reminded her of when they'd first arrived. It had been a weird but wonderful summer, excitement mounting as the exhibition grew nearer. Daisy stared down at her freshly laundered candy-striped outfit. Much to Claude's delight, she'd attracted lots of extra attention when she'd posed on the pier as he added the final touches.

'You look wonderful,' Claude told her, as ever in tune with her thoughts. 'All you need to do is stand beside your portrait and smile. When it sells, I shall be rich enough to pay my dues. I really appreciate your patience,' he told her, for once being serious.

The narrow streets of Newlyn were crowded with artistes. Some were on foot, others like them travelling in laden carts and jingles.

'Thank heavens we've booked rooms,' Claude said, turning into the entrance of a large Victorian guest house. 'I'll drop you here then take the portrait to the gallery,' he said, jumping down.

'I'll help,' Daisy offered, but he shook his head. 'Here, boy, see to the horse then take our bags up to our rooms,' he said, handing the reins to a young lad whose cheeky grin reminded Daisy of Ginge. She was just wondering how he was when she heard Grace calling.

'Daisy, how lovely to see you again. You're looking well. Obviously, life with Claude can't have been that bad,' she chuckled. 'I can't wait to see his finished portrait. Let me introduce Denzil, my fiancé,' she added, turning to the tall man behind her.

'Good to meet you, Daisy,' he said, eyes like sloes surveying her as he shook her hand. With his dark curls tied back in a ribbon, he was handsome in a rugged kind of way, and Daisy could see why her friend was enamoured.

'I've so been looking forward to seeing you again,' Grace told her, leading her inside. She was looking radiant in a soft green dress with pink flowers on the collar and cuffs, and it was obvious life with Denzil suited her. With a pang, Daisy thought of Harry and her hand automatically strayed to her bangle.

'The others are already here so Claude can join us when he appears.'

The bar was thronging with brightly dressed people, the atmosphere festive.

'Darling,' Mae cried, throwing her arms around Daisy, 'you look wonderful in that outfit. Doesn't she look all grown-up, Sean?'

'Grown and gorgeous,' he replied in that lilting voice of his. 'Come on, we've saved a table,' he added, gesturing to the bay window.

'Tell us how you've been getting on, darling,' Mae said, as soon as Sean had set drinks before them. 'We know Claude persuaded you to model for him and can't wait to see his exhibit. What are you showing, Grace?'

'Just a flower brooch I've fashioned. I've been too busy

to do much designing recently,' she added, smiling happily at Denzil, who lovingly took her hand in his.

'Sean's fashioned the most exquisite silver dish,' Mae told them. 'I don't suppose you've done anything yet, darling?' she asked Daisy.

'Daisy's been sketching the local flora and Celtic signs,' Claude said, sinking into the seat next to her. 'She's really good, so don't be surprised to see her exhibiting next year.'

'Oh yes, you were at the Fun Factory before you ended up with that terrible man in Bransum, weren't you?' Mae said.

'Well, you've nothing to fear from him anymore,' Sean told her.

'So, the police charged him then?' Claude asked, leaning forward in his seat.

'Yes, and his merry men too. Thanks to a certain picture,' he said beaming at Daisy. 'Got sent down for ten years for smuggling and handling stolen jewellery, he did.'

'Good,' Daisy cried.

'Ah, but then he was found dead in his cell. Rumour has it there was a price on his head.'

Almost weak with relief, Daisy felt as if a burden had been lifted from her. However her uncle's demise had come about, he'd put her through hell and she was pleased justice had been done.

Chapter 35

The atmosphere in the gallery was exhilarating, the exhibitors barely able to suppress their excitement as they milled around waiting to gauge the visitors' reaction to their work.

'That really is a work of art, darling,' Mae enthused, staring at the portrait of Daisy, which now graced the front wall. 'So much better than all those nasty, dark swirls.'

'Calling it *Enigma* is pure genius, adding to the mystery of who your model can be,' Sean added.

'Glad you approve,' Claude beamed. 'Daisy parading around in her outfit will hopefully generate more interest. Now, it's getting busy so let's go and see your creations while we can still move. It'll give the patrons more space to admire my picture.' He gave Daisy an outrageous wink. Clearly Claude was on good form.

They moved on, stopping in front of a two-handled silver bowl set on a plinth. It was entitled *Quaiche, the Cup of Friendship*.

'That workmanship is superb, Sean,' Grace marvelled. 'I feel the urge to reach out and touch it.'

'That surely was the reaction I was hoping for,' he replied, blue eyes sparkling.

'And your brooch is simply exquisite. The cloisonné violet looks just like it's crying,' Mae marvelled.

'Thank you, I was rather pleased with the effect the seed pearls gave,' Grace admitted, blushing when Denzil shot her a proud smile.

'*Tears of Joy*?' Claude quirked a brow as he gestured to the title. 'Ah, I remember you mentioning that when we were on Bodmin.'

'And now it's named in honour of my sister, for at last she's with child.'

'That's wonderful news, I'm so pleased for her,' Daisy cried, for she'd really taken to the warm, generous-hearted woman who'd kindly given her the clothes more suited to the climate on the moors.

'If you're interested, darlings, you'll find my humble offering over there,' Mae told them, gesturing to a pair of blue enamelled silver buckles, each with a pearlescent shell in the centre. It was entitled *Pieux*.

'What is that shell?' Daisy asked, having never seen anything like it before.

'Abalone, darling, and quite effective even if I do say so myself. I crafted them for Sean,' she said, lowering her voice. 'Do you think he'll approve?' The uncertainty in her voice surprised Daisy and she saw a vulnerable side to the woman she'd previously thought so self-confident.

'He'll love them,' Daisy assured her. 'Especially as you made them.'

'The shells have magical properties that magnify the energy around you. Apparently, if you meditate on what truly matters to you, those thoughts transfer themselves to the other person. *Pieux* means wishful thinking,' she whispered, her eyes sliding to where Sean stood chatting to Claude.

'Well, I wish you every luck in the world, although Sean obviously adores you, so I'm sure you won't need it.' Daisy smiled.

'If we've seen everyone's work, I think it's time for you to circulate, Daisy. Don't forget to twirl your parasol from time to time, get people to really notice those amethyst eyes,' Claude told her.

It was strange, she never normally liked attracting attention but this outfit made her feel more self-assured. Maybe that's how actresses like Sybella felt when they put on their costumes, she mused, gravitating towards a large group in the centre of the adjoining room. Gently whirling the parasol, she smiled demurely as people turned and stared at her curiously.

'Finest example of a posie ring I've ever seen,' one man murmured. As the little crowd began to move on to the next exhibit, Daisy gasped.

Leaning over the cabinet, she studied the ring before her. Crafted in silver with a daisy chain flowing around the circumference, its flower petals worked in shiny white enamel, it was a work of art, she thought, tears welling. The card bearing the name Harry Wylde declared he'd been awarded student of the year. Her heart swelled with pride and she suddenly had an overwhelming desire to see him to congratulate him on his success. She would also ask him why he hadn't written.

Before her courage failed her, she hurried out to the desk

where two curators were carefully watching over the proceedings, while a young man handed leaflets to visitors as they entered.

'I'd like to speak with Harry Wylde,' she stated.

'Impossible,' one told her officiously, before turning to speak to someone else. How rude, Daisy thought, determined not to be put off.

'But you don't understand, I'm Daisy from Camberwell, the subject of his—'

'I don't care if you're the flaming Empress of Egypt, I am not at liberty to divulge information about any of the exhibitors.'

'Suppose I want to purchase the ring?' she persisted.

'It's not for sale,' he retorted. 'Don't know why anyone would exhibit if they're not prepared to sell,' he muttered. 'I'm going for my break,' he told his colleague, getting to his feet and striding away. The man waited until he'd disappeared through a door behind them then turned to Daisy.

'Don't mind Fred, he's a stickler for the rules.' Leaning forward, he lowered his voice. 'Mr Wylde and his companion have just left to visit some tin mines on the way back to their workshop in St Ives. If you hurry you may catch them.'

Daisy dashed out of the exhibition just in time to see a smartly dressed Harry and a young lady passing by in a two-wheeled open carriage.

'Harry, Harry,' she shouted, but her voice was drowned by the clatter of the horse's hooves on the cobbles, and he didn't hear her.

Seeing him with another woman was a shock and Daisy

felt herself go cold. However, she knew she needed to speak to him and, running back inside, she spoke to the friendly man at the desk.

'Do you know when Mr Wylde will be coming back?' she gasped.

'He said he'd be back in the next day or so,' the man replied.

'Oh, but we're leaving this evening,' she cried, in dismay. 'Do you have an address for him?' Seeing her desperation, he nodded and pushed an exhibition catalogue towards her.

'You'll find details of his workshop in there,' he told her.

'Thank you,' she murmured, turning despondently away.

'Anything to help the *Enigma* Lady,' he called after her.

Suddenly the excitement had gone out of the day. Having been elated when she'd spotted Harry's work, she'd steeled herself to speak with him, but the sight of him laughing with that pretty woman made her angry. She'd write to him and demand an explanation.

'You'll never guess what?' Claude cried, appearing at her side. His face was flushed and he was beaming from ear to ear. 'Someone's bought *Enigma*. Apparently, interest was shown prior to the opening and the buyer offered the full price. Look.' He pointed to the wall where a large red sticker had been placed alongside the picture. 'I asked for a ridiculous amount, fully expecting to be knocked down if someone wanted to buy it but ...' He shrugged, evidently lost for words.

'Well done, darling,' Mae cooed, rushing over and throwing her arms around him. 'I dare say you want to go and celebrate.'

'No, I want to return home and start working on another picture straightaway. I'm on a roll and want to capitalise on it. Come on, my lucky muse,' he said to Daisy. 'We'll go and collect our things. Tell the others to come to Rosemerryn at the weekend and I'll throw the biggest bash ever.'

'You're on, darling,' Mae drawled. 'We love it here in Newlyn so much that we've decided to look for somewhere to rent for a while.' Daisy's spirits rose a little; to have her friends so close would make life more bearable.

They journeyed back to Lamorna in silence, each lost in their own thoughts. Claude was obviously visualising his next painting whilst Daisy pondered on the posie ring and the lady in the carriage. She just hoped Harry would have the decency to respond to her letter this time. To have come so near to speaking to him and getting answers to her questions was frustrating. It had been silly to get her hopes up when she'd spotted the ring, for having designed it as part of his project, he'd probably been encouraged to exhibit it at Newlyn.

Realising she had to face up to the fact Harry had someone else, and no longer cared about her, Daisy concentrated her energies into developing her own artwork. She kept house and helped Claude when needed, yet couldn't help feeling disappointed that Harry hadn't been in touch with news of her mother.

With the season drawing to a close, the guest house was quieter now and her hours reduced. However, her savings had mounted and with Claude promising to pay her as soon as he received his fee, she would have enough for her train fare home.

The day of the party dawned and Daisy enjoyed celebrating

Claude's success with their friends, particularly Mae, Sean and Cadan, and she was pleased to see Grace and Denzil so happy together.

A few days later, Daisy was preparing a stew for their supper when the doorbell rang.

'You have a visitor,' Claude announced grandly.

She turned to see Harry standing in the kitchen doorway. Her heart flipped and her mouth went dry.

'Hello, Daisy. I got your letter,' he said, and, although he smiled, his eyes surveyed her warily.

'Took your time, didn't you?' she retorted, then cursed herself for being so sharp. 'I thought you were only going to be away a couple of days.' She tried to return his smile but her face felt frozen.

'That was the plan, but the tin proved ideal for my next project so I took some straight back to the workshop to try it out. I didn't get your letter until yesterday. To say I was surprised to hear from you is an understatement.'

'Show your guest through to the parlour and I'll bring some refreshments,' Claude suggested, reappearing and frowning at Daisy. Suddenly conscious she was still holding the wooden spoon, she hastily put it on the table.

'Thank you,' she replied. 'Follow me,' she told Harry, leading the way as if he were an unknown guest. They were standing in the middle of the room, staring awkwardly at each other, when Claude bustled in with a tray.

'Oh, take a seat, old chap. Where are your manners, Daisy?' he chided.

'Do sit down, Harry,' she murmured, gesturing to the chair opposite.

'Harry?' Claude repeated.

'This is Harry Wylde, the—'

'Talented jeweller,' Claude cried, holding out his hand. 'Great to meet such a gifted artiste. Claude Noir at your service.'

'You're Claude Noir, painter of the *Enigma*?' he asked, looking shocked as he shook the proffered hand. 'Why sir, you must let me settle my dues,' he said, his hand going to his inside pocket.

'You mean it was you who purchased my picture?' Claude asked incredulously.

'As soon as I saw those distinctive eyes, I knew it was Daisy, and wanted it as a reminder. We used to know each other, you see.'

'More than that,' Daisy burst out. 'We were engaged until my parents were involved in that accident. And Harry here promised to let me know how my mother was recovering.'

'So, you're ...' Claude began, his eyes narrowing. Then held up his hands. 'No, it's not for me to interfere. I will leave you good folks to sort out your, er, differences. But I'll be in my studio if you need me,' he said, looking pointedly at Daisy as he backed out of the room.

'But I did write to you, Daisy,' Harry told her as soon as the door had closed.

'Well I never received any letters. I had to stay working in that horrid alehouse, not knowing how Mother's operation went.'

'What operation?' Harry frowned. 'And why did you have to work in an alehouse? I thought your uncle was taking you to stay with his family.'

'For heaven's sake, Harry, sit down; you're making me nervous pacing up and down like that.'

'Sorry,' he murmured, sinking into the chair she'd indicated earlier.

'It turned out Uncle was never married. He ran an alehouse in deepest Devonshire and had me working to help repay the hospital and funeral bills. Then he said the hospital needed more money for Mother's operation on her legs and …' she shrugged. There was silence as Harry's frown deepened.

'I think there's been some misunderstanding,' he said. He leaned forward in his seat and she could see the confusion in his eyes. 'Your uncle never paid any bills, which is why your father was buried in a pauper's grave.'

'What? But that's terrible,' she gasped, her hand flying to her mouth. His glance went to her bangle, but all she could think of was her beloved father sharing a burial place with hordes of unknown people. No wonder Cadan had said he felt he was with many others.

'But Uncle said he'd paid the hospital for Father's burial and Mother's hospital fees. They were going to let him know when the funeral was to be so I could attend.'

'Your uncle never paid the hospital any money, Daisy,' Harry said softly. The pity in his eyes was almost more than she could bear and she had to take a steadying breath before continuing.

'He had me working in the kitchen and waiting on tables,

because paying the bills for my family meant he couldn't afford to employ any new staff. He said I owed it to him, Harry.' She stared directly at him. 'He also said you couldn't care about me because you hadn't written to let me know how Mother was or ask after me.'

'As I said, I did write, nearly every day at first. I knew you'd be fretting about your mother and wanted to keep you updated on her progress.' He let out a long sigh. 'Though I can see you don't believe me.'

'I never saw any letters,' she told him truthfully. He stared at her then shrugged.

'I was so worried when I never heard anything, I travelled to Bransum to see you. It was in the spring. I remember because I had to wait for the heavy snow to clear although it was still quite a journey. Then, when I finally arrived, your uncle told me you'd left to live with an artist friend called Claude. I suppose that's him?' He nodded to the door.

'Well, yes, but it wasn't li—'

'Anyway,' he said, getting to his feet. 'For what it's worth, I visited your mother often, even helped her move her things into the workhouse.' Daisy stared at him, convinced she'd misheard.

'For a moment, I thought you said Mother was in the workhouse.'

'I'm afraid she is,' he replied sadly. 'When the hospital's bill remained unpaid, they insisted she leave. Of course, by then, the rooms in Tiger Yard had been filled and your neighbours hadn't heard anything from you, so she had no choice.' He shrugged. 'Still, water under the bridge and all that. Had you cared about either of us you would have returned to Camberwell, wouldn't you?'

'But I've explained …' she began then stopped as another thought struck her. 'Claude's picture? It was far from cheap. How on earth did you afford to purchase it?'

'I bought it legitimately, if that's what you're worried about,' he snorted. 'My grandmother died recently and left me a modest inheritance.'

'I didn't even know you had one,' Daisy replied, shaking her head.

'She and Father fell out when he insisted on marrying Mother. Seemed she was right about that,' he said wryly. 'Anyhow, she lived north of the river so I didn't get to see her often. Despite being fond of her, it came as a shock when she told me I was to be her heir.' His sad smile softened his features, and for a moment Daisy was tempted to reach out to him. 'When I asked your father for permission to marry you, he asked what my prospects were and I told him I would be able to make us a nice home.' A look of anguish flitted across his face, but it was gone in an instant. 'Anyway, now we both know the truth of things, I really must be going.'

'I still don't …' she began, trying to take in everything he'd said.

But he ignored her, and without a backward look, strode from the room.

Chapter 36

As Daisy sat there in a state of shock, she was vaguely aware of the murmur of voices, but it was only when she heard the front door closing that she came to her senses. Dashing into the hallway, she almost knocked Claude over in her haste.

'Harry,' she shouted, but by the time she reached the garden gate, the coach was disappearing into the distance. Kicking the gate post in frustration, she trudged back indoors.

'Why did you tell Harry that I was your husband?' Claude asked, when she reappeared in the hallway.

'What?' she cried, her eyes widening in shock.

'He apologised for leaving so abruptly, said he had urgent business to attend to, and was sorry for upsetting my wife. Didn't you explain that you kept house for me?'

'He didn't give me a chance,' she murmured. Apparently, my uncle told him I'd left Devonshire with a male artist called Claude, and he jumped to conclusions. I was about to explain and ask about his lady companion, but then he told me my mother's in the workhouse and …' she cried, shaking her head. 'Uncle never paid any hospital bills.'

'Bastard,' Claude murmured, his expression grave. 'You

must go and see her straightaway.' Daisy nodded and looked at him expectantly.

'Ah, trouble is Harry rushed off without paying for the picture. Just said I'd be getting the money in the next few days. Of course, as soon as I receive it, I'll pay your fare home. Though I have to say, having seen how young the chap is, I do wonder if he can actually afford it.'

'Harry would never purchase something he hadn't the money for,' Daisy declared hotly, quite forgetting that only minutes earlier she'd asked the same question.

Suddenly, it all became too much and she felt her knees go weak. Taking her arm, Claude gently guided her back to the seat beside the fire, promising to return with a warm drink.

As Daisy sat there, her thoughts in turmoil, she hardly noticed the shadows gathering in the corners of the room. All she could think about was her respectable father buried in a pauper's grave, her poor house-proud mother in the workhouse and Harry's uncompromising look as he'd strode from the room.

Had he really travelled all the way to Bransum? Then, she realised he must have been telling the truth about that or he wouldn't have known she'd left with Claude.

'Oh, mercy me,' she cried, jumping to her feet.

'What's the matter?' Claude asked, hurrying into the room.

'I must go to Newlyn and see Harry,' she exclaimed, heading for the door. Claude put out a hand to restrain her.

'Agreed. You have much to sort out. Like me not being your husband for one,' he replied, grimacing theatrically to try and lighten the atmosphere. 'However, you can't go now.

Night is falling and it would be too dangerous. I'll drive you in the jingle first thing tomorrow as I need to visit the exhibition to see my painting.'

As soon as the sun peeped above the horizon, they set off for Newlyn. But when they reached the museum there was no sign of the friendly curator, only the pedantic man who seemed to delight in telling them that Mr Wylde had left for home.

'Will he be returning?' Daisy asked, her spirits sinking to her boots.

'Shouldn't think so, Miss; he's taken his ring and picture with him,' he told her, glaring at the spot on the wall where her portrait had been. 'Now if there's nothing else, we're very busy,' he said, turning back to the papers on his desk.

'But there is,' Claude said. 'Did you receive payment for the picture before you let Mr Wylde take it away?' he demanded.

'Bloody man made off with it whilst my back was turned,' the curator blustered.

'You mean you weren't here so he didn't pay?' Claude exploded. 'Give me the address of his residence in St Ives immediately, before I make a formal complaint about your conduct to the trustees of this gallery.' As the man reluctantly handed over the information, Claude stormed out of the exhibition followed by an astonished Daisy. She'd never seen Claude so assertive.

'I'm off to get my money from Harry flippin' Wylde. Are you coming?'

'After what he's just done, I don't think I want anything

more to do with him. I'll use the time to find out about trains to Camberwell.'

'I'll see you back here later, then,' he told her, his expression grim as he set off to find Harry. She couldn't believe he'd taken the painting without paying for it. Although he'd made it plain he'd made it plain he had no desire to see her again, she still needed to find out the truth about her mother.

The promenade was busy with holidaymakers making the most of the clement weather as, thoughts running amok, Daisy headed towards the station. She couldn't see why Harry didn't approve of the way she'd acted, and how he could even think she'd married Claude, when she was engaged to him, beggared belief. Besides, although she was fond of Claude, he was old enough to be her father.

'Daisy, how lovely to see you.' As the sound of the familiar voice penetrated her thoughts, she looked up to see Nancy Noble staring at her. 'My dear, you're looking pale. Are you alright?'

'I'm fine, really,' she replied.

'Why don't we go and order a nice reviving drink,' Nancy said, looking at her sceptically. Before she could answer, Daisy found herself being guided towards the quaint little café that fronted the beach.

The woman made small talk until mugs of hot tea were placed before them, then her expression became serious.

'I'm pleased I bumped into you, Daisy. You must have thought me very rude leaving the guest house without saying goodbye, but I was so upset about Grandmother's pendant, I lost all enthusiasm for my embroidery. I can't tell you how delighted I was when Susan contacted me to say that terrible woman Tulla had been caught red-handed.' Nancy smiled as she stroked the purple stone adorning the front of her dress.

'I'm pleased you got it back; I know how much it means to you. But should you be wearing something so valuable while out walking by yourself?' To her surprise, the woman laughed.

'It's actually made of glass, my dear. Invaluable doesn't necessarily equate to valuable in monetary terms, as that Tulla would have found out when she tried to sell it.' She chuckled, then looked directly at Daisy. 'It's a bit like people, really. How they appear isn't necessarily a true reflection of how they really are. What they say, not necessarily what they mean.'

Daisy stared at the woman, suddenly remembering what Harry had said about buying the portrait as a reminder. If he truly didn't care about her, he wouldn't have used his precious inheritance to buy it, would he?

'Oh heavens,' she groaned.

'Can I help, my dear? Sometimes talking gets things into perspective.' The sympathy in the woman's eyes brought tears to her own, and before she knew it, the events of the past few months came tumbling out. Nancy listened without interrupting, reaching across the table and taking her hand as Daisy finally came to a halt.

'Poor girl,' she murmured. 'You know what you need to do though, don't you?'

'Go home,' Daisy replied.

'Yes, my dear. You must see your mother and then have

a heart-to-heart with that young man if you can. Clear the air. If love truly binds you, it will find a way.'

'Thank you, Nancy,' Daisy whispered, staring at the woman in surprise.

'Don't let pride stand in your way or you'll regret it. As I do,' she murmured, a faraway look in her eye. 'So, when will you leave?' she asked, pulling herself back to the present.

'I've been saving for my fare, although I thought I was going to visit Mother in hospital not the wor … workhouse.' She shuddered.

'I could always help, if you wouldn't be offended,' Nancy said, reaching for her bag.

'Thank you but no.' Daisy smiled, touched by the woman's offer. 'Just listening has helped me enormously. There are only two more days left before Susan closes for the winter and then I shall go home.'

'Good luck, my dear. I hope to see you next year when I return, for I too have made a resolve. I shall finish my bedspread and show it at next year's exhibition. In the meantime, I just might write a much overdue letter. Our little chat has helped clarify things for me too.' Nancy smiled, the shadow leaving her eyes.

After visiting the station, Daisy waited outside the gallery until Claude returned. When he stopped, she could see from his grim face that something was badly wrong.

'Harry left St Ives in a hurry, and didn't say where he was going,' he growled as he urged the pony up the hill and past the church of Paul. 'So, I have no painting and no money.'

'I can't believe that of Harry, though perhaps he's changed

over the past months,' Daisy sighed. 'Anyway, we don't know if he actually inherited any money,' she muttered, wondering if she'd ever really known him at all.

Although Daisy felt sorry for Claude, she had her own problems to resolve. Having discovered her wages added to what she'd saved throughout the summer would be enough to purchase a single ticket home, she was desperate to return to Camberwell and see her mother. Knowing she wouldn't be able to leave her in the workhouse, she needed to find them somewhere to live and a job to pay the rent. She'd go and see Blue and ask for her job back, after which she would try to see Harry. It would be good to clear the air between them, if possible, as there was also the matter of Claude's painting to have out with him.

When they reached Rosemerryn, Claude poured a glass of red wine and sat at the table, while Daisy made supper.

'I shall speak with Constable Penpraze, then if I want to pay the rent, I shall have to make a start on another painting,' Claude said, having obviously resigned himself to the events of the day. 'Would you sit for me again?' he asked, staring hopefully across the table at her.

'Not just now, Claude, the first thing I need to do is go and see Mother.'

'But I don't have the money to pay you.'

'I can manage,' she assured him. 'I also need to find Harry.'

'That thief? What's brought all this on?' Claude asked, narrowing his eyes. Daisy explained about her meeting with Nancy.

'So, you see, Claude, I need to find out the truth about everything so I can move on,' she finished.

'I guess that makes sense. For Harry's sake, I hope you catch up with him before I do,' he growled. 'This place won't be the same without you, Daisy; when everything's sorted, I hope you'll come back.'

Daisy smiled but made no promises.

Being the end of the season, the boarding house was quiet and, with little to do, Daisy's thoughts were on her journey home.

'You're like a cat on hot bricks,' Susan said as they finished their lunch. 'The last person has left so you might as well go home. I appreciate all your help and you've been so good with Simon and our guests I've added a little extra.' She smiled, holding out a little envelope.

'There's no need for that,' Daisy replied, knowing Susan couldn't really afford it.

'Please take it. And Simon's got some produce for you,' Susan said, ignoring her protest.

'I picked the biggest and best,' he beamed.

'Thank you, Simon. I'm going to miss you,' Daisy told him.

'Well, I am going to be too busy to miss you,' he replied gravely. 'The colonel said he's going to train me to track his pheasants for the shoot. He said I was eagle-eyed, which I told him was stupid cos only eagles can have them eyes. Then he said, I had sharp eyes but I felt them and they're not sharp at all. He doesn't know what he's talking about.'

'That's a bit rude, Simon,' Susan chided.

'But it's true,' he replied solemnly.

Daisy turned away to hide her smile. Simon might take

things literally but there was no denying his sharp observation had helped to catch Tulla red-handed.

'There'll be a job here for you next season, always supposing you decide to return,' Susan said, smiling sadly as she unconsciously echoed Claude's earlier words.

'Thank you,' Daisy murmured, swallowing down the lump in her throat as she took the basket. She'd enjoyed working here and would miss Susan and Simon.

Outside, she stared down at the beautiful turquoise cove she'd come to love. Then, straightening her shoulders, she turned towards Rosemerryn, vowing to return one day.

Chapter 37

As Daisy neared the house, she saw a carriage waiting outside. She glanced down at her basket, hoping she'd have the makings of a meal for visitors. Since his success with *Engima*, Claude had received a number of commissions and was becoming quite free with his invitations for people to visit.

'Hello, Daisy.'

'Oh,' she cried, jumping in astonishment and dropping the basket. Her heart flipped as she found herself staring into cornflower blue eyes. 'Harry, what are you doing here?'

'That's a fine greeting when I've travelled halfway up the country and back,' he grimaced. 'Well, you might not be happy to see me, but you'll love the surprise waiting in the parlour.' Before Daisy could reply, she found herself being propelled through the door. As the woman sitting beside the fire smiled, her heart flipped again.

'Mother,' she squealed, racing across the room and throwing her arms around her. 'I can't believe it's really you,' she gasped.

'I never thought this day would come,' Mabel murmured, tears coursing down her cheeks.

'But how did you get here?' Daisy asked.

'You can thank Harry,' her mother replied, smiling at him over Daisy's shoulder. 'Turned up at the workhouse and announced he was taking me on holiday,' she added, glancing fondly at him. 'You should have seen the matron's face. Ordered me to finish my work before I left, but Harry soon put her straight.'

'You had to work?' Daisy cried. 'But what about your legs?'

'You sit down for sewing.' Mabel shrugged. 'Have to earn your dish of gruel and bed for the night, or you get thrown out.'

'That's terrible. I had no idea. Uncle said—'

'Harry's told me all about that swine,' Mabel snorted. 'Poor Arthur, God rest his soul. He'd be turning in his grave if he knew how you'd been treated,' she cried. 'His own kith and kin too. Cors they never did speak properly after it were Arthur I chose to wed.'

Daisy stared at her in dismay. 'You don't mean Uncle Rich courted you as well?'

'Don't look so surprised, young lady,' Mabel chided. 'It were a long time ago now, and of course Rich only wanted me because Arthur did. Always had to have what his brother did and always one to bear a grudge when he didn't get it. Even tried again after we were married.'

'But that's terrible.'

'He always was,' Mabel nodded sadly.

'Uncle said you were still in hospital, that I had to work to pay for your operation.'

'He always was a liar as well. I didn't need any operation. It were poor Arthur who copped it. Threw his body across mine to shield me from the impact, he did. My hero to the end,' she sniffed, her words coming out in a sob.

'Oh, Mother.' Daisy squeezed her tighter, never wanting to let her go. 'I had no idea you were locked up in the workhouse.' How ironic, she'd gone with her uncle to avoid being sent to the workhouse and then her mother had ended up in it.

'They don't actually lock you up, well unless you commit some crime, which many do out of desperation,' Mabel said, fumbling in her pocket for a handkerchief. Daisy hid a smile as her mother brought out a pristine, snowy cloth and dabbed her eyes. Even in the workhouse she hadn't let her standards slip. But Mabel, who was obviously finding it a relief to talk, hadn't finished her story.

'They say you're not a prisoner and can leave at any time, but of course they know you have no money for food or rent, so you're well and truly stuck. Still, they were impressed with my sewing and had me making clothes for the inmates rather than hemming sacks for sheets. Anyhow, enough about me. How are you, Daisy? Claude explained you've been staying with him.'

'Yes, but as his housekeeper not his wife,' she said, blushing as she looked at Harry. He gave a wry grin.

'Claude made sure I understand the situation. I've paid him for his picture and explained that the curator wasn't at his post when I returned to the museum after the exhibition was over. And that the lady companion you saw in the carriage was another artist from the workshop in St Ives, who was also showing at the exhibition,' Harry told her.

'As everything seems to have been resolved, I've invited your mother and Harry to stay for a few days; I hope that's alright with you, Daisy?' Claude asked. 'I know you all have a lot of catching up to do,' he added, shooting her a knowing look.

'Susan insisted I bring some produce home even though she knows you grow your own, so we'll have plenty to eat,' Daisy gabbled, feeling Harry's gaze upon her.

'Garden produce, now there's a treat.' Mabel beamed. 'Can't remember when I last had anything fresh.'

'You must try the fish from Newlyn, Mrs T. Straight off the boat, and no need to add salt as you can taste the sea on it,' Harry enthused.

'Now, Harry, remember what I told you on the way here, if you're going to be fam … well, call me Mabel anyway,' she added quickly, noting his discomfort. 'We get winkles and jellied eels where we live,' she told Claude.

'Very tasty too, I'm sure,' he smiled. 'Why don't you show Harry the vegetable plot we have here, Daisy?' She looked at Harry, who nodded and got to his feet.

Together they wandered out into the garden. The sky was suffused with bands of crimson and gold, the fragrance of honeysuckle floating on the evening breeze. It was a romantic setting yet neither of them said anything, each waiting for the other to speak. Although her heart was beating wildly, she didn't want him to realise how his presence affected her. After all, she'd spent the past months forging a new life for herself and wasn't just the naïve girl dutifully waiting for him.

'Why did you …'

'Shall I find …'

They began in unison, then smiled awkwardly.

'Ladies first,' Harry said, and Daisy had to bite down the quip she'd have made a year ago when their relationship was free and easy. How she longed for them to be like that again, but Harry was looking grave as he waited for her to speak.

'I was going to ask why you didn't tell me you were returning to Camberwell. I could have come with you,' she told him. He seemed to be choosing his words as they ventured further down the path. Physically, they might have been walking side by side but mentally they were poles apart, and Daisy could have wept. His next words didn't help.

'It was obvious from our last conversation that you didn't believe a word I said. I thought it would be a good idea to bring Mabel to see you and prove I had been telling the truth when I said she was alive.'

'Oh, I see,' she murmured, disappointed by his response. Of course, seeing her mother again was splendid, but it wasn't what she'd been hoping to hear. 'Was that the only reason?' she ventured when he remained silent. In spite of her resolve, her heart flopped as the hope she'd been harbouring that he'd returned to see her died.

'I also had to pay Claude for his painting,' he admitted, staring at the oak tree by the fence as if it was the most fascinating thing he'd ever seen.

'The one to remind you of someone you once knew. And does it?'

'It most certainly does, so there's no reason for me to stay. I can rent a room in town and return for Mabel when she's ready to leave.' Daisy's heart sank further, but she was determined not to let him see how hurt she was.

'I don't think Claude would be happy if you did that,' she managed to reply. 'He prides himself on his hospitality.'

'In that case, I'd better stay for the night. Perhaps I could bed down in one of those outhouses,' he said, gesturing to Claude's workshop.

'For heaven's sake,' she burst out. 'Can you really not bear to spend one night in the same house as me?'

'There's nothing I'd like better.' He stopped walking and turned towards her.

'Pardon?' she gasped, staring at him in surprise.

'Look, Daisy, at the risk of making a complete fool of myself, I'll be honest with you. I've loved you from the moment I first saw you and, despite the infuriating way you continue placing obstacles in the way of my trying to rekindle our relationship, I still do.' As her heart began to soar, he nodded to her wrist. 'Although you're still wearing your silver bangle, you've made it quite clear your feelings towards me have changed, so I won't put any further pressure on you. They have changed, haven't they?' he asked. As he continued gazing at her with those clear-blue eyes, she knew she had to tell him the truth.

'Yes, they have,' she admitted. Seeing his forlorn expression, she went on quickly, 'During my time away my feelings for you have deepened, Harry Wylde.'

'What?' he exclaimed. 'You mean you've put me through hell and back when all along you ...' he groaned, then reached out and pulled her into his arms. As warmth spread through her body, Daisy snuggled into his chest. She might be far from Camberwell, but in her heart she'd come home. This was where she belonged.

Suddenly, he pushed her away but as she stared at him in dismay he reached into his pocket. Heedless of the dew forming on the grass he went down on one knee and held out the posie ring.

'Daisy Tucker, would you please do me the honour of marrying me?' he asked solemnly.

'I thought you'd never ask,' she laughed. As tears coursed down her cheeks, he slipped the ring he'd designed and made onto her finger.

'Honestly, Daisy, only you could laugh and cry at such a serious time,' he said, shaking his head. 'I can see I shall have to take you in hand when I become your husband.'

'Has nobody told you those archaic ways died out in the Middle Ages?' she exclaimed. 'I'll have you know I'm an ambitious, determined woman who thinks for herself.'

'Thank heavens for that,' he replied, feigning relief. 'So, how about Christmas?'

'How about it?' she asked, trying to keep a straight face. Although she knew only too well what he meant, after all the anguish he'd put her through, she intended making him work for things now. After all, a girl had her pride. Then she remembered what Nancy had told her and relented. 'A Christmas wedding would be perfect,' she told him.

'God, Daisy, you don't half know how to make a man sweat,' Harry smiled. 'Now come here,' he ordered, holding out his arms. Powerless to resist, she willingly walked towards him.

When they finally managed to tear themselves apart, a cheer rang out and looking up they saw Claude and Mabel smiling at them.

'Oh, I didn't know you were there,' Daisy mumbled, a flush creeping up her cheeks.

'I've prepared cheese omelettes with chives for supper, but there's no rush,' said Mabel.

'But you've only just arrived and shouldn't have to cook,' Daisy protested.

'On the contrary, it's been a pleasure putting together a decent meal in a clean kitchen. Thin, watery gruel doesn't do much to whet the appetite, I can tell you. Now, is that a ring I spy on your finger, girl?'

'It's the one Harry made,' Daisy said proudly, holding out her hand.

'That's a labour of love if ever I saw one,' Claude whistled, as he studied the white enamelled petals of the daisy gleaming in its silver setting.

'I told you Harry was a gifted craftsman,' Daisy said, smiling at the man she loved.

'Indeed, he is. It complements that silver bangle you always wear,' Claude agreed.

'Let's go and open a bottle of wine so we can toast this auspicious occasion. It's not every day I get a beautiful woman visiting my humble home.' To Daisy's surprise, Claude turned and smiled at her mother, who blushed prettily. 'And of course, we must celebrate the sale of my picture,' he added. 'Haven't forgotten anything, have I?' he teased, smiling at the happy couple.

'Nothing important,' Daisy retorted.

'We'll throw a party to celebrate, invite Grace and Denzil, Mae and Sean, and, of course, Cadan, if he's around,' Claude announced.

'Wonderful,' Daisy cried, clapping her hands in excitement. 'You'll love them, Harry. They're also highly skilled craftspeople who had pieces on show at the exhibition.'

'Cadan took our budding artist here around the local Celtic sites and it appears she has a talent for bringing these designs to life.'

'Cadan is a Cornish Charmer, Mother,' Daisy explained. 'He has this special gift and although I was sceptical of some of the things he told me, it turns out he was right all along.'

'I hope you will both stay for a while,' Claude said, looking at Mabel and Harry in turn.

'I'd love to, if you're sure I won't be in the way. Daisy and I have so much to catch up on, and plans to make, of course,' Mabel replied, beaming at the couple. 'I've never been to Cornwall before and would love to see some of these sights Daisy's mentioned.'

'Perhaps you would let me have the honour of showing you around, Mabel. I've been much too busy of late and the change would do me good,' Claude added, as she began to demur.

Daisy smiled, knowing the sea air and good food would help rebuild her mother's strength.

'And what about you, Harry?' Claude asked. 'Can you stay or do you have to return to Camberwell?'

'I'd love to stay. My time at the workshop was only a temporary arrangement and I need to move my things out of there this week.'

'As long as you're not going back to that pretty lady I saw you with?' Daisy teased.

'Decisions, decisions,' Harry replied, only to receive a dig in the ribs.

'You two stay here while we finish getting supper. It's not every day you get engaged,' Mabel said. 'Arthur would have been pleased; he always said you were made for each other,' she told them, smiling sadly at the memory. 'Though with you two, it's a case of the unstoppable force meets the immovable object. You need to be more tolerant or you'll be forever trying to get the better of each other.'

'Oh, Mother,' Daisy groaned, rolling her eyes at Harry. Although she knew it was true; they were both stubborn and would have to be more understanding of each other.

Harry settled onto the settee in front of the crackling log fire and pulled Daisy down beside him.

'I can't thank you enough for bringing Mother here,' she murmured, throwing her arms around him.

'If I'd known I'd get that reaction, I'd have fetched her sooner,' he said with a grin.

'This really is beautiful,' she told him, pulling the ring from her finger.

'So beautiful you no longer want to wear it?' he frowned.

'I haven't seen what's inscribed on the inside yet. "Daisy, love of my life",' she read. 'That's really lovely.'

'I thought of engraving "Potty Petal" but knew my tutor would have a fit.'

'Quite right too,' she cried, digging him in the ribs again.

'I always knew I was destined to be a battered husband,' he cried.

'But what does *"amor vincit omnia"* mean?' she asked, ignoring him as she read the words etched on the other side of the circle.

'It's Latin for "love conquers all",' he replied. 'Quite appropriate after all we've been through, don't you think?'

'I do, and we'll make it our family motto so we never forget,' she told him, leaning over and kissing him passionately on the lips.

Epilogue

Newlyn, two years later

Daisy added her signature white daisy to the corner of the blue agapanthus picture, entitled *Secret Love*. Recalling her days at the Fun Factory when she could only dream of doing such a thing, she wondered how Blue and Scarlett were faring.

Around her, the workshop buzzed with activity as craftsmen worked on their specialist silver and Cornish tin jewellery. Feeling Harry's gaze upon her, Daisy looked up from her easel and smiled at her husband. They made a good team in every way with him crafting her Celtic designs into exquisite creations. Never in her wildest dreams had she imagined their combined work would prove so popular.

In the next room, Grace and Mae worked at their high benches creating the cloisonné flower brooches and enamelled silver buckles people coveted. While Sean, having finessed his repousse ware, was building up his own following.

On the wall of their Wylde at Heart gallery next door, the picture *Enigma* had pride of place, its red *not for sale* sticker still firmly in place. Daisy had suggested selling it to fund starting their co-operative but Harry had refused, declaring it their good luck talisman. Her mother, wearing the blue and white striped dress she'd made to reflect the ocean, was helping a client. Fully restored to health, she was explaining that a bangle with the Cornish knot depicted the continuity of life, while a pendant incorporating the Celtic Triskeles design represented the past, the present, the future. The woman purchased both and her mother beamed delightedly.

Perched at his easel in the corner, Claude put the finishing touches to his latest portrait, *Loveable*, which he declared his best work ever. Knowing it was the meaning of Mabel, her mother's name, Daisy smiled. She'd never forget her father, Arthur, but her mother had the rest of her life to live and Daisy wanted her to be happy.

Embracing the spirit of the Arts and Crafts movement, they all worked together, giving mutual support and encouragement. Promoting the beauty of handmade crafts that could never be replicated by machine was their mission.

A true union in all respects, Daisy thought, her hand going to her stomach as it fluttered with the first movement of new life. Her latest Celtic design was for a baby's rattle and she smiled, imagining Harry's expression when he realised the significance. The new arrival was due at Christmas, and if it was a girl, he would be busy designing another silver bangle, she thought, gazing fondly down at her own.

Acknowledgements

To Pern: your continued support and encouragement is very much appreciated.

To Kate Mills and her wonderful team at HQ, who have continued their sterling work during these difficult times.

To Teresa Chris for those extra nuggets of wisdom.

To BWC, who have been so generous with their time, not only by listening and giving helpful feedback, but also providing insight into the world of art and the materials used.

ONE PLACE. MANY STORIES

Bold, innovative and
empowering publishing.

FOLLOW US ON:

@HQStories